Praise for the authors of Unleashed

REBECCA YORK

"[Her] books . . . deliver what they promise:
excitement, mystery, romance."
—*The Washington Post Book World*

SUSAN KEARNEY

"A master storyteller."
—Virginia Henley

DIANE WHITESIDE

"Whiteside rules the night."
—Angela Knight

"Whiteside has captured the volcanic passion
that a scene can arouse."
—*Sensual Romance*

LUCY MONROE

"Love scenes that go off the thermometer with their heat."
—*The Romance Reader's Connection*

UNLEASHED

Rebecca York
Susan Kearney
Diane Whiteside
Lucy Monroe

BERKLEY SENSATION, NEW YORK

THE BERKLEY PUBLISHING GROUP
Published by the Penguin Group
Penguin Group (USA) Inc.
375 Hudson Street, New York, New York 10014, USA
Penguin Group (Canada), 90 Eglinton Avenue East, Suite 700, Toronto, Ontario M4P 2Y3, Canada
(a division of Pearson Penguin Canada Inc.)
Penguin Books Ltd., 80 Strand, London WC2R 0RL, England
Penguin Group Ireland, 25 St. Stephen's Green, Dublin 2, Ireland (a division of Penguin Books Ltd.)
Penguin Group (Australia), 250 Camberwell Road, Camberwell, Victoria 3124, Australia
(a division of Pearson Australia Group Pty. Ltd.)
Penguin Books India Pvt. Ltd., 11 Community Centre, Panchsheel Park, New Delhi—110 017, India
Penguin Group (NZ), Cnr. Airborne and Rosedale Roads, Albany, Auckland 1310, New Zealand
(a division of Pearson New Zealand Ltd.)
Penguin Books (South Africa) (Pty.) Ltd., 24 Sturdee Avenue, Rosebank, Johannesburg 2196,
South Africa

Penguin Books Ltd., Registered Offices: 80 Strand, London WC2R 0RL, England

This book is an original publication of The Berkley Publishing Group.

This is a work of fiction. Names, characters, places, and incidents either are the product of the authors' imaginations or are used fictitiously, and any resemblance to actual persons, living or dead, business establishments, events, or locales is entirely coincidental. The publisher does not have any control over and does not assume any responsibility for author or third-party websites or their content.

First edition: December 2006

Library of Congress Cataloging-in-Publication Data

Unleashed / Rebecca York . . . [et al.].—1st ed.
    p. cm.
  ISBN 0-425-21211-4
  1. Erotic stories, American. 2. Occult fiction, American. 3. Supernatural—fiction. 4. American fiction—Women authors. 5. American fiction—21st century. I. York, Rebecca.

PS648.E7U55 2006
813'.01083538—dc22   2006025860

PRINTED IN THE UNITED STATES OF AMERICA

10   9   8   7   6   5   4   3   2   1

contents

BOND OF SILVER

REBECCA YORK

Ruth Glick writing as Rebecca York

one

This couldn't be reality. He knew that in some hidden corner of his mind. But it felt real. Smelled real. Sounded real. And when a streak of fire blasted toward him, he gasped as pain shot through the flesh of his arm. He smelled it, too. It was like a piece of meat left too long on the barbecue.

He looked down, seeing that he was dressed in a shirt, dark pants, and leather boots. His feet were bare, and his hand was clenched around something hard and metal. He realized it was the hilt of a sword—the burnished silver intricately decorated with a delicate tracery.

He was an artist, known for his skill with granite—as well as precious metal—and normally he might have stopped to admire the workmanship. In this reality he was more interested in how well the weapon would defend him against the fire-breathing beast advancing on him. Experimentally he swished the blade through the air, testing the weight of the weapon, getting used to the way it felt in his hand.

He had dueled for fun, but this was life and death—even if the killing ground was a manicured park with broad stretches of grass surrounded by carefully tended flower beds.

He grasped the cold metal of the sword. "Couldn't you come up with something more original than a classic dragon?" he muttered aloud. "One of those helicopter things? Or a flock of harpies?"

Well, he couldn't change the rules now. And the dragon's breath was sufficient to reduce him to ashes. Another man might have run. Alexander stood his ground, knowing that he could lose his life in this fantasy, which had transformed from dream to nightmare in the space of a heartbeat.

As the monster rushed him, he studied the gray blue scales the size of Roman shields, the flame-thrower of a snout, the three-inch claws that tore a path of destruction through the grass.

The beast homed in on the puny enemy facing it, probably thinking that it could kill him as easily as a man could swat a fly.

But Alexander wasn't planning on losing his life on this field of battle. He stiffened his legs, standing his ground until the dragon was almost upon him, then ducked low and under the monster's neck, striking upward, plunging the sword into the tender flesh just under the beast's jawbone. The dragon gave a screech of pain like a clap of thunder, then lurched to the side, spurting blood and belching black smoke.

Alexander leaped back, barely avoiding getting crushed under the massive body as it toppled to the grass and lay writhing, its death throes shaking the ground.

In the heat of battle, Alexander had vowed to stand his ground. Still, he was mildly surprised that he was alive.

He had not known what to expect when he stepped into this dream landscape that looked like an illustration from one of the books his mother had read to him when he was a little boy.

Maybe it actually was one of those illustrations, for all he knew. And his mind had translated the early memory into the dream to give himself a context he could understand.

"Keep an open mind," the priest had said as he'd led Alexander to one of the sleeping rooms in the Temple of Onaros—the Temple of Dreams. "You could find yourself anywhere you have been or anywhere you could imagine."

He laughed harshly now. Too bad he had a very vivid imagination. That probably wasn't the best trait for survival in the dream of bonding.

Or perhaps he was wrong.

"Bring it on," he muttered, a phrase he'd learned from watching an American television show. He liked the sound of the challenge. Now that he had the luxury of inspecting his surroundings, he looked past the dragon's body, his gaze probing the landscape that had turned from late afternoon to moon-silvered night.

When he saw the figure of a man surrounded by a low, clipped hedge, he froze, ready for an attack—until he realized he was looking at a very classical Greek statue. Much like something he might have seen in the sculpture garden near the center of Unoria—the only city on the island where he lived.

The wind riffled his hair and shook the branches of nearby trees, creating a strangely eerie sound. To his right, he spotted a dark tower, barely visible against the night sky. It was the only building he could see anywhere in the park, and he knew instinctively that it must be his destination.

He set off across the grass at a fast pace, watching for new monsters that might be lurking in the shadows, but he made it to the base of the tower without encountering any other perils.

The building, which stood in the center of a paved circle, was made of rough stones, rising fifty feet into the air. The door at the base was barred.

Which should be no problem to someone who routinely traveled on the currents of the wind to far-flung mountains where he used his mental powers to dig huge slabs of granite and marble from the living rock.

Walking five feet back from the door, he focused on the wood and steel barrier, sending his mind into the locking mechanism. He could see exactly how it worked. But in this land where dragons dwelled, his special talents seemed to be nullified.

He muttered a curse. Taking several more steps back, he looked toward the top of the tower and saw a window directly above the door.

It was high—almost near the top. If he fell from that height onto the pavement, he would be seriously injured. But he had no intention of letting the tower defeat him.

He grasped one of the rocks beside the door, pulling himself up, then wedging his foot into a crevice before finding another handhold farther up.

He had many skills, and because of his work, rock climbing was one of them. He looked around, wondering if a rope would magically appear the way the sword had come to his hand.

But this time he was on his own. Working without a safety line was dangerous, but he didn't hesitate to find a higher handhold and then a foothold, climbing steadily upward.

Just as he reached the sill, a face and shoulders appeared at the window. He stopped short, catching his breath. He had made no noise in his climb, but somehow this woman in the tower room had known he was there. She was looking out at him as though she couldn't believe her eyes.

In the moonlight he saw that her hair was raven dark, her features delicate. As he drew closer, her bow-shaped lips parted.

Transfixed, he drank in her face and her large luminous eyes. Although she might not be a classic beauty, the sight of her set off a longing deep inside him. He was no poet, but he felt suddenly that he had always been meant to climb to the top of this tower. And the woman who dwelt here was meant to live the rest of her life at his side.

He hadn't known exactly what to expect of the dream. He had

been told that the woman he would meet might be sleeping, that she might not even know he was there. But she had felt his presence and come to the window. They had connected at once—and that realization was thrilling.

Quickly he climbed the rest of the way to her tower room—like the prince coming to rescue Rapunzel in the fairy tale.

But her reaction wasn't what he was expecting.

Go back, she mouthed through the window, then stepped away.

Not likely. Instead, he pushed the sash up, threw his leg over the sill, and climbed into the room, keeping his movements slow and even. From where he stood near the window, he spoke in a low, reassuring voice. "I mean you no harm. This is . . . the dream where we begin to forge a bond with each other."

She stopped and faced him squarely, her shoulders rigid, her hands clasped in front of her. He caught his breath as he looked at her. She was wearing a light cotton gown, through which he saw the outline of her body. Her breasts, her hips. The shadows of her nipples and a triangle of dark hair at the juncture of her legs.

He ached to scoop her into his arms and carry her across the room to the bed. But the tight expression on her face kept him standing by the window.

"Go back," she repeated.

"Don't be afraid of me." For the last few weeks he'd been consumed by thoughts of this meeting. He'd spun out countless scenarios of what might happen when he and his soul mate shared this dream. But so far, nothing was going the way he had expected—from the dragon to the look of distress on his soul mate's face.

She reached out a graceful hand toward him, then drew her arm quickly back. "I'm not afraid for myself." Her eyes took on a haunted look. "But you are in danger here."

Yet another thing he'd not expected. He looked around the room, searching for new enemies.

There was no visible source of light in the room, yet somehow the chamber was suffused with a warm golden glow, so that he could see everything clearly.

The floorboards beneath his feet were old and worn. A strange kind of circular rug covered the center of the floor. He knew from something he'd read that it was called a rag rug.

He knew the honey-colored furniture was made of oak. And that the pieces must be very old.

Antiques they were called.

But he saw no other living creature besides the woman.

"You must leave. Before the witch comes for you."

His features hardened. "I just killed a dragon. I think I can handle a witch."

She clasped her hands in front of her. "She guards me jealously."

"Then you must leave with me."

She looked over her shoulder at the door, then back at him.

"Tell me your name," he asked.

"Claire."

"Come away with me, Claire." He held out his hand and at the same time held his breath. If she didn't accept him, he knew his heart would shrivel and die.

Unable to draw a full breath, he waited to hear her answer.

He saw emotions warring on her features, and when she reached for his hand, he felt the tightness in his chest ease.

He had tried to use his special talent to climb to the tower. It hadn't worked then. Now he was praying that the two of them could do it together.

"I'm Alexander," he told her quickly. "The man who was destined to be your soul mate."

"I . . . don't understand."

"You will." He stroked his hands up and down her arms, feeling the goose bumps peppering her skin. "But first you must lend me your power."

TWO

Alexander felt her whole body go rigid.

"What power?" she asked in a trembling voice.

"The force of your mind."

She drew in a sharp breath. "I hide that from everyone. How do *you* know?"

"It's the reason I'm here."

She tried to pull away, but he held her facing him.

Finally she whispered, "It made people afraid of me."

The look of sadness on her face melted his heart. He folded her into his arms, holding her tightly against the length of his body. "I'm so sorry."

"Only the witch knows."

He didn't want to talk about the mysterious witch. He wanted to get Claire away from here.

He hugged her to him, trying to lend her the warmth of his body, even as he asked for what she didn't want to give. But he sensed it—

the power that simmered inside her. Only another adept would have known of that hidden treasure. And he could do more than sense her concealed depths. Tentatively at first, and then with more intensity, he connected to it, locked his talent with hers.

She lifted her head, staring at him in wonder. "What . . ."

"I'm linking our minds. You don't have to do anything. Just stay joined to me and together we can work magic." He grinned at her, then slowly, carefully lifted the two of them a few inches off the floor.

"Oh!"

"Hold tight. Have you ever flown before? I mean—not in an airplane."

"No!"

She twined her arms around his waist. As he held her against his body, he knew that their linking minds were part of the magic of the dream. In this place, he had no power on his own, but with her—everything changed.

To get her used to the sensation of lighter-than-air travel, he turned her around, holding her a foot off the floor, as though they were dancing but not touching the ground.

"Okay?" he asked.

"It's so strange."

"But nice?"

"Um-hum," she answered, laying her head on his shoulder.

"It's going to get stranger. We're getting out of here," he whispered.

He heard her breath catch, but she didn't pull away. Elated, he clasped her to him, then floated the two of them to the window and out into the park.

She gasped, and he felt the mental connection between them stretch. Quickly, before they fell, he bound them closer.

"It's okay. I've got you."

He moved them away from the tower, into the woods, looking for a place where the two of them could be sure of privacy.

"The summer house," she whispered as though she were reading his mind. And perhaps she was—bonded couples could often do that.

"Where is it?" he asked.

"On the cliff. Overlooking the ocean."

He headed for the cliffs that towered over the breaking surf. And when he spotted a building standing out against the sky, he focused on the shingled roof, using it as a homing beacon, bringing them down. They landed beside a small structure with huge glass windows that faced the ocean. Before he took Claire inside, he used their joint power to rearrange the interior, making them a wide, comfortable bed with an ornate brass headboard, a puffy comforter, and soft white sheets. Then, so he could see her, he hung a small, glowing lantern in the corner.

Finally, he scooped her up in his arms and carried her through the door.

She looked around in wonder. "It looks so different. Where did the bed come from?"

"My imagination," he answered as he laid her on the satin coverlet.

She gazed up at him as though she could hardly believe what was happening. And in truth, he was having the same problem. He felt like he had been caught by a riptide and swept out to sea.

He hadn't expected so much. So fast.

But though it seemed to be happening at the speed of light, he wasn't alarmed. This dream had already brought him happiness beyond his imagining. Soon he would be with Claire in person. But this encounter was the first connection between them and an important link in the joining of their lives. He ached for it to be as perfect as he could make it—for her and for himself as well.

"Thank you for trusting me," he murmured.

She gave him a look that almost broke his heart. "How could I not?"

As he watched her lying on the bed, staring up at him in wonder and confusion, he felt an overwhelming need to make her understand what they meant to each other—what they *would* mean to each other.

Quickly, he pulled off his boots, then his shirt, before coming down on the bed beside her.

He had been fighting to hold his arousal in check. But now that they were horizontal together, his senses swam. The dream was like a precious memory forgotten and then recovered—with an immediacy that took his breath away.

He was a man of action. A man who was seldom unsure of himself. But tonight he didn't want to make any mistakes. So he gave her a light kiss, then raised a hand and stroked her cheek, her jaw, her neck, watching her face as he moved downward toward the tops of her breasts.

And just that light contact had his hand trembling. When he heard her breath quicken, he followed his hand with his gaze and saw that beneath the fabric of her cotton gown, her nipples had contracted into hard peaks.

"You want me," he murmured.

"Yes," she sighed out. "But I shouldn't."

"Why not?"

"I don't even know you."

He laughed. "You have the rest of your life to get to know me. Every way a woman and man can know each other."

He brought his mouth back to hers, tracing the seam of her lips with his tongue, silently asking for admission.

She opened for him as she made a small sound in her throat, a sound of surrender that traveled along his nerve endings, arousing him almost beyond endurance.

It was ecstasy to half lie on top of her, his erection pressed to her leg as his hands drifted over her, stroking her shoulders, her arms, and then her breasts, feeling her response to him.

And when her hands began to move over his body, he felt a surge of elation. She wanted to touch him as much as he wanted to touch her. She slid her palms over his shoulders, then down the front of his chest, winnowing her fingers into his chest hair, then finding his nipples and rubbing back and forth across them.

His own breath caught, and he felt her smile against his mouth, then take his lower lip between her teeth, teasing and inciting.

From far away he heard the waves crashing against the rocks below. But in this little house, the world was of no importance.

When the kiss broke, she stroked his lips with her finger. "Why do I feel so safe with you?"

He nibbled at her knuckle. "Because we were meant for each other—since the beginning of time."

"You believe in destiny?"

"Yes."

"I thought mine was . . . to be alone."

"Oh no! You belong with me."

It was suddenly impossible to hold back the emotions surging through him. He kissed her with unleashed passion, as he reached to play with her knee, then slid his hand up under her gown, pausing to see if she wanted him to stop. When she gave him back the passion of the kiss, he slid his hand higher, his fingers gliding between her thighs and up to that warm, wet place at the juncture of her legs.

She was hot and swollen. As he stroked between her folds, she lifted her hips and pressed more firmly against his hand.

He had been told that there was no one way for the dream to play itself out, but he knew she was ready for sex—ready for him. And he was more than ready for her.

But though he ached to join his body with hers more than anything he had ever wanted in his life, he held back. If he made love with her now, that would take away the pleasure of doing it for the first time in real life.

So he stroked between her legs with one hand, and caressed her breasts with the other, feeling her excitement climb as he urged her toward climax.

She cried out, her body shivering against his hand as orgasm took her.

He kept his eyes on her face, seeing her pleasure shimmering there. She settled against him, knitting her fingers with his, then slid her free hand down his body and cupped her palm over his erection.

Her touch was exquisite. And he almost gave in to temptation. But he managed to answer, "There's time for me later."

Still, he knew that later would be only a matter of seconds if her hand stayed where it was. He lifted it away from his body, then rolled to his back, dragging in drafts of air.

She tightened her fingers on his. "Let me . . ."

"Next time."

Because he ached to pull her back into his arms, he eased away from her, then climbed out of bed and stood on legs that weren't quite steady.

She looked up at him, regret in her eyes. "I don't want it to end this way."

"This isn't an ending. It's a beginning," he answered.

Before he had time to pull his shirt back on, he heard a sound outside. The wind was rising, swirling debris into the air and sending sand pelting against the windowpane. The waves below the cliffs suddenly began crashing against the rocks with terrible force.

Claire sat up, alarm tightening her features. "It's her."

"Who?"

"The witch."

The wind roared around the house like a giant cat prowling, and beyond the windows utter blackness descended on the landscape.

Rain suddenly lashed the roof, as the door burst open, and a woman, dressed in a severe black robe strode into the room. Her hair was streaked with gray, and lines marred her once smooth features. Still, from her appearance, he could tell that she and Claire were related.

Her furious gaze bored into the woman on the bed. "What have you done?"

"Nothing!"

"Don't lie to me." When the witch advanced on Claire, Alexander stepped between them. "Leave her alone."

"Who are you to give me orders?" He saw anger—and determination—in her eyes. When she spoke, she turned his dream from burnished silver to ashes.

"Did he send you? Is that it? Did he send you to steal my treasure? Or are you going to get her pregnant—then disappear, the way Bendon did with me?"

He couldn't hold back a choking sound as he heard the familiar name.

Her unblinking gaze remained fixed on him. She raised her hand, pointing a gnarled finger at him. "Go back. Go back to where you came from. Leave me and my daughter in peace—or you will come to grief."

THREE

Alexander awoke, his body drenched in sweat. He lay with his heart pounding, his eyes slitted, his whole body coiled into a spring, as though to defend himself from an attack.

He was alone—back on the island of New Atlantis—but the dream still held him by the throat, making it difficult to breathe.

He was in a small, windowless sleep chamber. The bed on which he lay was a narrow platform, topped with a comfortable down mattress. A plump pillow cushioned his head. The bedding was soft white, as were the gently curved walls of the chamber. When he had entered the room, the ceiling above his head had been a calm blue sky, with fluffy clouds drifting serenely above him. Now the clouds had turned dark and menacing, with bolts of lightning flashing in their depths. And the low rumble of thunder came a few seconds after each flash.

The room was tuned to his mood, and he knew his own grim emotions had generated the stormy weather.

He'd had plenty of disappointments in his life. This time, he'd thought . . .

He squeezed his hands into fists.

It didn't matter what he'd thought coming into the Temple of Onaros. He had to deal with reality.

When a low knock sounded at the door, he sat up and ran a hand quickly through his hair, then called out, "Come in."

Immediately, a man clad in deep blue robes stepped into the room. It was Father Daldis. The man looked like he was in his mid-forties, but Alexander knew that he was more than four hundred years old.

The priest's features were filled with concern. "Storm clouds and lightning," he murmured. "You must be troubled, my son."

Alexander answered with a tight nod.

"When you sent your mind winging from this place, did you fail to find your soul mate?"

Alexander dragged in a breath and let it out. "I found a woman, but she can't be the one," he blurted, then wished he'd thought about what he wanted to say before his lips started moving.

"You had a sexual encounter with her, and it was unsatisfactory?" Father Daldis asked as though he were a waiter in a restaurant inquiring why the patron wished to send back his perfectly cooked sea bass.

Memories poured over him, through him. A sexual encounter. "Yes. It was good," he whispered. "But that's not the problem. She can't be the right one."

"If you linked up with a female—then she is your soul mate."

"No. That's impossible." He spoke rapidly, with conviction, even when he had no absolute proof. "She is the daughter of Bendon Demos. My adoptive father," he added unnecessarily.

For just a moment, the priest's eyes widened. But he quickly recovered his calm demeanor. "How do you know?"

"The dream was a fantasy. We went off together, to a little house by the sea. But then a—a witch burst in on us. She asked if Bendon had sent me, and she warned me to leave her and her daughter alone."

The priest's tone was measured as he said, "When Bendon came back from his courtship, he was in despair. His soul mate wouldn't come to New Atlantis with him, and he knew he had lost the love of his life."

Alexander nodded. He knew the pain his adoptive father had endured. After that episode he had never married, but he had wanted to give the love within him to another human being. So when his good friends Erasmus and Anna Konstantinopoulos died in a freak accident out in the world, he took in their young son. As a boy of ten, Alexander had been devastated by his parents' deaths. It wasn't unusual for his people to live more than three hundred years. And his parents' early deaths had robbed him of so much. But Bendon had been warm and loving and patient with the orphaned boy.

Gradually Alexander had come to feel that he truly had a new home. Not in a typical New Atlantis family, because Bendon had no wife. But Alexander knew that he had been adopted by a good man who had taught him the responsibility of being a citizen of the island.

The priest began to speak again.

"You don't go through the dream ceremony simply to find your soul mate. You come to the temple to serve your people."

Alexander nodded. New Atlantis was in the Caribbean Sea, hidden from detection by a force field that repelled all recognition of the island. The inhabitants all had psychic powers, and those powers kept the force field in place around their home. But it was impossible for the relatively small population to sustain the field. So young men and women entered the Temple of Onaros to send their dreaming mind outward and find a life partner with psychic abilities who would renounce the outside world and come home to New Atlantis with the lover to whom they had bonded.

A few had failed in that mission, and Bendon had been one of them. His lover had stayed in a place called California.

But Bendon must have left her pregnant. And Claire must be his daughter.

Alexander's own mother had come from out in the world. And he thought that bonding with a wife from outside New Atlantis would not be a problem for him.

Maybe his head had been too swollen with success. He was skilled at telekinesis—the ability to affect the material world with his mind. Joining natural materials together and forming them into useful and artful shapes came naturally to him. He could melt precious metals and make them flow into the walls or the ceiling of a house. He could carve a block of marble from the earth, transport it back to New Atlantis, and form it into a soaking tub.

His talents were already sought after by the island's population. But even while establishing his professional reputation, he had begun studying the dream rituals. And he had walked into the Temple of Onaros confident that he would succeed in his mission.

The priest's voice stabbed into him. "The woman is not related to you."

Alexander's head jerked up. He wanted to shout that that wasn't the point at all. Instead he kept his tone calm and his words logical.

"If I go back to the outside world to court Claire, I must also come into contact with her mother. And she will poison her daughter against me."

The priest shook his head. "If you are asking to have a second chance, that is impossible. Over the years, we have learned that an initiate can only bond with the first woman he meets in the dream state. But you do have an option. If you choose to abandon the quest now, we can erase this outworlder from your memory, and you can marry a woman from the island."

Alexander raised his eyes to the priest. "No. I will accept the mission."

"Good. Then let us go to the locator and find out exactly where she lives and her full name."

Alexander climbed to his feet. A plan was already forming in his mind, a plan that would help him fool the mother and win the daughter for his own.

Claire Winston lay in bed, staring at the crack in the ceiling that had been in her room since they had moved to Sweetwater fifteen years ago. The crack looked like a road, disappearing into the hills. Sometimes, when her spirits were low, she would imagine that the road was magic, and she could somehow climb up to it and escape into another country where life was different.

Maybe she dreamed of escaping because her father had come from far away. Mom had told her that much, although she rarely talked about the man named Ben who had gotten her pregnant, then disappeared. But Claire had always thought Ben must have had magical powers—and that he had left her his legacy.

A knock at the door made her stiffen. "Yes?" she called out.

Her mother's voice came from the other side of the door. "Are you sick? I heard you call out in the night."

"No. I'm fine," Claire answered quickly, grateful that Jeanie hadn't opened the door. "I'll be down in a little while."

When she heard footsteps recede down the hall, she breathed out a little sigh. Her mother had heard her cry out? Like when she'd climaxed with her dream lover?

Embarrassed, she pressed her face into her hands—wishing she'd moved out when she'd bought the building that housed her pottery studio and gallery. There was room there for her to live, too.

But when she'd told Mom her plans, her distress had been painfully obvious. So Claire was still under her mother's roof—paying her emotional debts.

When Claire had been little, the other kids in elementary school had teased her unmercifully after that incident with Ted Schrader and the frog. Even now when the memory leaped into her mind, she tried to blot it out.

Too bad half the class had been there. They'd started whispering about her, and after that, nobody wanted to play with her, fearing guilt by association.

Then, lucky for her, Mom had gotten some money from the will of a relative she hadn't even known existed. So they'd moved from Monterey to Sweetwater—where nobody knew them. Claire had been so grateful. But she'd realized her mother had her own reasons for the move. In this new community, Jeanie could pretend to have gone through a bitter divorce, instead of being a single mother who had never married.

In Sweetwater, Claire had been careful to hide her special gifts—unless she was alone. Only her mother knew her secret. And Jeanie wasn't going to tell. That was one reason Claire was still here—instead of striking out on her own.

Or maybe as part of a couple? A lot of guys up here had been interested in her. She'd dated in high school. And she often went out with men vacationing in town. A time or two, she had allowed a man to get close. There had been Craig Cooper a few years ago. And more recently Sam Atholton. Each time, she'd felt like she was walking around on eggshells, afraid every second that she would reveal too much about herself. She'd ended up precipitating the very things she was afraid of. Craig said she was weird—and had broken off with her. Sam had said she was too closed up.

With each rejection, Jeanie had acted sympathetic. But Claire was sure her mother had been secretly pleased. She wasn't going to lose her daughter any time soon.

So Claire had given up thinking her life could ever change—until the stranger with a profile like a Greek god climbed into the high tower and carried her off to the summer house.

She snorted. He'd told her his name, but now she couldn't even remember it.

She stared off into space, trying to recall her dream lover. He was tall and appealing, with dark hair and dark eyes, very sensual lips. And hands that knew how to bring a woman pleasure.

Her other vivid memory was of his scent. Some men wore strong aftershave. His scent was much more individual, a temptingly masculine aroma that came directly from his skin.

She pressed her hand against her lips, struggling with needs and emotions he had stirred up. He had brought her sexual fulfillment— and so much more. He had understood her better than any real man ever had.

"Stop it!" she warned herself. "You conjured him up in a dream. And you can't even remember his name."

Still, the encounter had seemed so real. His touch had been light, yet it had felt like a hot flame flickering over her flesh, igniting fires deep within her. She had allowed herself to reach out to him, and it had been glorious. He'd taken her higher and higher toward a sharp peak of pleasure.

Then the witch had come in and spoiled it all.

Claire laughed. The witch. Lord, she'd turned her mother into a wicked witch!

That was as Freudian as the rest of the dream.

With a sigh, Claire heaved herself out of bed.

Her assistant, Vanessa, would open the showroom. But Claire had a commission she needed to finish.

four

After the disaster of his dream, Alexander avoided Bendon for the next few days. He knew his adoptive father wanted a report of what had transpired in the Temple of Dreams. But he simply couldn't talk about it.

Instead he picked a time when he knew Bendon would not be home and left a message, keeping details to a minimum, saying that he had to complete a project for an important client before he left to meet his soul mate in person.

But it wasn't that easy to avoid someone on the small island of New Atlantis. The next thing he knew, Bendon showed up at the building site where Alexander was working.

He had already used his mind to chip a patio area out of a hillside—in a location where no conventional construction method could have been successful. When the area was perfectly flat, he'd floated in a slab of solid granite he'd carved out of a Colorado mountain to use as a patio surface. After melting the bottom of the slab into the rock below, he was etching a bold design into the surface of the polished stone.

"Beautiful workmanship."

Alexander looked up to confront his adoptive father.

In the early years, Bendon had dropped by often to see his work. But it had been a while since he'd come to one of Alexander's construction sites.

"That patio is stunning. You've acquired a great deal of skill."

Alexander wiped the sweat off his forehead with the sleeve of his shirt. The work might not be physical labor, but it took a great deal of mental focus. "Thanks."

"You're already one of the most sought after artisans on the island. Your reputation will only grow when people see this work."

Again Alexander proffered his thanks, waiting for the real subject of the conversation.

Bendon shifted his weight from one foot to the other.

"So I expect you'll be leaving soon."

"Uh-huh. I'm trying to finish up this job so I can firm up my plans."

Bendon didn't take the hint. "Where are you headed?"

Striving to sound casual, Alexander answered, "The United States."

The next question came swiftly. "That's a big area. Where exactly?"

Alexander saw the tension on the older man's face. "Northern California."

"Oh."

Alexander swallowed. If he was successful in his quest, Claire would meet Bendon. Alexander would have to tell her about her father before he brought his soul mate to the island. Would that change her mind about coming?

Bendon must have caught the flicker of doubt in his expression. "It will work out for you. Fate wouldn't permit two failures in the same family."

"You're not a failure."

"We won't get into that debate."

Alexander nodded.

Bendon made a dismissive gesture. "Well, I just wanted to drop by and talk for a minute. But I'll let you get back to work."

"Thanks for thinking about me," Alexander answered stiffly. He had never felt more awkward with Bendon. They stood facing each other across the stone patio for several moments. Then the older man stepped forward and embraced him. "I wish you every success," he murmured before turning and walking away, leaving Alexander feeling strangely hollow.

Emotionally, he felt like he was betraying the man who had been his loving father since he was a little boy. Yet at the same time, he knew that he could never turn away from this mission.

And if he didn't succeed? He dismissed failure from his mind.

It was tempting to rush through the patio job. But he never gave less than his best to his work—which was one of the reasons he'd come so far so fast. And there was no point in being modest. He had a lot of talent, too.

Bendon had the same gift. Although he worked on government projects instead of as a private contractor, he had taught Alexander many skills and tricks of the trade. And Alexander knew he had passed his telekinetic ability on to his daughter. He'd been researching Claire Winston—and her mother, Jeanie Winston. Claire was a ceramic artist, and he suspected some of her pieces were formed as much with her mind as with conventional tools. He had seen pictures of her work in a catalogue from an exclusive gallery in San Francisco. The photos had impressed him, and he knew that if she was selling at the Cormack Gallery, she was well regarded.

That brought him a spurt of pride. His woman was making a reputation as an artist in her world.

His woman!

Well, not quite yet. One dream didn't form a bond. And what if her career made it harder for her to come to New Atlantis with him? Or would she have other reasons for refusing to leave?

He watched Bendon stride away, his back straight and rigid. Alexander wanted to run after him and ask the questions he'd never dared to ask, because he knew they were painful. If he found out what went wrong with Jeanie Winston, he might be able to avoid the same problems with her daughter. But he simply couldn't open that conversation. Bendon had kept those memories to himself. If he'd wanted to share the information, he would have.

So Alexander's only option was to make his own judgments—as best he could. And that way, if he failed, he would have no one to blame but himself.

FIVE

One of the secret air cars used by the residents of New Atlantis flew Alexander to Sausalito, where he would rent an automobile to drive up the coast, because nobody arrived in Sweetwater, California, on foot unless he was a homeless person.

Alexander had practiced his travel skills out in the world and at the school set up on New Atlantis for those who accepted the challenge of finding a soul mate off the island.

Still he was nervous about giving the whole show away as he stepped up to the car rental counter. But the temple had provided him with fake credentials—a working credit card and a driver's license from Barbados. Pretending to be from that island helped explain some of his strange speech patterns and the gaps in his knowledge about contemporary American life.

He had also practiced driving on the test course New Atlantis provided for residents who needed to handle a motor vehicle. His driving skills were adequate, and if he thought he was going to crash into something, he could always use his mind to cushion the impact.

After he left the rental car office, he had a bad moment when he entered a traffic circle and couldn't figure out how to get out again. He had to go around three times, watching what the other drivers did before finally exiting.

He knew that he must be on guard for the unexpected—starting with his own reactions. As he rounded a curve in the mountains and looked down on Sweetwater, the reality was like slamming into a solid rock wall at a hundred miles a hour.

He had to pull onto the shoulder of the road and catch his breath as he gazed down on the little resort town nestled between the mountains and the sea.

The main industry in the area was tourism. But the town had remained small because it was isolated. Which was good for him. A big city would have been harder to manage for someone from New Atlantis.

As he stared down at the little community, his heart began pounding so hard that he could barely catch his breath. Claire lived there. He would see her in person soon, not in a fairy-tale dream, and the thought filled him with as much dread as excitement.

He had come up with a plan to make himself look nonthreatening, but he could still mess this whole thing up if he wasn't careful. Yet there was no thought of turning back. Putting the car into gear, he started down the hill toward Sweetwater.

He knew where to find Claire's shop and pottery studio. They were outside the main business district on a road that ran parallel to the ocean. And the bed and breakfast that Jeanie owned was only a five-minute drive farther along the same road.

Claire was in her studio—trying to work. Each night after the dream, she had gone to bed expecting her midnight visitor to return. And each morning she woke up, knowing that she had spent the hours alone.

Now she struggled with a mixture of disappointment, relief, and uncertainty. But one thing she knew for sure: her work was suffering. She had been asked by Mr. Edgewater to make a set of tall, slab-sided vases, and she was way behind on the project.

He was a good customer. He'd bought extensively from her when she'd opened her studio, and he'd sent others to her shop.

Two of the vases she was making for him had been fired once, glazed, and had gone back into the kiln. But the third had cracked during the first firing, and she was starting over with slabs of porcelain, using a tapered wooden stick to seal the joints. Well, she was partly using the stick.

She was going for a subtle twist to the sides of the vase, so she gave it a push with her mind, changing the shape in a way that would be difficult to achieve with just her hands and tools.

Out in the front of the shop, the bell over the door rang, but she kept working. Her assistant, Vanessa, would take care of the customer while she stayed in the back at her worktable.

A short hall separated her studio and a small apartment from the shop, and she caught the faint sound of voices out front. The conversation stopped, and she assumed the customer was looking at her work. Some pieces were sculptural. Others were practical objects like pitchers and bowls.

But the customer didn't remain in the showroom. Instead she heard somewhat awkward footsteps proceeding down the hall. Not Vanessa's footsteps.

Claire froze, instantly transported back to that terrible day in school when she'd used her special talent and turned the class against her. She'd been using her talent to shape the clay with her mind, and now someone was going to catch her in the act!

Even as her hand faltered, she recognized her emotions had no grounds in reality. She'd been so off balance during the past few days that even the smallest thing could send a wave of cold panic over her.

She was sitting here in her own studio, and nobody could intuit her work method. As far as anyone knew, she was just doing the same thing as every other ceramic artist.

Still her stomach was in knots as she heard the footsteps approach. Struggling to seem like nothing was wrong, she kept her eyes on the vase for several heartbeats. When she looked up, she saw a large hand grasp the curtain that screened off her work area—as though the person on the other side felt the same hesitation that she did.

Then in one quick motion, the hand swept the curtain aside, and a man stepped into her work area. He looked to be in his late twenties. He was tall, with dark hair and dark eyes, and she felt a jolt of recognition when she gazed at his face.

SIX

Claire opened her mouth to say something. She wasn't even sure what it might have been. In the next second, she saw that the man's free hand gripped a cane. When he took a step forward, his left leg seemed to give him pain.

Any reference to the night in her room died behind her lips. Instead she asked, "Can I help you?"

"I hope so," he said in a deep voice that sent a little shiver over her skin. "I've traveled a long way to see you."

"Because?" she inquired.

"I've seen your work on a number of websites, and I wanted to meet you."

She didn't allow the flattery to turn her head. Instead she studied the man. When she'd seen his face she would have sworn . . .

No, that was impossible. The phantom lover who had come to her room hadn't walked with a limp. His body had been perfect—tall and straight and strong. And he hadn't been using a cane with a beautifully carved reptile head for a handle. It was very realistic, and she could almost imagine the mouth opening and a forked tongue darting out.

He followed her gaze. "If I have to lean on a walking stick, I want it to be amusing."

"Yes," she answered, wondering if she really agreed. She would have picked some other form of amusement.

He shifted the subject away from his infirmity. "I'm building a house for myself, and I wanted to commission some artworks specifically for the property."

"What kind of works?"

"Some dramatic sculptures similar to the ones you had on display in the Cormack Gallery a few months ago."

"You saw them?"

"Not in person. On the web."

She nodded. The web had changed the way people did business.

"I want something similar for the garden and also the interior. I've considered several artists, but I think you'd be the perfect one to take the commission."

She felt bound to tell him, "I . . . I'm working on something for a client now."

"That's fine. The house isn't finished."

"Where is it?"

"On a small island in the Caribbean. Near Barbados," he added.

He reached into the pocket of his sports jacket and took out several pictures.

She held up her hands. "I'd get wet clay all over them."

"Oh, right. I can hold them for you." He limped forward, one hand on the cane and the other holding the pictures. When he saw her watching him, he murmured, "Rock climbing accident."

She would have preferred to keep him on the other side of the table. Instead, he rounded it and closed the distance between them.

Despite the limp, his walk had a forceful quality that made her throat tighten.

She went very still, then dragged in a deep breath and let it out slowly. This close, she caught his very unique, very familiar scent. She turned to look quickly at him, and saw the Greek-god profile she remembered.

She wanted to say, *It's you, isn't it?* But then what? What was he going to answer? It seemed obvious that if he'd wanted to talk about the night in her room, he would have said something. Or was he playing some kind of game with her, waiting to see if she recognized him?

On the other hand, that might not be it at all. Perhaps her overactive imagination was playing tricks on her. Since the other night, she'd hardly thought of anything else besides her dream lover. She wanted to reconnect with him, so she was looking for signs that he and this man were one and the same.

He seemed calm and composed—like they'd just met and he really was approaching her with a job offer.

Struggling to hold her voice steady, she asked, "When did you hurt your leg?"

"A few months ago. It's taking a long time to heal," he answered, and she detected just a hint of strain in his voice.

When she didn't speak, he filled the silence. "Look at the pictures."

She'd forgotten all about the photographs. Bending her head, she saw a soaring modern house perched on the side of a hillside, the white stone contrasting with the green of the foliage around it and the blue of the ocean below.

"That's spectacular," she breathed. "Who's building it?"

"I am."

She turned her face toward him. "How do you get the structure to perch on the side of the hill like that?"

He grinned. "Trade secret. I have access to techniques that aren't available to conventional builders."

The way he said it raised goose bumps on her arms.

He shuffled the pictures, displaying a close-up. It showed an empty courtyard, completely open to the interior on two sides.

"Won't the rain come in?" she asked.

"I've built it to take the prevailing winds into consideration. And there's a screen that can slide into place if absolutely necessary." He moved the picture to the back and showed another, this one of a patio that jutted out from the cliff, seemingly defying gravity. "You can see there are lots of places for decorative artwork," he said.

"Yes."

"I want to surround myself with beautiful things."

She nodded.

"We can talk about some of my ideas—and yours. But for now, I'd like to know that you'll take the job."

She should give the offer some thought. Instead she heard herself say, "All right." Then added quickly, "At my usual rate, of course."

"Of course. I can leave you the pictures, so you'll be able to dream up something that goes with the actual setting."

"Dream?"

"Sometimes I dream about work that I want to create. Do you?"

She swallowed. "Did you use that word deliberately?"

"Why would I do that?"

She shrugged, then raised her chin. "Yes, sometimes I dream about a project—or a person."

"I find it's an effective shortcut." As he spoke, he set the photos down on the worktable, his hand brushing against her arm.

The light touch sent a shiver skittering across her skin.

She looked up, her gaze locking with his. He was the one who broke the contact first.

"I'm taking some time off to give the leg a rest. Can you recommend a place in town where I could stay?"

"My mother owns a bed-and-breakfast," she heard herself answering.

"That's perfect. Then we can talk about the commission in the evenings."

"Her place is called the Voice of the Dolphin."

"That's unusual. Where did she get the name?"

"I don't know," she answered. "But she was very sure about what she wanted to call the house. It's about a five-minute walk from here—down toward the cliff." She stopped. "Sorry. Maybe that's a long walk for you—I mean right now . . ." She stopped again, feeling like she was digging herself into a hole.

"I have a rental car. I'll drive." He paused as if to think for a moment. "It's probably too early to check in. Could I use the phone in the shop to call and make a reservation? Then I can look around town before I go over there."

"Of course. Vanessa can show you where to find the phone."

"Thanks."

He took a step back.

"Wait! I don't even know your name."

He stopped, looking suddenly like a small boy who had gotten caught with a bouquet of flowers he'd picked from a neighbor's yard. "Right. We've had a whole conversation and I haven't told you." He hesitated for just a second. "I'm Alexander Konnors."

Alexander. The name resonated inside her head. Inside her heart. But she only said, "Okay. Thanks."

Later, on the web, she would look for an architect with that name.

As she watched him limp down the hallway, she felt like he'd cast a spell over her—a spell that was lifting.

All at once, it seemed like he'd just pulled off something tricky, although she had no idea what it was.

She stood up, thinking to call him back and ask what was going

on. Instead, she sat down and picked up the stick she'd been using
to shape the vase.

Alexander's hand clamped around the snake's head at the top of the
cane, as he walked back to the front of the shop. He could feel perspiration filming his brow, and he resisted the impulse to wipe it with
his sleeve. It came from nerves—and from pain. Most of his life, he'd
been a stranger to any real discomfort. If he injured himself, he could
easily fix it. Bendon had taught him the skill before his teens.

He'd never gone the other way before—deliberately inflaming a
tendon to create the look and feel of an injured leg.

The damn thing felt foreign—like part of someone else's body.

Probably he shouldn't have gone for so much realism when he'd
manufactured the effects of a supposed rock-climbing accident. He
could heal it anytime he wanted, but that was a bad idea. If it didn't
hurt to walk on the leg, he'd forget to limp. And that little detail
might make Jeanie suspicious.

In his work, he'd learned that details could make or break a
project, so he'd bitten the bullet and gone for realism.

When he reached the front of the building, he told the salesclerk
that he would be staying in town and Claire had said he could call
the Voice of the Dolphin.

But for a moment, his mind went blank, and he didn't know how
to use the damn phone. Then his training kicked in, and he remembered you punched the numbers to send a signal to the person you
wanted to reach.

His hand clenched around the receiver as he listened to the ringing sound.

"My name is Konnors," he said when Jeanie answered, once
again using the name he'd chosen for an alias. Although it was easier to pronounce than his real name, it began with the same sound.
So, hopefully, he'd answer when spoken to. "Is there a room available?"

"Yes. But it's our most expensive one."

"I saw it on your website. The corner room on the first floor—right off the garden?"

"Yes."

"I'll take it. I'd like to stay for a week, if possible."

"A week would be fine."

As they talked, he was pretty sure that she didn't connect him with the dream. The next test would be when they met in person.

That prospect made his mouth go dry. Suddenly the interior of the shop felt stifling, although it had been fine a few minutes ago. He needed to get out into the sunshine and the wind. On Atlantis, most people spent a lot of their time out of doors. One side benefit of the force field was control of ultraviolet radiation, so it was possible to bask in the fresh air without worrying about the deleterious effects of the sun.

He walked out of Claire's shop and stood for a moment in the sunshine. The building was in an isolated location at the end of a roughly paved road. Looking toward the ocean, he could have been in the wilderness.

The sea drew him. Leaning on the cane, he hobbled down the steps, then started across a field of scrubby, windblown plants. They were nothing like the lush tropical vegetation on New Atlantis.

Still leaning on his cane with each step, he crossed the stretch of uneven ground, breathing in the salt air. Thorns clutched at his pants legs as he headed for the edge of the cliff. It was hard going, but the closer he got to the sea, the better he felt. He had never lived far from the water, and the sound of the surf had a soothing effect on his jangled nerves.

Claire lived by the sea, too. Which would help her feel at home on New Atlantis. Wouldn't it?

His mind went back over their meeting. He should have been more honest with her. From the look on her face, he was pretty sure she knew he was the dragonslayer who had shared her dream. At the very least, she suspected. And he'd wanted to confirm it. But he still had the hurdle of meeting Jeanie in front of him. Which had made him reluctant to come clean with Claire.

The circular reasoning made his head ache. He had been so sure he was prepared. Now he was wondering if he was making a mess of this whole thing when he'd barely gotten started.

After Alexander Konnors left her studio, Claire went back to her work. Or at least, she tried to. She had to finish shaping the vase so she could fire it, let it cool, dip it in the glaze and fire it again. There was no way to speed up the process, and she knew that time was slipping through her fingers. Mr. Edgewater had been a good customer, and she hated to disappoint him.

Yet her visitor had broken her train of thought. She sat staring at the vase on the table in front of her. Then, when she couldn't force herself back to work, she covered the clay with a damp cloth and turned to stare out the window.

Her workroom faced a wide, open stretch of rough land that bordered the ocean, and the view usually soothed her. Today as she gazed at the scrubby field, she drew in a sharp breath.

Someone was crossing the stretch of wild vegetation between her building and the ocean. Someone leaning on a cane.

Alexander!

Her heart leaped into her throat. He wasn't from around here. He didn't know that when the sea was high, it lapped at the undersides of the cliffs, eating away the soft rock and dirt, making the coastline unstable. Closer to the center of town, there were warning signs to keep people away from the edge. But not out here.

She leaped up, threw open the back door of the studio, and then started running across the field, heedless of the brambles catching on her skirt and scratching her legs.

"Alexander!" she shouted as she dashed toward him. But the sound of the waves pounding the shoreline drowned out her voice.

seven

Alexander headed for the edge of the cliff, his eyes focused on the horizon. He was hardly thinking about where he was going. The sea pulled him forward . . . until the ground suddenly gave way under his feet, sending him plunging toward the rocky beach thirty feet below him.

Pain shot through his bad leg, and he lost the cane as he fell toward the rocks.

Pieces of the cliff rained around him, falling past him and hitting the edge of the waves. He made a desperate grab for a clump of grass, even as he mentally groped for the side of the cliff, slowing his fall and pulling himself against the dirt and rock wall. Under ordinary circumstances he could have easily flown to safety. Now he found that the pain in his leg reduced his telekinetic ability, and he couldn't lift his entire weight. Damn, he hadn't realized that would happen.

Above him, he heard a voice call his name, and he knew it was Claire.

Fear leaped into his throat. Not for himself, but for her. If the ground had given way and sent him falling over the edge, the same thing could happen to her.

"Stay back!" he shouted.

"Alexander? Where are you?"

"I'm okay. Stay back," he called out desperately as he pictured her tumbling over the edge and crashing to the beach. He could try to break her fall, but he didn't know if he could cling to the cliff himself while he was doing it.

The wind whipped at his clothing and tore at his fingers as he clung to the vertical surface, searching for a place where his feet could find purchase. When he encountered a small indentation in the crumbling rock, he used his mind to scoop out a larger area for his right foot, then did the same for his left hand, so that he clung to the cliff like a mountain climber who had lost his rope.

"Alexander?"

His head jerked up, and his breath froze as he saw Claire looking down at him from about six feet above.

"Thank God," she breathed. "I thought . . ."

"Go back," he shouted, hearing the wind carry his voice out over the ocean.

"I have to get you up here."

"No! You'll get hurt." When he tried to shift himself into a better position, the tendon in his leg pulled, and he couldn't hold back a gasp of pain.

"Alexander!"

"Just the leg," he muttered.

Damn. The injury had seemed like such a good disguise. Now he cursed himself for thinking of such a harebrained idea.

He tried to pull himself up, and more debris shifted under his feet, tumbling down the side of the cliff and making Claire gasp.

"It's only rocks," he called out. "Get away from the edge. If it gave way once, it could do it again."

Ignoring him, she said, "We need a rope . . . or something."

"A tree branch."

"I'll look."

To his vast relief, she moved back, and he could hear her scurrying across the dry ground, searching for a branch.

While she was out of danger, he focused on getting to safety, grasping the cliff side with his fingernails but augmenting the process with his mind, creating a connection between his body and the rocky surface.

In that fashion, he ascended another couple of feet, then stopped to evaluate the cliff wall with his mind. His weight was a destabilizing factor, and his probing mind detected a crack developing farther back from the edge.

When he heard a noise, he looked up. Claire had picked that moment to return, holding a bamboo pole and looking hopeful.

"Somebody dropped this. Can we use it?"

"No. It's too dangerous. You have to go back; the wall is going to crack again."

"But . . ."

As he spoke, he reached up with one arm and used his fingers and his mind to scoop out another handhold. Then he carefully shifted his weight, moving upward another few inches.

With the exception of the artificially injured leg, he was in good shape. Good enough for this unexpected gymnastics.

Claire still hovered above him, and he would have bellowed at her again to go back, but he didn't have the resources to spare.

He focused on getting back to solid ground, but he kept part of his mind on the structure of the cliff. And when he felt a subtle tremor, he knew that he was in big trouble.

"Claire, where are you?" he called out.

"Right here."

Her voice was close—too close.

"I need your help," he bit out.

"The pole?"

"No! Move three feet back," he shouted.

"But . . ."

"For Kagan's sake, move back!"

"Kagan?"

He knew that in the heat of the crisis, he'd made a mistake. But he didn't have time to correct it now.

"Move back!" he bellowed.

He heard her feet shuffle across the ground, but he couldn't see how far she'd gone.

"Think about the edge of the cliff," he said. "Think about the rock and the dirt. Think about holding the ground together."

"What?" she gasped.

"Use your mind. Hold the cliff together for me. If it breaks off, I'm going down."

"I . . ."

"Maybe you can't do it," he bit out. "But it would help me a lot if you'd try."

He heard only silence from above. But he felt something different about the cliff face. It felt more solid. Maybe together they could stabilize it long enough for him to get to the top.

He kept part of his mind on the cliff, pulling her mental energy into a nexus with his own while he used the rest of his strength to get himself to firm ground.

He might have asked if she felt the mental bond between them—the way she had in the dream. But he couldn't spare the energy.

When he had to shift his weight to his bad leg, he gritted his teeth to keep from crying out. The last thing he needed was to have Claire more worried.

He'd told her to get back where the ground was stable. But when he was within a foot of the top, he felt her reach down and grab his jacket.

He cursed silently as she yanked upward. But she had given him the extra power he needed. Not just with her arms and hands; he sensed that she was yanking him up with her mind, as well.

He redoubled his own efforts, clawing upward until he toppled onto the ground at the cliff's edge.

Claire crouched over him, and he lay there panting for several seconds, but he couldn't spare himself the luxury of relaxing. Not yet.

"The edge is going," he gasped out as he grabbed Claire and staggered away from the shoreline. More dirt and rock gave way behind them, but he managed to get them to solid earth before his leg buckled, and he toppled into a heap on the ground, pulling Claire with him and twisting his body so that she landed on top of him, not on the hard ground.

They both lay there panting.

As he felt the vibrations around them, he held her close.

"I was so scared," she breathed, her face pressed to his chest.

"I was, too. For you. You could have gotten hurt."

She raised her head and looked down at him. "You were the one who went over the edge."

He managed a small laugh. "But I'm a mountain climber, remember."

"And you already hurt your leg."

"Yeah," he admitted. At the moment the damn thing was throbbing like a son of a bitch. But that wasn't the sensation that absorbed the bulk of his attention. He was much more aware of Claire's breasts pressed to his chest, her hips resting on his.

"What did you mean about using my mind?" she whispered.

"We can talk about that later," he muttered.

He had planned . . .

Didn't they have a saying here about the best laid plans of mice and men?

He'd thought he knew what he was getting into. But he might

have ended his life on the rocks below the cliff, and now he was damn glad to be alive.

When he looked up and saw her staring down at his mouth, his heart contracted. For a charged moment, neither of them moved. Then he reached up and cupped his hand around the back of her head.

Slowly, he drew her toward him, giving her time to pull away. But she came willingly.

He had kissed her in his dream. He had thought that experience was magic. It was nothing compared to real life.

The first touch of his lips on hers was like a bolt of lightning striking in a dry forest.

Heat blazed through him, the intensity startling.

He was instantly ready for sex, and he heard her make a sound deep in her throat as she felt his erection nestled in the juncture of her legs.

Until this moment, he had been able to fool himself into thinking that he could survive without her—if his quest ended like Bendon's. Now he knew he had been deluding himself. The needs he felt were too sharp, too urgent.

This was the woman who had been ordained for him since the beginning of time. When she opened her mouth for him, begging him for more intimate contact, he gladly accepted the invitation, angling his head to deepen the kiss, devouring her with his lips, his tongue, his teeth, even as his hands slid down her body, pressing her more tightly against his aching cock.

Claire had become his only reality. And he felt his heart slamming against his chest as he rocked her against himself.

She tasted of honey and sunshine and the same fevered urgency that he felt.

He rolled her to her side, then lifted himself so that he could cup her breast, squeezing the soft mound, then finding her pebble-hard nipple through the thin fabric of her shirt and bra.

She arched against him, making a sound of pleasure, and he knew that he would die if he didn't love her now. In some part of his mind, he was conscious of the blue sky above him, the sun beating down, the surf pounding the shore.

They were outside in the middle of the day, in a place where some tourist or resident might stumble over them, but that hardly mattered.

Growling deep in his throat, he gathered her close and rolled her to her back.

As he twisted to come down on top of her, a jolt of pain shot through his injured leg.

He must have made a sound, because her eyes blinked open.

"Oh Lord, Alexander. Your leg."

"Forget about it."

She looked around, and he saw her take in their surroundings.

"What was I thinking?" she whispered.

Alexander answered with a quick laugh. "That my timing isn't so great?"

"It's not funny. We need to get you . . ."

"Into bed?"

"You need to see a doctor."

"I don't think so."

"Someone should check you over."

He considered telling her he didn't have medical insurance, a complication in this society. But he thought better of that explanation. Instead, he sat up.

"I'm fine."

She brushed back her hair and looked out toward the sea. "I don't know what came over me."

As he stared into her eyes, a stanza of poetry leaped into his mind.

It was from a book on Bendon's bookshelves. Ironically, the name was *The Voice of the Dolphin*.

It had been written five hundred years ago by a prominent New Atlantian poet. And it was one of Bendon's favorites. He knew a lot of the poems in the book by heart—including the title piece. Had he recited them to Jeanie? Was that where she'd gotten the name for her B and B? It seemed like too much of a coincidence to be otherwise.

"What are you thinking?" Claire demanded.

"About a poem—

"Like the spirit of the forest, she will greet you in the morning mist.

"And you must reach for her and hold on fast.

"For when the sun shines out and burns away the haze.

"The world around the two of you will change."

"That's beautiful," she murmured.

"Yes." He remembered those lines but not the rest of the poem. He had never applied those words to himself. Now he felt a shiver travel over his skin, as he considered the implications. Everything *had* changed. But he still didn't know the future.

EIGHT

Alexander dragged in a breath and let it out. If Claire were the only other person involved, he would come clean with her—here and now. Too bad he couldn't sweep her off to some deserted island and make love to her. It would be like the fantasy environment of the other night, and with no distractions he'd probably be able to persuade her to his point of view.

But he wasn't free to do that. He had to consider Jeanie and the pain it would cause her if her only daughter vanished into thin air.

As though trying to read his thoughts, Claire was staring at him intently. And when she spoke, it wasn't about the poem. "When you were dangling off the cliff, you asked me to use my mind—to stabilize the ground."

He sighed. "Yes."

"How did you know about that?"

As he saw her waiting with the breath frozen in her lungs, he searched for an honest answer—one that wouldn't give away too much. "We have similar talents in my family, and we try to find people who can understand us."

"You . . . had the same problems when you were little?" she breathed. "The other kids made fun of you?"

"No. I come from a place where most of the people are like me."

She took that in with amazement.

"But the population of our island is small—and we don't want to intermarry. One way we look for a mate is by sending out our mind—in a dream. When we find the right man or woman we know it."

She caught her breath, then swallowed hard. "So you're admitting it was you in that dream I had a few nights ago."

"Yes."

Her cheeks reddened. "And you remember everything that happened?"

"Every lovely moment with you."

Her flush deepened.

He reached out to cup his hand over her shoulder and draw her close. "I wanted to give you pleasure. I knew you were the woman meant for me, and I wanted to forge the bond between us."

He stroked her hair. "I'd appreciate it if you didn't say anything to anyone about what I've told you."

He heard her swallow. "Okay."

She stayed where she was for a few seconds, then drew back, and he knew she couldn't quite accept what he was saying.

No surprise, since it was a strange story from her point of view.

She confirmed his assessment by changing the subject. "We should do something about your leg."

"Like what?"

"I'm a volunteer paramedic. If you won't go to a doctor, let me take a look at it."

He looked around. "Where?"

"At my studio."

He stood. When he put some weight on the leg, he had to clench his teeth to keep from crying out. He ran his hands through his hair, brushing off the dirt from the cliff side, then brushed at his clothing.

"I guess I look like I've been in an earthquake," he muttered.

"You look fine."

"Sure."

"Did your cane go over the cliff?" she asked.

"No. But it's too close to the edge to be safe to go back there." He made a quick decision, then turned and scanned the brush. When he located the cane, he held out his hand. The bushes stirred, and the wooden stick came gliding toward him across the scrappy ground.

Claire gasped as she watched it speed up, like a snake on steroids. When it reached his side, it stood upward, ready for his hand to grasp.

"How . . . how did you do that?"

"The same way you shape clay. Only on a larger scale. I can teach you."

"I'm having trouble taking all this in."

"I understand," he answered, hoping that she wouldn't have *too much* trouble. Not like her mother.

He would have to tell her about Jeanie and Bendon. But not until the bond was stronger.

She slung her arm around his waist. He leaned on her and the cane, but he held up some of the weight with his mind as they made their slow way back to the studio.

The sky had been blue. As they crossed the field, dark clouds blew in. Like the clouds after his dream, he thought with a pang. That made him think about the tower where Claire had been imprisoned. In some ways it was like the cliff. So what about the other elements—like the witch. He hoped she wasn't a foreshadowing of his relationship with Jeanie.

Before they reached the back door, the skies opened up, and they picked up their pace, hurrying inside.

They stepped into her workroom, and she led him farther into the building, to a bedroom at the opposite side of the old house.

"Lie down," she said. "I'll be back soon."

She walked down the hall again, and he heard low voices as she said something to her assistant.

She had told him to lie down, but when he looked at the white coverlet on the bed, he couldn't picture getting mud all over it. Instead, he hobbled to the bathroom, closed the door and turned on the shower, then began stripping off his wet clothes.

It felt heavenly to step under the hot water and wash the dirt from his hair and body. When he turned off the water, he heard the bathroom door open.

"I told you to get off the leg."

"And make a mess of your bed?"

He thought of stepping around the curtain as naked as a Greek athlete. That would serve her right. But he chickened out and reached around the curtain to grab a towel off the rack. After drying his hair, he fastened the towel around his waist and stepped out.

Claire was leaning against the doorway, her arms folded across her chest, her brows drawn into a scowl. She had on a clean shirt and jeans, and he suspected that she'd washed up at the sink in her workroom while he was in the shower.

She looked ready to tackle a mountain lion—and so damn appealing that his breath caught.

"I was going to examine your leg."

"The leg's tolerable," he muttered. "If you want to know how tolerable, I'll show you."

Without giving himself time to think, he crossed the bathroom and folded her into his arms. Instantly, desire came leaping back.

She made a strangled sound and clutched at him, and he hoped she was as aroused as he, because he didn't think he could stop this time.

As he gathered her close, he felt her trembling in his arms, but she didn't draw back. And when she began to run her hands over his back and shoulders, he knew that everything was going to be all right.

"Did you lock the door between the showroom and back here?" he asked, hearing the gritty sound of his own voice.

"Yes. And I told my assistant I wouldn't be available for the rest of the day."

"Good."

The need to bond with her was like a primal longing deep inside his soul. And he knew there was only one way to deal with it.

Outside, rain drummed on the roof. But he was barely aware of anything besides Claire.

When he tipped her head up, he saw his arousal reflected in her eyes.

Yet when she spoke, her voice was shaky. "Relationships haven't worked out so well for me."

"Because guys sensed your hidden talents?"

She swallowed hard. "Yes."

"You don't have to worry about that with me. Not at all."

He took a step back, then another. Because standing on the leg was still problematic, he propped his hips against the sink and cupped his hands over the porcelain edge. His gaze never left her, and he saw disappointment flash in her eyes.

He wiped it quickly away. Without physically touching her, he used an imaginary finger to trace the beautiful shape of her lips, then eased his way inside, playing with the sensitive tissue along the interior.

Her eyes widened.

"How . . . how are you doing that?"

"The same way I got the walking stick to come to me." As he spoke, he stroked back her gorgeous dark hair with an imaginary hand, exposing the sweet curl of one small ear. He gave her a wicked grin. Still not moving away from the sink, he used his imaginary mouth instead of his hand, nibbling at the curve of that ear, then stiffening his tongue and probing the interior.

He had never made love like this before. It had its points, he decided. Like standing a few feet away so that he could take in her heated reaction.

A new idea came to him, and he grinned.

"What?" she challenged.

He remained silent, his hands still gripping the sink as he reached for the front of the blouse she'd just put on and began to slip the buttons open one by one.

When the buttons were open, he pushed the fabric back and exposed the cups of a lacy white bra.

"Very pretty," he whispered.

He saw her sway on her feet. From where he was standing, he eased her against the edge of the doorway, giving her some support.

In one smooth motion, he worked the front catch of her bra and pushed the cups out of the way.

"Beautiful," he breathed, even as he pulled the shirt off her shoulders and down her arms, trapping them at her sides.

She stood before him, the front of her body naked to the waist, her arms imprisoned.

"Beautiful," he said again, lifting her breasts, cupping and shaping them. "This time, you're not getting away from me."

He heard her breath catch as he delicately began to inscribe circles around her breasts, drawing closer and closer to her pebbled nipples. He felt them tighten even more as he reached the raised centers.

He plucked at both nipples with imaginary fingers and used one more invisible hand to open the snap on her waistband. As he slicked her jeans down her legs, taking her panties with them, she made a strangled sound.

Struggling with her arms, she pulled them from the imprisoning sleeves and kicked her pants away.

"Alexander," she breathed. "You can't stay across the room from me."

The sight of her standing there naked in front of him and the pleading tone of her voice had him pushing away from the sink. He quickly discarded the towel as he crossed the space between them. When he folded her into his arms, the feel of her body against his made him gasp.

She raised her face toward him, and he lowered his mouth, drinking in the intoxicating taste of her.

The flavor, the feel of her was like a jolt of molten electricity that flowed to every nerve ending in his body.

He devoured her, and she gave him back the frantic passion. Together they staggered toward the bed, falling onto the coverlet in a tangle of arms and legs.

Somewhere in the back of his brain, the pain in his leg registered. But it was the least of what he felt.

His hand slid down to her hips, reveling in the feel of her silken skin. The sensation of touching her with his virtual hands had been exquisite. The real thing was even better.

He stroked his fingers over her back, down her flanks, as her hands moving over him intensified his pleasure.

When she made a whimpering sound and twisted against him, he felt as if his body was going to ignite and set the bedclothes on fire.

He bent to rub his face against her breasts, then took one distended nipple into his mouth. As he sucked, he felt her arch into the caress, heard a strangled moan escape her lips.

They rocked together on the bed.

He ached to be on top of her, inside her. Yet his own satisfaction was only a small part of what he craved. His pleasure was tied to hers. And he needed to bring her to the same peak of urgency that clawed at him.

"Claire," he murmured through trembling lips.

Ignoring the clamoring of his own body, he focused on her pleasure, taking one pebble-hard nipple between his thumb and fingers, doing the same with a phantom hand on the other side, while he trailed his other hand down her body, finding the hot, slick core of her.

When he dipped his finger into her silken folds, she made a low, needy sound and pressed her hips upward, telling him wordlessly that she craved more.

He thanked Kagan that she was ready for him because he knew that he would go insane if he didn't have her.

He rolled her to her back, his gaze locked with hers as he entered her in one swift stroke.

She stared up at him in wonder, then circled his shoulders with her arms. Smiling down at her, he began to move within her—slowly at first. But the rhythm quickly picked up, fast and hard.

She matched him stroke for stroke, her nails digging into his buttocks, intensifying the sensations. But that wasn't the only technique she was using.

He felt her inner muscles tightening and contracting around him, the squeezing like small shocks to his system.

"You're going to send me over the edge," he gasped out.

"Good . . ." Her voice trailed off as a spasm of pleasure seized her. The rhythm quickly carried them to a peak of ecstasy. He felt her topple off the edge of the world, then followed her into free fall.

He struggled to catch his breath, shaken to the depths of his soul.

She pulled him close against herself, cupping her hand around the back of his head, then smoothed her fingers through his hair.

He turned his head to the side so that he could stroke his lips against the silky skin of her cheek.

"I feel like I've come home," he whispered.

"Yes."

Outside, rain still drummed on the roof.

"Does it usually storm like this?" he asked.

"Not usually. Well, when my mom is upset."

His throat tightened, but he managed to say, "Your mom?"

"Yes. Somehow, when she's in a bad mood . . . a storm comes."

He felt suddenly light-headed. Bendon had never told him the special talent of the woman who had sent him away. Now he thought about the weather raging outside. Was she doing it? Why? Because she sensed her daughter bonding with a man from New Atlantis?

The temptation to simply let things drift along for a while was powerful. He had connected with Claire, and the experience had been soul shattering. Yet he knew that nothing was settled. Everything could still blow up in his face—the way it had for Bendon. And he suspected that he didn't have long to wait for disaster.

NINE

Claire felt Alexander reach down and twine his fingers with hers. She squeezed his hand, then shifted to her side so that the length of her body was pressed to his.

She should feel peaceful. She had just enjoyed the most satisfying sexual experience of her life. But something gnawed at her. Something she needed to understand.

Moving back a little, she searched Alexander's face. "You said you came from an island in the Caribbean," she said.

His features tensed. "Yes."

"So." She swallowed hard, wishing she could skip this subject but knowing she had to understand their parameters. "So you're not going to stay here, right?"

"I can't," he said, his voice gritty.

"Not even to be with . . . your soul mate?" she asked, using the phrase he had used earlier.

His face contorted. But he spoke with conviction. "I have obligations back home."

She felt her breath still.

"I was hoping you would come with me," he said quietly yet firmly.

"That might be difficult."

"Because?"

"I have my own obligations here. . . ."

"Your mother," he finished for her.

"How do you know?"

"I told you, I looked for background information about you before I came here. It would have made sense for you to move to a larger city where you'd have better access to the art world. But you stayed here. I figured it must be out of loyalty to her."

She answered with a small nod. "She brought me here when . . . when everything turned horrible for me." Her expression became fierce. "If you want to know, it was after I made a big mistake and used my . . . talent in school. When a boy put a frog down my neck. I threw it away from me. And I threw him across the room. Talk about making a spectacle of yourself. After that, the other kids treated me like a . . . a freak," she managed to say.

He reached for her and drew her toward him, stroking one hand across her back and shoulders, and caressing her hair with the other. "I'm so, so sorry. That would never happen on my island. Nobody would think anything about that in our schools. It wouldn't have happened to you. And it won't happen to our children."

She raised her head and looked at him. "Our children?" she murmured.

"Yes. Your children would never have to suffer what you did." He focused on her with an intensity that made her heart contract. "I want you for my wife. I want to raise a family with you—grow old with you."

"This is all happening so fast," she whispered.

"I know. And I understand. It was faster for me. As soon as I woke up from the dream, I *knew*. But it's just filtering into your reality. That's why I planned to stay here for a week."

"A week! Are you saying you want me to make a decision that will affect my whole life—and I have to do it so fast?"

"Yes," he answered, looking regretful. "I know you're the right woman for me, or I wouldn't have come to you in my dream. It wasn't like I visited a lot of candidates. I came straight to you."

When she didn't speak, he went on.

"And I understand loyalty to a parent. My own mother and father died when I was ten. My adoptive father was their friend, and he took me into his home. So I was like you in a way. Everything changed suddenly. Bendon knew I was sad and frightened. He worked hard to bring me out of my shell and help me understand that I had my whole life ahead of me. So I . . . get what you feel for your mother."

"You lost your parents when you were very young," she murmured.

"Yes. It was terrible. It shattered my world. But my adoptive father got me through it."

He pulled her to him, holding on as though he was the one who needed comfort. What he'd just told her helped her understand him better. Yet she knew there was more to it.

"What aren't you telling me?" she asked and felt him stiffen.

Alexander gave her a direct look. "The secrets of my island."

"Which are?"

His voice turned low. "We call our island New Atlantis because Atlantis was our original home."

"Atlantis!" She tipped her head to the side, staring at him. "You're talking about a mythical island."

"But it's no myth. It's real."

"Then why doesn't anyone know about it?"

He heaved in a breath and let it out. "For the same reason your mother took you out of that school and moved you up here. To prevent people from attacking you because you were different. We had similar problems with our neighbors, the ancient Greeks. So we moved away. And we let ourselves fade into myth—as far as the rest of the planet was concerned."

"But how can you keep your island hidden?"

That was one of the crucial questions they would have to deal with. Being as straightforward as he dared, he said, "It's hard to talk about our island. We are taught secrecy at a very early age. Still, you have the right to know about us. We protect it with a force field generated from the psychic abilities our people. But there aren't enough of us to keep it at full strength. So men and women of marriageable age go to the Temple of Dreams and send their minds out into the world to find a soul mate. Someone we know will be like us."

He watched her trying to take all that in.

"If someone else told me that wild story, I'd think they were lying—or insane."

"But you believe me, because you remember our first meeting—in a dream. A very vivid dream."

"Yes." She licked her lips, then asked a question. "All of your people can . . . can affect the physical world with their minds?"

"We have different talents. Some of us can view scenes at faraway locations. Some can change to different shapes. Others can communicate with the dead."

He took in her incredulous expression and gave a small laugh. "I was hoping to break that to you a little more gradually."

"I'll bet," she managed.

"Some of us can communicate mind to mind." He stopped speaking and focused in a way he'd never tried before, finding he could send his thoughts directly to her. *Soul mates can do that.*

"Oh!"

I've never communicated through thought before. Only with you.

While she was still grappling with that, he went on. "Something else that might interest you. We have a special way to regenerate cells. If you come to New Atlantis, you could expect to live three or four hundred years."

Her eyes widened.

"It's one of the advantages of our island. Another is having your soul mate by your side."

She considered that silently, then asked. "Could I go home to visit my mother?"

"Of course."

"But?"

"You'd be far away most of the time."

"I have to think about it."

"I know."

"On the cliff you said, 'Thank Kagan.' Is that your name for . . . God?"

"No. It's the name of the man who came up with the plan for moving our people to our new home. He's a hero to us." He stroked his hands over her back. "Maybe I can help you think about the advantages of living there with me." He lowered his head and brought his mouth down on hers.

"No fair," she breathed.

"Very fair," he said, speaking against her mouth.

It started off as a sweet kiss but quickly turned fierce. She wanted to tell him that he couldn't sweep her off her feet with sexual magnetism. Whatever she decided must be done calmly and rationally. But as soon as his lips touched hers and his hands moved from her back to her breasts, rational thought became impossible.

Heat leaped between them, around them, inside them. And she was helpless to do anything besides give herself over to the magic of the connection they'd forged.

"My soul mate," he murmured. "Oh, Claire, I didn't know it could be like this."

As he spoke, he kissed her breasts, then moved so that he could slide his mouth down her body, pausing to tickle her ribs with his tongue, circle her navel, and settle at the juncture of her legs.

She gasped as he parted her with his mouth, then found her clit, circling it with his tongue, then sucking delicately.

She called out his name, then tangled her fingers in his hair. "Come back up here."

He raised his head, grinning with male arrogance, as he took her into his arms and rolled to his back.

"This time when we make love, I want to see you on top of me. I want to see your hands on your breasts as you move up and down on me."

She might have been embarrassed by such directness. But not with this man. Not with Alexander.

ten

They slept, warm and intimate, under the covers. It was late in the afternoon when they stirred on the bed.

"Do you want me to go to the Voice of the Dolphin with you?"

He considered the offer. "If you do, looking so happy and satisfied, your mother will know we've been together."

She sat up and gave him an appraising look. "Are you planning to be dishonest with her?"

He felt a small chill travel over his skin. "I wasn't planning to burst into her house and announce that I wanted to take her daughter away."

She answered with a tight nod.

"But I hate orchestrating the meeting."

She thought for a moment. "Sometimes I work late. You could go ahead and check in. Then I'll come."

As he got out of bed, he thought about the jeans and shirt he'd ruined when he'd climbed back up the cliff.

"I need to change my clothing." He looked ruefully outside at the rain. "I could levitate my duffle bag in here. But maybe it would be more discreet if you got it for me."

"Yes."

While she got dressed and grabbed an umbrella, he dug his car keys out of his pocket. When she'd brought him the bag, he changed into a clean pair of jeans and a button-down shirt.

After he finished dressing, he walked to the window where she was standing, looking out at the rain.

"This is terrible weather. I'll bet some of my mom's customers have canceled."

"Yeah." He shifted his weight from one foot to the other, reluctant to leave. He felt like he had forged a true bond with Claire in this room. The two of them were fine on their own. But what would happen when they had to deal with the reality of her life?

He heard himself make a rough sound.

When she whirled to see what was wrong, he reached for her, pulling her close, hanging on. As she wrapped her arms around him, he let out the breath he'd been holding.

"I hate being separated, now that I've found you."

"Yes," she murmured.

But he wasn't sure her agreement carried the deep conviction that he felt. What had happened between her mother and Bendon? He cursed himself for not having the courage to ask. Because now he was operating blind.

"I'll see you later. After dinner."

"Yes," he agreed, although he wanted to suggest that as soon as she got home, they'd go to Jeanie and say they were getting married. But the rational part of his mind knew that rushing things was the wrong approach, so he wrapped his arms tightly around Claire for one more moment, then forced himself to step away from her and walk to the door.

It was still raining hard when he exited her workroom, and he shuddered. All that rain felt abnormal.

Where he came from, it might rain hard in the late afternoon in the spring and summer. But it never poured all day.

Of course, the elders could have arranged for controlled rain. Alexander had always taken the weather for granted, so he had never asked about it.

Was this constant storm normal? Or was Jeanie displaying her temper? And if so, what was he going to do about it?

Feeling like he was being forced into a trap, he drove to the Voice of the Dolphin. When he pulled to a stop in front of the sprawling Victorian, he was hoping the owner might be busy with other guests. But, through the rain, he saw a figure huddled in a chair on the front porch and knew it was Jeanie.

Resigned to some sort of confrontation, he climbed out of the car and limped toward the stairs, leaning heavily on the cane, moving as fast as he could through the downpour. By the time he reached the porch, he felt like he'd stepped out of the shower again.

She looked up as he approached, and he saw that she had once been pretty—a lot prettier than the witch in the dream. Still, her dark hair was streaked with gray, and deep lines were etched beside her mouth and her eyes.

"Mrs. Winston?" he asked, using the title that she had given herself without benefit of marriage.

She nodded, looking him up and down, taking in his face and the cane.

"I'm Alexander Konnors."

She didn't bother to put on a friendly face, and he wondered how she stayed in business if she acted this way with all her guests. Or was this special for him?

He had to remind himself that she hadn't been sad and bitter as a young woman. Her life had made her the way she was. But she had always been there for her daughter. Maybe that was the key. If Claire was happily settled down, perhaps that would make up for all the sadness and pain.

But he couldn't change her circumstances all at once. He had to take it one step at a time.

"I'd like to see that room," he said.

She stood, her arms folded across her chest. "Where are you from?"

He'd already told Claire he was from New Atlantis. He wasn't going to be that explicit with her mother.

"I live on a small island, not far from the Florida coast."

She took that in, then tipped her head to the side, studying him. "Have we met before?"

"I don't think so."

"How did you hurt your leg?"

"Rock-climbing accident," he answered, the lie sticking in his throat.

"Will you be able to manage the steps?"

"I've made it to the porch. The room is on the first floor. Right?"

She looked like she wanted to say she was putting him in the attic. Instead, she said, "I'd like payment for the first three days in advance."

"Certainly." He got out the credit card and handed it over. She turned it over, examining it like she expected it to grow a layer of mold.

He followed her to the office, fighting the tightness in his chest.

He wanted to tell her he understood what she had been through with Bendon—and then with a daughter who was different from the other children. He wanted to thank her for taking such good care of Claire. But he stayed away from anything personal.

"So how many other guests do you have?" he asked.

"None. I had several reservations. But they canceled because of the bad weather."

Oh great, there would be nobody besides Claire to act as a buffer between himself and Jeanie.

He went out into the rain again to get his duffle bag from the trunk. Jeanie could have offered to help, but she let him carry it awkwardly up the porch steps, then into the house.

He followed her down the hall to a large bedroom with a sitting room attached and French doors that opened onto a private patio.

The decor ran to flowered wallpaper and lace curtains, nothing like his sleek bedroom at home.

"Probably not your taste," she murmured.

"It's charming. I see why the Voice of the Dolphin is so popular."

That seemed to thaw her a bit. After reciting the hours she served breakfast, she finally left him alone, and he was free to turn down the coverlet. Lying down on the bed, he imagined Claire there beside him and was instantly aroused.

Still, it felt good to get off his leg. He was tempted again to fix the ligaments he'd deliberately injured. But he knew he needed to stay in character. So he relaxed for an hour, then ordered himself to get up again.

By way of being friendly, he asked Jeanie about the restaurants in town, and she directed him to the book of menus that she kept on a table in the sitting room.

Without much interest he selected one, then forced himself to go out in the rain again. It was a lonely meal at a table by the window in the North Country Lodge. But he ate a little of each course, because he didn't want Jeanie to know he'd finished the meal in half an hour.

Leaning on his cane and cursing the injured leg, he sloshed through the rain back to his car, then from the car to the B and B.

The lights were turned low in the front hall and the sitting room. But the moment he entered his own room, he knew someone was in there. Jeanie, sneaking a look through his belongings?

He stiffened, then saw a shadow detach itself from the wall.

"Claire!"

Suddenly energized, he tossed the cane onto the easy chair and crossed to her, taking her in his arms, holding on for dear life.

"Being away from you was agony," he said.

"Yes." She lifted her face for a long, drugging kiss. He wrapped her close, slid his hand down her back to her hips, pressing her against the erection that strained behind the fly of his jeans.

She reached under his T-shirt, pushing it up as she splayed her hands against his back. Her touch on his heated skin was heavenly.

He eased far enough away so that he could start opening the buttons down the front of her blouse.

She made a small sound in her throat, telling him that she approved.

He had made love to her only a few hours before, but he was as aroused as he'd been when he'd first taken her in his arms.

And she seemed just as needy. But the sound of the door opening made her go rigid.

eleven

When the overhead light snapped on, he stood blinking in the light, then focused on Jeanie, who was standing in the doorway. She held a small circular object in one hand. When he saw it, he felt sickness rise in his throat.

"I remember," she said in a deadly quiet tone, then added, "Everything."

"What?" Claire gasped. "What are you doing here?"

"He came to steal you away from me, didn't he? And you were going with him!"

Claire's gaze shot to Alexander, then back to her mother. "I wasn't going to sneak away. I was going to tell you about Alexander. He comes from an island in the Caribbean."

"I know all about New Atlantis," Jeanie ground out.

"She went through my luggage and took out something that belongs to me," Alexander explained in a flat voice. "It's a memory disk. Sometimes one of us goes out into the world and the experience makes him lose his memory. The stone brings back memories of New Atlantis."

Claire kept her focus on her mother. "Did you snoop though his belongings?"

"I had to."

"Why?"

"Because I suspected what was going on. From the dream."

"You were really there—with us?"

"Yes," she spat out. "And I'll bet there's a lot he hasn't shared with you. I told you your father came from far away—then left me pregnant. He was from New Atlantis. That's where your . . . special talents come from. Your father."

"He didn't leave you," Alexander broke in. "He asked you to go back with him, and you wouldn't do it. And if he left, then he didn't know you were pregnant."

"How do you know all that?" Jeanie demanded.

"Because that's not the way our people behave. We go out into the world to find our soul mate. And we want to bring that person back with us."

"To help shore up your precious force field," Jeanie added.

"Yes. What's wrong with that?"

"You take our people captive."

"You're turning it into something base. You don't know how much Bendon suffered after you rejected him." As soon as he had said that, he wished he'd kept his mouth shut.

Claire stared at him in sick fascination. "Bendon? The man you said was your adoptive father."

"Yes," he said quietly.

"You knew all about him and my mother? You knew I was his daughter, and you didn't say anything to me?"

"I couldn't. Not yet."

"You lied to me."

"No. I just didn't tell you everything—yet."

Claire took a step back, and he saw that all the color had drained from her face.

"Bendon loved your mother. When she refused to go with him, she broke his heart."

"I didn't refuse. He told me it was a critical time for the force field—and we had to go back right then. My mother was dying, and I needed to stay with her, but he couldn't give that time. So he left."

Alexander was pretty sure there was more to it. "You're not telling me all of it are you? Just your warped point of view." He could see from her expression that he'd scored a point.

But before he could get some clarification, she went on the attack again.

"Now that we're letting it all hang out, you might as well explain why you're going around with a bum leg when all you have to do is fix it with your mind—the way you'd fix anything else," Jeanie demanded.

Claire gasped as the impact of that question hit her.

He whirled back toward her, feeling like he was standing on the side of a crumbling mountain. "I thought I'd be less threatening to both of you if I . . ." He gulped. "Give me a chance to explain. I knew about Bendon. As soon as I saw your mother in the dream, I knew she presented a tremendous complication for me. I needed . . ."

She looked at him in horror. "A tremendous complication! That's just great. I'm tired of listening to your lying explanations." Claire turned and ran from the room. He staggered after her, but from the corner of his eye, he could see Jeanie's triumphant expression.

Claire threw the front door open and ran into the rain, heading for the hills in back of the house. He sent his mind toward her. He couldn't interfere with the will of another person, so he couldn't stop her, but when his probing thoughts bounced against the mountain, he gasped.

All the water had made the ground unstable. The vibration of her running feet was going to bring mud and rock raining down on her.

"Claire, for Kagan's sake. Come back Claire," he shouted into the rain.

She didn't stop, and he quickly lost sight of her in the downpour.

Cursing the leg, Alexander considered his options. He could try to follow her with the damn self-inflicted injury making it impossible for him to run. He chose to take precious seconds to send his thoughts into the muscle and sinew of his injured leg, making quick, inexact repairs.

Jeanie came up behind him.

"You've lost her."

"So have you, you damn fool woman. You've soaked the mountain with water, and now it's going to come tumbling down on her."

He shot Jeanie a look that would have killed her if he'd had the force of his mind behind it. But he had more important uses for his energy.

As Jeanie gasped he ran out into the rain. The leg wasn't exactly healed, and every step brought a jolt of pain, but he pushed himself, dividing his mental energy between himself, the mountain, and Claire.

He ran through the rain and darkness, following her trail. He could hardly see with his eyes. But he had forged a connection with his soul mate, and he could tell where she was.

"Come back," he shouted. "Claire, come back. The mountain's coming down."

The rain suddenly stopped as though it had never been. But he spared little energy for tracking the weather.

His focus was on Claire. Either she didn't hear him, or she didn't care what he was saying. His only choice was to follow her up the slope. And when he felt the ground begin to shake under his feet, he speeded up.

He was still calling his soul mate when rocks and mud high up the mountain broke loose and began crashing down the slope toward her.

He had moved massive slabs and granite with his mind, but he had never stopped a mountain sliding downhill. He tried to do it now, sending a mighty invisible hand upward to shield Claire from the debris. He couldn't repel gravity, but he found he could divert the falling mud and rock. Gasping for breath, he climbed upward until he found Claire, huddled in a crevice in the rock.

"Down," he cried out. "Get down."

He threw himself on top of her, sheltering her with his body as he tried to shield her with his mind.

But it was too much effort. He was already exhausted, and more debris was raining down. He could feel a tremendous boulder tearing loose above them, hurtling toward them.

"Help me," he panted. "Give me your energy."

"How?" she gasped out.

Like we did at the cliff. Just like that.

He prayed that she trusted him enough to merge her mental power with his. If she rejected him now, they were both dead. And if she didn't trust him, maybe death was best, because he had lived with Bendon and seen his misery. And he had seen what Jeanie's misery and anger had done to her.

The ground shook, as the boulder came rolling down the mountain toward them. Alexander clenched his hand on Claire's shoulder and turned her toward him, his fingers digging into her flesh.

I love you, he shouted into her mind. *I love you. Help me save our lives.*

The massive rock was seconds from crashing into them when he felt her add the force he needed to stop it. He pulled her energy inside himself, then expanded it outward.

He huddled protectively over her, directing energy to a mental shield as more debris rumbled over them. Finally it passed, traveling on down the mountain, headed for the house.

As his mental sensors followed it, Claire gasped. "Mom! Oh Lord, Mom."

It was so tempting to tell her he had no energy left, that there was nothing he could do about the woman who had tried her best to tear them apart. And—in the end—perhaps she had succeeded. Yet Alexander's conscience wouldn't let him lie. Not again. Not when a life was in danger.

He tightened his grip on Claire's hand. "We can shift it to the right."

"Yes!" She pumped a current of mental power into him.

Working together, they swerved the river of mud and rock around the Voice of the Dolphin, diverting it onto the field next to the house and then over the cliff and into the sea.

He heard the tremendous roar as the rock slide hit the water, and he knew it would have flattened the house, then buried it.

Finally the noise stopped reverberating in his ears, and the ground stopped shaking.

"Thank you," Claire breathed.

Exhausted, he tried to sit up and fell back against the rocks.

All he could do was lie there, dragging in air. He felt sick and dizzy. He'd never expended that kind of enormous mental energy before, and he knew the physical effect had been more than he ever should have attempted.

But he'd had no other choice if he wanted to save Claire and her mother.

If he'd been on the island, his own people would have gathered around him, lending him their life force. But he was alone here—a stranger in a strange land.

He began to shiver in his soaking clothes.

Claire's hand tightened on his. "Alexander," he heard her cry out.

But her voice seemed very far away.

I love you. He wanted her to know that.

"Alexander, tell me what to do for you!" she cried.

Energy . . . He was too spent to say more. As he lay there, he began to lose sensation in his body. And he felt his mind sinking into a cold place. A deep, freezing pit. If he landed at the bottom, he knew he wouldn't have the strength to claw his way back up.

The cold grew more intense, enveloping him, chilling him to the bone. And he thought this wouldn't be such a bad way to die. Like freezing to death, where you just went to sleep and never woke up.

His senses were almost dead, yet he still felt Claire's fingers gripping his hand. And he could hear her voice, but it seemed to come from miles away.

"Alexander, come back to me. Alexander! I don't want to be like my mother. I want the man I love with me. My soul mate. I want you with me."

The man she loved. The words registered in his fogged mind.

His lips moved, and he tried to speak her name. But no sound came out.

Her fingers clutched at his cold flesh, and he felt the warmth of her hand. Not just her hand, he felt her warm thoughts pressing themselves into his mind.

Alexander, don't you dare leave me. You saved my life! And Mom's. Don't you dare leave me now. Alexander, I was a fool to run away. I didn't understand. I didn't understand the pain of breaking the link with your soul mate. But if you die, I will, too.

She loved him! He had to see her, so his eyes fluttered open.

"Alexander. Oh Lord, yes. Alexander, stay with me. Please."

Before he could answer, something moved in the darkness. And all at once, it wasn't just Claire, crouching over him. Someone else was there, too.

"Mr. Edgewater?" Claire gasped out. "What are you doing here?"

"We'll talk later," he answered gruffly. "First we have to bring Alexander back."

Bendon!

"I'm here, son. I'm here."

He wrapped Alexander in his warmth, wrapped Claire, too. And the three of them huddled together on the mountain. As Bendon added his power to Claire's, Alexander felt the cold lifting from him.

When Alexander closed his fingers around Claire's hand, she sobbed out her relief. And when he used his mind to pull her to him, she nestled against him, her tears wetting his already soaked shirt.

"We need to get you inside," Bendon said.

"Yes," he managed, then looked from Claire to the tall man who stood beside her. "Your father came to help us," he whispered.

"My father!" Her head whipped toward Bendon. "Mr. Edgewater? You are . . . my father?"

"I watched over you. I did what I could for you and your mother after she asked me to leave," he said gruffly. "I wanted to be part of your life, so I did it the only way I could. I knew if you were ever in trouble—which is how I got here in time to save Alexander. And right now, we need to get him back to the house."

"Yes," she agreed.

Bendon helped him up, and Alexander knew he was using his mind as much as his muscles. While he supported Alexander on one side, Claire supported him on the other, and together they made their slow way down the mountain.

As they drew near the Voice of the Dolphin, Alexander saw Jeanie standing on the front lawn, staring up at them.

"Thank God," she breathed when she saw her daughter.

Then she realized Bendon was on the other side of Alexander, and she gasped. "You! Good lord, you hardly look a day older than when you left."

He ignored the last comment. "I wasn't going to let Alexander die," he said in a gruff voice. "Even for you."

"I didn't want him to die," she choked out. "I just . . . I just . . . didn't want him to take Claire away."

"It's not a question of taking away. But you never did understand that, did you?"

As she stared mutely at him, he continued. "Anytime you needed me, you could have called out to me. When I could, I helped you. I made sure you had the money to buy this property."

"Oh Lord," Jeanie gasped.

Claire stared at him. "And you helped me get my business established. You were one of my best customers."

He nodded.

All the defiance went out of Jeanie's features. She looked down at her hands, then raised her face to Bendon. Her lips trembled as she said, "I . . . I was afraid to go with you. Then I was too proud to admit I'd made a mistake."

He answered with a rough sound. "So your pride kept both of us miserable all these years. But I'm here now, because I knew Claire and Alexander needed me. And . . . if you want to have an honest conversation with me, we can."

She looked overwhelmed. Then she went to him and fell sobbing into his arms.

Claire stared in wonder at her mother and the man who was her father, the man who had kept himself in her life all along.

Alexander tugged on her hand. "I need to lie down, and I want you with me."

"Yes."

She kept her arm around him, helping him into the bedroom, and he flopped onto the bed.

He was too tired to use his powers to make his clothing disappear, so he let her ease off his shoes, then tug his jeans down. He raised his hips to help her get them off, then raised his head and shoulders to help her with his T-shirt.

After that, she brought a washcloth and towel, and bathed his face and hands. When she came back, she had taken off her own shirt and jeans. Climbing in beside him, she covered them both and clasped him close, stroking her lips against his cheek.

He brought his arm up to cradle her against him.

"I'm so sorry I ran away," she whispered.

"It worked out okay."

"It was a terrible shock . . . to find out your adoptive father was my father."

"And all this time your mother had been acting like he abandoned you."

She stiffened. "She thought . . . I guess I don't know what was really in her mind."

"Maybe I shouldn't have mentioned that," he muttered.

"No. We need to be honest and open with each other."

He swallowed. "Yes. I'm sorry I came to you with . . . a leg I injured. It turned out to be a dumb idea."

"It caused you a lot of pain."

"Yeah. Well, I guess that's my punishment."

"It's fitting."

She softened the words by laying her head on his shoulder.

Because he needed to hear her say it, he asked, "And everything's okay? With us?"

"You mean, do I know you risked your life to save me and Mom? And after that, I figured out that living without you would be like living in hell?"

His grip tightened on her. "Yeah, that."

"I want you with me. I don't know how Mom could have sent my father . . . Bendon away. But he came back, to watch over me."

"I hope they can work out their problems." Alexander dragged in a breath and let it out in a rush. "But the important thing right now is—are you coming home with me?"

"It's kind of scary, leaving everything I know."

"You already know your father. And you'll make lots of friends on New Atlantis. We're always grateful to the new members of our society for joining us. But you're bringing more than just your mental energy. You'll be acclaimed for your artistic talent. And we'll be together."

"Yes, that's the important thing, being with you."

He wrapped his arms around her. "Claire, I love you so much. And I was so afraid I'd lose you. Right from the beginning—when I saw your mother in the dream. I knew she would try and stop me from bonding with you."

She raised up so she could meet his eyes. "I think trying to work around her was the only thing you could do."

"Even when it blew up in my face?"

"You didn't know she was going to go through your luggage."

"She was desperate. It made sense from her point of view."

"Are you defending her?"

"I understand how it is to fear losing someone you love." His hold on her tightened. "Claire. You are my love. My soul mate. The light of my life." He felt his breath hitch. "And I can't wait to show my island to you."

"You're supposed to be resting."

"Am I?" he asked, feeling a wicked grin spread across his face. He pulled her on top of him, stroking his hands down her back, pressing her center against the erection that had bloomed as he lay in bed next to his love.

With his virtual hand, he cupped the back of her head and brought her lips down to his.

Her mouth opened, and her body melted against the length of his.

He gave her long, luxurious kisses, secure that she really did belong to him. And she returned the greedy intensity of his ardor.

He wanted to cup her breasts, tease her nipples. But he couldn't stand the idea of lifting her away from him to do it, so he inserted two phantom hands between them—the hands he was beginning to enjoy very much.

She gasped when she felt what he was doing. "You shouldn't," she moaned.

"No. This is exactly what I need."

"You're not supposed to exert yourself."

"Says who?"

"Lie back and let me do the work."

He grinned. "Well, if you put it that way."

He settled comfortably against the sheet, arranging the pillow behind his head and closing his eyes. When he felt the feather-light touch of Claire's fingers on his cheek, he opened his eyes again and smiled at her. Then he saw the look of concentration on her face—and also saw that her arms were folded across her chest.

He knew instantly what she was doing—practicing the skill he had used on her.

When her phantom fingers moved down his body, circling his nipples the way he had done to her, then plucking at them, he made a sound of pleasure, and she grinned at him looking triumphant.

Then her invisible hands drifted lower. Unseen fingers dipped into his navel while her touch trailed over his hip bones and down his thighs. He held his breath, aching for her touch, but she made him wait for a few more moments before closing her invisible hand around his cock.

He made a strangled sound, arching into the caress.

He had forgotten he was still wearing his briefs until she pulled them down with her real hands, then leaned over him, her beautiful raven hair brushing against his midsection as her tongue delicately circled the head of his cock.

When she took him into her mouth, he thought he would go up in flames.

He let her keep up the sweet torture for less than a minute, because he was too close to the edge to take more.

She drove him almost to orgasm, but he managed to cry out, "Stop."

She lifted her mouth from him. "I want . . ."

"Everything," he finished for her.

He was in too much of a hurry for finesse. With his unseen hands, he reached down for her, lifting her up and over him, holding her hips so that he could settle her onto his erection.

He thanked Kagan that she was wet and slick for him.

She cried out and began to move, and as she did, he caressed her breasts, wringing a shuddering gasp from her. After she drove them both to a shattering climax, he cradled her sweet, slick body against his, kissing her cheek, her neck, her ear, marveling at the utter peace he felt.

Claire nestled against him. For so long she had felt like she had to guard herself around other people—lest she do something that made her seem weird. Now she marveled at finding a man who accepted her for what she was. More than accepted. He loved her for what she was.

They slept curled in each other's arms for a few hours, then got up and took a long, luxurious shower. It was three in the morning when they went in search of something to eat.

To her surprise, Bendon and Jeanie were at the kitchen table, each with a mug of coffee. Between them was a plate with cinnamon buns and apple tarts.

Claire was a little embarrassed. She wasn't used to getting out of bed with her lover and finding they weren't alone.

"Baking. Mom's solution to stress," she commented.

Bendon glanced up. "I've missed her cooking."

Alexander gave him a long look. "That's why you did all that baking stuff? I thought you were trying to cheer me up after my parents died."

"No. I was trying to stay connected with Jeanie—trying to make the things she'd made for me," he said, his voice thick.

Jeanie reached for his hand and held on tightly. He smiled at her. "It's a novelty, daring to be happy."

"I'm so sorry," she whispered.

"You have a lot of years to make it up to me." He looked toward Claire. "But having such an accomplished daughter *is* some compensation." He stood and held out his arms to her, and she crossed the room and went into them. He hugged her tightly. "It was so hard, dipping into your life and not being able to tell you who I was. We're going to get to know each other. You and I . . . and . . ."

He stopped and looked at Jeanie.

"And I'm coming to New Atlantis with you," she said in a trembling voice.

Then she turned to Alexander. "Bendon forgives me. I hope you will, too."

"Of course," he answered.

Finally she looked at Claire. "And you."

Claire felt tears gather in her eyes. "Mom, there's nothing to forgive."

"Yes there is. I kept you from your father. From your people. From your heritage."

"That's behind us. All the bad times are behind us," Bendon said, pulling Jeanie into his embrace along with Claire, who drew Alexander into the circle so that they were all hugging—and crying.

They held each other for long moments, then Claire drew back a little.

"How are we going to manage it? Disappearing."

Jeanie answered. "Ben and I have been talking about that. I'm putting the bed-and-breakfast up for sale. He'll stay with me until we can find a buyer. He tells me we don't need the money, so we can make the price very attractive. And you can either sell your shop or have Vanessa run the showroom—and transport your goods from New Atlantis. You and Alexander can go on to your new home. And we'll join you when we get things settled here."

Claire nodded. Her head was spinning. It was all happening so fast. But when she leaned into Alexander's warmth, she knew how right it was.

Already she felt happier than she ever had in her life.

Alexander grabbed a cinnamon bun and took a bite. "These are wonderful. Better than Bendon ever made." He looked at Claire. "I hope you can get the recipe from your mother."

"I already know it."

She grinned at him, letting her happiness expand. Knowing that she was headed for a life she had never imagined.

"It started off like a fairy tale . . ." she said.

"But reality is going to be even better," he answered. And she knew he spoke the truth.

Red Skies at Night

DIANE WHITESIDE

Thank you, Gillian and Ben

one

Travis eyed the leaden skies over New York Harbor, stomped his feet, and clutched his triple mocha espresso a little closer in his gloved hands. A sullen red line marked the dawn, as if the sun itself was ill-tempered about facing the record-breaking cold. "Thank God for decent coffee, not the poison in the station house. A guy needs encouragement to be out in these temperatures."

His best friend laughed. "What did you expect with that on the horizon? Red skies in the morning, sailor take warning," Frank D'Angelo remarked, jerking his head significantly at the eastern sky, and sipped his organic Sumatran coffee.

"Are you repeating the weather forecast for the past month?" Travis drawled, slipping back into his Texas accent. Twenty-five years in the New York Police Department, now a lieutenant, and he still carried Amarillo in his voice. He hunched his shoulders in his uniform greatcoat and wished for a vacation in the Bahamas or at least Florida.

"Nope, just glad you were able to meet me here after you got off duty," Frank retorted.

By unspoken consent, both men moved into the shelter of an as-yet-unopened store between the coffee shop and the alley. From here they could see in both directions down the block of old cast-iron warehouses that was being remodeled into trendy shops and co-ops.

"Hard to believe it's been fifteen years since we were partners." Travis grinned, remembering the old NYPD jokes about how mismatched they were and how closely they'd stood together for the ten years they'd been partners.

"When I had to teach you how to find occasional shelter from the weather, while still being able to see what was happening?" Frank shook his head. "Man, those were the days. Who would have thought any cowboy could be so grass green about hunting bad guys?"

"Who'd have thought a city kid needed help learning how to wrestle?" Travis shot back, reminding Frank of the hours he'd put in teaching Frank the unarmed combat skills his grandfather had first taught him.

"Yeah, good times," Frank agreed. "Most of 'em, anyway."

Travis's mouth tightened. Twenty-two years ago, he'd married Frank's kid sister, Maria, and counted himself the happiest man in the world. Three years later, Maria was dead of leukemia and he'd stumbled through the funeral, guided by Frank's hand on his elbow. Ever since then, Frank's family was the only family he had.

"Feels like old times, drinking coffee together." Frank buried his nose in the steam. "You must have a ton of things lined up to do."

"Nothing as important as harassing an old pal for a few minutes."

They both laughed and bumped their elbows, before returning to the steaming hot liquid.

"Hope Peters doesn't come too soon to pick me up. It's nice having even a few quiet minutes with friends," Frank mused, staring at the almost empty street. It was so bitterly cold that no cars were moving and only one miserable pedestrian scuttled down the street.

Travis shot a sideways look at his friend, judging the deeply etched lines of exhaustion. "Thought you were investigating that affair down in Washington," he remarked, referring to a group of terrorists who'd splattered a military convoy across a Potomac bridge.

"Still am—but hope to wrap it up soon." Frank yawned. "Christ, I'd like to be home just once for Katrina's birthday."

"Gossip says you made arrests but you needed to find how they got into this country."

Frank grunted a coded assent. "You're fishing in deep waters, Travis. We may have been partners once, for ten years, but I can't tell you everything."

Travis's mind started to work, sorting through bits and pieces picked up at his job. "The terrorists' papers were very good, as in better than excellent, or you wouldn't be so far from Washington."

Frank's face turned impassive, a sure sign to his old partner.

"Newspapers said they came in legally, through the airports." Travis connected the dots. "Mother of God, Frank, is somebody making fake passports?"

Frank grimaced. "Not counterfeit. Real. And it's Morelli," he added in a bare whisper.

The biggest mobster in New York?

A chill ran down Travis's spine. "Jesus." Instinctively, he dropped his hand to his gun. "My God, if every foreign asshole with a little cash can bring his pissant fight over here . . ."

"Yeah." Frank's expression was as grim as his own. "But the door won't be open for much longer. As soon as I get back to the office, we'll slam it shut so fast and so hard, those assholes won't have time to bleed before they're six feet under." He tapped his chest, just above his breast pocket, where he always kept his investigator's notebook.

Travis's grin was savage, stretching his skin against the harsh cold. "Say the word and I'm with you all the way."

Frank snorted. "FBI doesn't need help from any ESU pukes."

Travis chuckled at the old joke. "They should! We're a better tactical unit than your HRT guys, any day."

"Wimps!"

Travis had just opened his mouth to frame another friendly insult when Frank's cell phone rang. Frank pulled it out of his pocket, looked at the display, and cursed.

Travis raised an eyebrow. A pedestrian dived into the coffee shop, clutching his parka to his throat.

"D'Angelo." Frank's expression became absorbed as he listened.

Travis lifted a hand, pointing toward the coffee shop.

Frank nodded distractedly, totally focused on his conversation.

Travis shook his head and went off to give Frank some privacy. Frank was capable of forgetting almost anything when he was on the trail.

Inside the shop, he quickly grabbed a fresh round of coffees and headed back outside.

He looked up and down the street for Peters, Frank's assistant from the FBI. Nothing.

More worrisome, there was no sign of Frank, who hated cold weather. He should be pacing the sidewalk by now, trying to stay warm. . . .

Instinct growled at him, trained on too many hard streets over too many bitter years. Travis threw both coffees into the trash can in front of the shop.

A patrol car turned into the street.

Something thudded into the alley next door—something heavy, about Frank's weight. The hair on the nape of his neck rose. *What the hell?*

He grabbed for his gun, his gloves making him too damn clumsy. *Dear God, please let Frank be okay. . . .*

He ran into the narrow alley, his Beretta in his hand, and stopped cold.

Frank lay against the old warehouse's cast-iron wall, edged in the thin fog rising from his wounds, with his blue eyes staring straight ahead and blood pouring onto the ground around him. His wound was so recent that his body heat was turning the frigid air into a wispy shroud.

Chilled to the bone by more than the temperature, Travis rushed forward to see if he could help.

The steam swayed and disappeared before him.

Travis jerked to a stop, unable to breathe.

Frank had been gutted so completely that even his heart had been ripped. His entrails were spilled onto the ground and his privates were stuffed into his mouth. His overcoat pooled on the ground at his sides, oddly unbalanced.

His notebook was gone from his breast pocket but his wallet and service weapon remained.

How the hell had this happened, so quickly and so silently? It looked as if someone immensely strong had held Frank up by the throat, then ripped him open with a knife from his pelvis to his ribs, notching his heart—and thus killing him almost instantly. But according to Travis's family legends, only a *vampiro* was that strong—and no *vampiro* would be stupid enough to kill a federal agent.

The legends faded as Travis tried to think logically.

The patrol car's flashing lights burst over the scene and stopped, unable to proceed farther down the narrow little alley, with its trash cans and Dumpsters.

An engine raced and tires spun on gravel at the alley's other end. Travis's head snapped around to see a big, black SUV's rear end slipping on a patch of ice.

The patrol car would never be able to move past Frank's body and chase the SUV. Its doors slammed open and two patrolmen jumped out.

Travis flung up his hand, showing his NYPD lieutenant's badge, and pointed at Frank's corpse. "Officer down!"

Comprehension flashed over the patrolmen's faces. One reached for his handset.

The SUV gained traction and sped off, scattering gravel behind it.

Travis raced down the alley but reached the opposite end too late to see anything, even a fragment of the license plate number.

"Morelli, you bastard, you'll pay for this!" he shouted at the fleeing murderers, just as the first ice pellet pounded out of the sky.

TWO

"Coffee?" Evans asked. "It's good stuff; we keep it for our art dealer friends when they come begging."

A half smile touched Travis's lips, the first in over a month, since Frank's assassination. "Don't mind if I do."

He settled into a side chair and stretched out his legs. The coffee was better than claimed, while the office furniture was genuine NYPD: battered, functional, and tolerable only thanks to long familiarity with its kin. Evans fit somewhere in between the two: as the lieutenant on NYPD's major case squad in charge of solving art thefts from museums and galleries, he was both urbane and nobody to have as an enemy. The city's major case squad itself was the equivalent or better than that of many countries' major case squads, given the great galleries and museums in Manhattan.

Evans closed the office door and sat down behind his desk. "Heard you wanted to know anything unusual about Morelli."

Travis came alert on the inside. "That's right. Of course, it's a federal agent's murder so it's a federal case. I'm just keeping an unofficial eye on things to make sure information flows smoothly to the feds."

Evans nodded, his eyes showing his understanding of—and dislike for—the need for politically correct phrases. He knew, just as everyone else in NYPD probably did, how badly Travis wanted to find Frank's murderer. He'd also probably heard that Travis had called in every favor owed to him in order to get leads. That had been a formality though, since Frank was a former NYPD cop. Every cop in New York was doing his best to solve this case.

"Morelli put out a twenty-five-million-dollar contract on the Jaguar."

Travis raised an eyebrow at the unusual alias. "The Jaguar?"

"One of the best burglars in the world."

"So?"

"The strange part is that he's offering an additional five million dollars for the recovery of a leather notebook, as well."

Travis froze, puzzle pieces snapping together with an almost audible click. "Any description of the notebook?" His voice didn't seem to belong to himself.

"Yeah. High-quality black leather, embossed with gilt wings and the name D'Angelo."

Travis's eyes met Evans's. "Bingo," he said very softly.

"Is it Frank's?"

"Oh, hell yeah. But that's probably nothing the feds are saying."

"One of those critical crime scene details." Evans nodded. He'd spent five years in Homicide so he'd know very well the importance of keeping secret the critical details about a crime.

A lead. Finally Travis had a real lead. *Find the notebook and follow it back to Morelli.* If nothing else, it must have Frank's notes, since Morelli wanted it so much. *So find the notebook—and close*

down Morelli's passport ring. Break that murderous bastard any
way possible, damn him to hell.

And find out who the crooked FBI agent was, who'd set Frank
up by telling Morelli where to find Frank that last morning. Peters
had a great alibi, not that it totally excused him in Travis's eyes.

Travis stood up and began to pace. "Did you tell the FBI?"

Evans snorted in derision. "Of course. They said—and I'm quoting—'We're investigating all available leads. Thank you for your assistance.' "

Travis stared unseeingly at a certificate of appreciation from Interpol. "In other words, they're not talking about what is or isn't important in their investigation. They probably also don't want to admit just how good NYPD's major case squad is, compared to their own sources."

Evans shrugged and stirred cream into his coffee, watching Travis closely. "How can I help you?"

Travis's mind was revolving. He wasn't a homicide detective and never had been. But he'd been studying Morelli like a cockroach under glass for the last month, looking for a crack in the bastard's armor. "Tell me about the Jaguar. Any outstanding warrants?"

Evans threw back his head and laughed. "Are you kidding? At her level"—*Her? She's a girl?*—"we're lucky to get enough on her to have a rumor, let alone probable cause. No, no warrants, not here or anywhere else in the world. We do think she might have stolen the Five Blessings Jade Bowl for Morelli from a Chinese tong."

Travis frowned. "So?"

"Morelli's cheap, especially with hired help. He's shortchanged more than one—but that wouldn't work with the Jaguar. She's been around a long time and knows all the games. Whenever someone tries that on her, she just steals something of theirs and holds it captive until they pay up."

"Like the notebook."

"That's my guess. She stole the Five Blessings Jade Bowl for

Morelli, he stiffed her on the fee, she stole the notebook to hold hostage. Pure speculation but she's done similar things at least twice before."

Travis's pulse was pounding. *Find her, and you find the notebook.* "Where is she?"

Evans raised an eyebrow. "Just how good do you think my sources really are?"

"Better than the FBI's," Travis retorted.

Evans looked back at him, his mouth open to deliver a stinging comeback. He shook his head, a slow smile spreading across his face. "Okay, you have me there. I did hear one more rumor, which I haven't gotten around to passing on to the FBI yet."

They must have really pissed him off. "Which is?"

"Seems that a fence, who likes to ski in New Mexico every year and needed to trade some info"—*Yeah, I'll just bet he did*—"saw the Jaguar out there last week."

Travis clenched his fist. *A location for the Jaguar? Yes.* "What town? Which resort?"

Evans spread his hands. "Who knows? She's damn smart so she's undoubtedly moving around frequently. I'd just say she's probably in the Southern Rockies."

Travis arched an eyebrow at Evans, who shrugged. "That's the best I'll commit to."

Travis nodded and went for the next step in finding her. "What does she look like?"

"You really think my sources are excellent, don't you?" He turned to his computer and Travis came around his desk to watch. A few clicks later and they were both staring at the same poor-quality video of a woman striding through an airport. A few more clicks and the video slowed, then stopped to show a grainy image of her face.

"Gillian Fitzgerald," Evans announced softly. "At least, that's her most frequent alias."

Travis's breath stopped and he leaned forward to memorize her face.

Gillian had an almost classic beauty, touched by what Katrina D'Angelo would have called Celtic elegance. Oval face, straight nose, slanted eyes, strong chin. Was that really a carnal mouth or just a trick of the camera and the awkward lighting? Her head's confident tilt and her gliding walk portrayed her as a woman of courage and strong appetites.

In other words, damn attractive.

Travis reminded himself fiercely that she was a top art thief, hunted by police forces around the world.

Evans slid her dossier over, opened to the half-page summary. The dry prose underneath her photo attempted to define her physical dimensions but left only the impression of a fine-boned woman, with reddish-blond hair and green eyes.

Green eyes. They didn't matter, of course, not compared with laying hands on Frank's notebook and bringing down Morelli and that bastard G-man.

Travis took one last, long look at her passionate mouth and turned away. "Can I have a copy of that?"

"Sure. Good hunting, Travis."

A quick smile acknowledged the wish. "Thanks."

No matter what it cost, personally or professionally, Travis was going to New Mexico after Gillian Fitzgerald. The biggest loss could be professional but he was still willing to risk it all, especially since he had no family or even a girlfriend to be hurt by his recklessness. While he'd hardly been celibate, he hadn't seriously dated anyone since Maria's death either.

Oh, he'd considered it from time to time, especially recently, wondered what it would be like to have someone to go to dinner or a movie with. Somebody he could do simple things with—drink a glass of wine, maybe dance on his terrace, just because the moon was out.

He thrust the images away angrily. A guy had to focus, not dream, if he wanted to stay alive.

What else could he put on the line? He'd even call old family friends in Texas, like Don Rafael Perez, if he thought they could help. Which they couldn't, since he'd be hundreds of miles away.

Four hours later, he was in his captain's office.

"You really think it's D'Angelo's notebook?" O'Halloran leaned back in his chair, steepling his fingers.

Travis spread his hands. "What other leather notebook would Morelli offer *five million dollars* for?"

"True. But murder of an FBI agent is a federal crime, not ours," the captain pointed out, still using the same overly gentle tone. It was a dead giveaway that he was thinking hard about politics.

"Yeah—and how far have they gotten hunting the killer? Besides, Frank was set up. Somebody knew Frank was going to be standing at that corner at that hour—and it had to be somebody in the FBI. Maybe the same person is slowing down the investigation."

O'Halloran's face turned granite hard and the room's temperature noticeably dropped. Every cop hated a cop killer. "Go on."

"But they won't suspect us of looking into it, especially if we do it as quietly as possible. I'd recognize Frank's notebook immediately because it's exactly like mine, except for the name on the outside."

O'Halloran drummed his fingers on the table, staring straight ahead. Travis held his breath. He'd hunt Gillian Fitzgerald on his own time, if he had to, but he'd rather do so officially.

Finally, O'Halloran nodded. "D'Angelo was NYPD before he was FBI and he was killed on our turf. That makes his murder our business. You have permission to follow up this lead."

Inside, Travis could have turned cartwheels. Outwardly, he came to attention. "Thank you, sir."

"Take Santini with you from Homicide, since he's worked interagency task forces before. This smells to high heaven and you'll need a good partner."

Their eyes met and Travis nodded, suspecting he looked just as grim as O'Halloran did. Frank's murder investigation stank to high heaven and he'd need all the backup he could get.

THREE

Travis leaned against the bar, considering the Thursday night crowd and wondering if he'd ever been as young as everyone else there seemed to be.

Probably not.

Small West Texas ranches took a lot of work from everyone involved to keep them running, no matter how young you were. When he was fourteen, his parents were killed in a Midland gas station robbery, just because they'd stopped at the wrong time in the wrong place.

His fingers tightened reflexively around his beer and he forced them to open, one by one. He'd decided to become a cop that night but he'd wanted to serve someplace where he'd be useful. Not a small West Texas town where cops did little more than drive around in cars for hours at a time and hope to find a speeder or drunk to harass. New York City had been perfect, with thousands of criminals to arrest and people to rescue. He'd been happy there for twenty-five years.

But being a New York cop had led back to this small western town—Pine Falls, New Mexico, a small ski resort in the high mountains on the eastern edge of New Mexico. Population: seven hundred in the off-season. Three thousand on a winter weekend, if there was a lot of snow. Like tonight.

He took another swig of his beer, measuring the crowd around him. At least West Texas cowboys were nothing like these weekend skiers, college-age idiots who seemed to think all they had to do was smile at a girl to get her to dance with them or go outside. Worse, two different sets of school colors were in sight, with their wearers snarling like wolverines at each other, especially when one side tried to snatch another's pretty girl.

Travis shook his head, wondering if it would take fifteen minutes or twenty for the first fight to break out. Santini would have had some pithy comments about the idiocy displayed on all sides and the utter lack of police presence here. However, he was flat on his back in Angel Fire, contemplating life from a hospital bed. Yesterday afternoon, he'd enthusiastically raced onto the ski slopes, forgetting to make allowances for differences between the West's deep powdery snow and the East's more icy version. Thankfully, the resulting fall had broken no more than both legs, even if it had immobilized him.

Travis had made his way up here late today without him, to a resort so small that even Santini thought Travis was just sightseeing, not investigating. If he didn't find Fitzgerald here tonight—or if a fight started—he'd have to move on.

But instinct insisted he was close.

So he sat in this noisy bar, with cowboy music pumped into his ears at rock-concert levels, and waited, senses open to everything that went on.

The door blew open from the street, bringing a brief, welcome spurt of cool air. For a moment, a slim figure was framed in the doorway, her red hair catching glints of light.

Travis came erect, his heart racing. *Fitzgerald?*

Then the two men with her pulled the door shut behind them and shouldered their way into the crowd.

Taller than most in the bar, Travis had no difficulty tracing their path. They found a momentary gap in the crowd and the woman took a few quick, clean steps—with the same vibrant stride she'd used in the airport video. It was confirmation of her identity, as inarguable as any mug shot.

Gillian Fitzgerald was standing before him, the key to catching Frank's murderer.

A surge of energy washed through Travis. He was completely and utterly focused on her, to the point where nothing else existed. Unaware of his movements, he set his beer down on the bar and slipped through the crowd toward her.

Her two escorts were certainly very pretty with their smooth, young faces and their brilliant blue college sweaters. But right now, they were arguing about exactly how many bottles of tequila to take back to her house with them.

Idiots. Were they planning to pay attention to a beautiful woman or booze?

Gillian stepped back and stretched slightly, letting her young men talk to the bartender. Travis sidled closer on her other side, careful not to spook her. She reminded him of a mustang he'd seen once—cautious, observant, wild, and so beautiful she took a man's breath away.

The music ended with a flourish and the dancers poured off the floor toward their tables. Somebody jostled one of Gillian's boy toys, spilling tequila on the bar. He spun around furiously, cursing, and shoved the intruder, sending him to the floor.

But his target was wearing the other school's black-and-gold colors. A cry went up, "West Tech!" Half a dozen fellows charged her escorts.

An answering shout sounded. "Carson State!" Fists swung and bodies surged forward. Girls squealed.

A beer bottle flew through the air, probably aimed at Gillian's escort but heading for her.

Instantly, Travis pulled her between him and the wall. The missile thudded against his shoulder and dropped onto the sawdust-covered floor, splashing his boots.

Travis automatically pulled her even closer against him, angling himself to protect her from the fool wielding a long-necked beer bottle like a baseball bat. Although wearing cowboy boots, Gillian easily fit under his chin. She seemed incredibly fragile and warm against him, even with her hands spread against his chest. Her hair brushed his throat, teasing his nostrils with the faint scent of roses.

His heart stuttered. He stared down at her, shaken more than a small bar fight could account for. Why the hell did he have such an overwhelming need to defend her at all costs from all comers?

Her green eyes flashed over him, brilliant with surprise. Damn, she was even prettier close up. *Forget about that, Travis; just think about Frank and the notebook.*

Behind them, a man yelped and somebody else crashed against a wall.

Gillian's eyes flickered sideways toward the bar and her erstwhile escorts, now totally absorbed in their fistfights. She snorted in derision. "Boys."

A pair of fighters lurched into the wall next to Travis and pushed off again, too engaged in their combat to pay attention to anyone else. She glanced up at Travis then toward the door. With one accord, Travis and Gillian slipped out the side door, emerging onto a street edged with parked cars.

The frosty air, brisk winds, and snowflakes here were a welcome change from the thoughtless brawling indoors. A single police siren sounded in the distance and Travis shook his head disbelievingly. Just one—to handle that many troublemakers? Still, it wasn't his problem, not when the key to the notebook was so close.

"You okay, ma'am?" he asked, lengthening his Texas drawl to sound less like a New York cop.

"Fine, thank you. Shall we walk?"

"Sure. The name's Travis."

"How very—cowboy, to use only one name," she observed, stepping carefully around a patch of ice on the sidewalk. "Mine's Gillian."

A louder series of crashes sounded from inside the bar, counterpointed by the rising wail of the approaching police siren coming from a mile away. He refrained from rolling his eyes: Surely this town was big enough on Saturday nights during tourist season that they could afford to hire more police protection.

She didn't break stride but her pace definitely speeded up. The siren was spooking her.

A muscle ticked in Travis's jaw. Dammit, he needed to get the notebook, no matter who or what she was. "Care for a new partner? Someone who knows how to handle his equipment and keep his nose out of trouble?"

Gillian turned to assess him, standing in a pool of light outside a public parking garage.

Mother of God, how she wanted to feed on somebody who wasn't a self-absorbed, narcissistic fool like those last two idiots. Or all the other ski bums she'd been forced to live off for the past three months.

Travis was damn attractive. Six feet two and a swordsman's grace, he was a mature man, past forty, quietly self-confident, and full of power. His coloring was unremarkable, with black hair and amber eyes that had seen far too much, even by her standards. His features were too harshly masculine to be called pretty, dominated by those sharp eyes, a strong nose, high cheekbones, and a stubborn jaw.

He was incredibly focused on her, almost desperate to spend time with her. *Why?* There had been other, prettier women in that grubby bar. Had he been sent by Morelli to trap her?

She allowed a slow smile to dawn and pulled him back with her, like lovers, against the wall and away from the street. She cupped his face in her hands and probed his mind, using all the skills she'd learned when she first became a *vampiro* three hundred years ago.

She touched his outermost thoughts and met a slick surface, capable of turning aside most mind probes. She frowned slightly. She'd encountered it before, in well-trained *vampiros*—and *prosaicos* from ancient *comitivas*, where survival had depended for generations on such protection.

Gillian tried again, narrowing her focus to the clear question: *What do you want here and now?* That subject shouldn't be life-threatening and therefore shouldn't raise his full shields.

More wary than ever, she slipped between a crack in his outermost thoughts and found her answer.

Notebook. Travis wanted the notebook—because he hated Morelli. Well, she could agree with him about hating Morelli, even if she wouldn't give him the notebook.

But who the hell was he?

She backed out and reformulated her question, ready to fight for the answer. When she touched his thoughts about this—they slammed up at her like dragons' teeth. She forced them back into place, where they could harm neither her nor him.

She probed, thinking of her question as a scalpel slicing deep to expose the answers.

Her skin crawled at the answer.

He was a policeman? Well, so much for her seduction plans. She'd never, not in three centuries as a *vampiro*, slept with a cop for pleasure.

Travis was a lieutenant in New York's Emergency Services Unit, which other cities would call SWAT. Goddamn bastards who wore armor and carried the heaviest weapons possible, just to break in doors and arrest innocent people.

She started to pull away from him, instinctively wanting to rid herself of him. He couldn't use force against her, only persuasion. Since he was an ordinary mortal—a *prosaico*—she could break his neck in an instant.

She'd reluctantly decided centuries ago she couldn't kill every cop she met, no matter how much she wanted to. Three hundred years ago, a constable had deliberately sent her mother to die on trumped-up charges. In all the years since, she'd never met a single lawman who was worth even a quick meal, especially since she fed on carnal passion. Now, if she fed on death and terror, like most *vampiros*, it might have been different. But she didn't kill unless she had to.

Travis's eyes widened at her retreat. "Gillian," he crooned, in that deep rum-and-sugar voice of his. He caressed her hip, his big fingers gliding over her ass in just the right way—a pleasurable reminder of a strong man's possession, not a painful grope by a greedy bore.

Despite everything she'd learned about betrayal over the years, she felt a flicker of interest, enjoying the surge of warmth flooding through her.

Both hands slid up her back, stroking her, reminding her just how securely he could hold her during lovemaking. How passionately he could shape her body for maximum pleasure when meeting his thrusts.

She leaned forward against his chest, sighing softly. Those strong fingers knew exactly where all the tension had built up during encounters with those boors over the last few months.

He kissed her hair, crooning to her softly. His clever, clever hands began to seek out the pleasure points hidden in her back, sending the most delicious spirals snaking through her.

She widened her legs slightly and he slipped one knee in between her knees, rubbing his jeans' rough denim against her ski pants. A subtle hint of pleasures to come, given that he hadn't yet touched her mound.

Dammit, so far he was proving as skillful as he'd claimed. And the ski bums she'd met over the last few months had been too self-absorbed to be of much use in the bedroom.

She'd never had a cop as a pet. Perhaps just for one night, she could make an exception. In the morning, it would be easy to erase his memories and kick him out. It might just be worth it.

Especially when the cop looked like Travis, someone who had assets and knew how to use them.

She'd need to bite him as soon as possible, of course. Once he experienced that exhilaration, he'd be more trustworthy toward her—if only so he could repeat the pleasure.

Travis and Gillian sat together in the Suburban, looking across the valley. The falling snow gilded the ski jump, making it look more like a rocket to the stars than a concrete tower. The pine forest closed behind them, turning the currently closed miniature golf parking lot into a private verandah.

"Beautiful," Travis said finally, breaking the silence.

"Exquisite." Gillian sighed.

"Especially redheads with green eyes."

She swung around to look at him. "Travis!"

But her remonstrance contained more laughter than objection.

He winked at her, taking a chance on seducing her. Just a little making out, nothing too serious. His heart was pounding as fast as on any run as an E-cop. "Not that I can tell about the eye color when you're all the way over there," he drawled.

She tilted her head, a slow smile curving her mouth. Even in the dark, he could see her eyes sparkling. "There's a big, bad piece of plastic in between us that Chevrolet calls a center console but I'd call a chaperone. To come closer, I might just have to climb onto your lap. Do you think there's room?"

Christ, how he surged with agreement! "Yeah, I think we can find some, if I push my seat back. Care to come on over, Gillian?"

She promptly unbuckled her seat belt and sat up. She knelt on the seat, limber as a cat, and stretched.

He watched her greedily, wondering whether to first explore her curves with his mouth or his hand. Or maybe a little teeth and tongue, to go with the lips. Or some fingernails and palms, to match the fingertips.

And the way her hair turned into a brilliant cap, which highlighted the vulnerable curve of her neck and the strong lines of her shoulder. It just begged to be investigated by some serious kissing.

She peeled off her ski jacket, exposing a fine woolen sweater, and tossed the jacket into the backseat. Her breasts bounced and settled, her nipples very much erect.

So were Travis's.

Christ, she had beautiful breasts for such a fine-boned woman. Not too big, nothing that looked purchased—just enough to make her every inch a woman. His body heartily approved.

He took a deep breath and told himself to think, dammit, think.

The most basic logic emerged from the mists. He unfastened his seat belt, took off his ski jacket, and dumped it in the backseat.

An instant later, he'd pushed his seat all the way back and pulled Gillian over into his lap. She sat astride him, supple as any yoga instructor and comfortable as a cat.

"Much better," she purred, nestling against his chest.

Damn, she was so delicate against him. Soft, feminine—and the top of her head barely reached his chin. Would she be strong enough to handle him? He'd manage to be gentle somehow.

She fanned her fingers over his shoulders, comparing their strength and breadth to her fragility. Lord, he felt ten times bigger at the visual contrast and her wide-eyed appreciation, no matter how studied it might be.

"Travis, ah, Travis," she murmured, her finger gliding back and forth in time to the syllables of his name.

He kissed her very gently, a light sweep of tongue over lip, a moist caress to awaken and tease. She answered in kind, their tongues flickering against each other, gradually building strength and interest until their mouths opened. She sighed in pleasure, turning her face up to him, and settled against him with her hand wrapped around his waist under his cashmere sweater.

Damn, Gillian was good at kissing and she wasn't trying to do anything else.

Warmth flooded through him, until he felt achingly alive. He had always loved to kiss, but most women saw it as the beginning to something more, not a pleasure in itself. He closed his eyes, enjoying himself with a woman who took kissing the same way he did— with no strings attached.

Of course, he ran his hands down Gillian's back, pulling her closer and enjoying her little moans. And she slipped her fingers inside his trousers and kneaded his hips, which made it damn hard to concentrate on her slim waist.

He groaned her name and she slid her fingers around to the front, coming to within inches of his belt buckle.

Travis froze. His cock was also damn close to his belt buckle, albeit inside his pants.

Gillian gave him a teasing grin and slid down onto the floor between his legs. She pulled his black cashmere sweater up slightly until his breath stopped with an audible gasp.

She nuzzled him through his T-shirt and he shuddered. She drew his cashmere sweater up, little by little, with a few teasing nudges and kisses through his T-shirt. Then she went to work on his T-shirt, drawing it loose, kissing and licking the bare skin underneath.

Every time she tasted him, fire crackled through him. She unbuckled his jeans and slowly unzipped them, gently stroking him through his briefs. His hips circled restlessly, while he watched her, groaning in anticipation.

Gillian outlined his ribs with her teeth then kissed them, sending shudders through him. She rhythmically kneaded his left chest, gradually centering on his nipple. His balls were drawn up high and tight, under his throbbing, eager cock.

He tried to peel his sweater and T-shirt off but Gillian licked Travis's abs at his solar plexus. The fever singed him again. His hands tightened on her shoulders and he threw his head back, his breath catching in his throat. Dear God in heaven, how could anything feel that good?

She hummed her encouragement and flicked his nipples with her fingers, sending vibrations through his skin and into his lungs. The fire gained a new dimension inside his body. He bucked, desperate for more, frantic to come.

Gillian came up higher between his legs until her head was just below his shoulder, palming his glans through his briefs. If he got the damn sweater off, he could pull her up and finish this to their mutual satisfaction. . . .

She kissed his chest and bit down, just above his nipple, where he'd lightly nipped women for their pleasure before. Drawing his blood into her mouth as if it were the sweetest wine . . .

An inferno exploded through him, ripping him into an orgasm like nothing he'd ever known before. Every atom of his body was etched in ecstasy for what seemed like an hour, rather than the usual few seconds or maybe minute. The cataclysm shook him to the bone and beyond.

Even as Travis sagged bonelessly into his seat, he managed to wonder how easy it would be to seduce and walk away from a woman who had this effect on him.

four

"Wow," Gillian gasped and sheathed her fangs. Travis's fifth orgasm had packed just as strong a punch as his first. Goddammit, why did a one-night stand—and a cop, at that—have to be so very delicious? Especially that first time—when his taste had rendered her so intoxicated, she'd had a difficult time stopping.

Travis rolled over, freeing her of his weight but staying possessively close. "You're very special yourself, Gillian," he rumbled, kissing the top of her head.

"Hmm." She blinked a little blearily at his latest bite mark, checking to be sure it had started to heal. Satisfied it would disappear within a few hours, she snuggled back against him. She could wait to wipe his memories since it was only nine a.m. There was plenty of time left to enjoy him.

She'd be leaving this little New Mexico mountain resort as soon as she was done, driven by the sure instinct that Vicente Morelli's men were getting too damn close. A pity—she'd enjoyed this town more than most of her recent hideouts. Small ski resorts at the end of the season were useful, when landlords were hungry for a couple more good rentals and ski bums were eager for just a few more good times. This so-called cabin was surprisingly luxurious, with its enormous living room and expansive views, one bedroom, and an immense private bathroom to counterbalance the wide deck with its de rigueur hot tub.

Travis stroked her back gently and she stretched against him, almost purring. Long body, hard muscles, prickly hair—all the lovely details of masculinity.

His stomach rumbled. Loudly. He froze.

She choked. Despite her best efforts, a chirp of laughter escaped and he chuckled ruefully. She tilted her head back to consider him, walking her fingers up his chest. "Would you like some coffee? Maybe some breakfast? I don't usually eat in the morning"—at least nothing *prosaicos* would call food—"but I can probably find something for you."

His eyes lit up, the harsh grooves around his mouth almost gentle enough now to be called laugh lines. "Coffee? The real stuff?"

"Coming right up. You can have the first shower; I'll take the bathroom by the kitchen."

"Thanks." He disentangled himself with an affectionate kiss and strode off to the bathroom, unabashedly naked.

She allowed herself a moment to admire the view. Last night, he'd more than proven the value of that harshly sculpted, incredibly masculine body. When his tightly controlled mouth relaxed and allowed its full sensual potential to show, and he started talking in that deep West Texas drawl, and he displayed his naked body, which any of Morgan's pirates would have envied for its predatory strength and grace . . . Why, any woman would immediately melt at his feet.

Even though he did have a great many scars. At least two bullet scars, one knife scar, and three surgical scars. He was carrying a Beretta but that was little threat to her, since he'd have to stop her heart or blow off her head with it to kill her.

Water began to run in the bathroom, bringing Gillian back to the present. She shrugged into her quilted robe and slipped the black leather notebook into its pocket. The damn notebook that had sent her on the run.

Travis fastened his jeans, whistling softly, the rich smell of genuine Java coffee drifting up from the mug at his elbow. His sweater hung by the bedroom door, while his jacket was in the living room. The cabin was laid out in a straight line—kitchen, living room, bedroom, bathroom. Plate-glass windows and sliding glass doors showed the spectacular mountain views. Mirrors covered two walls of the bedroom, which made it easy to watch either the outdoors or see into the living room.

Along the cabin's full length, a wooden deck was cantilevered over the canyon. Only a wooden balustrade kept the unwary from diving three thousand feet onto the rocks below. Personally, Travis had no intention of going near the rickety old structure. He'd rather climb to the top of the Brooklyn Bridge, without ropes, and try to talk down a jumper.

A few hours earlier, he'd cuddled Gillian and admired a mountain sunrise out those windows, shimmering red above the snow-capped peaks. He didn't need to have the old saying come true again, not after January's events.

Red skies in the morning, sailors take warning.
Red skies at night, sailors' delight.

There was a bad storm coming in. The deck was iced over and snow was starting to fall. But worse was forecast to the east. The weathermen had predicted the Blue Norther of the Century for the Texas Panhandle tonight.

Hell, he didn't need to worry about the weather. He was hours west of Texas and had no intention of driving there.

He cracked open the door into the living room, so he could hear her moving around, over the weather forecaster bleating about the big blizzard, and sat down to pull on his boots.

Gillian was a very feminine creature, a few inches over five feet, red hair, creamy skin with a touch of golden freckles across that straight little nose, a slender figure that looked breakable. But she had more stamina and passion than Police Officer Patricia Murphy on the mayor's detail had displayed two years ago, the last time he'd dated anyone.

He grinned, remembering some of Gillian's more inventive moves. Pity she was a cat burglar and his only interest was in Frank's notebook. Otherwise, he'd be tempted to take some of the vacation the captain was always trying to shove down his throat and spend it with the little redhead.

Gravel skittered down the hill and splattered against the house.

Travis stiffened. Was that natural—or had Morelli's men followed him here? Could the crooked fed have informed Morelli about Gillian this damn fast? Or maybe Morelli had just tracked Gillian down the same way he had.

He yanked his other boot on.

Slugs crashed into the front door lock, an all-too-familiar sound.

Reflexes, honed by twenty-five years on New York's toughest streets, took over. Travis immediately dived onto the floor, drawing his big Beretta Mini Cougar. "Gillian, get down!"

Simultaneously, the front door burst inward, followed by the bastard firing a shotgun. He knew that face—Big Charlie, Morelli's toughest hit man and a vicious Jamaican sadist.

Glass and furniture shattered. Walls crumbled. The weatherman abruptly stopped foretelling catastrophe in the Texas Panhandle.

Travis lifted his head and risked a quick glance into the big mirror at the living room. *Was Gillian safe in the kitchen?*

Massive holes showed in the walls. *What the hell kind of shot was Big Charlie using to cause so much damage? More than just slugs. Maybe linked by chain?*

Travis slithered backward through the bedroom. He cracked the sliding door open and went silently onto the big deck, cautiously moving over the inch of ice hidden by the gently falling snow. A rope and a full harness would have been useful, especially since he was hanging over a canyon. But what part of this old wooden cabin could he have tied on to? He shook his head and stayed close to the cabin.

Christ, if Big Charlie tried some of his nastier tricks on her before Travis could stop him . . .

The shooting finally stopped and a man spoke, clearly audible through the shattered glass doors. He had an Eastern European accent, not Big Charlie's Jamaican accent. "You were supposed to be sleeping, Fitzgerald. Now we will have to do this the hard way. Give me the notebook and Morelli will call it quits."

Crap, Big Charlie was working with an accomplice. He was so vicious that it took someone even nastier to work with him.

Travis smiled without mirth, his brain working as coldly as on any job in the 7-5, his old Brooklyn precinct. *Stall, Gillian honey, and let me get into position. You're a great cat burglar. Now's the time to show your stuff.*

He crept forward, using first the hot tub then the table for cover, until he could just see the intruders through a gap in the living room's shredded curtains.

Gillian faced a dour-looking fellow in an Armani suit, startling attire for a family ski resort in late March. He was sneering at her, his lips curled like a drug dealer's guard dog desperate to attack. Big Charlie flanked him, his shotgun restlessly sweeping everything in Gillian's cabin except where she stood. His ammunition had left the walls and furniture looking like Swiss cheese.

"Did Morelli send my money?" Gillian countered, her voice as calm as her demeanor. Only her green eyes' intensity betrayed that this was anything more than a casual conversation.

The Armani suit wearer snickered. "Pay good money to you, a whore? When he could send a *vampiro mayor* to recover what she had stolen? Not likely, bitch."

"No matter what he paid you, it'll rot in the bank. You're not leaving here."

"But now I'll get a bonus," the Armani suit wearer sneered, "since I've learned you too are a *vampiro mayor*."

His body dissolved into mist and a Rottweiler sprang at Gillian, the silk suit collapsing onto the floor underneath it.

Travis opened his mouth to shout a warning but she too had already evaporated. In her place, a cougar's svelte dusky gold blur snarled and sliced into the enemy's bigger, black and tan body. Her quilted robe crumpled into a fluffy pink heap.

A shape-shifter duel?

Half-forgotten family legends rose up in his mind, wrestling for his attention. *Vampiros* and *compañeros* and *prosaicos*, loyalty unto death, Don Rafael Perez and the Santiago Trust . . .

Big Charlie headed for the bedroom, shotgun at the ready.

The fight in the living room was a whirling, yowling mass of teeth and claws and blood. Slender streaks of gold flashing against lunging, bulky black and tan. *And Gillian was in there fighting for her life? Don't think about that now, Travis, just fight.*

Big Charlie emerged onto the balcony, shotgun at the ready. Travis ran for the only cover available—behind the hot tub.

BAM! Big Charlie shot at him, shattering the trellis between them. Shards of wood rained over Travis. His foot slipped on the ice and he fell flat on his stomach, only to start sliding across the deck like a toboggan.

BAM! BAM! Keeping his back to the cabin, Big Charlie shot again at Travis. His damn slugs shattered the deck's railing, leaving a gap big enough for two men.

Travis was skidding off the balcony, headed straight for the hole in the railing—and a two-thousand-foot drop into the canyon below.

Shit, he could really use a rope right now. . . .

His flailing foot caught against a single post, stopping the fall but swinging him around on the ice like an Olympic skater. He caught himself against the hot tub's base with one hand, one leg hanging over the edge above the canyon.

A freezing wind roared up the inside of his jeans, reminding him of just how far down he could fall. Snowflakes blurred his vision but he still held his Beretta.

BAM! Big Charlie blasted the hot tub's cover. It shattered, sending knife-edged fiberglass shards shooting in all directions. Blood trickled down Travis's face.

Would he make it back to Gillian in time?

BAM! Big Charlie shot at the hot tub, obviously trying to carve it away, as he'd done to the cabin's interior. Water poured out of it, gushing toward him, not Travis. The Jamaican yelped and dodged the flood, briefly emerging into view.

Travis shot him in the head.

Big Charlie dropped his shotgun and fell onto his face, dead before he hit the icy deck. That sure brought justice for a lot of murders.

Travis pulled himself completely back onto the balcony, desperate to reach Gillian. He half-crawled, half-slid back to the balcony door. He reached in through one of Big Charlie's holes and pulled the door open, then lunged back inside, reflexively glad of the comparative warmth.

Dammit, Gillian and the brute were moving too quickly, making it impossible for him to kill the bastard without hurting her. *Come on, Gillian, break away and give me a shot. Just an instant is all I ask. Just one lousy instant and I'll send the bastard to hell for you.* . . .

They closed on each other suddenly. Travis's finger tightened on the trigger. *Gillian* . . .

The Rottweiler reared up onto its hind legs, desperately trying to shake the cougar off its jugular. But its struggles were jerky and ineffective.

Holy hell, Gillian had a death grip on the paid assassin.

The cougar pulled back, mouth full of fur, covered in blood, and limping badly. But she was still in fighting mode, teeth bared to attack the enemy. Before Travis could fire, the Rottweiler's hindquarters collapsed onto the polished hardwood floor—and dissolved into dust. An instant later, it had completely changed into a small heap of pale gray powder, stirred by a draft from the shattered windows.

Blood splatters melted away and disappeared, until only Big Charlie's corpse lay in a large pool of blood on the deck.

The cougar settled onto the floor and shimmered. Then Gillian lay there, barely breathing, blood pumping from a dozen deadly wounds and a hundred minor ones.

Travis holstered his Beretta and raced over, dropping to his knees beside her. "Gillian!"

Before his stunned eyes, a small puncture in her hand slowly closed. An old family legend fell into place: Vampiros *heal themselves very quickly if they've eaten well.* Confirmation that he'd spent the previous night with a *vampiro*, or vampire. As if he'd needed it, given the shape-shifting.

Who hadn't harmed him in any way when she could have done so.

Christ, what was first aid for a *vampiro*? Blood, of course. She needed his blood. Now.

He slid his arm behind her head to support her. Then he made a quick, shallow cut on his forearm with his pocket knife to open a vein and held it to her mouth.

Her eyelids fluttered but her mouth didn't move.

"Gillian, honey," he crooned in his best paramedic's voice. Her head turned toward him. "Drink the blood quickly, sweetheart, and get well."

She kissed his arm.

He'd always been able to talk anyone into anything, one of the things other E-cops had teased him about. But this time, his concern for her was stronger than for any emotionally disturbed person on a New York City street. "Company's coming. You can do it, love; there's a good girl."

She licked gently. Then her mouth opened and she drank delicately, obviously careful of his welfare, despite her gaping wounds. His heart ached for her welfare and he urged her to drink everything she needed. But after only a half-dozen swallows, she turned her head away like a small child's polite refusal.

A moment later, she was asleep, her chest quietly rising and falling. The first deep scratch on her arm closed before his eyes.

He reached for her robe, desperate to keep her warm. The quilted silk was cool and soft in his hands, bringing what had been in her pocket. An elegant, black leather notebook, neatly tooled with the name *D'Angelo*.

Frank's notebook. Its twin was in his jacket pocket.

He could take it and leave now, while she was too weak to object. Then give it to the FBI in Albuquerque and say—say what? Morelli's hit men had probably found her so quickly by listening to the FBI and following the leads Travis had uncovered—starting with her presence here in New Mexico, maybe even tailing him. In that case, taking the notebook directly to the FBI would kill all hope of justice for Frank's murder.

The only alternative was to hide from both the FBI and Morelli, until he could take her back to New York for an honest investigation. But where could he hide her, since she was a *vampiro* and *vampiros* were hunting her?

The only place no sane person would go was Texas, where the blue norther was brewing. The FBI wouldn't be able to follow them there, at least not while the storm lasted, which could be as long as three or four days.

But would a blue norther stop Morelli's *vampiros* from following them? He'd need another *vampiro* for that, somebody close at hand and powerful. Maybe Don Rafael Perez of Texas, his family's protector for the past two hundred years.

When Travis's parents were killed, Travis's grandfather had sold the ranch and accepted a horse-training job in Upstate New York, far away from his only son's senseless murder. Don Rafael had bought the family's Andalusian cutting horses, descended from his own famous breeding stock. He hadn't tried to talk Travis's grandfather out of moving but he had spoken very quietly to Travis that last day.

"Every man has a right to make his own decisions but sometimes the time may come to rethink them," the Don had commented in the uncannily empty barn, the late afternoon light haloing his black hair until he almost looked like the angel he was named for. If you forgot about the scarred face and the slightly crooked nose, that is.

Fourteen-year-old Travis had simply stared at the graceful, massive man. He'd been so tired from working all day to clean and sell everything they had, then lying awake at night fighting not to cry, that he hadn't cared what the most powerful man in Texas had to say.

The Don had smiled slightly then offered Travis a business card, just as if Travis were an important adult. "If you ever need help, *amigo*, just call that number and ask for me."

Travis had cautiously accepted the small piece of pasteboard, carrying the Don's name, the words *Santiago Trust,* and a single phone number. "We're leaving tomorrow for New York."

"Your family has served me for centuries, Travis. Loyalty is a two-way street—and that phone number will always bring rescue for you."

Kneeling beside Gillian in the shattered living room, Travis touched his hip pocket above the wallet—and that business card. If old family legends were true, he'd need the most powerful man in Texas for protection against Morelli.

But first, he'd take Gillian as far away from here as he could. They'd been damn lucky that the cops hadn't shown up yet—and whoever was driving the getaway car for Big Charlie and the other hit man.

FIVE

Travis cast another look in the rearview mirror, looking for the damned elusive Jeep. The snow was coming down heavily now, thick enough to cover the pavement and make driving treacherous for a lesser vehicle than his big rented Suburban. Gillian slept behind him, nestled in a cocoon of blankets. At least, he hoped she slept and was still healing. She hadn't moved since he'd given her blood after the duel with the big Rottweiler.

All of her belongings had been packed and ready to go, something that had made him damn suspicious the night before. After the attempted assassination, he'd just thanked God for the time savings and thrown her gear into the back of her Ford Explorer. Then he'd taken the two of them back to his motel, watching for any followers, certain that the two assassins would have come with a getaway vehicle and driver.

But the highways had been crowded with tourists racing to leave town before the big blizzard hit. No single vehicle had seemed interested enough in him to be suspicious.

So he'd transferred Gillian and her gear to his Suburban, with all of his and Santini's cop gear, being careful not to be observed. Then he'd headed east, still looking for the rest of the assassination team.

He'd spotted the blue Jeep with the Arizona tags about twenty miles east of town, when the last tourists disappeared.

An hour later, in the middle of the blizzard, on a narrow state highway winding down from the Sangre de Cristo Mountains onto the grasslands of eastern New Mexico, Travis was damn sure he was being tailed by one of Big Charlie's men.

He'd put the bastard through backroads and startlingly sharp turns calculated to lose a professional tail. But the son of a bitch had stuck to them like a leech.

Even so, the hit man had little idea of how to drive in foul weather on a steep, curving road. Any deviation from straight and narrow tended to make him brake, skid, and fishtail all too close to the guardrails.

Travis had observed every one of those aggravations with some glee. He'd learned the art of driving in every kind of weather on every kind of road, while delivering thoroughbreds across Upstate New York. So far, the top-heavy Suburban was behaving itself on these mountain roads. But the worst would come when they reached the Panhandle and tonight's forecasted seventy-mile-an-hour winds and whipping snows.

The forecasted blue norther was on its way. So named for the great blue wall of clouds that rolled over the prairies from the north, it would cover everything beneath it with the wintry wrath of God.

Travis eyed the coming series of tight hairpin turns and the steep cliffs below, curling his lips. Every time he'd head away from the mountains, the wind would try to slide his truck toward the cliffs.

The big truck dipped and swayed, as if protesting his determination to stay on course. Canned food rattled loudly.

Gillian stirred behind him, her tousled red hair glinting in the dim light. It was late afternoon outside, although the falling snow made it look more like sunset. "Where are we?" she mumbled.

"Just east of Springer." He kept his voice deep and slow, trying to soothe her back to sleep.

She crawled into the front seat and peered out the window. "Springer?"

Another gust of wind shoved the truck up, trying to push it onto two wheels. Shit.

The blue Jeep pulled up close behind, almost nudging the Suburban's rear bumper.

"New Mexico," Travis answered curtly, gauging the distance between himself and his opponent—and the guardrails.

"That's in eastern New Mexico. Why the hell are we here?" Strength, however febrile, vibrated in her voice. He ignored it.

"Strap in *now*, Gillian, if you're going to sit up front."

She shot a hard glance at him but said nothing, simply pulled the seat belt hard and fast around her. He didn't care whether she'd done so out of obedience or comprehension; he simply thanked God he didn't have to worry about her.

He entered the first turn carefully, wary of any risk of sliding across the road. Then the blue Jeep came up on the inside and bumped him hard, sending him toward the guardrail.

Travis fought the wheel, forcing it to make the turn, grateful for four-wheel drive. The brakes pounded under his foot, whining their complaint. The wheels skidded silently on the snow, crossing the line into the next lane. Metal clicked and clanked in the back, probably his climbing gear.

The Suburban leaned toward the rail and he prayed, angling his body to give the truck what help he could. Gillian gripped the handhold over the door and leaned with him, her expression still hard-edged with suspicion, probably of his motives in helping her.

The truck settled abruptly back onto its wheels, sending the metal pieces clanking again, and scooted into the lane.

The Jeep fishtailed wildly but made it around the corner.

Travis set his jaw and gave the Suburban more gas. He'd make the Jeep's driver use all of his few driving skills to play this game. He bounced through first one pothole then another, and dodged a group of fallen rocks. Gillian silently braced herself. Her expression was focused and deadly, if edged with exhaustion. He didn't speak, concentrating on fighting the steering wheel.

By the time he came into the third turn, he was moving far too quickly for the very sloppy road. But he was on an interior line toward the mountainside, not the cliff. Instinct honed during thousands of runs, given that New York City drivers never yielded for screaming sirens, told him the road ahead was clear.

Gillian tightened her seat belt further.

He took the tightest turn possible, using evasive driving skills he'd learned from other policemen. The engine ground as it worked to obey and the axles squealed. The truck tilted hard and rose onto two wheels. Gillian braced herself between the handhold and the dashboard, her head craned around to watch the Jeep.

He fought the steering wheel with all his strength, the Suburban sliding toward the rail, every box in the back rattling loudly. *Come on, big boy, don't slide into the guardrail.*

With an audible groan, the big truck settled back onto the road with one wheel on the verge. Its rear bumper scraped the guardrail before Travis straightened it and sped ahead, allowing himself a little more caution.

Behind him, the blue Jeep tried to take the same curve at an even higher speed, a possibility with its greater stability. Its hit-man driver skidded, then hit the brakes hard, spraying snow and slush as the

Jeep slid across all the lanes. It slammed into the guardrail and popped through it, tumbling into the canyon below.

Shifting down to a safer gear, Travis carefully took the next hairpin, sparing a glance for the Jeep careering down the cliff. Two thousand feet later, it crashed onto a rocky ledge and disappeared in a puff of fire and smoke.

He spared a moment to wonder how long it would take for the next follower to find him and Gillian.

"Thank you for saving our lives, Travis." Gillian's voice was very precise and rang with surprisingly genuine emotion.

"My pleasure, Gillian."

She fumbled with her seat belt, a clumsy sound for someone as graceful as she was.

Several minutes passed before he dared glance over at her.

Gillian was sound asleep, her head flung back against the seat. But her left hand rested casually against his leg, almost trustingly.

Travis smiled wryly. He'd stop at the first turnout to loosen the seat belt, or maybe move her back into the backseat. She still needed to sleep and heal.

At least knocking off this hit man had bought enough time to call Don Rafael. With luck, the old family ties would still hold after twenty-five years in New York and he could beg shelter for himself and Gillian in Texas.

After that, he was just going to bet his life that she wasn't the type to butcher him or anyone else the way Frank had died. . . .

SIX

Gillian woke slowly, the sign of a bad injury, and lay still for a few minutes, taking stock of her situation. She arched cautiously, rolling her shoulders over the coarse cotton sheets. The bed billowed under her and around her, in a series of small squares. A feather drifted over her nose and she blew it away, testing the air currents. She was in a bed, a very old-fashioned one with quilts and featherbeds, not her cabin's high-thread-count sheets and basket-weave knit blankets.

The bedroom was simply furnished, boasting only a brass bed, pine dresser, straight chair, side table, and hooked rug. Its walls were plain wood, showing every plank and nail. A single door, currently shut, probably opened to the hallway, while a pale glow filtered around the edges of heavy curtains. *Prosaico* scent was faint, except for Travis's scent, which was recent and brief. There were no *vampiros* around so she and Travis were the only people here.

She listened, sending out her senses to the world around her. Winds howled outside, beating against the house like a thousand soldiers determined to tear it down. Trees groaned and swayed but managed not to break. The roof moaned in pain as the snow continued to fall, forcing it to carry more weight than it had been designed for. A diesel engine hummed, steadily working to keep lights and water flowing in the house. The rich scents of coffee and chocolate swirled inside the old house.

Damn, but she was thirsty. She ran her tongue over her lips, testing her own resources. Her skin was so tight and dry that it stretched taut over her cheekbones. Her tongue was thick, tasting of cotton. Her pulse was racing through her veins, yet her blood—the essence of life itself for every *vampiro*—seemed faint and thin.

She'd killed Morelli's hired assassin, at the price of losing far too much blood. For some unknown reason, Travis had given her enough blood to survive and heal herself, even though he knew she was a shape-shifter and a killer. No time now to worry about why, not when she desperately needed to feed, to replenish her lost reserves with the rich passion of another's carnal energy, as carried in his blood.

But on who? Travis? A damn cop?

Yet there wasn't anyone else around in this wintry desert.

She sighed and stretched again more slowly, rippling her spine over the soft old sheets. She was a cat burglar by trade and she'd always cherished the indirect arts. Seducing a fortress's guardian into revealing how to unlock it was so much more interesting than the brutally obvious takeover of a *prosaico*'s unprotected mind.

She hauled herself wearily upright and pulled the cotton robe around her, wincing at how every seam abraded her skin. At least she was alive enough to walk, thanks to Travis.

She grimaced at the debt to a cop and turned the shower on, the windows rattling from the wind's force. A moment later, the blessedly hot water was beating down on her, its steam enfolding her like a warm blanket. She leaned her forehead against the tile, shaken by the effort it had taken to come this far from the bed. Blessed Mary, Morelli's men and likely Morelli himself wouldn't be far away. She needed her strength back very soon.

The bathroom door opened and shut, sending a cold draft amid the shower curtains. Gillian stirred and recognized Travis's scent. Until this storm ended, he was her only hope of survival.

She cursed necessity's cruel humor and closed her eyes, just as Travis stepped into the shower with her.

He caressed her shoulders gently, with a quiet, "Mornin', Gillian. Glad to see you finally up and about."

"Hmm." He knew some wickedly effective ways to relax her neck and shoulders. She leaned forward, promising herself she'd revel with an actor, or anyone else, after she escaped the storm. "You're being very sweet."

His fingers carefully worked the knots out of her muscles. "You've been very sick." He kissed the nape of her neck, his mouth curving to hold her. His legs were steady and strong behind her.

Instinctively, she tilted her neck to give him access and purred when shivers ran down to her toes. Lovely, absolutely lovely, the way he could combine soft lips with the strength to hold a kiss and just a little touch of teeth for danger. Her hips circled against him, welcoming the hard ridge nudging her rump. Lassitude was shifting into a spiraling tension.

He kneaded her back and she rose up on her toes, arching her spine and quivering at the slow billows of heat floating through her. Her smile lingered over the thought of his superb body, the heavy muscles and the swirls of hair, all lightly spangled by beads of water.

A cop begging to serve a waif who'd grown up in the shadow of Tyburn's gallows.

Perhaps if she kept him for a while longer, her very own cop toy, they could stay together for days. . . .

His big hands shaped and rubbed the twin globes of her rump, unerringly finding every hidden knot in the deep muscles. Lifting her up and fondling her, centering the fires building inside her to deep within her core. She moaned, rippling herself over his gloriously hard masculine contours from shoulders to chest to stomach and hips, sighing over the heady waves of arousal surging through her every time his marvelously thick shaft found a new place to excite.

Groaning, he shoved his knee between her legs, lifting her onto her toes. She shamelessly rocked against him, desperate for more of the rasp of his harsh leg hair against her most sensitive flesh and the liquid fire of her cream flowing down her thigh as she melted.

He growled something under his breath and yanked her around to face him, his golden eyes fierce. "Gillian, are you well enough?"

She laughed and locked her arms around his neck. "Don't be a damn fool, Travis."

He shook his head, his expression both rueful and filled with lust, his calloused fingers a solid anchor in a world of steam and liquid desire. Muttering something profane, he braced himself with a hand against the wall and started to work himself into her. "Fuck, yeah," he murmured, his face softening with pleasure. Yet he continued to observe her reactions and adapt his movements to them.

She could have clawed his eyes out. Dammit, he was being just as careful as ever of her comfort. She didn't want him cautious; she needed him frenzied and hungry and passionate. She tightened her inner muscles around his big shaft in a move learned with a partner whose name she'd forgotten centuries ago.

"Gillian," Travis gasped and froze, shuddering.

Better, much better. She kissed his neck, nuzzling the strong cords of muscle. Returning to that deliciously sensitive spot under his ear, she lapped at it to increase its sensitivity to the steamy air, then delicately bit it to cause a ferocious spur of sensation.

"Oh yeah," he groaned, locking his arms around her shoulders. His thrusts speeded up, finally revealing the reckless lover she'd known before. Matching heedlessness burst into her veins. She chortled, dropped her fangs into her mouth, and raked them over his neck.

He groaned again and brought himself up into her with all the force of his powerful legs and hips. His musk perfumed the steamy air, ratcheting her desire higher and higher. Her fangs extended farther, pricking her lips, adding the scent of her blood to his musk. Half-maddened her with the combination of *vampiro* blood and fully-aroused *prosaico* . . .

She locked her legs behind his back and rode him, totally uncaring of the hard wall behind her or the dangers waiting outside. Only the tidal wave building in his body and blood, crying out to hers to be harvested, mattered now.

He chanted faster and faster, matching his desperate thrusts. He stiffened, his face taut as he fought to control himself. Immediately Gillian bit down hard on his throat, directly into his jugular, and catapulted him into orgasm. He groaned his ecstasy, a deep bellow that shook him to the bone.

Her own climax tumbled her, end over end, a rippling fire of satisfaction from head to toes. His blood covered her tongue—once, twice, thrice. She swallowed the mouthful of blood, the life-giving wave sweeping away all of her ailments.

She purred and delicately licked his throat, urging the small wound to heal faster—and permitting herself one more taste of his truly superb blood. Steam still swirled around them, while their bodies glowed scarlet from passion.

An idea occurred to her. "How much hot water do we have?"

He chuckled hoarsely. "Nothing to worry about there, honey. Electrical and plumbing here are brand-new, with a big backup generator and fuel tank. Both the fuel tank and pantry are full."

He gathered her close, turned off the water, and carried her out of the shower. She was well able to fend for herself now but it was very pleasant to let him take care of her. How he wrapped the big, fluffy towel around her, tenderly dried her off without fussing over how the dead skin and scabs peeled off . . .

Gillian placed a hand on his shoulder to balance herself, admiring how delicious he looked from this angle—the perfect combination of strength and tenderness, if one overlooked the three-inch knife scar on his cheek or those two bullet wounds in his shoulder. There was nothing inherently docile about that harsh profile, either. Yes, there was something to be said for having her very own cop toy. "Where are we?"

"Southeast of Dalhart, near White Springs Lake."

Dalhart? Gillian frowned, re-creating a map in her mind. "Texas?" *Texas? Dear God, not Don Rafael Perez's esfera . . .*

"Yup."

Hell, what was she going to do now? She couldn't stay here, not where Don Rafael could find her and carry out his threat.

She ground her teeth. She'd sworn when she left London at sixteen that she wouldn't freeze again unless somebody paid her to do so. Dammit, this was the first time in all these centuries she'd been forced to break that vow.

Travis stood up and wrapped a clean towel around her to form a sarong. "We'll be safe here, even if it gets as bad as the big blizzard of 1957."

She narrowed her eyes, intent on gathering all the bad news. "What do you mean?"

"The '57 blizzard was the worst in the twentieth century. Thirty-foot drifts, hurricane force winds, snow blowing so hard you couldn't see your hand in front of your face. If this one lasts four days, it'll match those records."

"We're stranded." *Shit.* Now what was she going to do, if she couldn't leave before Don Rafael found out she was here?

She followed Travis into the bedroom, thinking hard, and opened her suitcase, automatically blocking him from seeing her booby traps.

He stepped into his jeans on the other side of the bed. "Until the storm blows out. Then we can either dig ourselves out and drive away, if we're lucky. Or my friends will rescue us."

Everything along her spine to the fine hairs on her neck turned ice cold. "Friends?"

He shrugged on a T-shirt. "Don Rafael Perez and his *mesnaderos*. After I took some wrong turns and finally stumbled onto this place, I called him. Would have called sooner but I wanted to wait for a secure land line. They'll come as soon as possible once it stops snowing."

Don Rafael? Jesus, Mary, and Joseph, what had she gotten herself into? "You know the Texas *patrón*," she commented slowly, her brain frantically sorting and re-sorting options for escape. She was almost fully dressed now.

His amber eyes studied her, missing nothing, while he finished pulling on his boots. "My grandmother's family has served in his *comitiva* for over two hundred years," Travis drawled, his Texas twang much more apparent than before.

He'd been bred to serve Don Rafael? Her stomach headed for the floor, faster than when the alarms had sounded while she was escaping with those rubies from the Kremlin.

He stood up casually and leaned against the wall, his posture anything but threatening. But his eyes were as intent as a hawk watching for rabbits in a wheat field.

Her stomach twisted. The danger was too great. If there was one *patrón* in North America that no sane *vampiro* chose to challenge, it was Don Rafael. Given any chance at all to leave Texas before he arrived, she had to take it. Even though she could think of a thousand ways to play with Travis . . .

"Great story; wish I believed it. But unfortunately I need to leave Texas as quickly as possible, before Don Rafael finds me here. So give me the keys to the truck and I'll be gone."

His mouth tightened, highlighting the harsh strength of his features, and he shifted to block the door. "Gillian, honey, weren't you listening? Nobody's going anywhere until the blizzard stops."

"Travis, I'm damn well going to try. Let me through or I'll take command of your body."

"Gillian, even a *vampiro* can't travel in this storm." He reluctantly moved away from the door but followed her down the narrow hallway. "Otherwise Don Rafael would be here now."

"Don Rafael will kill me if he finds me here!"

"He doesn't kill women."

She spun to face him in the living room. "He destroyed Maggie Silver Tongue, who was the greatest con artist of her day. And Sarah Glengarry, who had the face of an angel—and led the largest criminal gang of the 1880s. Plus, there was—"

"They needed to be put down, Gillian. You don't."

"I make my living as a cat burglar and I sure as hell never asked permission to be in Texas. Every *esfera*'s *patrón* protects its borders by eliminating the undesirables who try to sneak in, Travis. Your precious Don Rafael kills criminals and trespassers, just like the others."

Travis's face hardened into stubborn lines. "Not you. I won't let him."

She'd have thrown her ski boots at him, if they were handy. "How the hell can you stop him? He rules Texas and he's been a *vampiro* for over seven hundred years!"

Outside the wind howled louder, swirling as if eager to tear this part of the house away. A tree groaned and cracked, shattering the air like a gunshot. Gillian jumped. "What the hell?"

"The storm has been continuously breaking trees." He ran his hands through his hair. "Come on; there's a weather station by the back door so you can see the conditions for yourself."

She cast a sharp look at the snow blowing past the windows and followed him.

"I've been a *vampiro* for three hundred years; I'm strong enough to get through anything."

He gave a harsh bark of laughter. "You're welcome to try. But if you go even a few paces from the door, I won't be able to find you in this whiteout. Do us both a favor: Tie a rope around your waist so I can haul you back in."

Hissing with fury, she spun around to face him in the small old-fashioned kitchen. "You underestimate me!"

Deadly earnestness shone in his eyes. "I've set foot outside in a blue norther and you haven't, Gillian. You tell me the same thing after you've tried it, and maybe I'll listen."

"Where's the garage?" she asked curtly.

"I won't tell you unless you tie this rope around your waist."

"That's a stupid precaution." She shook out her extreme cold weather overalls and parka, grateful she'd bought the best when she'd decided to hide from Morelli amid ski resorts.

Wood suddenly cracked and fell outside, thundering into the ground and sending tremors through the house's floor. Gillian jumped and her eyes caught the precise numbers flickering across the weather station's black panel.

Readings for indoors and outdoors were clearly provided. Wind, temperature, humidity, wind chill. The outdoor levels would have done credit to a storm at the North Pole.

Gillian blanched. Twenty years after she'd become a *vampiro*, she and her *creador* had been caught in a hurricane. He'd been a very powerful *vampiro* but the hurricane had dropped a tree across him, crushing his head and killing him, when he tried to cross their island. How many nights had she heard him screaming as the tree crashed into him and sent the blood pouring out of his skull, mixed with the rain, only to disappear as he dissolved into dust? Gone as if he'd never existed.

Eighty-two, read the wind speed. Eighty-four, eighty-five, eighty-six . . .

One degree Fahrenheit, read the temperature. Three, four, four . . .

The wind was too fast and the temperature too low for her to walk to the garage. She'd never get that big truck started so she could drive out of here.

Damn, damn, damn . . .

"Okay, Travis, you're right. I'll wait the storm out." *But if Don Rafael shows up while I'm still here, I swear to God I'll either kill him or run.*

seven

Gillian looked around the small living room and tried not to think *trap*. The entire house was small and decorated like a 1950s vision of the perfect hunting lodge. This room had a large stone fireplace, a comfortable sofa covered with multiple striped blankets, and several big leather armchairs. One wall featured a life-sized poster of John Wayne as Rooster Cogburn and an equally large picture of the Alamo, flanked by stuffed elk, antelope, and moose heads. Beautifully carved chess pieces stood ready in a glass-fronted cabinet. The only signs of modernity were a huge television in one corner and a large bay window, which currently showed a swirling cloud of snow and ice.

"More?" Travis offered, lifting a thermos.

"Thank you." She held up her cup, enjoying his casual grace as he leaned over to fill it. He'd stripped off his shirt and T-shirt in the living room's heat, baring his torso. His hard muscles rippled in the firelight, a light sweat gilding them. Superbly skillful, highly sensual, and generous with his emotions—in other words, the best possible prey for a *vampira* like herself, who lived on the energy carried in blood.

Travis was taking extremely good care of her, starting with that shower. She smiled softly, a lick of flame gliding over her nerves at the memory. His coffee was excellent too, belying the scuttlebutt about squad room coffee being black as tar and even worse to drink. But why was he being so kind when he knew she was a *vampira*?

She started to probe. "How long has the blizzard been going on?"

"Since yesterday morning. It's Saturday now and it's supposed to last into Monday night." He settled back onto the sofa beside her, his expression open.

Why wasn't he afraid?

"We're stuck together," she observed. "With Morelli out to kill both of us, and Don Rafael Perez, the most efficient killer of all North American *patrones*, heading in my direction."

"I've got my gear, plus my partner's. We should be able to hold off Morelli until Don Rafael arrives." Travis's voice was calm and confident.

"Now, why doesn't that make me feel better?" she mused and set her mug aside, the better to judge him. If she was about to spend three days cooped up with him, then she'd by God understand her cop's motives.

She came up onto her knees and plucked his mug away, placing it beside hers. He watched her, a half smile on his face, but made no move to stop her. If anything, he seemed very pleased. She faced him cross-legged less than an arm's length away.

"What am I supposed to call you? If we're going to spend three days together, Travis seems very formal."

"I answer to Travis on all occasions, Gillian."

She shot him a disbelieving look. "All? It's your surname, isn't it?"

"Yup—and it's the only handle I go by."

"Even on your wedding day?" Now why had she brought that up?

His face tightened briefly but his eyes remained steady on hers. "I used Travis when I was married at Saint Patrick's Cathedral."

She cocked her head, a little too curious for her own peace of mind about his wedding ceremony.

"My wife was a nurse, who died of leukemia and she called me Travis at all times."

She said a quick prayer for his wife.

Her eyes returned to him, considering her next move. He was leaning back against the sofa, displaying himself like an offering. *Why?* He was too cunning to do that unconsciously. She needed an answer.

"What do you have in mind while we're here, Travis?"

His eyes hooded and his mouth softened, transforming him into a being of pure carnality. "Whatever you want, Gillian. Whatever you want."

Damn, he was tempting but she wouldn't reach for him yet. "You know I'll drink your blood and I could easily kill you. Yet you'll come to my bed if I lift my finger?"

"Of course." He nodded, the pulse throbbing tantalizingly in his neck. "Anything, any time, Gillian."

"Why? And don't say it's because Thursday night was the best sex of your life."

His eyes flew open, golden with frustration. He controlled himself quickly and started to recompose his features into an eager lover's.

She grabbed his wrist, gripping it hard. "Tell me the truth, Travis, or I'll rip the answer out of your brain. You won't like that at all."

He snarled and yanked his hand free, a gesture she permitted him. "Dammit, Gillian!"

"The truth, Travis."

His pitiless eyes measured her for a long minute, a judgment as harsh as any she'd endured on London's hard streets or amid Morgan's pirates. She met his stare directly, impressed despite herself by a *prosaico* willing to lock eyes with a *vampira*. It took almost a minute before he was satisfied enough to reach over to the coffee table and pluck a small package out of his shirt pocket.

Travis held up a small leather book in a plastic bag. Her eyes widened and she blanched. Oh shit, the notebook she'd stolen from Morelli.

"This notebook belonged to my first partner and former brother-in-law, Frank D'Angelo. He became an FBI agent but was killed two months ago." His thumb rubbed lovingly over the winged logo, with its entwined lettering, on the corner.

Mother Mary, if Travis learns everything about the notebook, Morelli will certainly kill him. "I had nothing to do with his death."

He was standing now, only a breath away from her, as alluring and dangerous as an unleashed wildcat. "Never thought you did. But I'll do anything you want, if you'll tell me exactly how you came by his investigator's notebook."

She gaped at him, astounded by his offer. "You know I'm a *vampira* and you'll have sex with me—to do your job as a cop?"

He spread his hands wider, beckoning her to him. A hard ridge swelled behind his fly, emphasizing his eagerness. "Of course. Just say the words, Gillian, and you've got me. You want me naked? How about a strip tease? Whatever. Doesn't matter—as long as you tell me about Frank's notebook."

Blessed Virgin, he was everything a man should be. If she lifted her hand, she could run it up his thigh, palm the hard muscle, cup the fat swell of his balls, fondle his beautiful shaft . . .

Her breasts tightened with the urge to rub themselves over him.

"If I tell you the full story, he'll kill you." She wrenched her eyes away from the sweep of hair across his chest and the tight coppery nipples gleaming through it.

Travis shrugged. "I'm dead anyway, if he catches me. Let me show you a good time before then and you can whisper in my ear afterward." He pursed his lips in a kiss and waggled his fingers at her again.

A gurgle of laughter bubbled up. "Is that your idea of enticing a girl?"

"You want something else?" He began to unbutton his jeans very, very slowly.

Her breath stopped with an audible gasp. Dammit, if there was someone else to feed on, she might have had a chance to resist him. Or maybe not. His combination of strength and passion was unbelievably tempting.

She slipped her fingers between his thighs and he froze, one eyebrow flying up. "What?"

"Spread your legs." She gently moved her hand up and down an inch or two, to provide the lightest possible sensation in a very sensitive area.

He shuddered, sending an answering tremor up her arm.

"There isn't room," he protested hoarsely.

"Step back so you're not caught between the sofa and the table."

"That's not what I meant. These jeans are too tight to come down very far if I widen my legs." His shaft seemed to be pushing at his jeans' top button.

She veiled her smirk and continued to stroke his inner thighs. Heat was spiraling through her veins and down her spine. "Anything I want, remember?"

"Uh—yeah." He stepped back and spread his legs, setting his feet shoulder-width apart.

"Oh, very good," she purred and promptly rubbed the seams lightly against his inner thighs. She settled onto her knees before him.

He gaped down at her. "What?"

She leaned her cheek against his hip, swirling her hair past his abdomen. He trembled and leaned subtly closer. She caressed him again the same way, adding a touch of her breasts against his thigh. A warm glow of arousal was building in her core.

He moaned, his fists clenching and unclenching. "Can I touch you?"

She blinked, surprised that he'd asked permission first. "Yes, since you asked."

His fingers sank into her hair, softly kneading her scalp, matching their pace and tension to how she fondled him. "Slowly, Travis," she murmured. "We have time to enjoy ourselves."

He groaned in agreement, his pulse throbbing through the rich vein under her fingers.

She nuzzled and licked his stomach, reaching inside his waistband wherever possible. She explored his hipbones, raising shudders and moans that ran through her like hot brandy. She could have twined herself around his leg for hours, melting and flowing like hot sugar over a particularly delicious apple. Hot cream dripped onto her thighs but she was enjoying Travis's taste and sounds too much to reach for her own completion.

Aggravatingly, his jeans' denim was preventing her further enjoyment—and her test of how far he'd let a *vampira* go with him.

She began to unbutton his last item of clothing as slowly as possible.

"Damn, Gillian," he cursed, the first time the hard metal and cloth brushed his aroused shaft.

"Objecting?"

He stared down at her, panting. "Like hell. More likely, just wondering if you'll finish before I explode."

She chuckled and carefully eased him free of the first opening.

"I won't explode; I'll just be insane," he muttered and closed his eyes.

She bit her lip against a laugh. But her own body was throbbing with interest.

When the jeans were completely unbuttoned, he hooked his thumbs in the waistband but stopped. "Gillian . . ." he gritted.

"Oh yes, please do but only to the top of your thighs."

She lightly glided two fingers up and down the back of his shaft. His answering moan was music to her ears and to her arousal but he still managed to get his jeans down. "What next?"

She drew in a deep breath. How she loved the scent of an aroused man, the way it went straight to her core and sent her shuddering with eagerness. She tasted him delicately with her tongue.

He groaned, the tremor running through his every fiber and firing off flares in her veins. She had to close her eyes before she could truly start to lick him. Very, very slowly, of course, making pleasure a rich bed of fire, not a desperate lunge. Sliding the coarse denim slowly down his legs, every inch building her arousal higher.

Travis matched her step for step, his deep moans and strong, calloused hands telling her of his increasing enjoyment.

But finally, when the cloth was tossed against the wall and they were both almost breathless with anticipation, Gillian pressed deeply on the sensitive spot behind Travis's balls. Orgasm quickly rolled over him in a deep wave, sending jet after jet of cream spurting out. He groaned in rapture, his hands tightening on her shoulders.

Gillian promptly bit down on his femoral artery, deep in his thigh. His orgasm washed through her, rich as the finest Burgundy wine, and triggered her own climax, tumbling her over and over like a waterfall plummeting into a river of delight. She abandoned herself to it, luxuriating in his shared ecstasy.

EIGHT

Gillian recrossed her legs under her at the kitchen table and considered how to redecorate this room. Terrazzo floors, instead of linoleum, of course. But cherry cabinets, instead of knotty pine, or should she use oak? Granite countertops or soapstone, to replace the peeling laminate? It was all immaculately clean, though, as was the living room where they'd played chess and checkers—and laughed their way through a collection of Jeff Foxworthy DVDs.

Travis was working his way through an enormous plate of beef and beans. Plus corn bread and honey and beer. Like all *prosaicos* who were entertaining a *vampiro*, he was a ravenous eater in order to produce the necessary blood.

"Do the owners know we're here?" she asked. Sometimes she missed solid food. Enjoying it secondhand by kissing a *prosaico* or through the taste of his blood was close but not always good enough.

He nodded, buttering corn bread. "I called them last night after I spoke to Don Rafael."

She winced reflexively. A century ago, Don Rafael had warned her not to steal any more jewelry in Texas. In fact, the big brute had explicitly told her not to come back without an invitation and warned her of what would happen if she disobeyed. She managed a smile for Travis.

"They've been renting it out for vacations and fishing. It was stocked for someone else, who canceled because of the blizzard. I promised them we'd pay for what we use."

She nodded, trying to ignore the omnipresent noise of howling winds and falling branches. She decided to talk about more stable places to dwell. "Where do you live, back in New York?"

"An apartment on West Forty-seventh by the Port Authority."

"Hell's Kitchen?" Damn, she hadn't been there in decades and it had more than lived up to its name then.

He nodded. "It's coming back as a good address. After my grandfather died, I invested my inheritance and lived off my salary. Years later, I used my savings to buy a rundown pair of apartments, fixed them up and sold one for a big profit. Kept the other for myself—a great two-bedroom, two-bath with a terrace. Small private gym for myself, good kitchen . . ."

Realization sank in. "I'm stranded with a Manhattan real estate speculator."

He chuckled at that and waved his hand at their lackluster surroundings. "I'm no Donald Trump, Gillian, but I can afford to rent this place."

He went back to eating, apparently not holding a grudge. But she owed him an apology for insulting him by suggesting that he took bribes. That entailed an explanation.

Her stomach knotted. She hadn't spoken of those matters in so long. But he'd always treated her with courtesy and consideration; he deserved the same from her.

She swallowed hard and carefully stretched her fingers out across her legs, under the table.

"I'm sorry to have insulted you, Travis. I've never known a good cop so I'm afraid I jumped to the wrong conclusion."

His amber eyes studied her, far too observant now. "That's okay, Gillian. You don't have to like me."

Her mouth tightened at that. If they were going to spend days together during this storm and face Morelli at the end, there needed to be truth between them, even if there wasn't friendship. She bit her lip and plunged in.

"Three hundred years ago, a cop was responsible for my mother's death."

"What?"

Gillian went on in a flat tone without looking at him again. "Constable Peters lost his temper when Mother bloodied his nose for trying to rape a ten-year-old girl. He sent Mother to the Old Bailey on a trumped-up murder charge and she hung a few weeks later. I was fourteen and I swore revenge."

Travis's head came up fast, his eyes carrying the look of a man ready to do murder.

"I did whatever I had to, in order to stay alive. Somehow the constable and his friends hadn't felt safe."

"I wouldn't have either."

She glanced at him, startled. He smiled coldly back at her, slowly stroking the ball of his thumb over his knife blade in the ancient promise for bloodletting.

Gillian's own smile grew, as she remembered using the same gesture.

"So they bribed a judge to have me convicted of theft and sent to the West Indies, considered a sure death sentence given the tropical fevers. Instead, I met first pirates and later *vampiros*. I became one of those myself in order to finally gain revenge on my mother's killer."

"Couldn't you find justice within the law?" Travis asked quietly.

"Justice?" She hooted with laughter. "Not unless I bought it. No, I went to see Constable Peters myself. It was ten years since he'd seen me but he recognized me immediately."

"What happened?"

Gillian's fingers curled into claws. "He started to run—and I let him. The eight-year-old twins in his bed had already been through enough. They didn't need to see death meted out as well."

"Christ, I'm sorry, Gillian. I always want to string bad cops up by their balls."

She stared at him, totally at a loss for words.

He inclined his head to her, his eyes filled with hard-edged memories. "If he hadn't been executed, he'd have wished for death when he was sent up. Just like that rotten G-man will, the one who set Frank up to be murdered."

A ripple of belief ran through Gillian, showing her Constable Peters through Travis's eyes—wretched and miserable, forced to be one of the lowest of the low in Newgate, despised by both prisoners and guards.

The image was so strong, she could almost believe that there were good cops who'd make bad cops pay for abusing the law.

Travis stood up and began to clear the table. Gillian shook herself and helped him silently, wishing they could stay here in this cabin forever. Without thinking about today's problems like dead cops or Morelli or Don Rafael.

When they were done, Travis tipped up her chin. "Ready to talk now?"

She nodded. "Here or in the living room?"

"Easier to take notes here."

Her stomach knotted at the thought of another notebook but she nodded. "Fine."

She poured herself another cup of coffee and sat back down at the table, holding on to the ceramic like a lifeline.

Travis disappeared into the other room and returned with a neat leather notebook, a pen, and the plastic-encased notebook that had started this deadly affair.

His notebook brought her curiosity to full, raging life. "Your notebook—it looks just like the one in plastic."

"It should. It's exactly the same, except for the name and logo embossed on the cover. Frank's had a pair of wings and his last name. Mine has my name and a rearing horse."

"But from a distance, you can't tell them apart."

"Yeah, the guys always teased us like hell about that." He was silent for a moment, his face touched with old memories.

"Ready?" he asked, pen poised over his notebook.

"I'm a cat burglar," she began. "I won't give you all the names I've operated under, the crimes I've committed or been accused of. But I'm good and I'm well-known in certain circles."

"Go on." His face was calm, waiting for the real revelations.

"Vicente Morelli is the *capo di capi* of New York, which the NYPD probably knows already. In other words, the top mobster who all the other top mobsters report to. What you don't know is that he's a *vampiro*, like me."

Travis's jaw dropped. "You're joking."

"About Morelli? I wouldn't joke, not about that. He's a *vampiro mayor*, just over three hundred years old, so he can tolerate full daylight."

"What?"

"You have to be two hundred years old to even try your hand at twilight and three centuries old or so to be comfortable outside at high noon."

"I didn't know that about *vampiros*."

Gillian blinked. "You truly didn't grow up close to Don Rafael's principal estate, did you?"

"No, we left Texas when I was fourteen."

"Really?" If he'd left that young, Don Rafael would probably

not have considered recruiting him for his *mesnaderos*, his household guard. "Okay, back to Morelli. He hired me to recover a very
expensive jade bowl from a Chinese mobster. Knowing the difficulty
and Morelli's reputation as a cheap bastard, I set a high fee and
warned him that if he didn't pay me on time, I'd take something of
his hostage until he paid me. He told me there wouldn't be a
problem."

"And you believed him."

She rolled her eyes at him. "Yeah, just the same way I believe in
Santa Claus and the Tooth Fairy: not at all."

She stood up to pace restlessly up and down the kitchen.

"I stole the statue and returned it to him. Half my fee had been
paid in advance but I wanted the remainder. If I didn't get the rest,
every stinking SOB in the world would think they could stiff me. So
when time was up, I paid Morelli a visit."

She stopped, alternate waves of hot and cold running through
her as she remembered that night. She turned to face Travis, bracing herself against the counter.

"Morelli's estate in Long Island was a madhouse. Lights,
guards—both *prosaico* and *vampiro*. I've rarely seen anything like
it. It didn't stop me, of course, since I'd scouted the whole place before I took the job."

Travis was watching her, almost vibrating with tension. "Go
on," he growled, his amber eyes intent.

"Morelli was just leaving with a very polished blond, his arm
around the fellow's shoulder."

Travis froze. "Tall guy? Blond, bad acne scars? Notch in right
earlobe from an earring being yanked out?"

"That's him," Gillian acknowledged, watching her lover
cautiously.

Recognition flashed across his face to be replaced by a rage so
cold that it could sear through steel. Instinctively, Gillian looked for
the closest exit.

"Peters." Travis spat. He flung himself up and out from behind the table. "I swear, when I get back to New York, he will be arrested so fast, he won't have time to dial the area code of his single phone call." He pounded the refrigerator, his face hidden, before he turned to her. "Could you hear what they were saying?"

"No, even if I'd been listening, they were too far away."

"Damn. Go on."

"I made my way to Morelli's office and opened his safe." Really, the man should have had better equipment. Relying on guards, which were only one line of defense, was sheer laziness.

"There I found the notebook." She nodded toward it. "It was very carefully wrapped in multiple layers of silk, unlike anything else in there, even the most expensive jade. So I grabbed it. It wasn't until I was out of there and read it that I learned what I'd stolen." She gulped. "Have you read it?"

He nodded, his face haggard. "Frank told me. Morelli can make perfect U.S. passports. He's selling them to the highest bidder, which is how those terrorists made that mess in Washington just before Thanksgiving."

"Yes, Customs doesn't look twice at American citizens coming back from overseas vacations," she agreed, still as appalled as when she'd first read the notebook.

"That's what Frank was investigating—and what got him killed. The notebook has the conclusive details of his investigation. It can bring the bastard down."

Her gut unknotted at finally having someone else fighting against her enemies. "Yes, that's why Morelli wants me dead. The American government won't rest until Morelli is stamped out, a crusade that could easily result in finding out that *vampiros* exist. There isn't a *vampiro* in the world who wouldn't personally fry Morelli in order to stop that disaster from happening."

"Why haven't you gone to one of the big *patrones*, told your story, and asked for protection?"

"Who'd believe a cat burglar? Especially someone who's stolen from all of them at least once before." She shook her head, remembering all the nights she'd lain awake trying to think of a single *patrón* who might protect her. "No, that wouldn't work. The only answer has been to run. It's kept me alive for this long."

"Until Morelli's assassin caught up to you in Pine Falls, probably by following me."

She closed her eyes, remembering the dog's claws ripping into her. "Until then."

"Gillian, I'm going to radio in my report."

She swung around to face him. "What do you mean—radio in?"

"I can't call in from here. The phones are dead and email's down, because the satellite link is down. But the truck is in the garage, carrying a heavy-duty radio. It may be strong enough to get a message out."

"*Outside?* Jesus, Travis, are you some kind of masochist?" Instinctively, she glanced at the weather display. "Those are hurricane force winds! And the wind chill is what you'd see at the North Pole. You can't go out there."

His fierce golden eyes locked with hers and a muscle ticked in his jaw. "We should be able to dig out and join Don Rafael before Morelli arrives. But if things go bad, we want somebody else to know who's responsible."

"Is revenge worth your death?"

He gripped her shoulders, shaking her gently. "Justice, Gillian. We're the only ones alive who can bring Morelli to justice. You understand that need."

She glared at him, furious at being caught by her own past.

She began to laugh at the irony. "Hoist by my own petard, Travis? Very well, but only if I come with you."

He shot her an impatient glance and headed for the back door. "I've roped off the ranch's perimeter, so I can't wander away. Plus, I have full arctic gear. I'll be back in a few minutes."

"We'll be back in a few minutes," she corrected him, pulling down her own cold-weather gear. At least her own paranoia about winter weather had demanded that she buy the best.

"Gillian," he growled.

"Don't 'Gillian' me. I can walk to the garage and back." *No matter how much I hate the temperature.* "If you want to return in a few minutes without freezing any portion of your anatomy, you'll accept my help. Understand, you big chauvinist cop?"

He propped his fists on his hips and glared at her.

She ignored him and began to pull on her overalls. "Or are you planning to wait here and tell me what tools you want?"

"You're an infuriating woman, Gillian."

She laughed at him, genuinely amused. "No, I'm simply trying to return as quickly as possible to my own home in the Caribbean. A wonderful place of white sands, warm blue waters, and green gardens, where I don't have to wear heavy boots to go outside. Morelli's kept me away from there far too long."

He began to rapidly don his gear. "Sounds like we're partners."

"Partners? With a cop?"

"Partner—with a *thief*," he shot back and held out his hand. "Shake, partner."

Laughter bubbled up in her until she was leaning against the wall, holding her sides with tears streaming down her face. "Partners, it is then. At least until we're back in civilization."

They shook hands, mirth rippling through the air.

NINE

The world was composed of howling ice, beating at her like a thousand deadly whips held by one huge hand, determined to crush her. Gillian staggered but forced herself back upright through sheer determination. Blessed Mother be praised, at least the path to the garage was sheltered from the worst of the storm. So they were only wading through two feet of snow and not the enormous drifts they could glimpse on the other side.

Travis swayed, falling away from the wind's fury. She hauled him back upright, locking her arms around him. She'd never say so to his face but the damn fool man wouldn't have made it this far without her *vampiro* strength.

And may she never again go out in freezing weather without being paid for it. . . .

Travis bulled forward another step and she followed, near enough to stabilize him. They had to be close to the garage. She'd counted seventeen steps and it was only supposed to be fifteen.

Eighteen. Nineteen.

Travis stopped abruptly and Gillian barely managed not to step on his feet. A cautious glance around his shoulder showed that they'd found the garage. He sidled to his right, fumbled for the knob, and threw his weight against the door. Thankfully, it turned and they fell into the dark interior, together with a burst of shimmering, icy white.

Travis lunged at the door and slammed it shut. Gillian scrambled up and threw the light switch.

A bank of brilliant shop lights blazed into life overhead, displaying an ordinary garage large enough to hold three trucks. Workbenches surrounded most of the perimeter, while snow swirled under the pair of big doors that covered one side.

The Suburban sat squarely in the center, its once-proud black paint now hidden under mud and salt. But it smelled wrong.

Gillian pushed back her hood, peeled back her balaclava, and sniffed.

Travis headed for the truck but she grabbed him back.

He spun to face her. "What the hell was that for?"

"The scent is wrong."

He tilted his head curiously. "Just how good is a *vampiro*'s sense of smell?"

"Beats a bloodhound's any day." She walked around the truck, sampling the air at all levels. "Most of the truck's scent matches that on the supplies you brought inside. But there's one small trace, which reminds me of our Pine Falls attackers."

His eyes turned cold. "Morelli's assassins."

She stooped by the engine and looked underneath. "It's strongest here. Can you see anything?"

He produced a heavy flashlight, capable of being used as a weapon. "Where?"

She slid under the truck and pointed. "There."

The brilliant light picked out a small box on the truck's frame, scarcely larger than a pack of cigarettes, whose label included the words *covert* and *GPS*.

"Any chance the tracking signal didn't get through?" Gillian asked softly, ice forming faster in her stomach than on the snow banks outside.

Travis cursed viciously, as she slid rapidly out from under the truck. "No. The weather was only very nasty, not appalling, when we arrived."

"So company's coming."

"Yeah, they'll be here as soon as they can after the blizzard blows out, either by Humvee or helicopter." Travis shrugged off the heavy parka and opened the truck.

"So we'd better start preparing to fight, even if we have to do it in a blizzard."

"I wish to God we had more fighters on our side." Travis turned on the Suburban.

"There's only the two of us. We'll manage." Gillian swung herself up inside, cursing the builders of all big trucks who never thought of small women.

"But if we were both *vampiros*, I'd have the increased strength, speed, and senses."

Gillian snorted in derision. "Sorry, Travis. It takes at least three months, maybe years, for a *cachorro* to pass through *La Lujuria* and be of any use as a *vampiro* in a fight."

"Three months!"

"Well, occasionally two if the *cachorro* already knows and completely trusts his *creador*. He also has to be extremely clear about why he wishes to become a *vampiro*, before his *creador* gives him *El Abrazo*—the entire process of becoming a *vampiro*."

Silhouetted against the garage's light, his jaw's stubborn jut was all too apparent. "If we started now, I'd still have some of a *vampiro*'s strength. Every little bit would help."

"Not when you're insane! Travis, honey, after you first become a *vampiro*—when you're still a *cachorro*—all you can think about is blood and feeding your need for emotional energy. That time is called *La Lujuria*, because you're almost mindless with lust."

"For sex?"

"Or whatever is the first emotion you taste after awakening as a *vampiro*. It's almost always death or terror."

"Not for you."

"No, my *creador* made sure that I learned to feed only on carnal passions. But that's not the point. We only have two days so there's no time for you to become a *vampiro*."

He pounded his fist against the dash, making her jump. "Goddammit all, there must be something more! I will not sit here and wait for Morelli to slaughter us. Isn't there something you can turn me into, something more than just an ordinary mortal?"

She put her hand on his knee. "You're a very strong *prosaico*, Travis. It will be enough."

"Against Morelli's army? Is there anything else in your universe beside *prosaico* and *vampiro*?"

She hesitated. "Well, there are *compañeros* but they're rare."

His eyes caught a reflected beam of light, making them gleam like amber. "Tell me about these *compañeros*."

Gillian hesitated, made wary by too much intense interest. "If a *vampiro* licks a bite, it heals quickly, right?"

He shrugged. "Of course. Get to the point, Gillian."

"*Compañeros* are *prosaicos* who drink *vampiro* blood. They are healthy to begin with, whereas if you wish to become a *vampiro* you must be almost dead before you drink *vampiro* blood."

He flipped switches briskly on the big radio under the dash. "In order to become a *vampiro*, you have to be weakened by going into shock first. Makes sense. *Compañeros* aren't going into shock so they don't become *vampiros*."

"Correct. But they do get greatly increased healing abilities. It's enough that one *concubino compañero* can feed a *vampiro mayor*, such as myself, who requires only a few tablespoons of blood per day."

Lights glowed on the radio's display. Static poured out.

"*Vampiros* keep *compañeros* as concubines, your basic, old-fashioned sex slaves. So what?" He was trying to speed up her explanation.

"Old *vampiros* keep concubines and they also tend to be very secretive. Hence the lack of knowledge about *compañeros*."

He stared at the displays, cursed under his breath, and hit some more combinations of switches. The numbers on the display dropped. "How much do you know, Gillian?"

"Even after the first deep drink of *vampiro* blood, a *compañero* is noticeably stronger and faster than a *prosaico*. The longer a *compañero* drinks *vampiro* blood, the stronger a *compañero* grows until he can become almost a match for a weakling *vampiro*."

"How long does that take?"

"I don't know. Rumor says it depends on how often he drinks *vampiro* blood and . . ."

"And?" Travis prodded. His patience was clearly shredding.

"The strength of the *compañero*'s emotional attachment to his *vampiro primero*, the *vampiro* that he's drinking blood from."

Travis turned to face her. "Then let's start tonight."

She couldn't let him. He deserved better than that life. "No! A *compañero* becomes dependent upon, almost addicted to, his *vampiro primero*."

"How long does that take?"

She met his eyes honestly. "I don't know. I've heard anything from a few days to months."

"I'll take the chance."

"No way, Travis. You're going back to your life when this is done."

"It may be our only hope."

"We have cases of weapons and ammo inside the house."

"We need an edge, especially in knowing when and how to use them, Gillian!"

"What about afterward? Do you want to find yourself begging for a taste, just one taste of a thief who's also a blood drinker?"

He was silent for a long minute before he turned off the static-filled radio. Gillian reached for her door but he caught her arm.

"I'll do whatever it takes to bring my friend's killers to justice, Gillian. Do you understand that? Anything!"

His eyes were narrowed, intent on hers, demanding her understanding.

"You could live one, maybe two, centuries as my *compañero*, Travis. Are a few minutes of revenge worth that? Do you know how many times I've wished in the past three centuries that I'd left vengeance in the Lord's hands and refused to become a *vampiro*, just so I could live long enough to kill my mother's murderer?"

If anything, Travis's face grew harder. "Frank was gutted and his privates stuffed into his mouth. I cannot rest until his killer is brought to justice."

His friend had been given the ancient warning for trespassers.

Gillian gagged and closed her eyes.

Behind her eyelids she could see again her mother's broken, bloody body, as she'd laid it out for burial. As it had looked after the guards destroyed her during that last orgy of rape and knifeplay. As it had looked when she'd sworn to find justice herself, because there was none in England for a murdered poor woman.

"Ask me again after you've slept on it."

ten

Travis stood in the hallway before a framed picture of a long-horn herd and wondered if he was a damn smart cop for doing this, just thinking with his dick—or following his instincts. The wind howled, shaking the roof as if mocking his indecision.

Did it matter? There was no way he and Gillian could leave here before the storm stopped. Even then, it would take time to dig out, given the twenty-foot drifts currently blocking the garage's exit. Morelli wouldn't face those delays since he could come in from places like Arizona or Mexico, which were free of the blizzard. Don Rafael and his men would come but how soon?

And of course, there was the whole matter of spending decades having mind-blowing sex with a stunningly beautiful woman. One who was smart, tough, and funny, to boot. Played great chess and laughed at all the same jokes he did. Oh yeah, that didn't have any-thing to do with why he was standing here.

Or maybe it was because he'd spent seventeen years since Maria's death looking for the right woman and seeing the hell that could be found with the wrong one, in others' lives. Every instinct he had said Gillian was the right woman for him, even if it would take some extra effort to convince her.

He trusted his instincts; he'd bet his life on them, time and again as a cop. He'd do so now.

He slipped into the master bedroom, where Gillian was sleeping. His throat tightened at the sight of her, all tousled red hair and creamy skin sprawled across white sheets and green blankets, like a package of delights the fairies had left behind. She was so damn beautiful, so fragile and yet so tough, all at the same time.

This had to work. He was damn sure he couldn't survive watching another woman he loved die.

Her green eyes opened and blinked at the sight of him. Blinked again as she started to raise herself up on one elbow. "Travis . . ."

Like hell matters would go exactly the way she expected. It was his life that was changing so he'd do it the way he wanted.

A second later, he was above her, her wrists locked in his hand and his knee between her legs. "Gillian?" he mocked gently and rubbed his naked belly over her equally bare torso.

She wriggled under him. Not much; if she chose, the lady could probably throw him to the door. Blood rushed to his cock at that thought.

"Travis! What are you doing?" No objections in her eyes nor in those taut nipples nuzzling his aching chest.

"Going to have a taste of your blood, Gillian," he announced, deepening his accent as much as possible. "I figure we have a serial killer to stop. And if we don't stop him, he's just going to kill and kill all the good people."

She swallowed, lifting her chin to look him straight in the eye. "Are you very sure, Travis?"

He brushed a loose strand of hair back from her forehead with his free hand. "Isn't that why you went back for that constable after all those years? Because you knew he'd kill again and again unless he was stopped? And there was nobody around except you to do it."

A single silver tear gleamed high on her cheek. "You'll be sorry, once you start needing a thief."

"No, I won't." He was more certain of that than he'd been of anything else in his life, except why he'd joined the NYPD.

"It's more than that, Gillian, honey. I'll take a chance on forever, when it's with you."

Her eyes widened. "You don't know me well enough to say that!"

"Neither of us are inexperienced virgins who know nothing of the world. We've both seen enough of what we do and don't like to know when someone suits us, Gillian. So don't you think we've already been through enough—after fighting off enemies and then being cooped up in this cabin together for hours—to know when someone's the right person? To ask them to marry you?"

"Travis . . ."

"If you keep fussing, without giving me any good reasons, I'll keep proposing until you say yes."

She stuttered, her hands opening and closing against the sheets.

He leaned down and took her, slanting his mouth over hers, kissing her harder than he'd ever done before. She was his, goddammit, and he would not, could not, let her escape him.

She tensed under him. For a moment, he was afraid that she might reject him. He stroked her tongue, teasing her in the stroke she adored, gentling her with his breath and the touch of his lips and his teeth.

She quivered and moaned softly into his mouth. Her hands twisted in his and he tightened his grasp. He would not let her get away, not now, not the first woman who'd really mattered after Maria D'Angelo Travis.

Gillian's hips circled under him in a welcoming gesture as old as time. He growled into her mouth and hunched his back, rubbing his cock over her mound.

She moaned again, her breasts hardening under him. She twisted again, this time definitely to draw closer.

A wave of red lust clouded his vision, mixed with brilliant relief. "Gillian," he groaned. "Gillian." He kissed her face and her throat, flickering his tongue over her pulse points then gently scraping his teeth over them.

She shuddered, writhing under him. The rich, heady aroma of feminine musk crept into the air, clouding his brain until all he could think of was the desperate need to have her now.

He kissed her again, deeper. She sighed her approval and wrapped her legs around his waist, rubbing her creamy folds over his desperately hard cock.

"Oh yeah," he growled and used his free hand to guide himself into her. Her unbelievably strong inner muscles immediately clamped down hard on him, trapping his glans. He nearly came like a teenager, with more haste than stamina. "Goddammit, Gillian, wait!"

"Why? I want you now!"

Hell, that was even more exciting than having her body seize him. He lunged into her, driving his cock forward like a piledriver, until their bodies met with a hard wet slap.

"Yes!" she groaned. "Hurry up, you big cop. . . ."

Arousal reigned, sweeping logic before it. He locked his arms around her shoulders, forgetting to hold her wrists lest she try to not give him blood. He curved his spine and drove into her with the full power of his thighs and glutes, every muscle he'd built on the long hours in the gym and while running. She met him equally savagely, her nails raking his back and drawing blood. Her body fought to hold him but he came back into her again, their bodies meeting with hard wet slaps, as they gladly, fiercely took each other to the heights, with musk and blood scenting the air.

When it was all too terribly much, she raked her fangs over her wrist and spun into orgasm, her body locking down on his and wrenching him into a matching climax. He opened his mouth to shout in triumph when the first hard jet tore out of his cock, his seed just starting to rip out of his balls.

But Gillian shoved her bleeding wrist into his mouth. Caught by surprise, unable to stop, he bit down and drank, swallowing mouthful after mouthful.

Her blood tasted like whiskey and fire, burning through him, yet making him miraculously whole at the same time. It blasted through him like an exploding pipe bomb, firing through his veins and into his cells until every one of them was more vibrantly alive than ever before. He could have floated on the ceiling, he could have spun like a top, he could have danced across the room.

Afterward, he could not have lifted a finger to save his life.

"Travis," Gillian remarked, from somewhere underneath him.

"Hmm?" She gave him a small shove and he rolled them both over, pulling the sheet around them.

"You'll have to tell me your first name sooner or later, you know, now that you're my *compañero*."

Oh. Now that was alarming. He managed to think well enough to form an answer. "It's Beauregard Jackson Travis."

"Beauregard?" Amusement darkened her voice, like fine brandy.

He growled his disdain for the sissy name.

She chuckled softly and caressed his hair. "Go to sleep, Travis. You can have some more blood as soon as you wake up."

"Cool."

He was asleep almost before he uttered the final consonant.

ELEVEN

 "In Dalhart, the Red Cross has opened additional shelters at the following locations. . . ."

Gillian snapped off the radio and prowled restlessly around the living room. "Sounds like it's even worse in Dalhart than here."

Travis snapped the DVD case shut and slid it back into the big cabinet. They'd been enjoying a festival of Errol Flynn and John Wayne movies, among other activities. "They've got more trees than we do, so they're having power outages and destroyed roofs."

"Yeah." She considered the whirling cloud of white outside the windows.

"Think it'll stop soon?"

She extended her senses, the knack of reading her environment that had served her so well as a cat burglar. She reached out to the wind and the cold, reading the frozen ground, and the moisture-laden air rushing by. "Yes, sometime just before dawn. It will still be damn cold and windy, though."

"That's good to hear." Reflected in the window, she could see him studying the big map of the ranch, his intent features reflected in the snow's whirling patterns.

She turned to watch her *compañero* directly. After two days of sharing blood at every opportunity, he was as passionate, strong, and quick to heal as all the legends promised. He was still eating ravenously so he could produce enough blood for her—and for him by extension, although he now drank only a few drops at a time. He was also just as argumentative as he'd been before he'd first done so. Well, she'd never really expected slavish obedience from him.

She'd also never quite anticipated that the legends' claims of vibrant good health, to the point of astonishing physical attractiveness, would come true. She'd half-hoped he'd need her presence. She hadn't expected she'd long for his.

She glanced at the clock, calculating the hours until dawn.

"The forecasters say the storm should blow out just before dawn. Since Morelli can move around in daylight, when do you think he'll come?" His golden eyes were level, the deep-cut lines around his eyes and mouth clear to see.

Gillian blew out a breath, considering what to say. She'd worried over this question for so long but how to frame her answer?

"Gillian . . ." he warned.

She shook her head at her own optimism. Making Travis a *compañero* had definitely increased his independence of thought, as compared to the more typical quick obedience.

"What do you think Morelli is likely to do, as a *vampiro mayor*?" Travis repeated.

She gave him the truth. "Morelli's paid hit man said Morelli believes I'm a *vampira*, not a *vampira mayor*. In that case, he probably believes I put you under a compulsion to flee New Mexico and head east into the storm."

Travis pursed his lips, considering this. "All the same logic I used, but with you as the initiator. That would also explain why I took out the assassination team's driver on the highway."

"Correct." She chewed her lip, hunting for words.

"Go on."

She glanced up to meet his golden eyes, steady and calm. "It's unpleasant."

"What about Morelli is fun to talk about?"

She threw her shoulders back and gave him the worst of it. "If I were a typical *vampiro*, I'd have killed you by now. Probably on Saturday, the first day I was awake."

"What the hell?" He shook her by the shoulders. "Come on, Gillian, out with it."

"Most *vampiros* live on terror or death, as the emotion carried in the blood. Given how badly I was injured, I would have needed to kill the first *prosaico* I met to recover if I was like them. But I'm not!"

"No, of course you're not, honey. I never thought you were or I wouldn't have become your *compañero*." He hugged her comfortingly and she allowed herself to lean against him for a moment.

"Well, Morelli underestimates me in at least one way, even if he is about to arrive on our doorstep," she commented. "He has no idea I'm a *vampira mayor* and hence stronger and faster than any of his men except himself."

Travis nodded as a wicked grin blossomed on his face. "Still, we have one weapon he won't expect: me. He thinks I'm dead."

She shook her head, appalled by the nightmare vision of his bloody body sprawled across the snow. "It's not enough. He'll come with at least a dozen men, probably more. If you leave now in the Suburban, you can probably get far enough away that he won't find you."

"Like hell I'll leave you! I'm going to watch your back when you face that vicious bastard."

"You've only been a *compañero* for two days, Travis. Chances are it won't make any difference."

"I know I'm stronger and faster. You've experienced it—in the bedroom." His voice deepened suggestively but his amber eyes were still very intent on hers.

She flushed, caught in a morass of thoughts with only one clear thread through them: Travis.

"Are you afraid I'll make a suicide attack on Morelli?"

"Morelli will bring every man he possibly can, both *vampiros* and *prosaicos*. I may be able to sneak past them but you can't do that," she countered desperately, trying to keep the discussion logical. Fighting not to feel emotions she'd never allowed herself before.

"I won't let you go out there alone. If you make me go away with some *vampiro* tricks, I'll just come back as soon as I can."

She glared at him, weighing her chances of forcing him to reach New Mexico.

"We can defeat Morelli together, Gillian. We're partners, remember?"

"The cop and the thief?"

"The *vampira* and her *compañero*," he corrected her steadily. "When I drank your blood, I knew how I was spending the rest of my life. I love you and I plan to marry you."

Love? How could he say that so easily when it ripped out her throat to even think the word? "Travis! If . . . if anything happened to you, I don't know how I'd go on."

"Ah, Gillian." He caught her hands, his eyes blazing golden with battle hunger and something more, something that she didn't dare look at too closely. "We can do this together, Gillian. I've got a plan; just trust me."

She stared at him dubiously. They could easily die but if they did, they'd do so together. Something deep inside her that had been frozen for a long time shattered and fell away.

She kissed his hand. "Very well, Travis. We'll stand side by side against Morelli. And if we survive, I'll think about marriage."

TWELVE

The sun crept through the thick bank of storm clouds, as if concerned about its reception from the snow-covered prairies below. It was seven a.m. and the great blue norther had ended less than an hour ago. The entire world was a fairy tale of snow and ice, with great sweeping white waves poured over the barbed-wire fences and icicles hanging down from the buildings' eaves and the few remaining trees.

The pastures and roads were covered in snow, ruffled by the wind into symmetrical lines like cake frosting. The snow's surface looked even, except where it swept up to meet a barbed-wire fence or a building—hiding every dip and hollow in the ground underneath. As the forecasters had warned, the snow had fallen two to three feet but the drifts had covered up to twenty feet.

Three hours earlier, while the blizzard was still blowing, Travis and Gillian had fought their way up into the low hills overlooking the ranch on the west and built a hiding place amid a cottonwood grove. It was the only cover anywhere within sight on that great windswept, barren prairie, except for the ranch buildings themselves. The last winds had filled in their tracks. They'd made white smocks from bed sheets, daubed with black markers, to hide their parkas. While not perfect camouflage, Travis knew they'd be hard to see.

He also had a recorder hidden in his parka, set to tape everything said inside the ranch house or just outside it.

Now the two of them peeked over the crest of the hill, through the underbrush, and studied the scene.

The hills ran roughly north-south and contained the springs for which White Springs Lake was named and which formed the ranch's southern border.

The ranch was built on the higher ground above the lake, with the garage and other small outbuildings placed closest to the dropoff before the beach. The ranch house and immense old barn faced the main approach to the north, through the acres of what had once been prosperous cornfields and pastures. A road led from the barn, behind the garage and outbuildings, down to the beach, while a winding path led from the house to the shoreline. From his vantage point, Travis could see the lake only as far as the path's end, not to where the road ended at the boat dock.

An oval loop nestled between the ranch house, garage, and barn was generous enough to handle anything from a motorcycle to a limousine, and a wide range of farm vehicles.

All of the buildings, except the barn, were single story. The ranch house contained one picture window offering a superb view of the cottonwood grove, but none that could see the beach. Morelli could post a man there who could spot them easily.

God, do what you want with me. But please don't let anything happen to Gillian. . . .

He sniffed, checking his surroundings with other senses, and recoiled from the typically unpleasant scent of cottonwoods, far stronger than he remembered. Learning the complexities of Gillian's musk had been a great reason for becoming a *compañero*, but this? Damn, what would a New York subway smell like to him now?

He tried listening instead and heard ice crystals blowing across the snow. Waves beat on the boat dock and the canyon's cliffs, whipped up by the high winds.

There! The distant roar of big car engines or small trucks. It had to be Morelli.

Gillian's eyes met his, full of the same knowledge and equal resolve to kill their common enemy.

The big SUVs roared down the highway and up the long road to the ranch house with arrogant disregard for anyone within earshot. Three big Hummers, the commercial version of Hummvees, capable of going anywhere even in these conditions.

Gillian rolled her eyes and Travis had to agree. Morelli could hardly have shouted more clearly that he believed the only person present to be a *vampiro*, sound asleep to avoid daylight.

The Hummers screeched to a stop and more than a dozen men leaped out into the knee-deep snow, their heavy guns held high. Behind them came Morelli, a short, very stout fellow, dapper in the latest Italian ski fashion—and Peters, his blond hair stirring in the dying breeze.

Why, that Judas! That murderous bastard!

Gillian's hand clamped down on Travis's wrist.

He froze just before he would have broken cover. His pulse was pounding in his ears.

Gillian glanced over at him.

He forced his breathing to slow.

She searched his eyes, offering him her own bitterly learned discipline.

He nodded, the familiar coolness during an op taking control of him again. By God, he'd see Gillian alive and safe first. There'd be time later, especially with the recorder in his parka, to see Peters fry.

"Listen up, boys!" Morelli yelled, as clearly to Travis's enhanced hearing as if they stood next to each other. "Fitzgerald is hidden somewhere in this complex. Five million dollars to the man who kills her and brings me D'Angelo's notebook, understand?"

"Yes, sir!" the men responded, laden with a variety of heavy weapons.

"Then get to it!" Morelli snapped.

"Sir!" The men fanned out toward the different buildings, stumbling occasionally when they met chest-high drifts. Even the Hummers' drivers went to look.

Travis centered Morelli in his sights, wishing he had a long gun rather than his Beretta 9mm.

"Idiots," Morelli muttered, strolling west. "Sometimes you have to tell them every little thing."

Peters blew on his hands, his eyes restlessly searching the area. "How long do you think it will take? I didn't tell my boss I was taking time off."

Travis wondered how many guns Peters was carrying. The asshole was considered one of the feds' best marksmen.

"Not too long," Morelli growled and cupped his hands to light a cigar.

BAM! The Hummer closest to the barn blew up with a roar that shook the ground and blew out windows. Remote propelled grenades?

Thugs fell facedown into the snow. A man screamed.

Travis pulled Gillian under him, pressing them both into the ground.

BAM! BAM! An instant later, the other two Hummers flung themselves apart.

"Texas! Texas!" A wave of black-clad men flowed up and over

the bluff from the lake, led by a big warrior who wielded his heavy rifle as easily as a knight's sword.

Travis could have shouted for joy. Don Rafael and his *mesnaderos* had come at last.

Morelli immediately ran for the hills across the open pasture, closely followed by Peters, both of them fighting to break trail through thigh-high snow.

"Stop!" Travis came to his feet. If those assholes reached the highway and managed to steal a car, who knew what the hell would happen next? "Surrender, while you still have a chance. Or I'll shoot!"

Gillian stood up too, growling softly.

Morelli put his head down, his knees pistoning rapidly through the snow, and veered to the north, away from Travis. Peters stayed with him, clearly recognizing that his only chance lay with the criminal who'd bought him.

Travis fired a warning shot into the snow ahead of Morelli.

A column of mist shot out of Morelli's parka and coalesced into a tiger. It leaped forward onto the snow, leaving the clothes to collapse behind it like a discarded cocoon. Peters briefly broke stride but somehow kept moving forward, a pistol glowing darkly in his hand.

Angrily, Travis took a step out from the cottonwoods' protection. By God, he would not let that bastard get away.

Cloth brushed his elbow, making him jerk his head around.

Gillian shimmered briefly and resolved into a jaguar with great, black rosettes on dark brown skin—a sleek, almost pure black cat. She sprang forward and raced after Morelli, only half the size of her prey. But where he crashed through the snow with every stride, she was able to spring across the crust—which made her move far faster than he did.

Travis didn't know if he was more terrified by the thought that she might catch up to Morelli or that she wouldn't.

He started to run after her, forcing his way through the snow as fast as possible. He was too focused on watching Gillian's chase of Morelli to curse every time he found a sudden dip in the ground and the snow met him at the hip, instead of his calf.

Behind them, automatic weapons fire and grenades told of a vicious battle being waged at the ranch.

Gillian angled to meet Morelli, a slim black blur over the crystalline white snow, and bounded over a barbed-wire fence. Christ, she was going to catch him.

If Travis ran a little faster—and didn't break a leg—he should be able to help her.

Peters stopped, his breath a whiff of fog, and leveled his gun at Gillian.

No! Travis shot him in the shoulder.

Peters barely staggered, obviously wearing a bulletproof vest. He spun around and fired at Travis but the shot whistled past Travis's upper arm.

Then Peters flung himself down into the snow, disappearing out of sight. The thud came a fraction of a second too late to Travis's *compañero* hearing. The bastard had found a true hollow in the snow, more than three feet deep.

Gillian snarled and leaped onto Morelli, sinking her teeth into his spine and raking her claws across his hindquarters. He roared and rose up to try to shake her off.

God, Gillian, you're half the size he is. . . .

Travis fell on his face into the snow, praying for the first time that he'd find a hollow, and the two-feet-deep snow that would barely hide him from Peters.

He and Peters were about to have an old-fashioned western shootout, where they'd both peek over the snow and try to kill each other. But if Travis so much as twitched, Peters could see it. On the other hand, Peters could do anything he wanted in his much deeper hollow without being sighted.

Two great cats screamed in the distance. One staggered, crunching the snow under it.

Hang on, Gillian. . . .

Wait—he'd heard the cat's paws and its more solid hip, or leg, breaking into the snow. Could his *compañero* senses tell him what Peters was doing?

Travis listened as hard as he could, forcing himself to ignore the gunfire and breaking glass from the ranch, the yowl of a cat's battle cry and snick of fang slicing through fur. And found the faint thud and hiss of a boot kicking into snow.

Travis rolled up onto his elbow to greet the asshole.

An instant later, Peters's head showed over the skyline, gun in hand.

Travis shot Peters through his throat into the base of his skull. He crumpled without a sound.

Damn murderous bastard. Surely Satan would know just the right place to fry him.

Without a backward glance, Travis holstered his gun and raced up the rise to look for Gillian and Morelli. They were a whirling blur of yellow and black stripes against black, the air torn by yowls, with blood splattering onto the snow. The tiger broke free and swiped at the jaguar with one great paw, screaming its rage.

With an incredible serpentine twist, the jaguar evaded the grab and leaped onto the tiger's back. It bit the bigger cat at the base of the skull, striking through bone and muscle with an audible crunch.

The tiger staggered, swayed, and crumpled onto the snow. The jaguar leaped off and circled its enemy, warily scrutinizing the fallen giant's every move.

The tiger's head dropped onto the snow and its eyes fell shut. An instant later, it became a fine powder, starting with the tip of its tail.

The battered jaguar sat down on the snow and gave Morelli's remains a rude salute as they disappeared into the wind. Gillian's meaning couldn't have been more apparent if she'd shouted it.

Travis laughed and started to run through the snow, peeling off his gloves to expose his wrist. His lady would need blood immediately. "Goddamn, how I love you, Gillian Fitzgerald!"

Travis and Gillian strolled out of the cottonwood grove toward the ranch, hand in hand. Gillian was fully dressed, her injuries healed with the blood Travis had given her. He still continued to listen to her walk, checking for any residual damage; it would be a very long time before he'd forget seeing her twist through the tiger's outstretched claws.

A dozen men came out to greet them, all wearing body armor and armed to the teeth. The largest of them pulled off his helmet and smiled at Travis, white teeth flashing against his olive skin. "Hola, amigo!"

Travis recognized him instantly: the ancient black eyes that saw everything, the unself-conscious mastery of everyone and every situation. He bowed slightly, remembering old habits. "Buenos dias, Don Rafael. I believe you've already met Miss Gillian Fitzgerald, my fiancée?"

Gillian's hand twitched briefly on his arm at the last word but she didn't deny the appellation.

Don Rafael bowed very formally, like a medieval knight paying homage to a queen. "Good morning, Miss Fitzgerald."

Gillian nodded to him, equally polite, her expression a mask of punctilious courtesy. "Thank you for saving our lives, Don Rafael."

Don Rafael's eyes glinted briefly. "As the Texas patrón, it was my very great pleasure to crush those cockroaches, señorita. I will also enjoy ensuring that the cleanup is very thorough, to satisfy a lady's most demanding standards."

Travis hesitated. Don Rafael headed the Santiago Trust, whose methods were efficient, high-handed, and occasionally skirted the limits of the law. Still, explaining to the FBI that Morelli had been a vampiro so there wouldn't be a corpse was a task to daunt anyone.

He glanced at Gillian. She shrugged, her eyes asking him why he was hesitating. Perhaps some day he'd teach her to respect the law's more pedantic rules.

"Thank you, Don Rafael. We will be glad of whatever assistance you choose to provide," he said, yielding as graciously as possible.

"*De nada.*" Don Rafael bowed, the sunlight glinting off his black body armor. "When you left Texas twenty-five years ago, I'd hoped you'd one day return to join my *mesnaderos*," he said softly. "But now I congratulate you on allying yourself with another *vampiro* instead."

Travis nodded, wondering what this was leading up to.

"May I offer my assistance, in gratitude for all the aid your family has given me over the centuries?"

"What do you have in mind?" Travis asked.

"Unfortunately, I can't offer you a lifetime in Texas, since I am not Gillian's *creador*."

Travis blinked. "What?"

Gillian patted his arm soothingly. "It's illegal in the Texas *esfera*, dear, for *vampiros* to live here who were given *El Abrazo* by anyone other than Don Rafael."

Travis cast Gillian a disbelieving look but didn't demand an immediate explanation.

"However, I can guarantee you sanctuary in New Mexico, should you choose to live there immediately or after a few years. Don Lucien, its *patrón,* is my vassal and has different rules about which *vampiros* he'll accept as residents."

"More typical rules," Gillian muttered.

Don Rafael's mouth twitched. "If that's agreeable to you?"

Travis glanced down at Gillian. Their eyes met in a moment of perfect communion.

"It sounds perfect to me, sir. Thank you very much."

"My pleasure. I hope that I may one day kiss the bride, too," Don Rafael purred.

Gillian choked and Travis patted her reassuringly.

THIRTEEN

The apartment was awash in a sea of aromas from every known cuisine, topped by the sharp tang of beers and wines. An announcer's excited yammer, occasionally punctuated by deep roars, rose from upstairs where guests watched the Giants play football. Downstairs, Travis's superb (and brand-new) stereo system sampled Gillian's music collection.

Gillian wove through a maze of burly, sweating masculine bodies and expertly dodged a chopping hand, as one sergeant showed exactly how he'd pounded open a door to rescue a hostage. She shared a laugh with Evans, her new friend and occasional boss, when she consulted for his squad. Grinning with success at not having spilled a drop, she handed Katrina D'Angelo a glass of white wine sangria. Katrina murmured thanks and returned her attention to the very handsome lieutenant beside her.

Gillian stepped back, casting an experienced hostess's eye over the crowd. Parties like this were essential, if Travis was to obtain the promotions he deserved before he retired to New Mexico—and a lifetime as a *vampiro*.

The food and drinks were holding up, the conversation was flowing well, the scenery was excellent—especially if you enjoyed looking at very fit men's bodies, of which there was a remarkable display. Oh, there were wives and girlfriends present too. But she had to admit that NYPD's ESU officers could surely catch a girl's eye.

An arm slipped around her waist and yanked her up against one of those very fit men.

"Travis!" she protested halfheartedly, delightedly filling her nostrils with his clean scent. "We have guests, you know."

He eased her out onto the terrace, still wet from a heavy thunderstorm. Sinatra was crooning something that melted her bones. "Who cares about them?"

He caught her free hand. "Shall we dance, Mrs. Travis?"

Gillian chuckled hoarsely, set down her glass, and moved into his arms. "Somebody should worry about our company. Could you have packed any more cops into one apartment?"

He nuzzled her hair, his leg between hers, and made a half-turn, his body swaying slightly. "Not without bringing the fire marshals down on us."

She laid her cheek against his shoulder, her hips cradling his as they would when they were alone later. "You're a wild and crazy man, Travis. It's a good thing I love you so much."

He pivoted again, taking them beyond any watchers from inside. He tilted her chin up with a single finger. "And I adore you, Gillian. Eternity with you will be a pleasure."

She leaned up to meet his kiss, his heart beating steadily under her palm. Joy surged through her, the sheer ecstasy of relearning that they'd always be together.

A block away, a heavy corporate logo blinked red against the starlit sky.

Red skies at night, sailors' delight.

GLOSSARY

Pine Falls, New Mexico, and White Springs Lake, Texas, are entirely fictional.

The Texas Vampire universe is based on a scientific theory, which I vetted with top animal metabolism and behavioral experts. Every attempt has been made to stay consistent with that theory.

Terminology used in the Texas Vampire universe is taken whenever possible from medieval Spanish, supplemented by modern Spanish. The only exception is that *patrones* are given an honorific appropriate to their *esfera*'s ethnicity, e.g., *don* in Texas, madame in New Orleans, earl in England, etc.

Cachorro/cachorra/cachorros/cachorras. "Cub." Immature *vampiro*, who is unable to shape-shift except to feed.

Comitiva. "Retinue." Assemblage of *prosaicos* attached to a single *esfera*, *patrón*, or *vampiro*.

Compañero/compañera/compañeros. "Companion." Someone

who drinks *vampiro* blood regularly but has not become a *vampiro*. A *compañero* always has greater strength, speed, senses, and healing powers than a *prosaico*. The anticipated lifespan is a century, while surviving two centuries is extremely rare.

Concubino compañero. A *compañero* whose duties are confined to those of a sex slave.

Creador. "Creator." Sire of a *vampiro*.

El Abrazo. "The embrace." The entire process of becoming a *vampiro*.

Esfera/esferas. "Sphere," as in "sphere of influence." A *vampiro* territory, which does not necessarily exactly coincide with present-day geophysical territory. *Esferas'* boundaries are fluid and frequently fought over. The basic concept is adapted from gangster territories during Prohibition Chicago and New York.

La Lujuria. "Lechery." The Rut. Upon awakening as a *vampiro*, every *cachorro* will undergo months of insanity during which their only goal is to obtain blood and emotion.

Mesnadero/mesnaderos. A *vampiro* warrior and a member of a *patrón*'s personal guard. Taken from medieval Spanish, for a member of the royal household guard.

Patrón/patrona/patrones. The ruler, who is an absolute monarch of an *esfera*. He is also usually the *creador* of all the *esfera*'s *vampiros*.

Prosaico/prosaica/prosaicos. "Prosaic" or "mundane," similar to the Society for Creative Anachronism's usage. A mortal human, neither *vampiro* nor *compañero*. If he has drunk *vampiro* blood, it has happened so rarely and in such small quantities that it has not affected his everyday life in any noticeable manner.

Vampiro/vampira/vampiros. "Vampire." Someone who survives on the emotional energy carried through human blood. Mature *vampiros* can shape-shift to at least one other form (if only mist) and are resistant to telepathic suggestions.

Vampiro mayor/vampira mayor/vampiros mayores. "Elder vampire." A *vampiro* who has lived for at least three hundred years, can walk in full daylight, and drinks less than a quarter cup of blood per day (except in times of great physical need). He also becomes more and more difficult to detect, even with the heightened senses of other *vampiros mayores*.

Vampiro primero/vampira primera. "Primary vampire." The *vampiro* that a *compañero* is principally interested in drinking blood from. The *compañero* becomes utterly loyal to that *vampiro*, when fed from him long enough. The amount of time needed to form this bond is extremely varied.

come moonrise

LUCY MONROE

For Jean Gilsrud . . .
with thanks for your ongoing support of my dream,
your always kind comments about my books,
and bringing so much joy into my uncle's life
and to our family.

one

 Frankie watched the sleek brown wolf run toward her across the clearing, his powerful body moving with a fluid grace that took her breath away.

She should be frightened, but she wasn't. She'd met the wolf many times before, her mind told her, though she could not remember any single instance with clarity.

The summer sun warmed her bare skin where she reclined on the big diving rock beside the swimming hole. One foot dangled off the side, her toes trailing the water. She'd been skinny-dipping, but her nudity did not bother her. No one was there to see it, except the wolf.

He stopped about twenty feet away and fixed his blue gaze on her, his eyes glowing with an intelligence she could have sworn was human. He didn't growl or bare his teeth. His ears did not flatten. He made no signs whatsoever of aggression.

He simply looked at her.

She didn't understand why, but she tingled inside, and her body warmed with a blush that made no sense in the current situation. He was only a wolf, but the eyes that locked on hers were those of a man—or so her foolish imagination fancied.

She didn't move . . . couldn't move, though she felt a brief instinct to cover herself. The wolf came forward until he was within touching distance, a sound coming from deep in his chest, but it was not a growl. It almost sounded like pleasure.

He butted her shoulder with his muzzle and she gasped. His mouth opened . . . was he going to bite her?

He licked the droplets of water that had rolled down her neck from her still wet hair. She shivered and gasped again. Then, as if in a dream, she reached up and touched the wolf, running her fingers through his silky fur. The sound coming from his chest got louder.

Feeling like it was the most natural thing in the world, she nuzzled him like she did her pet German shepherd, Snoopy, and just like Snoopy, the wolf returned the affectionate gesture. Then his head came up, his ears perked, as if he could hear something she couldn't.

"What is it, boy?" she asked softly.

He shook his head and danced backward, his movements so graceful she envied him.

She had been known to trip over her own feet. Maybe that was why Ty never looked at her like a woman—he was as lithe as the wolf. Probably her clumsiness turned him off.

A sudden gust of wind lifted her hair and its damp mass swirled around her head, blocking her vision. When she brushed it from her eyes, the wolf was gone.

Had he ever been there?

Her hand lifted of its own volition and touched where the wolf had licked her neck. Yes, he had been real.

Disappointed he was gone, but moved by the encounter in a way she didn't understand, she climbed to her feet and dove into the swimming hole. The water closed over her naked flesh and caressed her like the lover's hands she had imagined, but never felt.

If only Ty were there. But if he were, she wouldn't be swimming naked, and he wouldn't touch her the way she craved.

The thought had barely formed when something splashed to her left, and she felt a hand grab her ankle and pull. Frankie kicked out with her other foot, but as quickly as she'd been grabbed, she was released, and she shot to the surface.

She gulped in air and twisted her head, trying to see who was in the water with her.

Ty's blond head broke from the water right in front of her as a pair of strong masculine hands latched on to her waist.

"Don't," she panted, unable to accept that her thoughts had taken physical form.

"Don't what?" he asked, his blue eyes reminding her so much of the wolf she'd seen that, for a second, she was speechless.

"You scared me . . . when you grabbed my foot," she finally forced out.

He grinned, pulling her closer through the water. "Did I?"

Their bodies brushed and she yelped.

"What's the matter, Frankie? The water too cold?"

"I'm naked, Ty!"

"I know. I saw you." His hands slid down to cup her bare bottom in a move that both shocked and intrigued her. "I can feel you too."

Oh, wow. She'd never been touched like this before, but she liked it. A lot. "I can feel you too," she whispered breathlessly, unable to believe what was happening.

It felt like she'd wanted Ty to see her as a woman forever, but never in a million years would she have expected him to touch her like this. He usually turned and headed the other way when there was a risk of them getting too physically intimate.

His mouth hovered over hers as his powerful legs kept them both afloat. "I want you, Frankie."

"I want you too, Ty . . . so much."

Her lips parted instinctively in preparation for his kiss.

His head came closer and closer while a buzzing sound went off in her brain. He stopped, his lips right above hers, so close she could taste his breath.

"Ty?" she whispered.

Frankie woke up, her mouth full of cotton pillowcase.

Aargh . . . not again. How many times had she had that dream? How many nights had she come so close to kissing the man she loved, only to be woken by something?

Her hand slammed down onto the buzzing alarm clock, and the offending noise abruptly ceased.

Darn it. When was she going to stop dreaming about the guy?

And that wolf . . . how many times had he been in the dreams? Even when she was dreaming in the city, the wolf was there, totally incongruous, and yet her subconscious mind accepted his presence without question. Maybe because that was the only part of the dream steeped in reality.

The encounter with the wolf had happened when she was fifteen. She'd gone to the swimming hole by herself that day, but she hadn't gone skinny-dipping. She'd just needed some time to herself. Ty had spent the day flirting with another girl at school, and it had hurt watching them together.

In reality, it had been her tears the wolf had licked from her cheek and her neck, not the water from the swimming hole. She hadn't been naked, but everything else in the dream was exactly as it had happened in reality.

Until she dove into the water. The part with Ty was pure imagination. The funny thing was, no one would ever believe her if she told them about the encounter with the wolf. Even Ty hadn't. He'd said she'd probably dozed off and dreamed it. She knew he was wrong.

Her encounter had been real, and it had sparked within her a lifelong love of wolves.

She had spent years researching them, had even at one time dreamed of doing a field behavioral study at Ty's father's ranch, the part dedicated to the wolf refuge.

But that dream had died, along with many others, the day the man she loved made it clear he wanted nothing more than friendship from her. That had been six years ago, and Ty McCanlup was still her best friend.

He was also still the man she measured every other male in her life against—and they all came up short.

Her feelings for him made it impossible for her to maintain a relationship with another man, and it was time she faced up to that. She'd moved to the city, away from him and the everyday proximity of their friendship. The move should have helped rid her of her unrequited love, and at first she'd believed it had.

She'd been dead wrong. Lately, it was getting even worse, the pain of loving him but not having him, the inability to see other men without the superimposed image of Ty's face in her mind. The dreams were becoming more frequent too.

Probably because she'd been offered that job on the West Coast. She knew that accepting would mean an irrevocable step in her life.

It had been summer in her dream, but it was November now and soon it would be Thanksgiving. A time for family and friends to be together.

It was also high time for her to do something about Ty.

She'd spent the four years after puberty trying to get him to notice she was female, and the last six trying to forget his gentle rejection. She'd been unsuccessful at both. If she was ever going to move on with her life, she should take the job in Washington State and let her friendship with Ty go.

The knowledge hurt, but it had been a long time coming.

Frankie was at a crossroads, both professionaly and personally. She couldn't keep living this awful half life. She hated city veterinary medicine, and the job in Washington would be working in a wolf haven. She was also tired of being lonely, of pining after a man who thought of her as a buddy without chest hair. Maybe if she moved away, cut him from her life completely, she could learn to care for someone else.

But was she still sure he still saw her that way? an insidious voice inside her head asked. There were times Ty looked at her the same way he had in the dream . . . as if he wanted her. He hadn't dated anyone seriously in the last six years either.

She made a decision, sitting there in her lonely bed, still tingling from a dream that could not make up for reality. It was time to fish or cut bait with Ty McCanlup. She would go home for the holidays and try one more time. If he rejected her again, she would cut him completely from her life.

She had no choice.

One way or another, this trip back home was going to determine both her future career and the future of her relationship with Ty.

"What do you mean we weren't invited? The McCanlups have been sharing Thanksgiving with our family since before I came here to live." Frankie stared at Aunt Rose, her stomach plummeting in disappointment.

Frankie had bought the perfect dress to wear for the dinner. It even made her look elegant and somewhat curvy, not like a beanpole with a couple of interesting bumps. She'd spent hours shopping—something she hated doing—in order to stock her arsenal of weapons.

"Something happened with Duke and Marigold," Aunt Rose replied.

Well, crud. Trust her cousin to mess things up. Whatever Marigold had done to Ty's older brother had to be serious for the annual Thanksgiving dinner invitation not to be extended. "Did they have a fight or something?"

Aunt Rose bit her lip and looked away with a sigh as she proceeded to roll out piecrust with a practiced hand. "She won't say, but Duke's fiancée left town and now he cuts your cousin dead whenever he sees her. No one in their family has stepped foot on our land since Leah left."

"Have you been over to see Carolyn?" Ty's mom and Aunt Rose had always been almost as close as sisters.

"It didn't feel right, not knowing what had gone on between my daughter and Duke." Rose's voice was calm, but Frankie could see losing the other woman's friendship had hurt her aunt deeply.

Younger than Frankie, Marigold had never tried to keep her crush on the older man a secret. Frankie would sympathize with her cousin if she didn't think that the idea of Duke's wealth and position in the community was even more tantalizing to Marigold than the man himself.

Besides, at barely twenty, Marigold wasn't exactly mature in her dealings with others. A professional prima donna, Frankie's cousin rarely thought of anyone else's feelings when going after something, or in this case, someone, she wanted.

"You wanted to see Ty," Aunt Rose guessed.

"Of course."

Her aunt's lips pursed in concern. "You're still in love with him."

"You don't have to look like that's the worst fate in the world. Ty's a good man."

"He's not going to marry you, baby." The sad certainty in Aunt Rose's voice scared her, but Frankie hadn't come this far to turn back at the first fence.

"I guess I've got to know that for sure."

Although, if her aunt was right, then her cousin's antics could turn out to be a favor instead of frustrating. Cutting her ties with the man she loved would be a lot easier if their families weren't so close.

"Another family moved into town. French Canadian. They've got a daughter about Ty's age."

"Really?"

"Her name is Olivia. She's real pretty."

"That's nice."

"Ty seems partial to her."

Frankie's heart stopped in her chest with a painful thump and then started beating so fast she could barely breathe. After all this time he was showing interest in another woman? *Why now?* "How does she feel about him?"

"The boy seems to irritate her more than anything, but with their kind you never know."

"You think French Canadian women are more likely to hide their interest in men behind dislike?" she asked, not really understanding what her aunt was getting at.

Aunt Rose frowned. "I wonder . . ." She shook her head. "No. A promise is a promise. Just don't get your heart set on Tyler McCanlup."

Her heart was already set on the gorgeous veterinarian. So was her body, for that matter. No other man had ever stirred her senses like Ty did, and he'd never even kissed her. It had gotten so bad that she couldn't even give herself orgasms without thinking about him.

"I think I'll go for a ride."

Aunt Rose shook her head. "Stubborn child. Give the McCanlups my regards."

Hardened snow crunched under Flash's feet as Frankie guided the big black gelding away from the barn. She'd missed him as much as she'd missed her family since moving to the city. She pulled her scarf down and breathed in the cold air.

Oh, man.

Her lungs seized on the freezing offering before expelling it all in a rush. She breathed in another big whiff of what she loved best— fresh, clean air that smelled like snow, wood smoke and nothing else. No car exhaust, no nearby restaurants cooking for the lunch crowd, none of the stale city smells she'd grown used to, but not fond of.

Pulling her scarf back up to muffle her nose and mouth, she kneed Flash and the horse sprang forward eagerly. Before long, they were galloping across the land between her aunt and uncle's ranch and the Rocking M. Even with Flash's speed, it was a fair ride to the McCanlup homestead.

She slowed Flash to a walk far enough away to cool the horse down. It was then that she noticed a trio of riders coming toward her.

All three men sat tall in their saddles and wore almost identical outfits of faded jeans, flannel shirts over dark Henleys and sheepskin jackets open down the front. She had no problem telling them apart, however. Not one of the men wore a hat. Their almost insane tolerance for the cold had always amazed her.

Duke rode on the left, his dark hair the same color as his dad's. King rode in the middle, and Ty, his golden-blond hair glistening in the stark sunlight, rode to his right. None of the men were smiling, but that didn't stop her heart from speeding up at the sight of Ty.

She reined in when she reached them. "Mr. McCanlup." She nodded toward the man in the center, then to the others. "Duke. Ty." Her voice softened just a little on his name and she smiled slightly.

His expression showed no matching welcome.

Had Marigold destroyed the relationship between their families completely?

"I'm surprised your people let you go riding alone right now," King McCanlup said with his usual emotionless stare.

He and her uncle got along well enough, but King had always been somewhat cold toward Frankie and she'd never understood why. His apparent disapproval of her had never stopped Ty from being her friend, so she'd never let it bother her.

She wasn't about to start now. "I always go for a ride when I first get home. No one was available to come along."

"Maybe your family didn't expect you to ride over this way." Ty shot a sidelong glance at his stone-faced older brother.

"I told Aunt Rose where I was going. She sends her regards, by the way. As for being out riding right now—I don't see the problem. The storm front isn't supposed to move in until tomorrow, tonight at the soonest." Which was why she'd traveled a couple of days earlier than she'd originally planned. She hadn't wanted to be snowbound in Billings on Thanksgiving. She'd felt an urgency about her trip home, a certainty that if she didn't figure out her relationship with Ty now, it would never happen.

"The full moon is in thirty-two hours," King said as if that explained everything.

She rolled her eyes. He probably assumed it did. He had the timing down to the hours, no less.

"I know you all think the full moon has some kind of weird effect on the wolves in the Rocking M's refuge—"

"It does," Ty cut in, his voice brusque, his blue eyes cold. "You don't have to believe it for it to be the truth. You had no business riding out here so close to a full moon."

She blinked in surprise at the painful rebuke. Ty might have held back from deepening their friendship to something more, but he'd always treated her like he was glad to see her.

Right now, she felt about as welcome as a skunk at a picnic. She lifted the reins, prepared to turn Flash around. "I'll just go back then."

"You're closer to the homestead," King said, staying her. "Ty can give you a lift back to your aunt and uncle's. One of the hands will ride Flash back."

"That's ridiculous. I can ride back now."

"You're on our land. You'll do as we say." Duke's voice lacked even an edge of warmth.

She opened her mouth, but Ty forestalled her. "Don't talk to her like that, Duke."

"You got a problem with it? Why? I thought you were interested in that little French Canadian bitch."

Frankie's jaw dropped. She'd never heard Duke refer to a woman with anything but unfailing respect. "Don't you like her?" she blurted.

"Ignore him; he's just feeling his age right now."

She would have laughed if she wasn't battling pain at their obvious rejection. "You're only going to be thirty. That's hardly ancient."

Duke said nothing, but wheeled his horse around. "Let her do what she wants," he called back over his shoulder. "But don't blame me if a wolf decides she looks damn tasty right now."

TWO

Ty wanted to smack his brother upside the head.

He knew Duke wasn't alluding to one of the pack eating Frankie, but to something that could be equally as devastating.

Beyond being a woman alone in the wild, she was single and she was ovulating. In heat.

Her scent would drive any unmated werewolf crazy . . . or to do something both the wolf and Frankie would end up regretting.

Hell, her scent was calling to the beast in him, and it was taking all he had to keep his wolf under control. He could see that his attitude had hurt her feelings, but why did she have to show up today? It was the last damn thing he needed when he was mentally preparing himself to mate with another female.

On top of that, Duke was right. She was definitely at risk out here on the range.

Many members of the pack gathered on the Rocking M before the change so they were someplace where it was safe to run when it happened. If another male found her alone out here this close to the full moon, there was every chance she could wake up tomorrow morning mated.

And that would be less than ideal for both her and the wolf. She'd have the trauma of overcoming an unwanted werewolf mating, and if it turned out to be a sacred bond, some poor bastard would be rendered effectively neutered when she refused to stay with him.

"Ride back to the homestead with us, Frankie," he said, forcing his voice into a friendlier tone, even though all he wanted to do was growl and rip off her clothes. "Mom'll have a fit if she finds out you were close enough to say hi and didn't."

Frankie was still watching Duke's disappearing figure, but at Ty's words she turned to face him, her soft brown eyes still filled with the wounding of their initial reaction to her. "Are you sure? Things are more strained between our families than I expected."

"It's not your fault," his dad said shortly. "Come on to the house."

For King, who hated the thought of either of his sons mating a non-wolf, it was practically an engraved invitation. He turned his horse and followed after Duke, his assumption Frankie would follow obvious in the set of the pack leader's shoulders.

Frankie looked at Ty, her expression troubled.

He smiled, letting the warm feelings he'd always had for her show in his expression. "You don't want to disappoint my mom, do you?"

"No."

"Then come on." He spurred his horse and went after his dad. With a muttered imprecation about arrogant men, which Ty was sure he wasn't supposed to hear, Frankie followed them.

They reached the yard a few minutes later and Frankie let Jed take Flash into the barn.

They walked into the house together. He picked up the scent of his mother's cinnamon snaps and her concern over having a human visitor this close to the full moon at the same time. She was smiling when she came into the living room, though.

It was something he hadn't managed when he'd first seen Frankie, but then, he'd been too busy trying to fight his reaction to her hot scent. He still was—and he wasn't winning.

Hell. The last thing he needed right now, or ever, was a hard-on for his best friend.

"Frankie, what an unexpected pleasure." His mom's voice held all the welcome his dad, his brother and he had not extended.

Frankie's pleasure at the greeting came off her in waves, and she rushed forward, her sexy hips swinging slightly with her graceful walk. She hugged his mom, dwarfing the smaller woman, and kissed her cheek. "It's been too long."

"You didn't come home this past summer."

"The partners all took their vacations over the summer."

"And left you to work the clinic while they were gone?" Ty asked, anger at her being treated like that boiling through him.

She turned one of her brilliant smiles on him. Apparently, she'd forgiven him for his earlier coldness. She was like that; she rarely held grudges, especially against him. It was one of the many things he liked about her.

Her doe eyes filled with a warmth he'd never been able to break his addiction to. "They didn't all go at once and it *is* my job, Ty."

"You could have come home and worked with me," he reminded her. "I wouldn't have forced you to go without a break all summer."

It had surprised him when she'd refused his job offer right out of college. It had hurt too. He'd thought that after she broke up with that pathetic fiancé of hers she'd be willing to come home, but she hadn't.

If he needed more proof that thinking of her as a possible mate was beyond idiotic, there it was. He didn't belong in the city, and she'd rejected life out here. Not to mention the fact that she was no more stable in relationships than any other human, as her ex-fiancé could attest.

There was no official pack law against taking a human mate, but it was strongly discouraged. While a werewolf mated for life, a human could leave his or her mate behind and seek another. It had happened often enough to make the pack leery. Werewolves were taught from the time they were cubs that humans made poor choices for mates.

That didn't stop it from happening, unfortunately.

Ty's own grandmother had been human, and had left Ty's grandfather to marry another man when the cubs were less than half grown. Ty's father had been more adamant than most about drilling into his sons the need to mate within the pack. Or if not within the pack, at least with their own kind.

His father's admonitions had not been necessary for Ty. After he had witnessed firsthand the grisly results of breaking the pack law about mating for life, he'd never considered mating a human anyway.

"Maybe I should have taken the job you offered, at that. Living in the city hasn't accomplished what I wanted it to." There was another layer to Frankie's words, his wolf senses said so, but he couldn't figure out what it was.

"Leah moved to Billings." Ty was glad his brother hadn't come into the house as his mom's words settled in the air between them.

Frankie reached down and squeezed his mom's hand. "I heard she left. I'm not carrying tales if I mention neither Uncle Ben nor Aunt Rose know what Marigold did to send her away."

"But they know their daughter was involved," Ty said.

"I guess it's kind of hard to miss how Duke cuts her now."

"She played one of her selfish, all-about-me games." Ty frowned. "Both Leah and Duke got hurt because of it, but in some ways, I think it was better in the long run."

His mother glared at him. "Not all human females are like your grandmother McCanlup."

He sensed that if she could have gotten into his head to yell at him some more without being overheard, she would have. He didn't understand why, but his mother and father did not agree on this issue of out-of-kind mating.

But she couldn't yell at him that way. The only one in the family who shared the telepathic link with him was his brother.

Duke and their father shared a bond too. It was even stronger than Ty's was with Duke. He had to be close to his brother to reach or to hear him, but Duke and their dad could be a mile apart and hear each other.

"Let's not get into this right now, Carolyn." His dad had come into the room and towered over his mom in a protective stance. "You know what they say . . ."

He guessed his dad finished the saying about werewolves mating with humans in his mom's head because she glared. She'd liked Leah. A lot.

"They say men aren't good for anything but shoveling horse manure and breeding babies too, but I don't buy that either."

"Um . . . I didn't mean to cause a family fight." Frankie had peeled off her outer layer while they'd been arguing and her soft brown hair crackled around her head from static after taking off her stocking cap.

Her hair was silky fine, and she wore it longer than you'd expect a tomboy like her to keep it. It brushed her bottom seductively when she walked, something Ty had started noticing when she was about fifteen, and had spent the last eleven years trying to ignore.

The rest of her was something of a surprise too. She was wearing her usual jeans, but they had little red rhinestone roses on the pockets and down one leg. They hugged her hips instead of her waist, and a narrow band of pale skin showed above the waistband when she reached up to finger comb her long hair.

The soft red sweater clung to her curves so lovingly it didn't take his wolf eyesight to see the evidence that she was either still cold or someone was having a profound affect on her libido. He could smell her stirring arousal and guessed it was the second. Since he knew she didn't have a thing for older men or women, he figured that someone was him.

The wolf in him sat up and howled, and he had to clamp his jaw tight to stop from snarling his need. He had to get away from her soon, or all of his plans were going to go up in smoke from the bonfire of his own stupidity.

"Frankie, it's been a long time."

Ty's head snapped around at the sound of the other werewolf's voice. Kurt Garrick was lounging in the doorway like he had every right to be there, his mouth crooked in a half smile, his eyes dark with interest as they rested on Frankie.

A low, level growl rumbled in Ty's throat. Too quiet for her human ears to hear, it nevertheless brought a frown of surprise to the other wolf's features.

"Kurt! I didn't expect to see you here." Frankie's obvious delight in his presence irritated Ty more than Kurt's intrusion.

"Same here, gorgeous."

She smiled at that, her cheeks turning a delicate pink that made Ty want to do more than growl.

She crossed the room in less time than it took him to figure out how to get rid of the other wolf and threw her arms around Kurt in a hug. He hugged her back, the scent of his instant arousal hitting Ty like a kick in the gut.

She kissed Kurt's cheek and the damn werewolf kissed her back, his lips coming perilously close to hers. Ty growled again, this time loud enough that even Frankie's dull human ears caught it.

She stepped back from Kurt, a look of concern on her face. "Something wrong, Ty?"

"Just wondering when I'd get my hug."

He could forgive her the look of surprise that crossed her face, because the last time he'd accepted one of her hugs gracefully, she'd been fifteen years old. He'd withdrawn from her physically after he got his first hard-on at her touch. So as not to hurt her feelings, he'd made it clear he didn't like hugging anyone.

However, he'd be damned if she was going to touch the other wolf and leave him standing around like some sixteenth-century wallflower in the king's court. The knowledge that his wolf was more in control right now than his human only registered vaguely as he reached out and pulled her into full body contact.

She wrapped her arms around his neck and pressed her breasts against him like they belonged nowhere else. She sighed against his neck, the fluttery sound one of obvious pleasure.

She hadn't done that with Kurt, and Ty would have smiled if he wasn't having such a hard time not stripping her clothes off to mate with her. He'd wanted her for years, but today she was in heat, and this close to the change, that was like kerosene on the fire of his libido.

She went to kiss his cheek, but he turned his head and their lips met for the first time. Hers were soft and opened around a surprised *oh*. He tasted cinnamon, sweetness and a special flavor he could easily get addicted to. *Frankie*.

Oh, hell. He was losing it. No wonder humans kissed on the lips. It was the sweetest sensation he'd ever known. Werewolves avoided physical intimacies until they were ready to mate. It prevented them from taking an irrevocable step based on pure physical need . . . usually.

Unlike humans, who experimented in ways he'd never comprehended. But then, they could move on when and if they wanted to.

That cold reminder brought his lips tearing from hers, and he thrust her from him a lot less gently than he wanted to.

Her eyes snapped open, mirroring more hurt at this rejection, and Ty wanted to fix it, but he couldn't. So he turned away.

His mom looked too damn smug and his dad looked angry and worried. Kurt . . . hell, he looked like a wolf on the verge of issuing a challenge.

"I thought you were sniffing around Olivia." Kurt's voice came out a rumble, just a hair shy of a growl.

A soft sound from behind him said that Frankie had heard every word. Ty couldn't fix that either. It was the truth. Damn it to hell, how had things gotten so complicated so fast?

"I thought you were down in the barn with Duke," he said to Kurt with pointed emphasis.

"I saw Flash and knew Frankie was up at the house." He smiled at her, his teeth showing. "I wanted to say hi."

More like he'd scented Frankie's pheromones on her horse's saddle and had followed the scent like the wolf close to the change that he was.

"I'm glad." She was probably giving Kurt that sweet smile that always pricked Ty's heart.

He gritted his teeth.

Kurt smiled back, confirming his guess. "Me too."

"Well, you need to get back to the barn," Ty said, sounding meaner than he had in a long time.

Kurt's eyes narrowed, his body shifting subtly into a stance that said he was ready to meet Ty's aggression. "Is that right?"

Ty glared, straightening to his full six foot three and flexing his hands with intent.

Kurt's eyes flared and then narrowed as if he was deciding whether or not Frankie was worth the challenge.

"That's right." This time it was his dad speaking and his voice brooked no opposition.

Kurt stiffened, but then he nodded, his expression one of grudging acceptance. "I take it the word is to stay in the barn for the time being?"

"Right." King McCanlup had been pack leader since his father's death, and kept the role with a strength of will that even his sons rarely challenged in any serious way.

The last time had been when Duke had insisted on taking a

human mate. King had been furious, but Duke had refused to back down—and look what had happened.

Leah had walked away, the way any human could.

Kurt left and Ty realized he'd better make tracks too, or he was going to end up just as bad off as his brother.

He turned back to face Frankie and just seeing her was enough to erode one more level of his self-control.

He figured he needed to get off the ranch completely. It also wouldn't hurt to see Olivia right now. According to his calculations, she should be in heat too. Exposing his wolf to her should counteract the effects of Frankie's pheromones on him.

"I, uh . . . I'll just leave you here visiting with Mom while I go check on the Delacroix's mare. She's ready to foal, but it's her first time and they're worried."

Frankie's eyes lit up and he could have kicked himself.

"I'd love to come with you. It's been so long since I tended a pregnant horse."

"That's not a good idea."

"Sure it is. Frankie will enjoy meeting Olivia and her parents. They moved to town since your last visit," his mom said, smiling at Frankie just as if she hadn't screwed over her own son with an electric Phillips.

"The French Canadian family?"

"You've heard about them?"

Frankie's face closed up, the joy that had been there seconds before now absent. "Yes. I'd like to go with you." She didn't sound anticipatory anymore so much as stubbornly resigned.

"Ty can drop you by home afterward."

He groaned inwardly at his dad's subtle reminder. They had to get her off the Rocking M, and the sooner the better.

Frankie sat beside Ty in the pickup cab and wondered how wise it had been to insist on coming with him to visit the horse.

She'd meet the competition, and that should be a good thing, but her heart shied away from being forced to witness his attraction to another woman. Then again, that was probably exactly what she needed. Time had done nothing to blunt her love for the man; maybe watching him fawn over some other woman would destroy it.

Or at least convince her, finally, of the hopelessness of her feelings.

But why the heck had he acted all territorial about her when Kurt came up to the house? And that kiss . . . it had been so good, but then he'd shoved her away like he'd gotten a whiff of three-day-old garbage. What was that all about?

Tyler McCanlup had been confusing her for more years than she wanted to deal with. It was time to excise him from her heart and move to Washington State—or seduce him until she was as deeply embedded in his as he was in hers.

One way or another, she was going forward with her life.

The Delacroix's ranch was a lot like Uncle Ben's. Not tiny, but certainly not on the same scale as the Rocking M either.

"So, this is a working ranch?" she asked as they walked toward the barn.

"They run a few cattle, but Olivia and her dad train horses mostly."

"What about her mom?"

"She's a teacher in town."

"What grade does she teach?"

"I don't know."

"Is Olivia the only child?"

If he noticed the conversation had turned into more of an inquisition, he didn't let on.

"She is now."

"What does that mean?"

"She had a little brother. He's gone."

"That's hard." She knew firsthand how much it hurt to lose a close family member.

"Yes, it is. They moved here to get away from the memories."

"I hope it works for them." Moving had done nothing to ease her memories—not in helping her forget her parents and not in helping her forget Ty.

"Me too." The way he said it made it sound like he was emotionally invested, or was she reading something into his voice?

Life had been so much easier when she was busy sublimating her love for Ty.

As they reached the barn, a beautiful woman walked out. She had long, curling dark hair, almond-shaped eyes the color of a deep-purple pansy and a figure that could have rivaled Marilyn Monroe's. Even dressed in jeans and ropers, Frankie had no problem seeing why Ty was interested.

"*Allo*, Tyler. Who is this?" She spoke with a slight French accent and smiled pleasantly at Frankie.

"My best friend, Frankie Random. We grew up roping cows and researching animal diseases together." He couldn't have made her role in his life clearer.

She was just another guy as far as he was concerned. Which is what he had said the one time she'd tried to take their friendship into the realm of male-female relationships. That he saw her as one of the guys.

It had devastated her enough to keep her libido in check around him after that, but she'd enjoyed his friendship too much to give it up. Now . . . well, now she had no choice. Not if she wanted a full life.

"Frankie, meet Olivia. Horses find her every bit as irresistible as the men around here."

Frankie forced her lips to smile, her eyes to warm and her heart to keep beating despite the mortal blow it had just received.

He was definitely interested in this goddess among women. No wonder he couldn't see Frankie for dust. His tastes ran to the exotic and beautiful. Because he'd never been much of a womanizer, she hadn't known that. Then, the town didn't boast that many women who could have modeled for Botticelli either.

"Hi, Olivia. It's nice to meet you." Frankie lied without so much as letting her smile falter.

Olivia's expression turned concerned anyway, her eyes filling with a knowing sadness as her gaze flicked back and forth between Ty and Frankie. Her insight surprised Frankie, who had never thought she wore her heart on her sleeve.

She shrugged her shoulders slightly to let the other woman know she had no intention of fighting the inevitable, but Olivia didn't look comforted. If anything, she looked more worried.

THREE

"If you're here about Circe, she's doing fine. I just checked on her." Olivia tucked a wayward curl behind her ear. "I don't think she'll foal for another few days."

"If I'm not around, have your dad call Frankie. She's staying at the Random's place. They're her people."

At one time the vote of confidence would have touched her, but now it just landed against the wall of numbness growing around her heart. Why had she let herself hope again? Because he never dated anyone else?

How stupid was that? What a flimsy excuse to come home ready to seduce a man who so obviously wasn't interested in his tomboy best friend.

There had been no Olivia before, was all.

"Then Frankie should meet Circe, I think," Olivia said.

"That's not necessary," Ty said. "Frankie's a trained vet with an affinity for animals. If you don't need me to look in on the mare, then we'll be on our way."

"*Sacre bleu*. I am not having a vet who has never met her tend my horse for her first birthing." Olivia's voice was hard with certainty, her eyes snapping annoyance at Ty.

Ty gave her a look of pure irritation. "If I say Frankie will do, she'll do."

"God is the only omnipotent being I know of, Tyler Mc-Canlup. I will have your friend meet the horse, if it is all the same to you."

"It isn't. I said I wanted to get her home."

"If you are in such a hurry to return to your ranch, then I will make sure Frankie gets home."

"No."

"Yes."

They glared at each other and Frankie couldn't help doubting her former certainty that Ty wanted the other woman. His expression was anything but loverlike—and shouldn't a man enamored of a woman be more indulgent?

Ty didn't love *her* that way and he had always been a lot more tolerant of her whims. Which meant what? That maybe there still was hope?

Her emotions were swinging like an overzealous metronome. She needed to get herself under control and stick with the plan. Either seduce Ty or walk away . . . completely.

"I'd love to meet the horse," she said, hoping to avert an all-out war between the two people still glaring at each other.

Frankie laid her hand on Ty's sleeve when he said nothing. "Please, Ty. It's been so long since I've seen a pregnant mare."

He turned to her with the indulgent smile she knew so well. "All right, Little Bit, if that's what you want."

She warmed at the familiar nickname. At six foot three, he was one of the few men who actually considered her five-foot-eight-inch frame little.

Olivia led the way back into the barn and stopped at a stall with a beautiful little brown mare in it. "This is Circe."

Frankie extended her hand to the horse's muzzle, letting the animal get her scent before she started scratching the mare's head and talking softly to her. "You're a beauty. I bet your baby is going to be just as pretty."

The horse responded to the soft words with a gentle neighing and butted her head against Frankie's shoulder. After that, Frankie insisted on meeting the rest of the animals in the barn.

She stopped at Circe's stall again on her way out and asked if she could examine the horse, just to get her used to having Frankie around. But the truth was, she wasn't sure Olivia was right. Frankie sensed the horse was ready to foal, even though she wasn't showing a lot of outward signs.

This affinity she had for pregnant animals had surprised her family at first, especially considering what a city girl she'd been when she came to live with them. However, her uncle had learned to listen when Frankie said a female was ready to give birth.

The more she touched the horse, the more certain she became. "She's going to drop her foal tonight."

Olivia stared at her, and Ty swore.

"Are you sure?" he asked.

"Yes, and I don't think she should be left alone. She's scared and new at this."

"You're not pack," Olivia said, her voice laced with disbelief.

"Pack?" she asked.

Ty shook his head. "Never mind. If she says it, it's true."

Olivia's shapely brow rose and the look she gave Ty was nothing short of mocking. "Oh, speaks the great oracle again?"

Frankie laughed. "You two fight like brother and sister." And the relief she felt at that was huge.

Ty glared at her, but Olivia nodded. "He's every bit as annoying as any little brother could be."

"Are you older?" Frankie asked.

"Less than a year," Ty groused.

"Sometimes it feels like a decade," Olivia said with an obvious bid at yanking his chain.

It worked and Ty glared at her.

"Well, this time you can believe him," Frankie said before the argument could escalate. "I can't explain how I know things about pregnant animals, but I do. It's one of the reasons I became a vet."

But she'd helped with a total of only six births in the two years she'd practiced in the city. Domestic animals usually had their babies at home without the assistance of a vet.

Olivia frowned, biting her lip, her agitation apparent. "I've got to go somewhere. Tonight. I should have left hours ago. I can't be *here*, not even for Circe."

"Where are you going?" Ty asked sharply.

"None of your business, *little brother*."

Ty's jaw twitched. "Rocking M land is the safest for running."

"That's not what you told me when I rode my horse across it today," Frankie said with a frown.

Ty looked like he couldn't decide what to say and Olivia just shook her head, her expression obdurate.

"Look, I don't mind staying with the horse if Ty has other animals he needs to tend to," she offered.

The life of a rural vet was a busy one, if extremely satisfying.

"No. I don't understand why you're leaving your mare right now, Olivia." Though something in his tone said he knew exactly why the other woman had to go, and it made him mad.

"I must leave," Olivia repeated, a stubborn edge to her voice. "And I think you understand very well why I might find it necessary."

"Fine, then I'll stay." Ty accepted the inevitable with bad grace.

"Will you drop Frankie off on your way to *wherever it is you're going?*" he asked with sarcastic emphasis.

"Certainly."

"No."

They spoke at the same time.

Frankie crossed her arms over her chest. "I want to be here for the foaling. Do you mind Olivia?"

"Not at all. I am very glad my mare will have you to comfort her. I sense things too, sometimes. About people. And I think you are kind."

Frankie's smile at the compliment faded with Ty's next words.

"Well, I mind."

"Why?" Frankie asked.

"I'm Circe's vet. I'm here now and I don't need your assistance."

"Stop being so cranky or I'm going to think you've got PMS," she joked. "You're a guy. You aren't supposed to have monthly hormonal imbalances."

Olivia snorted at that.

"You're not staying." He spoke so harshly, Frankie took a step backward.

Finally, she got it. "You don't want me around you."

The look on his face said it all, like a man caught in an unpalatable truth. She'd come with the noble intentions of breaking off their friendship if that was what it took to move forward with her life, but it had never occurred to her he was ready for it to end.

And the realization hurt more than she would have thought possible. "You've been trying to get rid of me since you first saw me this morning. I'm sorry it's taken me so long to catch on. I guess your family really wants a total break from mine."

If she thought it was more personal than that, her heart was going to break. Maybe it already had.

It felt like everything inside her had shattered. So much for the numbness she'd been feeling. She was in so much pain, she could barely breathe.

He said a word under his breath that was not very nice, but she kept backing up.

"I'll just ride back to the ranch with Olivia. I won't bug you again, Ty." Her voice broke on his name and she spun away before the stupid stinging sensation in her eyes manifested in something as embarrassing as tears.

A hand latched on to her arm, the hold unbreakable. "Damn it, Frankie. I'm not trying to kick you out of my life."

She kept her body averted, her face turned away from him. "Don't worry about it, Ty. It's time I grew up and moved on. I knew it, and I thought I was ready, but it's harder than I expected, is all."

He yanked her back around, the movement not gentle, but not painfully rough either. He glared down at her. "It is not time for you to move on. We'll be friends forever."

"No. We can't, Ty. I can't," she stressed.

"What the hell are you talking about?"

"This . . . all of it . . . you're right. I have no place in your life."

"I never said that!" His roar startled a loud whinny from Circe.

"Then I'm saying it. I can't be your friend anymore, Ty." The moisture in her eyes welled against her lids. If she blinked, it would trickle over.

"Don't you dare cry," he growled.

"I'm n-not," she said as two tears rolled hotly down her cheeks.

"Damn it!"

"D-don't swear at me!"

"What am I supposed to do? How do I fix this?" he asked as if the answers pained him as much as they did her.

She didn't get a chance to respond because his lips were claiming hers again. This time they were hot, hard and hungry against hers, confusing her even more. But nothing could dampen her response, this kiss had been so long in coming.

She wrapped her arms around his neck and pressed up against

him with all her might. His arms circled her and he held her as if he could never bear to let her go.

This time, he kissed her until she was a melting pool of feminine desire against him, until her mouth parted and his tongue tasted hers.

When he broke his lips from hers, he hugged her close and spoke into her neck. "I don't ever want to hurt you, Frankie."

"This doesn't hurt."

"But it will. If we keep doing it."

"Why?"

"I told you. I don't think of you that way."

"Then why are you hard?"

He swore again, but he didn't move away. "Biology. It still won't work between us."

"I don't understand."

"I know, baby. I know."

He swore again, this time even more viciously than before, and stepped away from her.

"What's the matter?"

"She left."

"Olivia?"

"Yes."

She looked around and sure enough the other woman was nowhere to be seen.

"She's probably up at the house. I'll leave with her if you want me to, Ty." She had too much pride to stay when she wasn't wanted.

"She's not at the house. She left."

"How—"

"I heard the car start."

"I didn't hear anything."

"You have your gifts. I have mine."

"There's probably time for you to drive me back to Uncle Ben's before anything happens with Circe."

"What did you mean you couldn't be my friend anymore?" he asked instead of answering.

She met his eyes, for once not trying to hide anything in hers. "I love you, Ty."

"I love you too, Little Bit."

"Not like that. Not like a friend. I want you."

"That's just . . ."

"Biology?" she asked, wondering if he really believed it.

"Yes," he gritted.

"It's not. Not for me anyway."

"Frankie, don't do this."

"Don't tell you the truth? I can't live a lie anymore, Ty."

"So, what, you're saying that if I don't let you be my girlfriend, you won't be my best friend anymore?"

"That's really oversimplified, but in essence . . . yes. I can't keep giving the best of myself to you when all you want is one part of me. I'm sorry."

"That's such a human load of crap."

She flinched from the disgust in his eyes. "I know you'd like to believe you aren't human, but you're fallible too, Ty."

"I'm not threatening you with walking away if you don't do what I want."

"Aren't you? Haven't you always made it clear that if I tried to be more than a friend, our friendship would end?"

"I never said that."

"No, you just lied to me."

"Never."

"Always. You said you didn't think of me like that, but you want me too. Isn't it worth trying to make a relationship work between us?"

"I'd get hard with any woman rubbing up against me like that."

"I don't believe you."

He opened his mouth, but a frightened whinny cut off the rest of their conversation.

They returned to the mare and by tacit agreement, both of them kept their conversation to Circe's condition and practicing veterinary medicine. Frankie used the phone in the barn to let her family know where she was and that it might be morning before they saw her.

Mr. Delacroix arrived with Mrs. Delacroix a couple of hours later. She insisted on feeding Ty and Frankie. Sometime after that, a hand came into the barn to inform Ty he'd be there to watch over the mare after the birth. Ty said nothing about having one of them take Frankie home, so she stayed, wanting this last chance to be with him.

Circe foaled at six forty-two in the evening.

By the time the mare had been tended to and Ty and Frankie had cleaned up, it was almost eight and the storm front had moved in. Frankie felt no fear at the prospect of Ty driving her home through the heavy snow mixed with sleet. He'd been driving in weather like this since before he was old enough to get a permit.

However, the car that almost hit them head-on and sent Ty's truck swerving toward the side of the road apparently hadn't. Frankie didn't scream, keeping her lips clamped tightly together as the big truck slid, bumped over what felt like some very big rocks and landed nose-down in a deep ditch with the back wheels off the ground.

"Are you okay?" he demanded, his voice grim.

"Yes."

"Idiot."

"They left," she said, looking out the back window. She could barely make out the red taillights retreating slowly in the swirling white, but they *were* retreating.

Ty grabbed his cell phone and flipped it open only to utter a pithy imprecation. "It's dead. Let me have yours."

"I don't have a cell phone."

"What? Everyone has a cell phone."

"I don't."

"Why not?"

"It's a luxury I can't afford on my salary as a junior vet."

He said something truly foul and she glared at him.

"Why don't you have a CB? Every ranch truck has one."

"My truck's new and I haven't had it installed yet." If his voice got any lower, he'd be growling.

"Do you think we can get the truck back on the road?"

"Maybe."

She went to get out when he did, but he snapped, "Stay inside where it's warm."

"I can help."

"If I can't get it, your strength isn't going to make any difference."

"You're so darn arrogant sometimes, I want to spit. I'm not a lightweight."

He smiled. "I know, Little Bit, but let me try first, all right?"

He was back sooner than she expected with more bad news.

"The drive line's broken. We're not going anywhere."

"We can stay inside the cab, turning the engine on to keep it warm every so often."

Ty shook his head decisively. "We cannot stay in the truck."

"It makes sense. Rescue will come along eventually."

"It could be hours." He said it like they'd die together in the cab if it took that long.

"But—"

"There's a cabin not too far from here. It belongs to a friend of my dad's, but he moved on."

"How far is it?"

He shrugged. "Close enough."

"I still think it would make more sense to wait for rescue."

"We're in a ditch off a secondary road in a snowstorm that is going to cover the truck before long. We can't depend on rescue."

*   *   *

Ty watched the emotions chase across Frankie's face as she thought about what he'd said. She might be right; they might get rescued if they waited in the truck, but he also might give in to the feelings clamoring inside him to mate with her.

He couldn't take that chance.

The cabin was maybe a half an hour's walk away. It was cold, but he had natural resistance and she had bundled up to ride her horse earlier. Her layers should protect her.

She sighed, her mouth turning down in defeat. "Okay. We'll go to the cabin."

She started putting the layers back on she'd taken off in the warmth of the truck cab. Soon she was as bundled up as he'd first seen her that morning. He pulled the horse blanket he kept behind the driver's seat and wrapped it over her head and around her like a shawl, as additional protection from the elements.

"Shouldn't you use it? You've only got your sheepskin. You don't even have a hat."

"I do." He pulled the wide-brimmed Australian oilskin hat from behind his seat and a pair of wool-lined leather gloves as well. Even werewolves knew better than to brave the Montana winters in their human skin without basic precautions. He put them on and cinched the string on the hat so it couldn't fly off. He even buttoned his coat.

When he was done, he said, "Come out my door. It'll be safer to exit the truck together."

She followed him without comment. As he lifted her from the truck, her scent reached out and enveloped him with such strength his knees almost buckled.

That half-hour walk to the cabin was looking almost pleasurable to him right now. Maybe it would cool his libido to manageable proportions. He'd never found it so hard to control his beast, and there was something else really bothering him.

He'd been right, Olivia had been in heat. He'd smelled it on her before she'd even come out of the barn, but he hadn't felt the urge to mate her. Not even a twinge. His senses had been full of Frankie's scent and no matter how hard he tried, he couldn't direct his wolf's interest to the other woman. Was it because he'd scented Frankie first?

He didn't know, but he wasn't mating with a human.

Not today, not ever.

His father was respected and feared as pack leader because he enforced pack law with no exceptions. His best friend had mated a human when they were both young. It had not been a sacred bond and the human female had never conceived. She'd wanted children more than she wanted her mate and she'd left him.

Five years later, Ty's father's friend had been caught mating a femwolf. His first wife was still living and according to pack law, that made both him and the femwolf guilty of adultery. Although they were divorced by human laws, they were found guilty by the pack and pack justice was carried out.

By Ty's father.

Both wolves had their throats ripped out by the pack leader and both Duke and Ty had been forced to watch, to see pack justice as well as the consequences of disobeying pack law.

Ty wasn't sure he agreed with the law, but he damn well wasn't going to risk ever becoming a casualty of it.

With a femwolf for his first and only mate, he wouldn't have to worry about that. Only werewolves foolish enough to marry humans did.

four

Frankie stumbled into the small cabin ahead of Ty, too numb from the cold to even appreciate being out of it.

The door slammed behind her, leaving them in darkness. From the sound of Ty's movements, that didn't seem to slow him down. The scratch of a match on a tinderbox came just before a small flame illuminated his hand on a kerosene lamp. Once lit, it bathed the main room in a soft yellow glow as Ty hung it from a hook in the ceiling.

Her first impression of the cabin surprised her. "I thought you said your dad's friend moved on."

She'd been expecting a bare floor and no furniture, and while the furnishings were simple, they were definitely adequate, and the woodstove partially recessed in the middle of the wall opposite the kitchen looked like it had been tended recently.

"He may come back. The pac—people take care of it for him."

"Oh. Lucky for us," she said through lips stiff from cold.

He winced as if he could feel the prickles of pain across the surface of her skin that speaking had caused her. "I'll get a fire going in the stove."

"Is there wood?"

"Yes." He found it and kindling in a wood box to the right of the stove and built the fire with an agility she envied.

"What are you, some kind of freak of nature? Doesn't the cold affect you at all?"

He shrugged. "I've always been this way."

"I know, but even you should be a Popsicle after that walk."

He wasn't human. If she didn't know better, she'd think he was some kind of supernatural being . . . and while she was at it, his brother and father as well. They all seemed superhuman sometimes.

"Maybe we should have stayed in the truck." He sounded like he was feeling guilty for her discomfort.

"The storm's only getting worse. You were right. The chances of rescue would have been slim. Besides, we made it and hopefully, we'll be warm again soon."

He took the hint and got the fire going. Then they both peeled off their wet outer layers and hung them on the indoor clothesline near the stove. The sexy little red sweater she'd bought to entice Ty made a poor barrier against the cold still permeating the cabin.

Shivering, she kicked off her boots and peeled her wet socks from her feet. "I don't suppose your dad's friend left any blankets behind."

"I'll look, but I'm sure he did." He opened a door on the other side of the woodstove and went through to what must have been the bedroom.

He came out a few seconds later carrying a quilt. He handed it to her with a jerky movement that said he didn't want to touch her.

She was too cold and too tired to worry about the implied rejection. "We should probably eat something and put on a pot of water for washing up later."

Although there was no electricity, thankfully, the cabin did have running water. Someone must have been taking care of that too.

She filled a big stew pot from the faucet and he lifted it to the stove before she got a chance.

"You're always doing that."

"What?" he asked.

"Taking care of me."

He was bent over, pulling something out of the canned goods cupboard. "That's what friends are for."

She didn't answer. She'd told him she didn't want to be his friend, and maybe he just thought it was feminine pique, but it hadn't been. It was the desperate act of a woman who didn't want to spend the rest of her life in love with a man who did not love her.

She saw that he'd retrieved a big can of stew from the cupboard and a couple of cans of vegetables to add to it, so she got another pot down from where they hung on the wall above the sink. She set it on the two-burner kerosene stove and lit the one under it.

They ate together at the table, her with the quilt wrapped around her shoulders like a cape and him peeled down to a single Henley. Sheesh, the man really wasn't human.

Afterward, she examined the cabin while he went to the lean-to off the back door and brought in more wood.

The single bedroom was small, but the bed was big. The wood-stove wasn't recessed in the wall so much as exposed on its backside to the bedroom through the shared wall. The room was warming up, if not with the same speed as the main room.

The closet was empty, as was the small dresser, but a picture of a man with his arms around a woman was on top. He looked about King's age, and the way he held the woman said everything important about how he felt about her.

Tears stung Frankie's eyes unexpectedly. Something so nice should not make her cry, but she turned away from the photo anyway.

"There's hot water on for coffee."

She pivoted to face the door at the sound of Ty's voice. He was looking at the bed with a pained expression, then his gaze snapped to hers, and the desire burning in his blue eyes was unmistakable. Even to her less-than-tutored eye.

She stepped toward him, "Ty . . ."

He moved back, his face shuttering with the speed of light. "There's no cream, but there's sugar."

The coffee. She sighed. "No, thanks. I'm tired. I think I'll just turn in if there's nothing you need me to do."

He shook his head and looked at the bed again.

"It's big enough for both of us."

"*No.*" The vehemence in his voice might not be warranted in her opinion, but she wasn't totally shocked by it.

"Why are you so against having a relationship with me?" she asked, unable to help herself. "You want me."

"It's a bad idea."

"Says who?"

"I say."

"Well, I say you're wrong."

This time when his eyes met hers, they were filled with anger. "I don't give a damn. You're my friend, Frankie, and that is all you will ever be."

The words hurt, but they didn't make sense and so she couldn't quite make herself accept them. "There's an old saying that friends make the best lovers."

"And sex can ruin a beautiful friendship."

"It wouldn't just be sex."

"Yes, it would."

Now that really did hurt. He was saying he might want her, but he didn't love her, not like that. And seriously, after all these years, what were the chances he ever would?

"I'll take the sofa. I'm shorter."

"Forget it. You'll sleep on the bed."

She didn't bother to argue. She'd learned long ago that he could be as stubborn as a mule with a behavior problem. She waited until he left the room before stripping her clothes and pulling on his flannel shirt, which she'd filched from the outer room. It smelled like Ty and covered her to her knees.

She rummaged in the closet and found another quilt. She grabbed it, picked up the quilt she'd dropped earlier and grabbed one of the pillows off the big bed before padding out to the main room in her bare feet. The sound of chopping came from the lean-to and she figured Ty would probably be out there long enough for her to fall asleep.

She really was tired.

She curled up on the sofa under both quilts and willed her mind to stop spinning around the insurmountable problem of her useless love for her best friend.

Ty walked into the cabin and was hit immediately by her scent. He wanted to howl at the moon, but even more than that . . . he wanted to taste her whole body, to soak that scent into every one of his pores.

He frowned when he realized her presence was so strong because she was sleeping on the couch.

Stubborn.

He smiled grudgingly. He should have known she'd do it when she didn't argue with him. She'd spent over a decade taking care of him too. He'd laughed at her efforts sometimes, finding it genuinely amazing that this small human woman could think he needed her to protect him in any way.

Even though she didn't know he was werewolf, she did know he was a strong man . . . and determined. Only this time, she would get her way. Normally, he would have just picked her up and put her in the bed, but he couldn't trust himself to touch her. He wanted her too badly. The full moon and his change were getting closer by the hour, making it more and more difficult to control his baser impulses.

He stoked the fire, trying to ignore the lure of her scent. After putting on another big log, he went into the bedroom and shut the door. Hoping for a respite from the seductive smell tormenting him, he groaned in real pain when he saw her clothes folded in a neat pile on top of the dresser.

He picked them up, holding them as far from his body as he could and carried them into the other room. He left them by the woodstove. He could tell her he wanted them to be warm for her in the morning if she asked about it.

Thankfully, the scent that lingered when he went back into the bedroom was muted. He shut the door and cracked the window, letting in frigid fresh air to help mask it.

As it was, he doubted he was going to get any sleep that night.

Frankie woke up pulsing between her legs from a dream about Ty, rolled over and fell off the narrow couch to the hard cabin floor.

"Ooph . . ." She climbed to her knees, still disoriented from sleep. "Jeez. Trust me to fall out of bed when I'm twenty-six years old."

Standing up, she winced with pain. Her neck and back hurt from the cramped position on the couch, and she would bet her favorite copy of the *Merck Veterinary Manual* she was going to have a big purple bruise on her hip tomorrow.

The main room was cooling off and she realized the fire needed to be stoked again. She was surprised Ty hadn't come out to do it. He must be sleeping pretty heavily. She took care of it and then tried to stretch out the kinks.

It only took a few seconds of stretching to realize that any attempt at sleeping the rest of the night on the sofa would be hopeless.

If she snuck into the bed with Ty, he wouldn't even notice. It was so big. His insistence they not share it was just plain stupid. So, okay . . . he didn't want to make love to her, but no one was asking him to. She just wanted a comfortable place to sleep without the guilt of knowing she was consigning her best friend to the purgatory of the too-short couch.

She opened the door to the bedroom as quietly as she could and tiptoed toward the bed. It was freezing. Goose bumps shivered down her arms.

"What are you doing, Frankie?" Ty's voice was gravelly and low, but not sleepy.

It was also not in the least welcoming.

Since he was awake, she made no effort to be quiet as she crossed to the window. "It's open. Are you nuts?"

"I like fresh air when I sleep."

"Well, you're going to have to go without tonight." She shut the window with a snap.

"To hell with the window; what are you doing in here?" It sounded like he took a deep breath and let it out slowly. "Damn. That wasn't smart. You're supposed to be on the couch." He said it like he was telling her she'd shirked her duty toward world peace or something.

"I fell off the couch." She grimaced at the admission.

"Are you okay?" All irritation had drained from his voice to be replaced by immediate concern.

How was she going to walk away from this man? "Not really." She sighed. "I bruised my hip and I can't get comfortable on the sofa again."

"You have to try."

"I don't want to. It's hopeless, Ty."

"You can't sleep in here with me," he ground out, the softness fading as fast as it had come to his voice.

She ignored him. Sometimes you just had to do that with bossy men. She crossed the room and climbed into the bed on the opposite side of Ty. "Just pretend I'm not here."

"I can't do that."

She rolled her eyes in the dark. "I promise not to kick."

"You're breathing. That's enough."

She turned on her side away from him. "Get over it, Ty. I'm not going back to the couch."

"You chose to sleep on it, to get your scent all over it. I can't sleep out there now."

Great, now he was saying she stank. Nice. "So, I made a mistake."

"Yes, you did."

She turned back to face him and realized he'd moved across the bed. His face was fewer than six inches from hers.

"You don't sound so good."

"You're wearing my shirt." He sounded equal parts amazed and pissed.

"Do you want me to take it off?"

"Yes."

She gasped.

"No. Damn it. Get back in the other room before I do something we'll both regret."

"Are you talking sex here?"

"Yes."

Her body pulsed with need at that one small affirmative and a truth she'd fought earlier settled inside her. "I won't regret it."

She was meant for him . . . even if he didn't want her in a forever-after kind of way.

"Yes. You. Will. *Now, go*." He sounded more like a wild animal than a man.

She put her hand out and touched his chest. "No. Even if it's only sex, I want it."

His big body shuddered and a low groan rumbled in his chest.

"Please, Ty, make love to me."

She wanted a memory to take with her. She'd always thought that was stupid when other women said the same thing, but now she understood. It was that whole "better to have loved and lost than never to have loved at all" thing.

Their friendship was over. He might have a hard time accepting it, but she couldn't go on like they had been. Tonight was all they had left of each other, and she wanted as much of him as he would give her. It might be stupid, but even if all he had to give her was sex, she'd take it.

This one night.

"It will change everything."

"I know."

"You will belong to me."

She only wished, but she replied with a truth he would never understand. "I already do."

He came over her in a rush that left her flattened into the bed. "I'm going to taste every inch of you, Little Bit."

She wrapped her arms around him, reveling in his heat. "Oh . . . yessss . . ."

His mouth clamped to hers in a kiss more voracious than anything she'd ever known. Hunger denied far too long surged up inside her to match his, and she touched him, exploring wherever her fingers could reach. He groaned when she traced the contours of his face around their locked lips and shivered when she brushed the nape of his neck with fluttery fingertips.

Her hands traveled downward.

The fact he hadn't worn anything to bed registered at the same time as his hard penis settled between her thighs, sending a thrill of pleasure through her.

His lips ripped from hers. "I want you now. No waiting."

"Yes." She widened her legs, prepared for him by her dream and the desire that had burned latently in her all day.

She didn't want to wait either. This was too primal to preface with tender touches. It was arousal at its most basic and they both vibrated with it.

He pushed inside her without any hesitation, his mouth moving to her neck and clamping down on the sensitive flesh at its base. She'd been given love bites before, but nothing like this. It felt like he would break her skin with his teeth, but he didn't and the pleasure was just this side of pain.

"Ty . . ." His name came out broken and husky.

He made a purring noise deep in his throat and thrust deeper, claiming her body with primitive power.

Her pleasure rocketed upward with no chance for her to prepare herself, or even imagine her climax could come as quickly and with the power that it did. She screamed his name as her body convulsed so hard she almost bucked him off her.

He threw his head back and howled just like a wolf.

It was the sexiest thing she'd ever heard and she climaxed again, right on the heels of the first one, her body going completely rigid under him.

He kept moving, his hot seed spurting inside her in the longest climax she'd ever known a man to experience.

Aftershocks shook her body and she jolted against him as he continued to pound out his pleasure.

Finally, she couldn't take any more and she collapsed in boneless disarray under him. With a final howl that shattered her senses, he joined her, his body falling across hers in a limp heap.

It felt so good to have him covering her, to be so intimately close to him that she did not make a big deal about the fact that breathing was a challenge.

But he must have noticed because he rolled onto his back. She followed him, snuggling into his body with a sense of rightness and belonging she hadn't known since her parents' deaths over a decade before.

It was an illusion, but she wallowed in it, wanting it to last.

"That was good." Ty's voice rumbled through his chest.

She laughed softly. "That's one word for it. Cataclysmic is another."

He slid out from under her, turning on his side so they faced each other and smiled. "Maybe we should go for Richter-eleven earth shaking."

The hot desire in his eyes after so much spent passion shocked her even as her body responded. "Right now? Aren't you done for a while?"

His climax had been so long and powerful, she didn't think he could get a hard-on for hours yet.

He took her wrist and guided her hand to his large and growing-bigger-by-the-second penis. "Does this feel like I'm done?"

"Uh . . . no . . ."

FIVE

He chuckled, the sound more dark than humorous, and pushed her on her back, looming over her in predatory expectation. "You do realize that means you're not done either?"

She curled her fingers around his hard length and stroked him. "That's okay by me. I've wanted you so long . . . I could make love to you forever."

She might be exhausted, but the part of her that was already dying to have him inside again gave no credence to that fact.

Something came and went in his blue gaze, but she didn't have time to ponder it because he bent down and licked from her collarbone to her ear, tickling her with his tongue.

She giggled.

She could feel his smile against her skin. "I told you I wanted to taste you."

"You're going to lick me?" She paused. "All over?"

"Yes."

"Only if I get return privileges." Her voice came out breathless and it was no wonder. The thought of tasting his big male body was enough to make her light-headed with hunger.

The hand resting on her hip contracted in an almost painful grip. *"I want that."*

But he made her wait until he'd used his tongue to torment every inch of her skin. The things he did to her nipples and inner thighs were probably against the law in some states . . . they were certainly decadent. He tasted bits of her flesh she'd never even thought about, and some she'd only dreamed of in her most secret fantasies.

When he reached her toes, he sucked on each one as if it were a lollipop. She shivered and moaned and rocked on the bed, spreading her legs in blatant invitation. "I need you, Ty . . . please."

He lifted his head and leaned over her at her feet, his expression wicked. "I thought you wanted to taste me too."

"I do, but I don't think I can move right now," she admitted.

He didn't give her the chance. More swiftly than she could imagine, he was beside her on the bed, turning her over, pulling her up on her knees and entering her from behind.

Oh, wow. He was big . . . so big . . . and hard, like cast iron hot from the forge inside her. She rocked back toward him, pressing her bottom into his stomach and whimpering with delight when he went deeper still.

"That's right, baby. Take all of me." He pulled back and then thrust forward again. "You're so tight, so wet."

His hands came around her front, one to touch her aching clitoris and the other to play with her rock-hard nipples and swollen breasts, going back and forth between them in a rhythm guaranteed to drive her insane.

She'd never been this turned on.

Not ever.

She groaned as he pushed in and out, hitting that place she'd only ever read about in women's magazines. Oh, man . . . she really did have a G-spot, and this was it. She laughed with triumph, but the sound choked off into a desperate moan as he took one tight nub between thumb and forefinger and squeezed.

"You're so good at this," she panted.

"Am I?" he asked, like he really didn't know.

"Oh, please, don't tell me no one has ever told you before." Not that she liked thinking of him with other women. More like, she hated it, but he was too amazing a lover not to be aware of his prowess.

He grabbed her hips with both hands and rammed into her. "No," he said, sounding angry, "no one has ever said that to me in this situation before."

Why was he mad?

She had no hope of figuring it out now. He was loving her so hard and so fast that her thoughts splintered to nothingness in a shower of exploding sparks.

Pleasure pounded through her, tightening her womb until she felt like she was going to die if she didn't come again.

She whimpered brokenly, not knowing what to do.

"What is it, baby?"

"I want to come."

"Then come."

"I can't." She threw her head back and hit his chest. "Touch me again. Please, Ty."

He nuzzled her ear, his breath hot and his tongue wet on sensitive flesh, sending shivers through her. "Touch yourself."

"No, I . . ." She'd never done that before with a man. "I can't," she gasped out.

"Yes, you can."

"I'll fall," she said desperately, snatching at excuses.

"I'll hold you up. *Do it*." Then he pulled her back so he was kneeling behind her and she was supported on his thighs.

He continued his thrusting, but his hands stayed maddeningly attached to her hips. She'd probably have bruises there later from the grip, but she didn't care, she just wanted to come. Every thrust hit her G-spot, sending sensation overload along her nerve endings, but it still wasn't enough.

She moaned.

"You know what you need to do," he whispered seductively in her ear. "Are you going to deny yourself?"

How could she do it? How could she make herself come when he was inside her, watching her, feeling every contraction, every jolt of her hips?

But her need for release was reaching an agonizing level and the pleasure plateau she was on had become more ordeal than delight. Desperate, she brought her hand between her legs. The wet silkiness there felt wonderful and her body shook with joy as she allowed herself to caress the swollen button that so needed touching.

His arms came around her, the fingers of one hand tangling with hers between her legs, and the other cupping her right breast. "That's right, Frankie. Oh, honey . . . you're so hot and soft. So perfect."

The combined effect of his words and the sensation of their fingers together on her clitoris sent her over the brink. She convulsed in one rapturous contraction after another, her body bucking and bowing. Ty held her to him by a feat of strength beyond her comprehension and yet the fingers doing their slow glide up and down her pulsating sweet spot remained gentle.

She screamed his name brokenly, letting him control the way she touched herself because she couldn't do anything else as he pushed her to and beyond pleasure limits she'd never even approached.

"That's good." He bit her earlobe. "Real good."

But it was too much. She tried to stop the torment, her climax over, the aftershocks so intense she could not bear them. "Stop . . . please . . . Ty . . . no more."

He stilled and pressed his hand over hers, cupping her mound in a gesture that felt both possessive and protective.

Tears of release and overwhelming sensual joy trickled down her cheeks as she relaxed against him. He held her body to his in total intimacy. The moment was profound and she had no desire to talk. Her breathing eventually returned to a more normal pattern, her body's tension draining away, but he remained hard inside her.

"Are you ready to taste me now?"

Incredibly, she was. "Yes."

He lifted her off of him and she turned to face him. They were both kneeling.

He reached out and brushed her tears away. "Are you all right?"

She nodded. "That was amazing. *You are amazing*, my love."

"Was it better than what you've had before?"

She couldn't believe he needed to ask. "I've never known anything like it."

His eyes burned her with feral possession. "Good."

"Will you stand up for me?" she asked.

He didn't answer, but he crawled off the bed and stood beside it, his big body seeming even taller and wider than usual. She reached out with both hands and laid them against his hair-roughened pectorals. Man, he was built.

She leaned forward and kissed the very center of his chest. "You're a large man," she breathed against his sweat-slick skin.

She tugged his head down and started her tasting with his mouth, kissing him. She tried to pour the love she felt for him through her lips into his mouth, not ready to give vent to the words in intimacy. She moved on to taste the scratchy surface of his unshaven jaw.

He was salty and yummy and everything in between. Her mouth slid to first one ear and then across his face to the other, tasting as she went, before traveling down his neck.

"You taste special . . . like nothing else on earth."

He said nothing, but she hadn't expected him to. If it felt half as good for him as it had for her, he would be incapable of speech.

She moved down his body, licking the salty sweat from his chest and then gently biting the small hard nubs of his male nipples. She went around to his back and continued her tasting and touching journey, her breathing growing rapid again as her fingers traced the well-developed muscles of his back.

When she came around to the front and dropped to her knees, he made a keening sound that sent shivers between her legs.

She kissed his shaft, amazed at the size and heat of it.

"Take me in your mouth," he demanded.

"*Yes.*" She opened her lips wide and took him inside.

His hips surged forward and he hit the back of her throat. She tried not to gag, but he was big and she wasn't used to this. She pressed against his hips until he let her set the depth and pace. She could taste herself on him and she'd never done that before either. It was strange and yet very exciting, more intimate than anything she'd ever known.

Pre-ejaculate slid across her tongue and its salty sweetness surprised her too. She'd never liked giving head with the one lover she'd had, but she liked this.

She used to think she hated the taste of a man's come, but she wouldn't mind him exploding in her mouth.

Ty had other ideas. He pushed her head away and lifted her against the wall. She wrapped her legs around him and then moaned brokenly as he surged inside of her swollen and hypersensitive passage.

He made love to her more gently this time, his thrusts tender and measured, as if he was prolonging their pleasure. She couldn't believe his stamina, that not only hadn't he come yet, but that he could maintain the pace when another man would have passed out from exhaustion by now.

Not to mention the fact that he was holding her up like she weighed no more than a toddler, and at five foot eight, she was no child.

He stopped thrusting to step back and move toward the bed. "I need to be on top of you."

"Yes." She didn't know why, but that seemed right.

Perfect, even.

He managed to get them both on the bed without breaking their intimate connection as he came down on top of her, his body completely surrounding her.

Their lovemaking took on a surreal property as he coaxed her to more orgasms without taking his own pleasure. When he finally came, she was a limp, sweaty bundle of pulsing nerve endings under him.

He howled again, this time longer and louder than the last.

The sound brought answering whimpers of pleasure from her throat and she reached up to brush his throat where the sound vibrated against her fingertips.

She loved this. Loved him, probably more than he would ever know or accept.

Afterward, to her delight, they cuddled together on the bed and slipped into an exhausted sleep.

He woke her three more times to make love, once at sunrise.

She was so tired and sated that she allowed him to do everything that time, and found a peculiar pleasure in her exhaustion-based submission. He seemed to like it too, praising her body and her response to him with words she'd never thought to hear coming from his mouth.

She came awake later curled up under a single quilt and toasty warm. The other side of the bed was empty, but Ty's scent and the fragrance from their lovemaking lingered. He must have gotten up to stoke the fire in the stove. The bedroom was certainly warm enough.

Her gaze flicked to the window. She couldn't believe he'd had it open last night. The storm was gone and the position of the sun in the sky said it was past noon already. Not surprising, considering how they'd spent the hours of the night and early morning.

"Ty?" she called.

He came in through the bedroom door, his cock semi-erect, and she wondered if it ever shut off completely. "Awake?"

She nodded, not sure what to say in the cold light of day. Would he start going on about how last night had been a mistake?

She didn't know if she could stand it if he did. She'd told him she wanted him even if it was only sex, but what had happened last night and that morning had not been restricted to the realm of the physical. She'd let him so deep into her heart, she'd never get him out without losing part of her soul.

His nudity and growing arousal implied *mistake* wasn't the word on the edge of his lips at the moment, but even so, she waited in silence as he approached the bed.

He didn't give her a chance to talk once he got there either, as he made it very clear what he wanted from her and it wasn't a postmortem. His touch was tender and gentle, but every time she opened her mouth, he closed it with his lips or with his finger pressed against her lips.

He didn't want to talk.

She could deal with that. At least he wasn't saying goodbye.

She didn't know how long he caressed her body, but it felt like hours before he positioned himself over her.

She winced with slight pain when he took possession of her, but he didn't see it because his mouth was busy suckling a throbbing nipple. And she said nothing. She was enjoying their intimacy too much, despite the soreness that proved she'd never been made love to so completely and that it had been a very long time since she'd made love at all.

This time they came together, her climax feeding off his prolonged orgasm until she reached a level of pleasure that sent her into semi-oblivion. She was aware only peripherally of his final thrust and the howl she'd come to expect on his completion.

As he settled against her afterward, the words she'd tried so hard not to repeat the night before rasped out of vocal cords strained by screams of ecstasy. "I love you, Ty."

He went stiff and rolled off her in an unmistakable physical repudiation of the words. Her heart squeezed and she turned her head, needing to see something in his face that said he hadn't meant the movement the way it had felt.

All she saw was stony coldness.

"Ty?"

"So you love me."

"Yes."

"So much that when I refused to have sex with you yesterday you told me you didn't want to be my friend anymore."

"I'm sorry I hurt you. It's not like you're thinking. I was at the end of my emotional tether with you, Ty. I wasn't trying to manipulate you."

"Weren't you? Human women are good at that."

"As opposed to what, female *animals*?" she asked, her voice laced with sarcasm.

"As opposed to my kind," he said, a kind of impotent rage throbbing in his voice.

"*Your kind?* What are you talking about?"

He grimaced as if he hadn't meant to say what he had. "I'll explain after you tell me if this so-called love of yours is going to lead to marriage."

She scooted into a sitting position, dragging the quilt with her as a covering over nudity she wasn't comfortable sharing with him at the moment. The sunlight coming in through the window put his features in harsh relief and there was no comfort there for her hungry soul.

"It's not *so-called* love, it's real, Ty." So real, his attitude was shredding her.

"Then you'll marry me."

"Are you saying you *want* to marry me?" she asked, unable to believe he was offering her dearest hope with such emotionless detachment.

On top of that, after everything he'd said yesterday, the proposal—such as it was—didn't make any sense.

He sat up beside her and she had to stifle an urge to reach out and touch the beautifully molded muscles of his chest. He was so perfect.

He raised one knee and draped his arm over it, his casual pose at odds with the tension emanating off him. "I don't have a choice." His hand fisted in the sheet, his knuckles white with tension. "According to pack law, we are already mated. Until death do us part."

"Pack law?" She felt vaguely disoriented, as if she'd stepped into one of those rooms at the fair where everything seemed farther away than it really was. "I think you need to explain now. This isn't adding up for me."

"*First* tell me if you're going to marry me."

"Is that what you want?" she asked again.

"I told you, I don't have a choice."

Which was an answer, she supposed. For some reason, he believed he had to marry her, but he patently did not want to.

She turned her head away, unable to stand one more second of his icy regard. "I see."

"No, you don't. I want you to marry me, all right?" He sighed, the sound impatient. "I need to know if you were telling me the truth last night when you said you belonged to me."

She swallowed, focusing on the white snow against the bright blue Montana sky out the window. "I've always belonged to you."

"I guess you believe that right now."

She jerked her gaze back to him. "Why are you so cynical?"

"I stopped believing in fairy tales a long time ago."

"And marriage between us, love . . . it's all a big fairy tale in your mind?"

"No." He cupped her chin, his gaze burning through her. "It's very real. I need to know if it's real for you too."

"It's real."

"Then we get married."

"Just like that?"

"If you love me like you say you do, you'll marry me."

"And do you love me?"

"Will you refuse to marry me if I don't?"

She considered that. He wasn't acting very excited about the prospect of marriage between them, even though he said he wanted it. In fact, he was downright cranky, but this was Ty, her best friend for more than a decade and the man she'd loved almost as long.

His current attitude notwithstanding, she knew he cared about her. A lot. He'd been watching out for her for years, and usually they enjoyed each other's company more than anyone else's. He'd also proven beyond the shadow of a doubt last night that he desired her physically. But was that enough for marriage to work between them?

"I'm not sure. Before I can answer that, I have to understand why you *say* you want to marry me, but *act like* you'd rather ride an unbroken bronco sidesaddle."

He took a deep breath and let it out before settling more comfortably against the headboard. "To understand, you'll have to learn some things about me, things that very few outsiders know. I can't tell you any of it unless you promise me that no matter what you decide, you'll keep my family's secrets safe."

"I promise," she said without hesitation.

"I'm a werewolf."

She shook her head, feeling like she had marbles rolling around inside it instead of brains. Ty was the most practical man she'd ever known. No way had he just said what she thought. *"Come again?"*

"I'm a werewolf." He paused, glaring at her impatiently when she remained silent. "A lycanthrope . . . *a shape changer.*"

"I know what a werewolf is. They're the guys who get all hairy during a full moon and go on killing rampages in movies . . ." Oh, yuck. This *revelation* had all the makings of a nightmare she wanted to wake up from. "Ty, this isn't funny. You're no killer."

"No, I'm not, but I am a werewolf. Werewolves aren't the myths of folklore." His face twisted with distaste. "Though most of what the world believes about our kind is no better than that. We're human and yet we're not. The animal nature humans fight to suppress plays a bigger role in our makeup, but we don't lose our humanity because of it."

"So, it's just an inward thing?" She couldn't believe they were having this conversation.

Of all the relationship-defining talks she had imagined having with Ty McCanlup, his trying to convince her he was some kind of monster was not one of them. He didn't look or sound crazed, but his words were the kind of thing that got people locked up on the funny farm.

"No. It's much more than an inner delusion," he said, indicating he knew the direction of her thoughts.

And why shouldn't he? He knew her better than anyone else in the world. But if what he was saying was true, she didn't know him at all. "You can't be serious, Ty."

"I am. Very. Moonrise comes at four sixteen this afternoon and with it, I will shape change into a wolf, but inside I will still be me— with all my knowledge, all my thoughts, all my feelings. You will still belong to me."

She wasn't even sort of going there. She belonged to a wolf? Not likely. *"Today?"* she asked in a squeak as the significance of what he was telling her hit her.

"Yes."

"You're going to get all hairy?"

"I'll get more than hairy; I will take on the form of a wolf completely."

For some reason, an image of the wolf she had met as a teenager came to her, but she pushed it away. The situation was bizarre enough without her getting fanciful. She wanted to dismiss Ty's words as a bad joke, or maybe even temporary insanity, but he was too serious, too obviously convinced himself for her to do that. "You mean it, don't you? You really think you're going to turn into a wolf later this afternoon."

"I don't just think it, I know it."

She shook her head, unable to believe, despite his strong conviction.

He let out an impatient breath. "Do you remember the wolf that came to you when you were crying by the swimming hole when you were fifteen?"

A shiver skated up her spine. "Yes, but I told you about him. I suppose now you're going to claim that was you, or something."

"It was. It was the first time I kissed you."

"You didn't kiss me."

"Yes, I did."

And she remembered how he'd licked the salty tears from her face. She made a strangled sound in her throat, but nothing would come out.

"It was me."

"No." She felt tears welling in her eyes. Either he was serious and needed psychological help, or he was trying very hard to drive her away. Either way, it hurt.

"You never told me what you did after the wolf ran away."

No, she hadn't. No way would she have told him that.

"You took your clothes off and you went swimming. I watched from the trees. You were so beautiful and I wanted to join you so bad, but I couldn't control my change and I knew if I went back to you I would scare you."

"I . . ."

"But you didn't just go swimming . . . you came out of the water and you dried off in the sun. Then you closed your eyes and you touched yourself. . . . You said my name when you came." His eyes burned into her with an angry passion she didn't understand. "I wanted to howl with frustration, you were so beautiful, but I couldn't have you."

Embarrassed heat climbed her cheeks and she averted her face. He'd seen her, all right, because he couldn't have guessed that happened. He'd watched her pleasure herself just like last night, only that time she hadn't known she'd had an audience.

"You couldn't have heard me say your name," she said, trying to stick within the realm of reality. "No one was close enough."

"I was. Wolves have far superior hearing to humans. You know that."

Yes, she did, but in order to accept that he had heard her, she had to believe he had been the wolf and it was too fantastic. And yet nothing else made any sense.

"You never even noticed me back then."

"You're wrong."

"But you always flirted with the other girls."

"They were safe. I didn't want them . . . or they were fem-wolves."

"Female werewolves?"

"Yes. Don't look so shocked. As a vet, you know every animal species has to have two sexes to mate."

"But you mated with me last night . . . I mean had sex." She couldn't call it making love because he'd said nothing about loving her.

"Werewolves and humans can mate."

"Can they have babies?" Her scientific mind demanded to know.

"Sometimes. When it's a sacred bond."

"What's that?"

"The simplest answer is that it is a mating between two were-wolves or a werewolf and a human that results in offspring."

"Oh." She wanted to ask more questions about that, but something else he'd said took precedence. "You said it was your family's secret? Is this like a genetic mutation?"

"From what our scientists can tell, werewolves have existed as long as their single-form counterparts."

"Humans."

"Yes. We coexist, but our ways are different. Pack law takes precedence over human law."

She stared at him and an irrefutable knowledge settled inside her. He totally believed what he was saying, but even more than that, she believed him too. She'd suspected for years that there was something different about Ty's family, but she'd dismissed her thoughts as foolish fancy. She couldn't dismiss that sense of rightness about what he was saying now.

That encounter with the wolf . . . Ty . . . oh, gosh, she still couldn't believe it had been him . . . but the encounter had been real. She'd never doubted it and now she had to accept that the reason it had such an impact on her was because she'd met not a wolf, but a werewolf.

"You belong to a pack?" she asked in barely a whisper, her mind still trying to wrap around this new reality she faced.

"Yes. Dad is pack leader."

That didn't sound nearly as farfetched as it should. King was definitely a leader among men, why not werewolves?

Oh, man . . . lycanthropes in rural Montana. She shook her head, trying to clear it, but her thoughts swirled like a motorized merry-go-round. "If what you're saying is true, why didn't I know about it? We've been friends since I was twelve years old."

"We're good at keeping our secret. We've had millennia of practice."

"But I've been your *best* friend for fourteen years . . . wouldn't you have told me?" The thought he'd kept something so integral to his nature from her for so long made her wonder again how well she really knew him.

"Obviously I didn't, but I always half expected your aunt or uncle to."

"They know? Who told them?" If all this was real, then her family knowing while she didn't would hurt as much as the fact he'd withheld the information from her in the first place. And it did hurt. She felt betrayed even if she might have no right to that feeling. "And Marigold?"

"Yes, she knows." His lip curled derisively. "Too much."

"Why them and not me?" she asked with a catch in her voice she was powerless to suppress.

It seemed to bother him and he frowned, then pulled one of her cold hands between his, rubbing her knuckles absently. He'd comforted her this way many times over the years and she wondered if he was even aware of doing it now.

"Your aunt's great-grandmother was a femwolf, a female werewolf, but there have been no wolves born in the family for two generations."

"Aunt Rose is a werewolf, femwolf . . . whatever?"

"No, I told you—"

"Her family. Okay, I understand, I think, but I still don't . . . I mean . . . why never tell me?"

He sighed. "You didn't need to know. It didn't impact our friendship."

Hadn't it? It seemed to her like he'd withheld a pretty big part of himself. So had her aunt for that matter.

"If we did get married and had children, would they be puppies?" she asked on a sudden thought that frightened the life out of her.

"No, cubs don't go through their first change until puberty. In a wolf-human mating, there is no guarantee any of the offspring will be born wolf."

"Does that bother you?"

He cocked his head to the side, as if thinking about it for the first time. "No. I don't think it does. I'll love my kids regardless of what they are, but even if they are human, as long as they choose to belong to the pack and participate in its rituals, they are subject to pack law."

"That sounds scary," she said with a shiver.

"It can be." His tone was grim and she didn't doubt him.

"And if they choose not to belong to the pack?"

"Then they are subject only to human law, but they also forgo the protection of the pack."

"And if I marry you, will I belong to the pack?"

"That's not a decision I can make. My father would have to approve your joining the pack and you would have to want to, but I will always protect you, no matter what."

Remembering the cold way King had always treated her, she thought her chances of being approved as a pack member were pretty slim.

"Is your father going to be angry if we get married?"

"Yes."

Her heart contracted. "Oh."

"But he will accept the marriage."

She said nothing to that, not as convinced as Ty was that his dad would accept anything.

"Is the werewolf gene the recessive one?" she asked, not wanting to dwell on future problems while her mind was all but mush dealing with the ramifications of what Ty was telling her.

He shrugged. "It's more complicated than that, but werewolf science still hasn't figured out the whys of it all. All we do know is that if it was a totally recessive gene, out-of-kind matings would never result in wolf offspring and sometimes they do."

"Out-of-kind?"

"When one partner is nonwerewolf."

"You didn't want to mate with a human," she remembered. "I mean it was a big thing with you if you've been avoiding me since I was fifteen." A lot of stuff was starting to make sense. "Even yesterday, you told me you didn't want that with me."

"Oh, I wanted you."

"Your body did, but your mind didn't."

"Right."

"You always tell the truth, even when it hurts," she said with a pain-filled laugh.

"It's a wolf trait. We're good at hiding what we are, but not lying outright."

She nodded, her knowledge of animals making perfect sense of that remark. "My aunt told me you were interested in Olivia. . . ."

"She's our kind."

"You wanted to marry her?" she asked. All the signs pointed to that, but still she couldn't quite believe it. Not after last night.

"Yes."

She stared at him in disbelief. "You don't mean that."

"I do. Mating with Olivia would have been natural."

"Your father likes her, I guess."

"Yes, he does."

"Because she's your kind."

"Yes."

"But you didn't want her!" Pain and anger was ripping through her in a torrent of devastation. "And she didn't want you."

"I planned to change that."

"Only I got in the way." If learning he was a werewolf was overwhelming, discovering he had truly planned to marry—mate with—another woman was devastating.

This conversation had moved from the realm of unbelievable to the torturous.

"Yes."

The confirmation of her fear hurt. It also made her mad. Really, really mad. She hadn't been alone in that bed last night and he hadn't been thinking of Olivia when they made love. Had he? What if he'd had sex with her because she was handy . . . because Olivia was not?

She would not live her life as a substitute for anybody.

"Just because we had sex doesn't mean you can't marry her," she said scathingly, her fury making her feel violent. She wasn't about to beg for his affection. She shouldn't have to. "That kind of thing happens all the time."

He seemed to grow with an anger that easily matched hers. "*You're wrong.* That kind of thing doesn't happen in the werewolf world. Once we mate, it's for life—a byproduct of our animal nature and pack law. Unlike humans, we have no infidelity and there is no provision for divorce in our pack."

"Are you saying that *making love* is equivalent to *mating* for a werewolf . . . *to marriage?*"

"Yes."

"Oh, please."

His face creased in a fierce frown, his blue eyes dark with obvious displeasure at her skepticism.

She frowned back. "That would mean that every woman you'd had sex with would be your mate." No way could that be true, but then . . . "Hold on a minute, you don't have multiple mates do you?" If her question came out more hysterical than not, she could be forgiven.

No way was she joining a harem.

But wouldn't she have noticed if he lived like some kind of lycanthropic sultan? Then again, she hadn't even noticed he was a werewolf.

And furthermore, did her questions indicate she accepted all that he was saying as truth?

It seemed she did. As implausible as his story might sound, Ty had never lied to her, nor was he the delusional type. And then there was the wolf incident . . . the things he knew he could not have known if he hadn't been there, hadn't had the sharp hearing of a wolf. This was all real. Too real.

His hand gripped hers more tightly, as if an involuntary reaction to her words. "One mate, one mating," he said, each word spaced for hard emphasis.

"That would mean that last night you were a virgin!" She was back to practically shrieking.

He winced at the volume of her voice. "Yes."

"Impossible."

His frown turned to a smug, mocking smile. "Thank you. I'd hate to think I didn't live up to your ex-fiancé and other lovers."

"There were no other lovers besides him, but . . ." Her voice trailed off because she didn't know what else she wanted to say. "I'm finding all of this really hard to digest."

She would not admit that the part she found hardest to digest was his affection for Olivia. She could live with him being a werewolf—she thought—but she couldn't live with that.

"Considering how hard we work to hide our existence from humans, that's no surprise. You're having to replace a lifetime of myth with a very different reality regarding our kind." The anger seemed to have drained out of him, leaving him thoughtful. "What does surprise me is the fact you seem to believe me. I thought it would take witnessing my change for you to accept what I am."

She wasn't bringing up the incident when she was fifteen. His knowledge of her self-pleasuring while she daydreamed of him was way too embarrassing. She settled for saying, "You've never lied to me."

"No, I haven't."

Thinking of a couple of things he'd said to her the day before made her heart cramp in pain. He'd said, or at least implied, he didn't love her like a woman he wanted to marry. He'd also said any physical intimacy between them would be nothing more than sex.

She didn't want to face those revelations right now, but the pain refused to be dismissed in order to be dealt with when she was ready. It pulsed inside her in a steady, aching rhythm.

She pulled her hand from his grasp and scooted toward the edge of her side of the bed.

His eyes narrowed at her movement.

"If I marry you, you're stuck with me as your mate for the rest of our lives?"

"I told you, I'm already stuck. The minute I put my cock inside you, we were mated."

"That can't be." Though if sex equaled mating and mating equaled some kind of permanent werewolf marriage ritual, then he really was stuck with her.

No matter how either of them felt about that.

"So, even if I walk away . . ."

"I cannot take another mate."

"That's not fair."

"Fair isn't in the equation."

No, it wasn't. She either consigned herself to marriage to a man who didn't love her, or consigned the man she loved to lifelong celibacy. After last night and this morning, she didn't think he would thank her for that. "You should have warned me of the consequences. I had a right to know."

"You didn't give me the chance. I told you to leave. You wouldn't go." His voice was rough, like he was angry again, and the expression in his blue eyes had turned accusing.

But remembering how he had responded to her presence made her balk at accepting all the guilt for their current predicament. "You didn't want me to. Not really."

"Like hell."

Disbelief rolled through her. She'd never known Ty to shirk responsibility for his own actions like this. Okay, so maybe he didn't like the results, but that didn't mean he got to blame her for them.

"You didn't try very darn hard to get rid of me," she reminded him.

"I couldn't," he gritted out, sounding really disgusted with himself.

"I don't buy it. You are one of the most self-disciplined people I know."

"Every man has his limits. I reached mine."

"Right. I'm irresistible."

"Last night you were . . . to me."

His obstinate denial of any culpability for their time together added more pain to the cauldron boiling inside her. This was so not the way she'd thought the morning after would be conducted. "How can you be like this after what we shared?"

"You mean the sex? I suppose I should take comfort in the fact that my mate is a real firecracker in the sack. Not all humans can keep up with a werewolf, but you held your own last night. I'm surprised your ex-fiancé let you go so easily. Most men would kill for a response like yours."

She stared at him. The words were borderline insulting, but he sounded jealous, not mocking. Only *he* had nothing to be jealous of. She wasn't the one who had made love to him after only the day before having plans to marry someone else.

She curled her lip with derision at his obtuseness. "If I'd been able to give it to my ex, we would be married right now and last night would never have happened."

But she hadn't loved the other man. She loved Ty, even if he was too stupid to see it.

"Well, you're with me now," he said through gritted teeth. "I suppose I should feel honored there haven't been any other men since your ex-fiancé. You obviously like sex."

That was definitely an insult and it was one too many.

She punched him in the chest. Hard. But it was like hitting a rock.

Her hand stung and she rubbed it. "You *jerk*."

"Maybe . . . probably . . ." he admitted with an angry shake of his head. "But I'm *your* jerk."

"Oh, no. Olivia can have you. With my blessing." It wasn't a rational thing to say, not after what he'd told her about the permanency of mating, but she was so mad, she almost meant it.

Did she really care if this condescending idiot spent the rest of his life without sex? She would do the same with the rest of hers. *If* she walked away . . . But it would be a cold day in Hades before she admitted that to him.

"*Oh, yes,*" he growled. "You knew I wanted her, but you seduced me anyway. Now, you get me, Frankie. For a lifetime."

"You didn't want Olivia!" she yelled in frustration, totally unwilling to stomach that lie on top of his nasty attitude.

Maybe he hadn't wanted to mate with Frankie, but he didn't desire Olivia either. Not really. His head might say the femwolf would make a better mate, but his body had not been engaged. She refused to believe on top of everything else that she'd been a stand-in for another woman.

Her heart could not accept it and she was going to make him admit it. "You two fight like brother and sister."

"Not everyone courts with roses and poetry."

"Even the most unromantic guy in the world treats a woman he wants with more warmth than you treated her yesterday."

"You saw us together one time. You are hardly in a position to judge. You have no idea what we were like together when we were alone."

She wrapped her arms around herself, trying to control the mushroom cloud of pain imploding inside of her. "I can't argue that, but you still went to bed with me last night. Not her."

There *had to be* some significance to that fact.

"I wouldn't have, if you had stayed on the couch."

The words slashed through her with a finality that left no room for rosy dreams and hopeful fantasies, decimating her defenses with the power of a nuclear blast. One time, fourteen years ago, she'd felt this way. Like someone had reached inside her chest and ripped out her heart.

The day she was told of her parents' deaths.

She'd felt just as empty, just as bereft, and every bit as scared then as she did right now.

"I *was* just a stand-in. She wasn't here and I was," she whispered in agonized acceptance.

SIX

She rolled out of the bed onto her feet, dragging the quilt with her and wrapping it around her now-trembling, naked body.

She slapped at his hands when he tried to grab her. *"Don't touch me."*

"Frankie, come back here."

"No."

"We're not done talking."

"Yes, we are."

He got out of the bed, not bothered by his own nudity as he stood in front of her, glowering down at her. "You are my mate, not Olivia. No matter how it came about. It is now a fact."

"So, you're resigned to it? And I suppose you expect me to re-sign myself to marriage with a man who's pining after another woman? *You think I should be okay with you using my body while you think of her?"*

"It wasn't like that!"

Her eyes burned with tears she'd be darned if she shed in front of him. "You just got through saying it was."

"I did not. I would never do that to you." He rubbed his hand over his face, frustration lining his chiseled features. "Look, you're right. The chemistry wasn't there between Olivia and me. She didn't want me any more than I wanted her. I realized that yesterday. I shouldn't have implied there was more to our relationship than what you saw. I was being a prick and I'm sorry."

He sounded more furious than apologetic, and was his explanation supposed to make Frankie feel better?

It didn't. It just gave her another possible reason for his making love to her that was extremely painful. Had the other woman's rejection caused him to accept Frankie's sensual overtures? Had he made love to her in order to assuage his hurt pride at realizing Olivia didn't want him?

Her mind was spinning with one scenario after another, all of them awful.

"What was last night?" she asked in a desperate bid to understand how something so beautiful could have ended in this sense of ugly desolation.

"It was our mating."

But what had it meant to him besides what pack law stated it meant?

"Why did you make love to me like that . . ." Like he could never get enough, like she was ambrosia to his soul. "So many times . . . if you didn't want me?"

"I couldn't help myself." He said it so flatly she couldn't argue.

True or not, he believed she had seduced him, believed she was at fault for them having sex.

Wasn't she? a voice inside her head whispered. Hadn't she chosen to make love, not caring what the future held? She'd known he hadn't wanted a future with her and she had wanted him anyway.

"I don't know what to do." All she knew was that she hurt. Everywhere. Both inside and out. She could barely walk, her thigh muscles were so sore. "I need some time to myself. To think."

"Come back to bed and think with me."

Was he serious?

She looked down his body and almost choked on her outrage. "You're excited."

"That surprises you after last night and today?"

"You just got through telling me that I'm the last woman in the world you would have chosen for a mate and you expect me to welcome you into my body?" she asked in angry amazement.

Was he crazy?

"I didn't say you were the last woman in the world I wanted. And you can blame this," he indicated his hard-on, "on the fact it's our first mating and the approaching full moon. My animal instincts are in the fore right now."

"There's a full moon every month and if what you told me is true, you've never succumbed to it in this way before."

"No, I haven't." He looked like he expected that to mean something to her and reached for her.

She backed up toward the bathroom. "Forget it."

He frowned. "Damn it, Frankie."

She glared. "You can stop swearing at me *wolf-man*! I hurt and you can at least take all the credit for that, since you want me to take all the blame for us having sex. I need a very long, very hot bath. I don't suppose you lit the water heater?"

"Early this morning. The water should be hot by now." He had the grace to look consternated. "Are you sore?"

She turned toward the bathroom. "Yes."

"I'm sorry."

"Aren't we both?" The pain in her heart was a lot worse than the ache between her legs.

"I could join you."

The man was pure Neanderthal, and brain-dead in the emotional department too. "I want you in my bath like I want a root canal right now."

"Are you sure about that?" Oh, man, even feeling the way she did, that voice was an invitation to decadence.

Nevertheless, she turned to face him again, about falling on her backside when she realized how close he'd come without making a sound. "Positive. While I'm sure your precious femwolf, Olivia, would have withstood a night like last night without the slightest discomfort, I'm just a lowly human and my whole body hurts."

He cupped her shoulders and rubbed her neck muscles with his thumbs. "I could give you a massage."

She shrugged him away, unwilling to accept anything from him right then, even comfort. "You can keep your hands to yourself. If you wanted postcoitus lovey-dovey, you shouldn't have been so quick to point out I'm everything you don't want in a mate. Believe it or not, that kind of talk has a very dampening effect on a woman's affectionate nature. I'm sore and I'm angry and I'm taking my bath *alone*."

He stepped back, his expression going blank. "Fine."

But it wasn't fine and she wasn't sure how it ever could be. She reached the sanctuary of the bathroom, then slammed and locked the door.

How could she have believed one night of ecstasy would be worth this kind of pain the next day? But then she hadn't expected things to turn out like this . . . for them to be stuck together in a lifelong mating he didn't want and blamed her for.

No, she never would have expected that outcome in her wildest imaginings.

Ty paced the outer room, his beast fighting with his man. Damn it. He'd hurt her. He hadn't meant to. He should never have made love to a human this close to his change.

His unruly body still wanted her, and it was taking all his self-control to stay out of the bathroom where the water conspicuously was not running. Was she in there crying? He couldn't hear any sniffling, but Frankie had always cried silently.

He wanted to comfort her, but she didn't want him anywhere near her. She'd made that clear. And he couldn't blame her. He'd given her none of the soft words and tenderness a woman expected after the kind of lovemaking they had shared.

But he'd woken that morning hard, aching for her and furious at how easily she had circumvented his will.

His lack of control the night before had lacerated his pride far more than the realization that Olivia would run alone, rather than with the pack to avoid mating with him in the fur. She'd realized his intention and acted to deny it. Or she'd simply wanted to avoid any mating that would have been damn hard with so many wolves in the pack still single and her in heat. She knew as well as he did that her instincts would have been to seek out a mate herself.

The fact he had planned to be that mate, even if it meant fighting another wolf for her was now a moot point. And right now, Olivia's actions and motivations were the last thing he needed to worry about.

He'd been unable to restrain his desire for Frankie and would spend the rest of his life mated to a human—the one thing he'd been determined not to do. The wolf in him did not take defeat well. He reacted like any predatory animal when challenged, he struck out.

The soreness between her legs wasn't the only pain he'd given her, and his beast was actually glad he had drawn emotional blood. It needed recompense for his defeat, but the man inside him felt like the jerk she'd called him. He'd hurt one of the most treasured people in his life and he hated knowing that.

He was furious with himself and the beast in him that had prompted sexual demands that left Frankie's body sore, and words that had hurt her.

He was such a prick.

But he wasn't entirely sure he really was *her* jerk like she'd claimed.

She'd said she was his last night, but she hadn't been acting like his this morning. And yesterday she'd told him she didn't want to be his friend anymore. She'd been prepared to cut him out of her life. *Just like a human.* He couldn't help but notice she hadn't said she would marry him either.

She could walk away, but he couldn't.

That made him feel helpless, which in turn infuriated him. A furious werewolf on the verge of the change was not the best companion for a tenderhearted woman who was soaking away the pain of an overzealous mating.

According to his father, it was always like that the first time. Ty had never known anything approaching the pleasure of being inside his mate, and if he didn't get away from here and her scent that permeated the cabin, he was going to go seeking that pleasure again.

It was less than an hour until the full moon. He had to go, for her sake as well as his own. She'd be okay until he could send rescue. There was plenty of wood and food in the pantry.

As he moved toward the bathroom door, the water started to run finally. He waited until it turned off again and then knocked.

"What?" She sounded surly.

Once again he wished he could fix it and make her okay with everything. He hated being at odds with his best friend, but he was more likely to make everything worse if he tried to talk to her again in his present state. His wolf wasn't ready to tuck tail and submit to a destiny he hadn't chosen with the grace she needed.

Better to get out and away from her until he was.

"I'm leaving. I'll send help as soon as I can, but it'll probably be moonset before I can talk to anyone. Don't get worried. Just sit tight, all right?"

The bath splashed like half the water was sloshing onto the tiny bathroom's floor and then the door was yanked open. "What?"

He turned away from the view of her naked body and the justified accusation in her gray eyes. "I'm leaving."

"You can't. It's below freezing out there."

"I'll be fine."

"You aren't superhuman."

"I'm a werewolf."

"But you're not a wolf right now."

"I will be soon enough. You don't have to worry about me." It shocked him that after all that had happened, all that he'd said, she was still afraid for him.

He wanted to kiss her, but didn't trust himself to keep it to a simple kiss. Even though this lack of control over his libido was to be expected right after mating, and was something most werewolves reveled in, right now he found it a total pain in the ass.

He turned to leave.

"Ty!"

He ignored her and walked out of the cabin, glad her naked state would stop her from following him.

She was smart enough to stay inside.

He hoped.

Just in case, he hung around the cabin, watching for a good half hour, but the front door didn't open and he had to figure she'd stuck with her plan to take a long, hot bath.

Frankie watched Ty walk out of the cabin with a sense of disbelief that paralyzed her.

As the door shut she accepted that he really was simply going to leave her there, by herself, to wait for rescue. The pain inside of her exploded in a blast of anger so intense, she shook with it. He'd always been so darn pigheaded and arrogant, so sure he knew what was right for her.

"Ty McCanlup, you are going to hear about this," she promised the empty cabin in a deadly voice he would have shuddered to hear.

Because he would have known exactly what that voice meant . . . just how angry she really was. And why would he know it? Because he was her best friend, darn it! And she was his, even if he hadn't seen fit to tell her he was a werewolf.

She could still hardly take that fact in, but no one except a totally insane person would have walked out the cabin door in this weather unless he was, well, a werewolf.

For some reason that acknowledgment cut through both her anger and her pain. Ty was a werewolf, and that meant his responses, his motivations, his feelings were going to be different from those of a simple human. Didn't it?

She started thinking like a woman smart enough to get a degree in veterinary medicine. Looking back over the last day and a half, she remembered more than just his rejections. What about the kisses he'd given her of his own volition, the day before? The kiss at his house had not been sparked by Olivia's rejection, because he hadn't been rejected yet.

He'd been acting possessive.

What did that mean? Male wolves were possessive of their mates, but they hadn't been mated yet. Which meant what? That he'd had those kinds of emotions engaged already? After all, he was more than a wolf, he was a man too.

Capable of feeling things a pure wolf would only know on an instinctual level.

Ty said he had wanted to marry Olivia, but he didn't really *want* her . . . not like a man should want the woman he planned to spend the rest of his life with. He wanted Frankie that way. No chance was hurt pride a strong enough motivator for the kind of lovemaking they had shared. As relatively inexperienced as she was, she still knew that.

And their lovemaking had not been mere animal sex. She had felt too much, and so had he. She was fairly certain that his humanity had been fully engaged even if he wanted to blame his wolf's instincts. He'd wanted her with the kind of passion a man *in love* exhibited. Certainly not a platonic friend, a big brother type or even a casual lover.

He'd marked her, inside and out.

He couldn't have gone that deep into her soul without letting her into his at least a little way too.

He might think he had. He might have convinced himself what they'd shared was nothing more than sex, but the way he'd cuddled her close to his body when they were sleeping was not about nooky. It was about tenderness, and an intimacy that had nothing to do with putting tab A into slot B.

So, why was he so determined to deny the depth of their feelings for each other? Why did he doubt her love for him?

She thought back over their argument, or conversation—whatever it was. He'd gotten really squirrelly every time the subject of her ex-fiancé had come up. Come to think of it, he had been the one to bring the other man into the conversation, along with her other supposed lovers.

Why had he gone off on that whole tangent? She'd sure never given him any reason to believe she had other lovers. If she didn't know better, she'd think he was jealous. And why not? He'd been a virgin—one mating, one mate. It probably chafed him big-time she'd shared her body with someone else before him.

Well, he'd have to get over that if he expected her to go through with this mating-marriage thing.

She had a hard time believing that was the only thing that had him so uptight about what had happened between them though.

He had a real thing about being mated to a human, but it couldn't be because it was a total taboo, or her aunt's great-grandmother—or whoever it was—could not have mated a human.

One thing was for sure . . . Ty had a lot of explaining to do when she saw him next. And she was not going to let her fear of him not loving her cloud her ability to reason and process data again.

She stepped into steaming water that filled the old-fashioned claw-footed tub and sighed with pleasure as she sank up to her chin.

Ty was stubborn, but she could be stubborn too, and she knew his weakness: her. Despite his rendition of Jerk Male of the Year just now, he hated to hurt her or see her hurt in any way. That, combined with the way he'd made love to her, spoke of feelings a lot deeper than friendship.

She soaked in the bath, refilling the hot water twice, until her fingertips were wrinkly and the lingering aches in her body were gone. She got out and dried off, still a little tender inside, but she couldn't do anything about that. She wasn't sure she wanted to.

As frustrated as she was with Ty, she nevertheless experienced a primitive satisfaction at having her body so blatantly impacted by his. It was like the scent she'd woken to that morning. His fragrance on her body. She didn't remember that from mornings after with her ex-fiancé.

Maybe it was because Ty was a werewolf. Or maybe it was just because she loved him and was more attuned to him than she'd ever been to anyone else.

Then a thought struck her and her hands stopped in their task of drying herself off. She stood in stunned disbelief for several seconds as something that should have concerned her a great deal the night before finally registered.

The reason Ty's scent had been so strong on her that morning was because they hadn't used condoms when making love. And since her last sexual relationship, her only sexual relationship—no matter what her foolishly jealous lover thought—had ended over two years ago, she wasn't on the pill.

Doing some quick mental calculations, she realized she was at the optimum time to get pregnant.

She sat down on the side of the tub as her legs gave out. That was all she needed, to be pregnant on top of everything else. Not that the idea of having Ty's baby was all that repellent, but right now she couldn't decide if she loved him or wanted to kill him.

That was not the kind of dichotomy of feelings a woman should have for the father of her child.

She spent the rest of the afternoon and evening vacillating between hope and terror at the prospect of being pregnant. She couldn't believe Ty had left her by herself, but then if he was close to the change maybe he didn't want her to see it.

Maybe it was really gross.

The thought was less than comforting.

She found a deck of cards in a drawer in the kitchen and played several games of solitaire before going to bed early. Rescue would not be coming tonight and she was still pretty exhausted from her long session of lovemaking with Ty.

The brown wolf stood outside the cabin, sniffing the air. He could smell her. So close. He wanted to see her. No lights were on, but then he hadn't expected there to be. The position of the moon said it was well past midnight.

He'd run with the pack, enjoying their companionship, but he couldn't stay away from her. She was his mate. It was his job to make sure she was safe. Protected.

He edged toward the window of the bedroom, his silent stealth as much a part of his wolf nature as his instinct to hunt. Once he reached it, he lifted his forepaws to the sill so he could look inside.

His wolf vision could make her out clearly under the quilts. She was curled around the pillow he'd used the night before, her silky brown hair spread across her own pillow.

He wanted to be in there with her.

Needed it.

He had to touch his mate. It was the first time he had ever wanted *inside* a building during the full moon, but the urge was irresistible. He scratched at the window with his claws.

* * *

Frankie woke feeling disoriented. Where was she? There were no branches outside her bedroom window, but something was scratching on it. Then she remembered. She wasn't home in her small apartment in Billings. She was stranded in a cabin out in the middle of nowhere . . . a cabin that also had no nearby trees.

She looked toward the window and screamed.

Monstrous, gleaming eyes and glowing white and sharp canine teeth in a big hairy head were illuminated by the moonlight reflecting off the snow outside. The head disappeared at the same moment she registered what the monster was.

A wolf.

Her heart beat very fast and she tried to breathe, but her lungs weren't cooperating.

Was it Ty? It could be another werewolf. According to him, there was an entire pack in the area. How big was a pack? Was it like wolf packs that could vary in size from two to thirty, or did werewolves have even bigger packs?

It could be a regular wolf too.

Oh, man . . . was the door locked? She thought so, but couldn't remember. She hadn't thought of any reason to lock it. After all, who was going to come by? She couldn't picture a marauding rapist tramping to the cabin in snowshoes.

There was a scratching sound at the front door and then the unmistakable sound of it opening.

She trembled, unsure what to do. If she got up and tried to shut the bedroom door, the wolf would reach her before she got to it. She could run for the bathroom, but again, she didn't think she could reach it in time. But she couldn't just stay there like a dolt, waiting to get eaten.

Wolves were hungry in the winter.

The door shut and her heart leapt into her throat, but then reason asserted itself. Would a wild wolf really take the time to shut the door? For that matter, wouldn't he already be in here, ripping into her throat?

Yuck. Icky imagery. Reminder to self: Do not think so much like a vet in the future.

The wolf came to the doorway and stood there, just looking at her. It was a dark color, she thought brown, but although the moonlight was bright, it was dimmer than the sun, or a lantern.

She swallowed. "T-Ty?"

The wolf barked once, but didn't move.

"Am I safe with you?"

He stepped into the room. Oh, gosh . . . he was big. Huge. Bigger than any wolf she'd ever seen.

He moved regally, but slowly, like he was afraid of spooking her. His canine head nodded up and down and she realized he was answering her question.

She was safe.

She let out the breath she'd been holding.

"Can I light the lamp?"

He barked once. She took that as a yes and gingerly climbed out of the bed. He didn't move, but his eyes followed her. Once the lamp was lit, she placed it on the tall dresser, illuminating a fair portion of the room.

He was brown, his coat sleek, but his eyes were Ty's . . . gentian blue. Beautiful.

It was her wolf . . . the wolf from that hot summer day when she was fifteen, and in its eyes she saw the man she had loved since then.

seven

She licked her lips. "You're gorgeous."

He padded forward until his head butted up against her torso. Even after his assurances, standing this close to such a large beast was terrifying. She hadn't been afraid when she was a teen, but then she'd been younger . . . hadn't studied wolves and their habits so thoroughly.

Now she knew just what one this size was capable of.

He nuzzled against her chest and whined.

Oh, wow.

She tentatively reached around and patted him, then buried her hand in the fur of his neck. He turned his head and licked her wrist. Tears filled her eyes. She didn't know why, just that she was moved unbearably by her wolf's presence in the house . . . his desire to be with her.

She leaned down and kissed his muzzle. He licked her face, his tongue warm and gentle.

She smiled. "I wish you could talk right now."

I do too. The voice was in her head, but it was Ty's voice. No doubt about it.

"Ty?"

He looked at her, his eyes questioning.

"I know this is going to sound crazy, but did you just talk in my head?"

You heard me?

"Yes." The tears spilled over. "This is so strange, but special too. Can all mates hear each other?"

No.

"Why can I hear you?"

Because you are meant to.

She laughed at that.

It's hot in here.

"If you wear a fur coat inside, what can you expect?"

A rumble sounded in his throat, almost like a laugh.

"Do you want me to open a window?" His wolf instincts would probably like the sense of easy escape that would give as well as the drop in room temperature it would bring.

He barked once.

She went over and did as she'd offered, opening it wide and letting in freezing air that made her lungs tight.

She scooted over to the door and shut it as well as the one to the bathroom, so the rest of the cabin's temperature wouldn't drop significantly. Her entire body was shivering by the time she reached the bed. She dove under the quilts and shook, despite their added warmth.

You are cold.

"A little."

I can keep you warm. He waited, as if he needed her permission to get close.

"Okay," she said softly.

He bounded onto the bed, his move powerful, but graceful. He lay down beside her. *Cuddle up to me.*

She did, sighing with pleasure as heat emanated from his body to her immediately. "This is nice."

He licked the side of her face. *Yes, it is.*

The sound of barking outside the cabin startled her and once again, her body jolted into fight-or-flight mode.

Don't be afraid, my mate. It's only my parents and Duke.

"Do they know about us?"

I told Duke. He must have told Dad and he would have told Mom, no question.

"Are they angry?"

I don't know. I can't talk with my parents in wolf form.

"But Duke can?"

Only with Dad.

"This is all pretty confusing."

I'll explain it all to you.

A large silver wolf's head appeared in the window, his forepaws on the sill.

She moved closer to Ty, fear a metallic taste in her mouth.

Duke told me to tell you to relax. He's already hunted and he's not hungry anymore.

"Thanks a lot. That's not all that funny."

The wolf in the window growled at her and she turned her face into Ty's fur.

He's just cranky. The growl meant nothing.

She lifted her head and glared at her future brother-in-law. "Stop trying to scare me, or I'm going to shoot you with a tranquilizer gun on the next full moon and dose you for worms."

That strange rumbling sound vibrated in Ty's throat again and Duke barked in obvious censure before disappearing out of the window.

"He's so surly."

He has reason.

"What did Marigold do?"

I'll tell you later. First, tell me how you're feeling.

"Nice and snuggly with you beside me."

I meant from our lovemaking. You were sore.

She blushed at the reminder and hid her face against his fur. She liked the feeling of the soft pelt against her skin and she nuzzled him. "I'm better."

An almost purring sound rumbled in his chest. *Good. Moonset is in less than four hours.*

"Is that when you return to your human form?"

Yes.

"And you want to make love?" She wasn't sure how she felt about that, but she wasn't as averse to the idea as she'd been right after their talk anyway.

Very much. I missed out on the kill in our hunt because I kept thinking about it . . . about you. I wanted . . . needed to be with you.

He talked about making a kill like it was so natural and for him it would be, she supposed. But was that so different from the men she'd known growing up who went hunting every season and weren't happy unless they came home with a deer or elk for their trouble?

Her own uncle had gone camping with his friends every year and brought home more than one trophy. But for wolves, hunting was also a way of establishing a wolf's role amid his peers. It was more than sport, it was necessity, and Ty had missed out on the most important part—for her.

"Funny, that doesn't sound like it's just sex for you. Not unless you're no more controlled than a horny adolescent."

He growled, the sound rumbling through his huge wolf's body and she grinned, but he couldn't see it because she was still nuzzling him with her face.

She yawned, the adrenaline rush draining from her body, leaving her exhausted. Now that Ty was back, she felt safe and her sleep up to now had been fitful.

Sleep. I will stay with you.

"Will you be here when I wake up?"

Yes. Duke is taking care of the truck and they'll come for us later today.

"Will you wake me up so I can watch you change?"

You want to see it?

"Of course." She leaned back so she could look in his animal-human eyes. "You can't seriously think I would want to miss it."

It's not anything special to watch. It just happens.

She shook her head. "Your view of interesting and mine don't match, obviously."

Okay. I'll wake you.

"Promise?"

Yes.

She snuggled down beside him. "Is it gross?"

No.

"Good."

You'd want to watch just the same, though, wouldn't you?

"What do you think? I'm a vet, just like you . . . gross is part of our job."

He nuzzled her and it felt really nice.

"You came back just to be with me?"

Yes.

"That's nice."

You are my mate. It is my duty to protect you.

She yawned again, cuddling in closer. "Stop trying to be such a hard-ass. I don't understand all that's going on here, but you could have watched over me from outside the cabin. And last night you made love to me like you meant it. Those facts say something about your feelings for me, even if you're too stupid or obstinate to see it. Or both."

He made a sound of frustration but it was drowned out by the eeriest growling she had ever heard.

She sat bolt upright and looked toward the window again. Another wolf was there. This one even bigger than Ty and he looked mean. His eyes had that same human quality as her lover's, but they were filled with a repudiation she had never seen in Ty's.

He bounded off the bed, putting himself between her and the window. He growled in unmistakable warning at the other wolf.

The wolf barked back and then bared his fangs.

"What's happening, Ty?" she demanded in a voice she couldn't quite keep steady.

My pack leader is not happy with our mating.

"You said he'd have to accept it. That there was no other option."

There isn't. But the words didn't ring true. They sounded desperate.

King barked viciously and she flinched beneath the quilt. "Don't lie to me, not even to protect me. I have a right to know what is happening. He looks like he'd like to rip my throat out."

King's attention shifted from Ty to her and his huge wolf's head nodded. He disappeared from the window and she sat in paralyzed fear, not understanding what that meant. A second later, the unmistakable sound of the front door opening could be heard and then King walked into the bedroom.

His naked human body gleamed pale in the moonlight.

Ty growled again, moving with blurring speed to position himself between them again, his muscles coiled to spring.

King ignored his son and his own nakedness, locking his attention solely on her. "Pack law states that until you die, my son is mated."

"So you want to kill me?" she asked, her body trembling with the implication of the big man's words.

"You trapped my son into a mating he did not want."

Ty barked and it sounded like he was disagreeing, but she couldn't know for sure.

"I didn't know," was all she could think to say.

Suddenly another wolf jumped in through the window, landing only a couple of feet from Ty and she screamed. She shoved her fist in her mouth to stop another sound from emerging as she recognized Duke, but that recognition gave her no comfort. Was he here to help his father get rid of the unwanted complication in Ty's life?

"He told you to leave him alone," King accused.

"He made love to me like he would never get enough," she responded, knowing only the unvarnished truth had a hope of saving her now.

Ty couldn't win against both of them.

"If you touch her I will leave this pack and never come back," a feminine voice sounded from the doorway.

Ty's mother was here—in human form—as well.

King spun to face her. "What the hell are you saying?"

"I watched you mete out pack justice on your best friend, a man you loved like a brother, because he broke pack law. I hated it. . . . I hated you for a while after you did it, but I understood the justice. It's been our way of life for millennia. But what you are proposing isn't justice, it's murder—and you will have to go through both your son and me to commit it."

"She tricked him into the mating; that has to be answered for."

"He withheld the truth from her even though she loved him. What did you expect, King? She needs him as much as I've always needed you. They made love. How that happened isn't as important as the fact that it did. They're mated and you have no right to undo that mating just because it angers you."

"She's a human."

"So is part of you, as much as you'd like to forget that."

Suddenly, Frankie realized that by staying in the bed, cowering, she was feeding the bad opinion King had of her. So, she stood up, but Ty wouldn't let her go near King.

She looked at him, her own eyes filled with a love she wasn't sure he would ever accept. "I'm not afraid of your father."

You should be. My mom's not exaggerating. He killed his best friend for breaking pack law.

"You saw it?" she asked.

Yes.

"You can hear my son in your head?" Carolyn asked.

Frankie looked at her. "Yes. He said mates could do that sometimes."

"Sacred mates, yes." She turned to her husband. "She could be pregnant with your grandchild right now. You will not hurt her."

King glared at Frankie. "Carolyn believes you love Ty."

"I do."

"I won't kill my own son for breaking pack law if you walk away and he can't stand the loneliness. I'll kill you first."

The words were meant to frighten, but they didn't scare her at all. "I'm not the one who's been running from a relationship between the two of us for the last decade."

King said nothing. He simply turned and walked away.

Carolyn smiled at Frankie. "Welcome to the family. Rose and I will so enjoy planning the wedding, and don't you worry about King. He'll soften up when the grandbabies come along."

Frankie didn't know what else to say, so she said, "Uh . . . thank you."

Then Carolyn was gone too.

She turned to Duke. "Do you want to kill me too?"

He shook his wolf's head, said something to his brother she thought by the way Ty's body clenched and then disappeared through the window.

She shivered and without her realizing how he got there, Ty was nudging at her back, pushing her toward the bed. *You need to get back under the covers. You still need to sleep.*

"I don't think I can after the adrenaline rush I just got. Your family certainly has an interesting way of welcoming a person into it."

Ty made that wolf sound that emulated humor again and climbed up onto the bed with her, so he could cuddle her like before. *You're safe now. You may not have realized it, but my dad actually put his seal of approval on the mating.*

"Is that what that was?" she asked, tongue in cheek, her heart rate finally slowing down a bit.

Yes. And Duke never intended to hurt you. He was here to fight by my side if I needed it.

"He would have fought your father with you?"

Yes.

"But he doesn't like me any more than King does now."

He likes you well enough.

She snorted.

He nuzzled her. *No more talking. Sleep, sweetheart, you're going to need it come moonset.*

Remembering what he wanted to do when he returned to his human form, she thought he might be right and did her very best.

Ty lay beside his sleeping mate, savoring the feel of her warm body against his fur, her scent and the sound she made when she breathed. She was fully human and yet she intrigued his wolf's senses like no femwolf ever had.

She also challenged him in a way few females of his species had the courage to do. She'd called him both obstinate and stupid and he had to wonder if she wasn't right. He had refused to acknowledge his feelings before because of his determination not to mate with a human, but there didn't seem to be much use in hiding from the truth any longer.

He loved Frankie.

He always had and God help him, he always would. She was more than his sacred mate, though that was miraculous enough. She was the mate of his heart and he never could have gone through with mating with Olivia in the fur because of it.

He could only hope that Frankie's ability to stick it out for the long haul was greater with him than it had been with her ex-fiancé.

He waited until just before the change to wake her up.

She came alert instantly and sat up to watch with the attention she'd always given her studies.

He felt the change overtake him, and he knew what she was seeing. Nothing. One minute he would be a wolf and the next a man. The change could take longer, he could even stop partway through now that he had control of it, now that he was mated. But right now was not a time to play with his new control over his dual nature.

She gasped as he took his human form and then screeched in shock when he reached and grabbed her to him.

He'd been aching to touch her like this all night.

"How do you feel?" he asked, barely in control of his primal urges.

She smiled, her eyes filled with a warmth that melted the icy places inside him. "Like I want you."

He was careful to arouse her before taking her. So careful that she was begging for his possession by the time he gave it to her. They came together again, the miracle of their shared pleasure rolling through him with a powerful force he no longer had any desire to deny.

This time, she let him bathe with her and they were both very clean and very sated when they got out of the claw-footed tub.

She was frying corned-beef hash while he opened a can of peaches for breakfast when she asked, "So, what did Marigold do that made Leah leave town and Duke hate her like poison?"

He didn't like having to tell her about her cousin's behavior, but he'd promised. "You know a werewolf only mates once, right?"

"That's what you said yesterday, but your dad implied that if a mate dies, the survivor could mate again."

"That's true, but once mated, it's for life."

"I got that part."

"Well, the closer to the change we are, the more in control our wolves become."

"That makes sense I guess."

"A wolf's first instinct is to mate and procreate."

"Well, you all certainly don't give in to it if you're anything to go by."

"No, we don't. We know that the decision is irrevocable, so we're careful to make the right one."

"I see."

"But we have a time limit. At least our breed does."

Breed? Oh, wow . . . there was so much she was going to have to get used to with all this. "What do you mean?"

"If a male of my breed doesn't mate by the age of thirty, he'll never control his change."

"What about the females?"

"Things are a little different for them. Mating any time gives femwolves control of the change after the age of twenty."

"There are no limits on time for them?"

"No."

"That seems really strange."

He shrugged. "It's just the way God made our breed."

"Okay . . . get back to Duke."

"Marigold knows all of this and she also knows that the scent of an ovulating female will put a werewolf into a lustful frenzy. His need to mate will become all but uncontrollable."

Frankie spun to face him, her expression horrified. "What do you mean?"

"It's pretty simple. A male werewolf stuck in close confines with an unmated ovulating female will try to mate. His only hope is for her to say no, but even then . . . it's iffy. We're careful to stay out of that kind of situation when we can."

"You mean an ovulating femwolf, right?"

"Or human."

She paled. "And Marigold . . ."

"Got Duke in a room alone close to his change and at the right time of month for her. To add incentive, she was stark naked."

"He mated her?"

"No, but it was damn close and his hand was between her legs when Leah walked in on them."

"Oh, my gosh. No wonder she left!"

"She didn't understand."

"Does she know about him being a werewolf?"

"Yes, but I don't think she knows about the other."

"The whole overpowering urge to screw a single female who is ovulating thing?"

"Right."

"Poor Leah."

"Poor Duke. He managed to turn Marigold away, but it was too late to fix things with Leah. And he'll be thirty in a few months."

"If Leah doesn't come back . . . he'll be unmated then?"

"Yes."

"Because he'd rather have her than control of the change?"

"Yes."

"He must really love her."

"I think he does, though the way he talks now, he can't stand her."

Frankie turned back to the stove, the set of her shoulders tense. Marigold's antics must really have upset her. A betraying sniff told him she was crying and he was across the room in a heartbeat.

He turned off the stove and pulled her around to face him. "What's the matter? Is it what Marigold did?"

Frankie shook her head, her face a mask of tragedy. "It's what I did," she said in a pain-filled voice.

"What you did?"

"I raped you . . . or as good as."

"What?"

"I was ovulating . . . in heat. I'm a vet. I know what kind of effect a female in heat has on the male of her species. You were close to your change . . . your wolf instincts were in control. You told me to go, but I wouldn't listen. I thought it meant you wanted me despite what you'd said, but now I know the truth. I might as well have held a gun to your head and forced you to have sex with me." She tore herself from his arms and ran to the bathroom, where she slammed and locked the door.

He raced after her, unable to fathom the workings of the female mind. He pounded on the door. "Open up, Frankie."

She didn't answer, but he could hear her hiccupping sobs from behind the door.

"We've got to talk, Little Bit. You took me wrong."

His words were met with nothing but the sound of her grief.

Shit. He had screwed up so badly, he should be a professional at it. He had to get to his mate. He couldn't stand the sound of her tears.

"Step away from the door, Little Bit."

His superior hearing could discern no movement on the other side of the door, but then there was a bump and sliding sound.

She was sitting against the door on the floor.

Now, what was he supposed to do? He couldn't knock down the door with her on the other side. Then he remembered the other one. The bathroom opened to both the bedroom and the living area.

He went quietly into the bedroom and approached the door. He tried the handle, but she'd locked it too. "Are you still against the door, Frankie?"

She didn't answer, but he put his ear to the wood and could hear no heartbeat on the other side.

He kicked, one swift hit against the handle and the door swung inward. She was sitting on the floor, huddled up in a little ball and sobbing as if her heart were broken.

It probably was and it was his fault.

He joined her on the floor, pulling her into his lap over her protests. "Let's get one thing straight: You did not rape me."

"I did too! No wonder your dad was furious at me. He had every right. I deserve to have to marry a man who doesn't love me. Rapists have to go to prison. I guess mine's a life sentence."

"Marriage to me is not a prison," he growled out, offended.

"No, but it will be for you, won't it? You didn't get to choose." She started crying again in earnest.

"You didn't rape me, damn it."

"What would you call it?" she demanded between sobs. "You told me a werewolf couldn't control himself around a female in heat."

"I said the urge to mate is *almost* uncontrollable."

"But you were really mad at me yesterday and now I understand why. It was all my fault! It really was. Oh, gosh . . . and I just thought you were shirking responsibility. You've never done that in all the time I've known you."

"No. Oh, baby . . . I'm sorry. I was mad and I said stuff I shouldn't have because I get stupid and stubborn when I'm angry."

She grabbed his shoulder and tried to shake him. "You've never lied to me. Don't start now."

"I'm not." He'd all but forgotten how unreasonable Frankie got in guilt mode. "Remember, I told you Duke didn't mate with Marigold. She was still in heat when Leah stormed out, but he walked away. Just like I could have walked away from you . . . if that's what I really wanted."

"No. I didn't give you the chance."

He'd have to tell her about Olivia and hope it helped, rather than hurt. "Olivia was in heat too."

She looked up at him with rainwater-gray eyes. "She was?"

"Yes, but I had no desire to mate with her."

"None? I don't believe you. You said you wanted to marry her."

"I thought we agreed I don't lie to you."

"Then you really don't want to marry me. You said so."

"I wasn't lying to you then, I was lying to myself."

She shook her head. "Olivia . . ."

"Was another moment of male idiocy for me. I never really courted her, but planned to mate her in the fur. She was in heat and I knew it. So did she. She would have sought a mate if she ran with the pack, she wouldn't have been able to help herself, and I planned to be the mate she found. But when we saw her at the ranch, the only female I wanted was you."

"You were going to use her impulses against her?"

"She would have had a choice."

"But you just said . . ."

"Even in our wolf forms, our humanity exists. If she really wanted to avoid a mating, she could have. In fact, she did."

"That's why she insisted on going out of town."

"Yes. She planned to run alone."

"Is that safe?"

"It depends on where she ran. I'm sure she chose where she went carefully, but that's not the point right now. The point is, *I made love to you because I wanted you.* And you are my mate because it is meant to be that way."

"If that's true then why were you so against mating a human? Why were you so furious this morning when you were telling me we had to be together forever?"

He explained about pack law and watching a man as close to him as an uncle have his throat ripped out by King.

"That must have been horrible."

"It was, and it made me determined never to risk putting myself in that position. King wanted it to be a life lesson for me and Duke, and it worked."

"A little too well. You just assumed that if we mated, I would walk away some day? That's ridiculous."

"The risk was there." He'd seen so many human relationships end, even ones where both parties said they loved each other more than life.

He'd spent high school watching one couple after another have sex, say they loved each other and then break up to move on to someone else. By the time he'd gone to college, he was totally convinced that affection between humans was a very precarious thing. As he'd gotten older, he'd seen more lasting relationships, but his mind had already been set.

She stared at him like he'd gone nuts. "I've spent over ten years loving you. Do you honestly think that's going to end one day? Ever? If I could have gotten over you, I would have. Believe me."

He didn't like hearing that and tightened his hold on her. "You got engaged to another man."

"After you told me we would never be more than friends. I tried to love him—"

"You had sex with him."

"And that really bothers you, doesn't it?"

"Hell, yes."

She smacked him on the chest, openhanded, unlike the day before. "It was your own darn fault."

Like hell. He hadn't shoved her into bed with another man. "How do you figure that?"

"I told you. I got engaged to another man trying to get over loving you. I made love with him for the same reason. It wasn't fair to him. It hurt me, but you can take a flying leap if it bothers you, because you shouldn't have rejected me in the first place. You loved me then, didn't you? But you were too stubborn to admit it."

There was no use denying it now, even if he'd blinded himself to it then. "Yes."

She went completely still, her gray eyes wide with vulnerability. "Say that again."

"I loved you then. I love you now. I'll love you tomorrow and every tomorrow after." The words were surprisingly easy to say, and he finally realized they should have been said a long time ago.

He would have saved them both a boatload of heartache.

She started to cry again, but she was hugging him and kissing him. "I love you too. So much. Oh, Ty, I thought I was going to die if I had to let you go."

"You never have to let me go again, and you can be damn sure I'll never walk away from you."

"Because of pack law?" she asked, shocking him with her uncertainty.

"Because I would rather face pack justice than live without you. I love you," he stressed.

She smiled and it was like the sun coming out after the rain. "I love you, too. So much, Ty, so much."

Finally, he believed her. "I have been stupid."

"But not anymore."

"No, not anymore." And he had a lifetime to prove it to her.

It took Duke until the next day to get them out of the cabin. He took them back to the ranch, correctly assuming Ty would not allow Frankie to sleep anywhere but with him in his den ever again.

They planned a Christmas wedding, and she said she intended to make sure Leah was one of the guests.

He didn't tell Duke, but his brother could do worse than to make it up with the mate of his heart.

Ty had never been happier and marveled at how stubbornly he had rejected that happiness. He couldn't believe he'd been capable of turning Frankie down six years before, but he'd never turn her away again.

She was his and he was hers.

Like he'd told her . . . werewolves mated for life and when it came to humans like his wife, they did too.

He was one lucky wolf.

BEYOND LIMITS

SUSAN KEARNEY

one

Never before had Ian Gordon shot Samantha Bessinger a devastating peel-off-the-panty-hose smile. "Why don't you take the copilot seat, Samantha?"

What had gotten into Ian? His suggestion to sit up front in her plane's cockpit right next to him floored her. Intrigued her.

Samantha gave him a thorough second look. Since when did her pilot exude pure male magnetism that sparkled like fine champagne? Maybe he'd been drinking. But his speech was crisp, his smoldering blue eyes clear as he met her gaze, his expression both burning and compelling.

Wow. Double wow. She'd known her pilot for more than a year and she'd never reacted to one of his smiles with a zing of pure female interest.

Strange how her normally reserved and businesslike employee called her Samantha—not Ms. Bessinger. Funny how an invite to sit in the cockpit and one suggestive smile had made her suddenly aware of his dark snappy eyes. Never before had he sent interested signals—not when he'd flown her to Chicago, Cleveland, Pittsburgh or LA. Even the night the two of them had been grounded during a thunderstorm, his demeanor had remained formal and respectful. Yet this invitation had sounded as if he were asking her on a date. His demeanor had most definitely been playful, his smile hot.

And every cell in her body wanted to sidle closer, even if she got burned. The idea of taking him up on the invite was inappropriate.

Oh really?

Since when had hot become inappropriate? Since when had sitting next to a sexy and interested man become wrong?

My God. Had she become so conditioned . . . so caught up in what was businesslike that she no longer responded to the signals of her own body? Her nerves jangled like a teenager's and her pulse accelerated. Strangely flattered by his interest, she forced her lips into a smile. And in the typical fashion that amazed her competitors and contributed to her success, Samantha altered her plans. Work could wait. She deserved a break and she would enjoy a change in scenery.

Putting her briefcase behind the copilot's seat, Samantha gazed back at Ian, wondering if she still remembered how to flirt. "Thanks for the offer."

He gestured to the empty seat. "Make yourself comfortable. Would you like a cup of coffee?"

"Thanks. Black, please."

He handed her an empty mug and poured steaming coffee from a stainless steel thermos. Since when had Ian cornered the market on virility? The delicious aroma filled the cabin, and her mouth watered—but it wasn't the coffee she was thinking about tasting.

Nevertheless, she settled for the hot java and took a bracing sip. Ah, caffeine kicked in and revved her exhausted motor. "It's good."

The glimmer in his eyes as he gazed at her with keen appreciation suggested he'd like to offer her more than coffee, making her glad she'd taken extra care with her makeup this morning. Wearing her custom Armani suit that matched the Gucci pumps and bag she'd picked up at Saks, and sporting the new haircut she'd just gotten from the brand-new stylist she'd found on Forty-second Street, who had done wonders with her baby-fine hair, Samantha looked her best. The glamorous cut softened her jawline and the new honey color brought out her brown eyes. Her dad would say she looked like a million bucks. But, of course, Samantha was worth much more.

And wealth made her a target. A target for the paparazzi. A target for scam artists. A target for men on the make. But she reminded herself that the shields she'd put up for her own protection were also shields she could pull down when the occasion warranted it.

As she sipped her coffee and Ian completed his preflight check, she recalled a time when she hadn't been suspicious of a hot smile and a charming man's interest, a time when coffee this good had been a luxury she couldn't afford. She'd grown up poor, worked her way through college and bought her first fixer-upper before she'd graduated. In the beginning, she'd done most of the renovations herself, sanding and painting, fixing plumbing and hanging curtains. Later, she'd had to deal with contractors and building inspectors—not an easy task for a woman, especially one so young. She supposed she'd begun erecting defensive walls then, in order to make men take her seriously.

As Samantha had expanded into duplexes, then apartments and finally New York City skyscrapers, she'd developed a tough exterior. She now owned a real estate enterprise that would soon rival Donald Trump's. Contractors no longer looked down their noses at her or assumed they could sell her cheap materials or shoddy workmanship. But somewhere along the way, regular workingmen had stopped asking her out. As she'd made the Bessinger name a household word, she'd become insulated from her working-class roots and protected by her executive assistants.

So Ian's charming invitation had taken her aback, but on second thought, there was no good reason to decline. She slid into the copilot's seat and caught the pleasant spicy scent of him, mixed with a clean male aroma. She relaxed into the plush leather, sipped her coffee and tried not to ogle the man beside her.

A change of pace would be good for her. She had been working too hard, and although she'd owned the jet for more than a year, she'd never sat up front. A little adventure would help clear her head of the business deals that dominated her life of late. If she had to be honest, Ian's handsome smile and twinkling eyes had caused tiny butterflies to alight in her stomach and had a lot to do with her decision.

He most definitely had a fit body. Military-straight shoulders tapered to a flat stomach and lean hips—from what she could see of them. At about five foot ten inches, his lean frame complemented his short military haircut and his clean-shaven jaw.

Still, no matter how unexpected and pleasant his attention might be, in this day and age of corporate kidnapping and terrorism, it paid to be careful, and Samantha had given Ian a thorough perusal. As chief executive officer, she could have assigned an underling to hire her pilot, but since she often flew, putting her life in her pilot's hands, last year she'd hired Ian herself. And Ian Gordon, an ex–military pilot with a reputation for meticulous detail and careful flying had proven a fine choice. She always felt safe aboard this airplane—but until today, she'd never thought of him in any capacity except pilot, and he'd certainly never caused these tingles of sexual magnetism that drew her closer.

When he leaned over to help with her seat belt—a totally unnecessary move since she could have placed the coffee mug in a holder—his hand grazed her arm, and she didn't think his touch an accident. She would have expected Ian to act with a bit more subtlety and discretion. Instead . . . he seemed . . . different. More sexual. More male. As if this flight were a hot date—not a business trip.

"Ready to go?" he asked.

She nodded and he slid a headset over his ears. As he taxied the plane toward the runway, he spoke with the air traffic controller and was all business. She ignored the gauges and meters before her, stared out the front windows and wondered how she could so suddenly be attracted to a man. But as the engines revved, their speed increased and the nose lifted, she was no closer to an answer.

Once they soared into the air and climbed to cruising altitude, heading for her meeting in Miami, Ian flicked on the autopilot and again turned his attention to her. "Miami Beach is scorching in August."

She shrugged. "I'll be in an air-conditioned office building during the entire time. Meetings."

"Doesn't sound like fun." His expression turned playful, his lips turning up at the corners. "Why don't I reroute us to the Caribbean?"

She conjured up the delicious idea of playing hooky with him, then shook her head and smiled. "I wish."

"When was the last time you drank a piña colada with a paper umbrella?"

She laughed. "I can't remember."

"Or the last time you sank your toes into a pink-sand beach?"

With his silky, smooth tone, he made a trip to the islands with him sound enticing. Still, she had too much profit riding on her upcoming meeting to consider taking an unplanned vacation. "Some of us work for a living."

"Come on. Tell me you don't have a yen to swim in emerald green waters? Or watch the sunset from a hammock, your bare feet cooling in the breeze? I could have you in Barbados or Aruba in less than five hours."

He could have her? If he kept talking so suggestively, she might just agree. She'd been working for so long without a break that she owed herself a vacation. In fact she owed herself a fling. Twenty-hour workdays led to weekends where she barely had time to catch up on desperately needed sleep, never mind put energy into a relationship.

It was a measure of how long it had been since she'd really relaxed that she was finding his offer so very tempting, so very difficult to refuse. "I've been working on this deal for months. I can't skip out now."

"After the meeting?"

Her heart hammered. "More meetings, I'm afraid." She eyed him over the rim of her mug. His eyes twinkled as if he knew the secret to a happy life and she was clueless. Perhaps she was. She certainly hadn't made time to enjoy her wealth. Her penthouse looked more like a hotel room than a home, but she was going to decorate, as soon as her top designers completed the color scheme for the new hotel. No, then they had to move on to the theater renovation, a huge project, which took up an entire city block. The moment she returned to New York, she had a full day of meetings about her newest project, but suddenly the idea of spending some time on extracurricular activities with Ian tempted her.

"So if we crashed and burned—not that we will," he assured her, "but if we went down, what would you regret most?"

"Not growing old?" she quipped.

"I'm talking about specifics."

The image of sweaty bodies entwined in silk sheets filled her mind. Yum. Kissing Ian on a starry rooftop. Bathing together in her personal hot tub? She cocked her head to one side. "What would you regret most?"

"You so do not want me to answer that question." He grinned again, a grin so charming it ought to be illegal.

His I'm-so-interested expression caused her stomach to twist and her pulse to dance. Ian Gordon *was* flirting. With her. In fact, she suspected he was going to make an outrageously sexy suggestion, but what astonished her even more was that instead of cutting him off, she yearned to encourage him.

"Come on," she prodded. "Why don't you tell me what you'd regret the most if we crashed and burned."

"That I'd never marry my soul mate."

She buried her gaze in her coffee cup to hide her rising embarrassment. Samantha was so out of practice with casual conversation that she'd thought he'd been about to say something playful, like he'd regret that he'd never kissed her underwater or romanced her on a beach. And when she dared to look at him again, she caught his eyes dancing with amusement, as if he could read her thoughts.

Thank God, he couldn't.

"You believe in soul mates?" she asked, recovering almost immediately.

"Of course. I've dreamed of her."

Okay, this conversation was getting a little weird. Ian Gordon, ex–military pilot believed he had a soul mate because he'd dreamed about her?

"I see." She started to put down her mug and release her seat belt. Time to retreat to real life and work in the plane's main cabin.

"No, you don't see. You think I'm . . . a little eccentric."

"We're all entitled to our dreams," she prevaricated, trying to withhold judgment.

"All the men in my family dream about their soul mates."

"Really?"

"We dream about the right woman and then we go out into the world and find her."

Samantha had read Ian's file. When he'd been a teenager, his father had died during a classified mission over Iraq. His mother had run off and Ian had ended up in foster care. He had no brothers. No uncles. No grandparents. One of the reasons she'd hired him was that he had no responsibilities and could leave on a moment's notice.

She kept her voice steady. "I've read your file. There are no men in your family."

His tone turned serious. "It's true that there are no men in *Ian Gordon's* family."

The way he'd emphasized his name shot a tingle of fear down her spine. It was as if he was implying his file was incorrect. She put down her coffee mug before her trembling fingers dropped it. "What are you saying?"

"I'm not Ian Gordon."

"You're not Ian?" She stared at him, fear racing up her throat.

"I'm Ari Dillon. And I have four brothers."

"But you look just like—"

"You aren't an easy woman to approach. You're never alone, except behind guarded doors, and you travel in a limo with very protective drivers. Since we had to meet, I arranged to take Ian's place." Ari spoke gently, as if understanding she was in shock.

"What have you done to my pilot?"

"Don't worry, he's fine. He has no idea we took off without him."

No wonder this man had seemed so different from Ian. She'd known from the first moment he'd smiled that charming grin and called her Samantha that something was odd. But she'd forced her mind to accept the evidence in front of her eyes, even as her body had recognized the differences, responding to Ari as she'd never done to Ian. "Your resemblance to my pilot is . . . astonishing."

Could Ian have an identical twin not even he knew about? Or had Ari undergone plastic surgery to take the place of her pilot? She tried to come up with a logical explanation. But extensive plastic surgery took years and that meant he'd been planning to come after her for longer than Ian had been in her employ. The facts made no sense.

His words haunted her. He'd said they had to meet. "So why are you here?"

Ari's voice remained calm, gentle. "Because you are the woman I dreamed about. *You* are my soul mate."

TWO

Ari wished he could draw Samantha into his arms and assure her that he wouldn't hurt her. However, he knew enough about the outside world to recognize fear in a woman's eyes. So he remained still and tried to look nonthreatening, allowing her to adjust to his words before he shocked her again with the rest of his story.

Samantha clenched her armrests, staring at him as if he'd grown four eyes and a tail. Her nostrils flared and her eyes dilated. She drew in a deep breath and let it out slowly, and finally a bit of color came back into her pale face.

"I don't know what to say." She licked her bottom lip, a nervous gesture, yet she was very good at hiding her feelings behind a mask he found difficult to read.

Clearly, she didn't believe him but at least she hadn't lapsed into hysterics. Supposedly the dreams were never wrong. After dreaming about and finding their soul mates, many New Atlantean men had returned home to brag that they'd felt an immediate and total connection with their soul mate at the first moment of meeting. But while Ari admired her intelligence, while he was attracted to her courage, he felt as if she was hiding most of herself behind a businesslike front. He wished he could have gotten to know her better under more normal circumstances before he'd inserted himself into her life.

But Samantha lived behind guarded gates. To even enter her office building required an appointment. Sure he could have slipped past security, but that wouldn't have gained him quality time with her.

So Ari had been forced to make extensive plans in order for them to spend time together. And he would make the best of the opportunity. "Would you like to know how I made myself look like Ian?"

"Sure."

"Do you remember high school biology class?" he asked, knowing he needed to explain before he showed her exactly who and what he was. Although shape-shifting was rare where he came from, no child would fear him or his ability. He prayed she wouldn't view him as a monster.

She frowned. "You learned how to make yourself look like my pilot in high school biology class?"

He laughed. "Not exactly. But do you recall how after a worm is cut in half, the head can grow a tail and the tail will grow a head?"

She shook her head. "I'm afraid I was never any good at science."

"Well, take my word for it. It happens all the time. And I use the same principle to change my shape."

"Change your shape? Uh-huh." She remained polite, but skepticism shined in her eyes.

"Now, don't freak out. I'm going to show you by growing another finger. Okay?"

She swallowed hard. "Sure. Go right ahead."

He could tell that, although she'd listened intently, she didn't believe him. Slowly, he lifted his hand and with a mental thought, he grew a second pinky.

"Oh . . . my God." Samantha's eyes widened, but she leaned forward in fascination, staring at his sixth finger. "Can I touch it?"

"Yes."

She poked his pinky and then massaged it between her thumb and index finger. Her touch didn't shoot an electric tingle through him as he'd hoped—however her touch was pleasant enough to urge him to reach out and place her hand in his. He remained still, forcing himself to let her proceed at her own pace. She might not have enjoyed science classes, but she took her time, thoroughly examining the newly grown finger.

Her voice rose in surprise. "It's genuine flesh and there's a bone in there—just like a real finger. Are you a magician?"

"Nope."

"You dropped down to Earth in a UFO?" she guessed.

"Wrong again."

"So you're a lower life-form?"

He shook his head and held back a sigh. The conversation wasn't going as he'd planned. "Have you ever heard of Atlantis?"

"The legendary ancient island that sank beneath the Mediterranean Sea? Of course I've heard of it. My interest in history is a bit better than biology. Why?" She picked up her coffee. For a moment he feared she might throw it on him but she remained too controlled for that. Instead, she took another sip, giving away nothing on a face once again composed.

He was pleased she had a good brain. That she hadn't run from him screaming. It was a start. And he couldn't help thinking that it was no wonder she'd achieved such success in the business world. He'd just showed her something she considered impossible and already she was adapting.

He leaned back into his seat. "My ancestors were born on Atlantis. They had special abilities that others did not."

"What kind of special abilities?"

"Our people have different talents. Some specialize in telekinesis, telepathy, empathy and shape-shifting."

"Go on."

"Thousands of years ago, our special abilities weren't understood by the masses and their distrust led to fear, persecution and jealousy. So we sank the island and disappeared to make a new home in the South Atlantic. We named it New Atlantis and that is where I call home."

He missed his house on the beach. The Caribbean breezes cooled him, the lapping waves soothed him, the palms rustled outside his windows—and a force shield protected them all from hurricanes and the prying eyes of outsiders. He couldn't imagine why anyone would want to live in a noisy, crowded city and was certain he could convince her of the advantages of moving into his home. But he was thinking ahead of himself. Right now, it didn't appear as if she even liked him.

She looked him straight in the eyes, her stare challenging. "I've never heard of New Atlantis."

"That's because it's hidden and very private." He couldn't wait to show off his home. While he couldn't offer her the high-rise skyscraper's view of one of the premier cities in the world, there was a serenity on New Atlantis that could be found nowhere else on Earth.

"How do you hide your island?"

"Remember the special abilities that I told you that my ancestors possessed?"

She eyed his second pinky. "Yes."

"We all use our abilities to keep a shield between the rest of the world and New Atlantis. Radar, sonar, photographs cannot see our island. To your scientific instruments, New Atlantis appears to be ocean."

"You're good at storytelling. You ought to write a book."

"If I did, then New Atlantis would no longer be a secret. My people have no wish to be studied or kidnapped and used for ill gain."

She raised her eyes to his and then lowered them again to his hand. Her eyes sparkled with wary curiosity. "I don't understand."

He made the pinky disappear. "I'm changing to my real face."

Ian's face morphed before her eyes. To her, Ian was there one moment, the next, a stranger appeared in his place. And while Ian had been an attractive man, Ari possessed the chiseled cheekbones of his Greek ancestors, a haughty brow, and a longish aristocratic nose. Never would Ari be mistaken for pretty.

Her eyes widened. "That's amazing."

"I didn't change the rest of me because my normal shape won't fit in these clothes."

"You can make yourself into any size? You can look like anyone?"

He nodded. "Down to fingerprints and retinal scans."

"I can see why you wouldn't want the world to know. My God . . . you could make yourself the president of the United States, infiltrate any bank, corporation or country. You could be the ultimate spy."

"You're beginning to understand."

"I don't understand anything." Her eyes narrowed with suspicion. "Maybe you put a hallucinogen in my coffee."

"I didn't. And I drank the coffee from the same thermos," he reminded her.

"Maybe you're an alien from Mars."

"Isn't it easier to believe I'm from this world? Besides, why would I lie?"

She frowned at him. "Maybe you're the Devil."

"Because you like me?"

"I don't know you well enough to like you," she snapped.

He laughed. "Come on, Samantha. You liked me well enough when you thought I was Ian."

"I know Ian."

Damn, she could be stubborn. But she'd been interested in him—
Ari. He'd seen it in the way her mouth had relaxed into a pleased
little smile when he'd invited her into the cockpit, the way her eyes
had returned his interest, the way she'd given him that thorough
once-over when she'd thought he hadn't been looking.

"And you're going to get to know me. I'm not a bad guy."

She rolled her eyes. "Can you land this plane?"

"Of course. I went to the trouble of learning to fly so we could
meet." He gestured to the instrument panel. "I assure you, I'm perfectly capable of operating every one of these—"

"Good." Her fingers drummed on her armrest. "If you intend to
keep New Atlantis a secret, why are you telling me about it?"

"Even if you wanted to tell others, who would believe you?"

"Exactly." She arched an eyebrow. "So why should *I* believe
you?"

"You've seen me shape-shift. And you've heard the legends
about Atlantis."

"You've made your point, but I've also read about Greek gods,
and I didn't expect to meet one of them." She leaned back in her
seat, stared out the window and her tone softened. "And you
dreamed about me?"

"Yes."

"By name?"

"Yes."

"And suppose I say no?"

"You're going to become one of us. Because you're my soul
mate."

If looks could kill, he would have frozen to death from her icy
stare. So much for his reputation for charm with the ladies. This
was one stubborn woman and he had the sinking sensation that
she'd put up one hell of a fight before agreeing to join him in
Atlantis—but her resistance made her interesting.

"What do you mean I'm going to become one of you?"

"The shield that protects New Atlantis from your world is weakening. We need fresh minds. New blood. So occasionally we go into the world to find those who can help us maintain the shield."

She shook her head. "I assure you, I don't have any special abilities—unless you count business acumen."

"That's where you're wrong." Down to earth, practical and logical, she wanted to know every detail and he would explain as best he could. Yet, understanding she was still fearful, he braced for any reaction from her. "I wouldn't have dreamed about you unless you possessed the genetic sequencing that allows *you* to shape-shift."

"Me?" She shook her head and snorted. "You place a lot of stock in dreams."

She was so intense, so cool and collected, and he had always longed for a mate with warmth and fun in her soul. "We trust our dreams because they are always accurate."

"So now what?" she asked.

"Excuse me?"

"What are your plans? You've told me your secret. I've listened. Now what?"

"We need to spend time alone together. So we can bond."

At his words, alarm darkened her eyes. Her lips pressed into a firm line. Her hand reached into her purse to retrieve her cell phone.

He didn't try to stop her. "Your phone won't work at this altitude."

She frowned at the lack of signal and turned off the battery. "Suppose I don't want to bond?"

"Please, try to relax. I mean you no harm." He took the plane off autopilot and adjusted their heading. Instead of almost due south, he turned southeast toward the south Atlantic Ocean.

"Where are you taking me?"

"To a private island."

"New Atlantis?"

He shook his head. "We need to be alone."

"Why?"

"I want to teach you how to shape-shift."

She turned shocked eyes on him. "Me? Shape-shift?"

"It's part of your genetic makeup."

"Yeah, right. What happens if I don't learn how?"

He didn't like scaring her. But shape-shifting was difficult to learn. To teach her, he needed to spend a lot of time under conditions that would eventually lead to trust. According to his teachers, the best way for him to earn her trust was for her to believe her life was at risk so she could learn to depend upon him for her own survival.

"If you don't learn to shape-shift, you could die."

Her mouth trembled and she bit her lower lip, no doubt to stop from showing weakness. "I thought you said you meant me no harm?"

"Once you adapt to who and what you really are, you'll be fine."

She glanced at the radio as if it could save her life. He flicked it off, removed a fuse and pocketed it. "Sorry. No one will be coming to your aid. To shape-shift you must look to yourself. You must look inward."

"Even if I believed that you could teach me to shape-shift, I don't want to live on New Atlantis. I have a life in New York. I have friends, a business. A sister."

"We do travel into the world. There's no reason you can't return to visit."

Samantha's fingers clenched into fists. "You have no right to take me from my life. Change our course back to Miami. I refuse to co-operate."

Sad that he must abduct her, he kept his voice gentle. "If you refuse to cooperate, you will die."

THREE

Despite the fact that the sexiest hunk on Earth seemed to have abducted her, Samantha had no intention of dying with him. When she and her plane vanished in the Bermuda Triangle, the news would make headlines. People would come looking for her. They'd discover her plane had taken off from New York and had never landed in Miami. A satellite would pick up the flight path and surely rescuers would come.

Ari flew the plane toward an island that possessed little more than a sand landing strip. As they'd approached by air, she'd seen no buildings, no people, no sign of civilization. Worse, she'd spied only limited vegetation on the spit of sand, indicating a lack of water.

So when the landing gear touched sand, she moved to the galley, dumped her contracts out of her briefcase and grabbed supplies. While Ari braked the plane, she loaded her now empty case with water bottles, grabbed a pack of matches, stuffed several low-carbohydrate Powerbars into her purse, placed a life jacket over her head and then clung to a seat back as the plane skidded and bumped across the sand.

A glance out the portal told her the landing strip was too short. The plane had slowed considerably, but they weren't going to stop before plunging into the ocean.

Hands shaking, feet shifting for balance, Samantha placed the briefcase's strap over her shoulder and yanked the plane door's emergency exit handle. The door rolled back with a smooth hiss. Wind whipped her hair and she breathed in hot, humid air and the tang of the sea. Below her, the ground passed by, but Ari braked and they slowed down to bicycle speed. She prayed they'd stop before rolling into the sea. Another glance told her they wouldn't, but, the slow speed made surviving a jump doable, even for her.

Still, her heart battered her ribs in fear. She looked ahead one more time. The plane was clearly about to dive into the water. Oh God. If she didn't want to drown, she had to jump.

Fear racing up her throat, she forced her quivering legs to launch her into the air. She dropped with sickening speed, landing hard, toppling, rolling and skinning a knee and an elbow. She ended up on her back and breathed in a mouthful of sand. She spit out the sand, shoved to her side, and turned to watch her plane taxi into the sea with just enough speed to carry it deep enough to submerge it completely.

Squinting in the bright sunlight, she pushed to her feet. She was now highly suspicious that Ari could have slowed the plane enough to have stopped on land if he'd wanted to. The bastard had deliberately run her plane into the sea.

She wasn't surprised when, a moment later, his head broke the surface of the calm turquoise water. He swam toward shore, using the steady, powerful strokes of a long-distance swimmer. Damn him. Not only had he ruined her radio, he'd destroyed a thirty million dollar airplane to hide their tracks. Finding her on this isolated spit had just become much more difficult, and she prayed the black box with a GPS locator beacon still worked, even as she tugged her cell phone from her purse and hit the power button.

No service.

Damn. Again, she switched off the power.

Now what?

She'd seen the island from the air. It wasn't larger than fifty acres and had few places to hide. All too aware Ari would soon catch up with her no matter what she did, she didn't bother to expend the energy to run.

She began to perspire in the heat and decided to head for the north shore where she'd seen several palm trees that might offer a bit of shade. Shrugging out of her suit jacket, she placed it over her head to wear as a hood to shield her from the Caribbean sun, worrying that the half dozen water bottles she'd grabbed wouldn't keep her alive for too many days.

Ari's irritating whistling warned of his approach. She'd never heard the tune and resented the cheerful tone.

She didn't bother turning to look at him, but kept trudging forward, her eyes straight ahead. "You ruined my airplane."

"You don't need it anymore. You have me."

"Right. Since you can teach me to shape-shift, I'll just grow myself a pair of wings and fly."

"You *can* fly, you know, but it's an advanced shape and shouldn't be attempted just yet."

She snorted. She supposed she should be grateful that he wasn't a rapist and didn't seem violent. However, her anger that he'd forced her into survival mode fed her temper. Samantha was a city girl and hadn't spent time in the woods. The only thing she had in her favor was common sense and that her favorite television show was *Survivor*. Unfortunately, her situation was far worse than a reality TV show.

When she turned to glare at Ari, her breath caught in her lungs.

Despite her fear, despite her harrowing leap from the plane, desire slammed her. And it wasn't natural. Now was no time to be bowled over by his awesome face and dynamite body.

He no longer stood at about five foot ten inches. Now he had to be at least six foot six. And he'd morphed out of his clothes. He'd lost his shirt, and his powerful chest could have graced a romance book cover.

When Ari had taken Ian's shape, the tug of attraction had been full-blown. But her response to Ari was over the top. Just looking at him seemed to set her nerve endings on a high simmer, and that she reacted to him at all annoyed her. That she could barely resist staring at the strong cords of bronzed neck muscle and the flat stomach that tapered to boxer shorts, muscular legs and bare feet rocked her.

He noted the direction of her gaze. "I left the boxers on for your comfort."

"Thanks. You're so considerate."

"Was that sarcasm I detected?"

"Is the moon round?"

"I'm sorry I had to sink the plane, but otherwise it would be too easy for rescuers to find you." He shot her a sideways glance. "You might as well know that I disabled the black box before you boarded the plane. The GPS won't lead anyone here."

She bit back a curse, as frustrated with him as her unwarranted reaction to him. "You seemed to have thought of everything— except bringing along food and water."

"I can forage from the land and the sea."

"Good for you."

He grinned. "You'll learn how to forage, too. Necessity is supposed to make you more determined to learn."

She saw no point in telling him again that she didn't want to learn how to shape-shift. Why should she learn to forage when she could afford to dine in the top gourmet restaurants in the world?

Unfortunately, none were on this island. Her credit card wouldn't buy her a drop of water.

Ignoring Ari, Samantha set her priorities and ignored the notion that if she was going to die, he could at least make her a happy woman and make delicious love to her. First, she intended to make a giant SOS in the sand that could be seen from the air. Then she would gather driftwood so she could start a fire to catch the attention of a passing boat. Third, she'd have to find water, food and shelter.

When she reached the palm trees, she sat and rested, her back propped against a tree trunk. She opened a bottle of water and drank, sipping slowly and appreciating the cool liquid as it wet her parched throat. Since Ari had claimed he could live off the land, she didn't offer him any and didn't feel the least bit guilty.

The ocean beckoned and she longed to take a swim, but she had work to do first. She decided, however, that although her beautiful suit and shoes belonged in the boardroom, not on a beach, she could at least get her feet wet. She kicked off the shoes, peeled off her knee-high hose, and unbuttoned her shirt's top buttons.

"Going for a swim?" Ari asked, his tone curious and slightly playful—almost as if he knew how difficult she found it to resist him.

"Just getting my feet wet." She ambled along the beach, keeping her eye out for driftwood and tried not to think about how pleasant the wet sand felt between her toes, tried not to think about the refreshing breeze in her hair or how much she wanted to go for a swim with Ari, lie on the hot sand and enjoy him and the beautiful island, instead of completing the tasks she'd assigned herself.

As if following the direction of her thoughts, Ari trailed behind her for a few steps. "I'm going for a swim."

"Whatever."

He held out a hand to her. "You could come with me. I'd enjoy the company."

Wanting to join him but holding back, Samantha refused to take his hand and saw disappointment in his eyes before he turned away and waded into the water, out past his hips. Then he sank below the surface and didn't come up, but the clear turquoise water allowed her to watch his smooth transition from man to dolphin. His bronze skin turned gray and shiny, his nose elongated, his arms retracted and his feet merged into a tail. Soon, a perfect-looking dolphin played in the surf, catching a wave and gracefully riding it to shore.

Amazing. Cool. Unbelievable.

When he swam near the beach and playfully splashed her, she had the urge to accept his invitation, plunge deep into the sea, grab his top fin and let him take her for a swim. But she wasn't about to start frolicking when she had work to do. Nor did she want to give him the idea that she was in a playful mood . . . she wasn't.

Perhaps some distance would help clear her mind from lusting over him. She had no idea what had gotten into her. Whenever she was near him, her pulse seemed to leap into overdrive and she was so keenly aware of his every glance. She should be thinking about survival, getting away, not his hot body.

But as she turned her back on the sea, she wondered for the first time what it would be like to swim in the sea like a dolphin, or fly like a bird. Or run as fast as a—

Stop it. While she couldn't doubt the evidence before her eyes, just because he could shape-shift didn't mean that she could. And even if she could shape-shift, did she really want to live a life like that?

However as she left the pleasant sea and walked along the beach, she had no doubt he'd gobble down a few fish for dinner and drink whatever dolphins drank. And the entire process amazed her. He really had a miraculous skill and she wondered if he ever put it to good use or only employed his abilities to play.

During her walk, she found three sticks, not enough for a fire, but she could use the longest branch to carve her giant SOS in the sand. Making sure she began above the high-tide mark, Samantha traced oversized letters, then returned to scoop out a deep trough of sand with her hands so her plea for help would be visible from the air.

Bending over in the hot sun and digging in the sand was sweaty work, and she promised herself a refreshing swim when she was done. And if that meant peeling down to her bra and panties, well, so be it—she wouldn't be revealing any more skin than she would if she were wearning a bikini on a public beach.

She didn't know what to think about Ari. Or her reactions to him. He'd flirted only a little since he'd told her about the shape-shifting. But her response to him—her absorption with the meaning behind his every glance was not like her usual self. What was it about him that she found so attractive—besides the obvious exterior beauty? If she could have forgotten what he'd told her about becoming soul mates, she might have accepted that it had simply been too long since she'd been with a man.

But the soul mate idea turned her on in a way that she recognized as trouble.

And she couldn't forget. *Soul mates*. He had to be insane. And yet, if he was correct, was that why she found him almost irresistible? Why she had to fight the compulsion to agree to what he asked? Perhaps pacing around before him only partly dressed might not be a good idea—because while he might ignore her bare skin, she would feel even sexier when he looked at her.

If she was lucky, Ari wouldn't return until after she'd put her clothes back on. Pausing to drink, Samantha calculated that at this rate, her water would be gone in two more days. She'd have to ration more carefully.

Two hours of sweaty labor later, she finished her giant SOS. Pleased with her efforts but tired and smelly, she peeled off her shirt and slacks, folded them and set her clothes next to her briefcase and purse. Then she plunged into the water, letting the cool sea restore her energy.

And now that she'd done what she could to be rescued, she finally admitted to herself she wouldn't mind staying awhile. The island was so peaceful and she couldn't recall ever being out of touch with the million details of running her business. In addition, she admitted that she wanted to get to know Ari better. Her soul mate? There was no denying the effect he had on her. Her own life hadn't served up anything resembling a date lately, let alone a gorgeous, sexy soul mate.

As she swam into deeper water, a dolphin appeared beside her, almost as if it had been waiting just for her. At first she wasn't certain it was Ari, but when it again splashed her playfully with a flipper, she had no doubts.

"Come here," she told him.

He swam right over and she had the strongest urge to pet him. Reminding herself he was a man in dolphin's skin and that stroking him was a no-no, she placed one hand around his fin. "Take me for a ride, Ari."

The dolphin raised and lowered his head, clearly signaling agreement. Placing both hands on the fin, she let her legs float. And then he swam, slowly at first. Water rushed by and she held her chin out of the water, enjoying the sensation of the fluttering ripples that were similar to the jets in a whirlpool tub, but much more exhilarating.

Ari swam parallel to the shore, staying where she could easily swim to the beach if she lost her hold on him. Samantha wondered if he could think like a human when he took the dolphin's shape. How much of Ari remained in this dolphin?

She didn't know. But it must be marvelous to swim to the ocean's depths, explore without the need for scuba tanks and fins. Hanging on for the ride was fun but how much better would it be to swim like this under her own power?

Ari took her to shore and then left her to swim out alone again before he joined her on the beach. He'd morphed back into his own shape and had donned the boxer shorts that he must have previously stashed underwater.

"You're a good swimmer," he told her, his voice warm and full of approval.

"I competed in college, but swimming with you was . . . incredible." All those years in the pool hadn't prepared her for the power of swimming with a man/dolphin.

"It'll be even more incredible when you can shape-shift, too."

With a wide grin, he glanced at her bare shoulders, her breasts, her slender waist, and every cell in her warmed at the obvious approval in his gaze. "One advantage of being a shape-shifter is that you can always have the body of your dreams. Or your soul mate's dreams."

She supposed it beat plastic surgery, but she had difficulty concentrating as she beat down the flutter of desire to kiss him, right now. She would have liked to laugh off his soul mate theory, but what else could explain her response to him, her compulsion to know him better in every way? All that delicious bronze flesh covered by water droplets distracted her. She ached to have those wonderful lips on hers, but forced herself to answer him. "You don't get old?"

His grin widened and the heat in his eyes flared, as if he knew exactly how difficult she found it not to reach out and touch him. "We don't get sick. Ever. Once you know how to maintain your immune system, health becomes automatic. And fit cells don't age as quickly."

She had to cover up before he noticed her nipples tightening. "So what's the life expectancy of a shape-shifter?" She put on her shirt, hoping he'd think she needed to shield her skin from the sun. She didn't bother with her slacks. It was simply too damn hot.

"We live three to four hundred years."

Her lower jaw dropped. "How old are you?"

"Thirty. My people believe we should find our soul mates early in life, before we become set in our ways—so we can grow together."

He made the idea sound so appealing, she had to know more. "How many people live in New Atlantis?"

"A few thousand. Maybe another five hundred of us are traveling in your world." He glanced at her again, his eyes darkening with an emotion she couldn't read. "You're no longer worried that I'd hurt you, are you?"

She hadn't thought about dying—except for lack of having him. The powerful needs racing through her simply had to be induced by stress—not the notion he was the perfect man for her. "You said I would die if I don't succeed. That's pretty harsh."

"So you don't trust me?"

"Let's see. You impersonated my pilot, flew my plane off course and crashed it, virtually holding me prisoner on a deserted island where there are no supplies. Do you think I should trust you?"

Her tone was sarcastic, but oddly, she did trust him—at least to not hurt her physically—unless one counted dying slowly from arousal. She was almost shaking with the need to touch him. For him to touch her.

He laughed, the tone deep and knowing. "Since you still don't trust me, I suppose I won't feel too bad about destroying your SOS in the sand."

She frowned, spun around, and placed her fists on her hips, about to yell at him, when he grew a long flat tail that reached the sand behind him, effectively silencing her. He strode over to her SOS, his steps tracing her lettering. As he walked, his tail swished over the sand, the back-and-forth motion wiping out hours of her work in just a few minutes.

Furious with him and furious with herself that, despite his actions, she still wanted to make love to him, she stomped off to search the beach for driftwood in a direction she had yet to explore. Damn him. She hated the way he toyed with her emotions, one moment acting friendly and concerned, the next a calculating bastard. Ari and the sexual tension he generated kept throwing her off balance.

Or maybe she shouldn't be blaming him for her vacillating feelings. Even as a part of her wanted nothing to do with him, she couldn't discount her physical reaction—but her reaction wasn't just lust. She could have handled lust. She couldn't so easily dismiss their swim, how he'd carefully stayed near the shore in order to make her feel secure, how he hadn't dived deep, how he seemed to care about her safety and her feelings.

Too many hours had passed for her to still question whether her coffee had been drugged. If it had, any mind-altering effect would have worn off by now. And while her doubts that *he* could shape-shift no longer lingered, she had plenty of concerns over *her* ability to shape-shift.

But most of all, her maddening, ferocious attraction to him made her less certain of herself than she'd ever been before. She didn't want to face the possibility that his dream of a soul mate, his dream of her, had been accurate. That she remained fascinated by him— despite the fact that one moment he was giving her a marvelous ride through the ocean, playfully splashing her, the next destroying her hard work—worried her. The man most definitely had an agenda, and she didn't believe he would hurt her, but it was her own reactions she didn't trust.

So what *did* she want? Did she want him to teach her how to shape-shift? If she could do it, her entire life would change. While learning to shape-shift might be the only way she'd escape this island, if she succeeded, would that really mean she'd found her soul mate?

four

While Ari admired Samantha's strong will to live and escape the island, her survival efforts were distracting her from his task to teach her how to shape-shift, but she intrigued him. One moment she looked as if she wanted to tackle him on the sand and have her way with him, the next she shut down into her business mode. Clearly Samantha didn't fully believe or trust him, but the complex body alterations took a level of belief and acceptance from one's partner that they had yet to establish.

However, if Ari waited until she weakened from lack of water or food, if he waited until she was desperate, she might not be able to learn what he had to teach her. His plan was coming apart because he'd overestimated their physical attraction, believing that lust alone would convince her they were soul mates. He'd mistakenly counted on her succumbing to their passionate connection. He hadn't expected her to be so stubborn. He'd thought once they arrived on the island that she would depend upon him and believe and trust him because he was the only other human being here and because she'd feel their connection as strongly as he did.

Although Samantha surrounded herself with assistants and ran a corporation of thousands of employees, Ari hadn't taken into account that the number-one person she depended upon was herself. She had an inner strength and fortitude that was working against him right now. Until they'd established a measure of trust, she couldn't learn what he must teach her.

He wracked his brain, trying to come up with a way to reassure her. And he could only think of one method. He would be taking a great risk with his own life, but if he wanted to earn her trust, he didn't see another choice.

Determined to do what must be done, he stripped, morphed into a wolf, picked up his shorts by the waistband of his canine teeth, sprinted down the beach and caught up to her in minutes. He morphed back into human form and dressed before she spied him.

Since scaring her was not part of the plan, he began whistling a tune to warn her of his presence. The wind teased her hair and the setting sun gave her skin a healthy pink glow. But it was the squared shoulders and the arms full of driftwood that caught his eye. She was ever industrious, and he had no doubt she was intent on building a signal fire.

He held out his arms for the wood. "Let me help you with that."

"Like you helped with the SOS in the sand?" she snapped at him, clearly still irritated.

"If I promise not to throw the wood out to sea, will you allow me to carry it?"

She stopped walking and looked at him, her eyes locked with his. "Why should I believe you?" Her tone remained slightly hostile and he realized he had to go through with his plan. He had to find a way to bring them into accord.

"I haven't lied to you," he said.

"Except by omission. I still haven't forgotten your Ian impersonation."

"Are you going to hold a grudge against me forever? I'd like to move on."

"So go. I'm certainly not asking you to stay here with me."

Her expression sent a different message than her fierce words. Her eyes called to him. Her lips softened.

He kept his tone reasonable. "You don't understand. It's time I showed you the different forms I can take. And if you're out here searching for driftwood and return to camp exhausted, you'll be too tired to learn."

"Fine." With a mischievous grin, she tossed the driftwood into his arms.

He lengthened his arms and increased the bone and muscle size to tuck the load under one arm, then placed his hand in hers with the other. When she tried to pull back, he tightened his fingers slightly. "I won't hurt you. Touch is necessary."

"Necessary for what?" Her voice trembled.

For bonding. But he couldn't tell her that. "Feel my hand. I'm going to slowly change the size and muscle tone. I want you to absorb the feel of the changes, not just see them."

"Okay, but if you do anything weird—"

"I won't. First, I'll soften my skin. Feel the calluses disappearing?"

"No. Wait. Yes."

"Good. Now I'll thin my bones. If you squeeze too hard, you could break them." This was her first test. Would she hurt him?

"But if I broke the bones, you could heal them, right?" She arched that knowing eyebrow, her gaze piercing and intelligent and very curious.

"You could cause me pain, but yes, I could knit the bones and repair the torn flesh."

She reached across her body to place one hand over his. He tensed, wondering what she would do now that both her hands were around his. But she didn't squeeze. She kept her touch light and explored the new shape of his hand.

"I'm about to grow fur on my hand, just like your cat." He changed the texture.

She ruffled his coat, her eyes showing excitement and curiosity. "You know about my cat?"

He laughed, happy that she was asking questions. He considered curiosity a very good sign that she was coming to accept him, what she could be, and that they were meant to be together. "I've studied everything I could learn about you for a year. If you hadn't kept yourself behind locked doors, I would have found a more casual approach for us to meet."

She kept stroking his fur. "But you could have impersonated anyone and walked right into my meetings."

"We don't use our skills unless we are certain the outside world won't learn of them."

She seemed to accept his explanation. "Can you do feathers?"

"Sure." He altered the fur, changing it to feathers. "And goose down." He changed again.

"Wow. That's awesome."

He knew better than to think that she was speaking directly about him. He'd thought she was talking about his shape-shifting abilities, but she'd stopped walking to take in the sunset. Magnificent slashes of orange and spears of pink streaked across the sky. The sun, a fiery red ball, appeared to sink into the sea.

He spoke with pride and longing. He ached to share his home with her, to show her how he lived. "On New Atlantis my home is at the foot of a mountain and overlooks the beach. I watch the sunset almost every night. And it's always different."

"I need to travel more. I've allowed work to take up too much of my time." She turned to him, her tone scolding, her eyes dilated, her nostrils flaring. "But that doesn't mean I'm interested in your offer."

Her words said one thing, her body told him another, yet, he didn't push what he sensed was her feminine interest in him—not yet.

When they returned to the spot she'd left her water bottles and Powerbars, he stacked the wood. She gathered dry grasses, stuffed it between the driftwood, and she started a fire with a pack of matches she must have scavenged from the plane before the landing.

With the fire crackling, the scene was almost cozy. She broke open a water bottle and helped herself to a Powerbar. Hesitating for a moment, she offered him a bar but he shook his head. "I ate while I swam in the sea."

Taking tiny bites, she made the food last a long time. Staring into the fire, she grew silent and the physical tension between them grew. When she finished her food, he knew it was time.

"I have more shapes to show you." His serious tone must have alerted her. She jerked her head up, caught his eyes and he swallowed down a gasp at the longing he saw there. And he prayed that longing was . . . for him. "Look what I can do."

He changed into a marble rock, shaped like Michelangelo's *David*, and his shorts fell by the wayside in the sand. Clothing was such a bother to a shape-shifter, since the only form that required clothing was the human one.

She leaned over to touch his rocky surface, her hand gentle, her strokes almost erotic. "Watching you change shape is better than television."

"And after your caresses, I'm so hot for you, I need to cool down." He morphed into a giant ice cube, but didn't allow himself to melt.

She chuckled. "If you're hoping I'm thirsty enough to lick you, you're wasting your time."

He compacted his cells down tight. And changed into a diamond. Leaning over, she picked him up and peered at his tiny, perfect lines. "What happened to your weight?"

He rolled from her palm, dropped into his shorts and changed back into human form. "When I don't need all my mass, I shove it into *Inf* space."

"*Inf?*"

"Short for infinity. Your scientists call *Inf* the fourth dimension."

"I thought the fourth dimension was time."

"It is." He thought she was going to ask him more about *Inf*, but her curiosity turned in a different direction.

She fed a stick into the fire, her face thoughtful, her hands shaking. "So size is limited to your mass. You can't become a whale?"

"I can do a small whale. Although I can't grow more cells, I can expand the ones I have."

"And what would have happened to you in ice cube form if you'd begun to melt?"

"As long as the water pooled around me, I would have been fine. If, however, you had decided to lick me"—at his reminder of her words, her face reddened, or perhaps it was the fire flickering off her skin—"I would have lost those cells forever."

"And if you lose a lot of cells?"

"Lose too many cells and I can't ever return to my human form." He kneeled beside her. "Some forms are very dangerous. If I became a bouquet of flowers, you could rip me apart."

Her gaze locked with his. "You would die?"

"Yes." He held her stare, gathered himself to place his life in her hands. "Pick me up again and I'll show you." Without further discussion, he morphed into a seed and waited for her to do as he'd asked. The moment he sprouted from the seed, Ari would be putting his life in her hands. He'd made certain to explain first, so she would understand. And he'd seen comprehension in her eyes, but he had no idea what she might do when he sprang into a blooming bouquet.

Time to find out.

Using his will to re-form his cells, he grew two dozen stems and made a variety of flowers bloom. Lilies, roses, carnations, pansies. He needn't conform to the rules of nature. With her hand around the stems, she could toss him into the fire before he could change to a shape in which he could defend himself. Or she could break him in half by slapping him against the remaining firewood, or shred him with her bare hands.

She sniffed, then very carefully placed the stems back inside his shorts. A few moments later, he was once again human, very relieved to be in one piece and trying not to pretend he'd had any doubts about what she'd do to him.

But she read him easily enough. "You weren't certain I wouldn't hurt you, were you?"

"What I must teach you requires trust." He spoke simply, watching her eyes flare with comprehension and heat. "To earn your trust I had to show you that I could give you mine."

She lowered her gaze and stared into the fire. "Just because I don't wish to harm you, doesn't mean the reverse is true."

"And knowing that, you were still careful with me." At his question, she shivered and he wanted to sling an arm over her shoulders and draw her against him. He wanted to hold her and tell her that shape-shifting was wonderful. But some things had to be done alone. She had to *want* the gift she'd been born with in order to make use of it. He'd tried to show her the pluses but like everything in life, there were minuses, too. "Why didn't you toss me into the fire?"

"Because you abducted me to help your people. And you've tried to make me feel safe when you could." She tilted her head up to meet his eyes and again he saw a burning curiosity. "I'm considering having you teach me to shape-shift, but first I'd like to hear more about the risks."

Wow. She certainly knew how to lay her cards on the table, making him realize that he'd lucked out when it came to dreaming about Samantha Bessinger for his soul mate. She was tough—deep down where it counted—yet reasonable. She didn't hide from the facts, no matter how difficult the truth might be, and so he hoped that eventually she'd even admit their growing attraction.

He could barely keep his hands off her. He ached to draw her into his arms—not to reassure her, but to find out if he could coax the simmering heat between them into a blazing inferno. But as much as he wanted her, his task required patience.

She seemed to have figured out that danger—if it came— wouldn't be caused by him or survival on the island, but how she adjusted to the shape-shifting process. But she'd taken the first step toward making a transformation, she wanted to know more, and from the intensity in her gaze and the hardening of her nipples, she was sexually aroused by the danger. Samantha really was one amazing woman and even as he ached to have her, he tamped down his impatience.

As the fire flickered over her skin, as the breeze toyed with her hair, as her long bare legs teased him, his heart lightened. For the first time, he believed they had a good chance of success. That they'd make a good team. That he'd dreamed of his true soul mate. Shape-shifters didn't judge people on their appearances since they could take any form. Instead, his abilities had made him look deeper into her character. And what he saw, he could love.

And as his hope flared, so did his desire for this beautiful and courageous woman.

FIVE

"Can attempting and failing to shape-shift cause my death?" Samantha asked, fighting her excitement and finding resisting almost impossible. What he offered was way too incredible, way too tempting—she owed it to herself to explore.

Although Ari had effectively trapped her here, giving her only one way off the island—by learning to shape-shift—she'd always enjoyed the challenge of trying new skills. And a tiny part of her wondered if there really was such a thing as a soul mate and if he could be hers.

She'd been alone for so long that she'd never really expected to meet the one right man for her. The one man above all others who would fill her needs and she his. The idea of him being her soul mate enticed her to dip in a finger and taste. Even if she'd been free to do so, she'd never forgive herself for walking away from all that Ari was offering—long life, healthy life—plus a mouthwatering man to share it with.

"Failing won't hurt you at all," he said. "But if you don't follow my exact directions, there can be . . . difficulties."

Samantha sensed that he'd chosen his words with care in order to avoid frightening her. However, if Samantha had had a life-threatening illness, she'd ask the doctor to be frank. If there was risk, she wanted to know the odds so she could assess her chances and increase her opportunity to achieve success. And if there was danger to her life, she wanted to know how and when and what to watch out for.

Samantha folded her jacket to form a pillow and made a bed in the sand, relaxing on her back. She'd never seen so many stars in the night sky and it made her feel as if life was precious, special.

She sensed a tremendous life-altering opportunity for her . . . and Ari, and her stomach tightened the way it often did when she was on the verge of a business deal—only more so. "Please, tell me about what can go wrong."

He lay next to her, rolled onto his side and rested his head in his palm. "I'm not supposed to dwell on the dangers."

"Says who?"

"Our dream instructors. New Atlantis doesn't just send us blindly out to find our soul mates. Esteemed professors instruct us how to teach. And they strongly recommend glossing over the dangers."

She turned her head to look at him, almost relaxed now that she'd decided to give the shape-shifting and Ari a try. He appeared so comfortable lying on the sand. With the fire dying, the embers glowing, just enough light remained to let her read his serious expression. "I hope there's a 'but' you're going to add to that statement."

"But"—he shot her a charming grin, then returned to serious mode—"I believe that you have a right to know exactly what you're facing, especially since shape-shifting is one of the most dangerous skills."

His calm and reasonable tone reassured her, and yet made her feel special, as if he were holding back his interest in her for fear of scaring her away. "I'm listening."

"It's important to learn simple shapes first. The danger of going too fast too soon is that you might become stuck in a form and not have the skill to change back."

She shuddered, recalling his diamond shape, a form where he couldn't move or talk, not until he'd morphed. "That sounds unpleasant. I wouldn't want to spend the next few days as, say, a rock."

"It would be more than the next few days. As a rock, you don't require food or air. You could live an eternity as a rock. That's why we'll pick a—"

"When you turn into a rock," she interrupted him, tried to ignore the clench of nerves in her stomach and punched her pillow into shape, "do you keep all your thoughts and memories?"

He nodded and curled an arm under her shoulder, offering himself as a pillow. She snuggled into his heat, enjoying the warmth of his flesh and appreciating how comfortable she felt in his arms—as if they were destined to fit. All her earlier lust was there, simmering, but she could ignore it and wait more easily now, now that she'd decided to make love.

Why not enjoy him? Why not find out if the connection between them was as electric as it seemed?

"No matter what shape we take," he said, "the brain goes into the *Inf* but we can tap into our thoughts. The second most common danger is panic. To me the morphing sensation feels like a combination of stretching and compression but it may seem very different to you. While it's not painful, you can't change your mind after you begin or you'll tear yourself apart."

She swallowed hard. "What else?"

For the first time, he avoided her gaze. "The best way to teach you is for us to link."

"Link?"

"Remember when you touched my hand? How you felt the changes?"

"You want us to hold hands?"

"I can wrap my body around you, so that I'm over you, under you. Inside you. Part of you."

Inside her? She assumed their atoms would mix on a very elemental level. And if she got stuck, it sounded like he would be stuck with her. "And what happens if we're linked and I panic?"

"We'll go real slow. You'll be fine. If our bodies are linked, I'll be right there with you. Knowing that should keep you calm."

"*Should?* You don't know?" She narrowed her eyes. "Have you ever linked before?"

"Not like this. We need to start by making love and then progress to—"

She turned onto her side, chuckled and splayed her fingers over his chest. "I've heard a lot of lines in my day, but yours has to be the most . . . outrageous."

"Touching is necessary," he insisted, clearly not understanding that she was teasing. "The more touching we do, the stronger the link and the greater the chance of success. In truth, I am not certain if it's possible to teach you to shape-shift without . . ." He tightened his lips. "I'm sorry you find the idea so distasteful."

She picked up on the hurt in his tone and sought to reassure him. "I won't deny that you fascinate me. Or that I want you. There's a connection growing between us that I'd like to explore."

"Thank you."

"For what?"

"Accepting a difficult situation. Giving us this chance."

Samantha had experienced lust. She'd experienced friendship. But she'd never known both at the same time. Ari appealed to her on the physical level—what woman wouldn't enjoy his masculine physique or his warm eyes following her every move? And his husky tone lapped with the same persistence as the waves rolling across the beach, soothing, caressing and exciting—all at the same time.

But what impressed her most was that he hadn't tried to use his physical beauty or his touch to convince her to do as he wished. Another man might have stolen a kiss, found excuses to touch her. He hadn't done more than hold her hand or offer his shoulder to pillow her head, mostly appealing to her intellect. And his plan was working. Once she'd gotten past the shock of his shape-shifting revelations, she'd realized that she wanted to know him better. She wanted to learn how he'd grown up, what he did for a living. She wanted to see his island. She wanted to kiss him and see where it led.

She wanted to make love.

Leaning toward his mouth, she kissed his lips. He tasted of the sea, slightly salty, fresh and with a tang of the wild. And best of all, he didn't hurry her, didn't grab her, allowed her to explore his mouth at her own pace.

She liked his patience and control almost as much as she liked the way his eyes sparkled in the reflected firelight. The way the pulse at his neck leaped. The way his hands threaded into her hair and massaged her scalp.

Yum.

With the starlight above, the warm sand cradling their bodies, the fire crackling and the waves lapping along the beach, she couldn't have asked for a more romantic setting. Or a more considerate partner. Ari kissed better than her best dream.

Although he didn't rush, she appreciated the intensity of his muscles, and heat coiled inside her. Wanting more of his flesh, so firm, so silky, so hot, she shrugged out of her shirt. She thought he might immediately disengage her bra. He didn't.

Ari seemed quite content to kiss her thoroughly, teasing her lips, their tongues dancing, their breaths merging. Her nipples tightened, her breasts swelled and her breath came in gulps. Inhaling Ari's scent, a combination of sea and wind and a male aroma all his own, she wriggled closer, breaking their kiss and toppling him to his back.

She ended up lying across his chest, her legs entwined with his. His sex strained against her, evidence of how her kiss had turned him on, and she filled with a joyful certainty that they would be good together.

His eyes glinted, searching hers, almost as if he needed reassurance that she wanted to proceed. "Being here with you . . . feels so very right." She whispered the startling truth into his ear, nibbled on his lobe, gently bit down, then licked away the sting.

He trailed fingers over her back, showing her with his hands and his mouth that angled and demanded another kiss what he didn't say in words. Never had a man's touch made her feel so cherished. He explored every hollow of her back, every dip, every exposed inch of needy flesh, until she could think of nothing but that she craved to be with this man.

Raising her hands to her bra, she was about to unclip it when he shook his head. "I'll do that."

But he didn't. Instead he lowered his head to her breasts and traced her exposed flesh. She yearned for more, and when he found her nipple right through the cloth, used his teeth to nip, she wanted nothing more than to be bare. She needed his flesh against hers, his mouth with all the heat he had to offer on her skin.

When she hooked her thumbs into his shorts, he lifted his hips and she freed him of them, which he kicked aside. As he did so, they rolled in the sand and she ended up on her back beneath him.

He wrapped her in heat and she couldn't wait to take him inside her. But he seemed content to begin kissing her mouth all over again. Her lips tingled, swelled, gave him more—even as her hands found his hips and tugged him to her.

"There's no hurry," he whispered.

"I'm ready. More than ready," she told him, her voice sounding needy and raw.

He nuzzled her neck and shot a shimmering thrill down her back. "We're going beyond lovemaking."

"Beyond?" What was he saying? Thinking was so difficult when with every breath she longed to get closer to him. She'd never known his hands could feel so good as he skimmed them over her bare shoulders.

"We can share the heat on a cellular level. And when we do, we'll shift into another shape together."

She couldn't focus on his words. She only knew that if his lovemaking had been a song, it would have been her favorite. If his lovemaking had been a movie, she would have watched it a hundred times. If his lovemaking had been a book, it would have been a number-one best-seller.

When he finally removed her bra, she didn't think her need could peak any higher. But she was wrong. He spent as much time kissing her breasts as he had her lips, and the wondrous sensations had her squirming for more of him. Her nipples tightened and when his lips teased her sensitive flesh, a corresponding sizzle ripped through her.

Gasping for air, her skin slick, she tilted up her hips and parted her thighs, groaning as she recalled she'd yet to remove her panties. Together they made short work of them, and he returned to press against her, chest to chest, stomach to stomach, thigh to thigh, remaining careful to keep most of his weight from crushing her. Ari's powerful shoulders had no difficulty holding his weight as he slid over her. She thought he might kiss her again. But instead he rubbed his flesh over hers, shooting a wild flame of sensations over her skin, under her skin, through her skin.

It was as if their touching flesh crackled with tiny jolts of electricity. Wondrous, but a bit unnerving, the sensation caused her muscles to tense in expectation of what would happen next.

Already this experience surpassed lovemaking. The heightened perceptions had an eerie and otherworldly impact that left her mind reeling.

"Relax. What you feel is our surface cells merging." He rubbed his chest over her breasts. At least she thought that was what he was doing. But when she stared at him, he didn't appear to be moving.

Oh God. It was as if the surface of her flesh were liquid and he was stirring the mix. Zinging bursts of pleasure sparked through her and she had to remember to breathe.

"Is this . . . going . . . right?"

He nodded. "Very right. We'll make love and merge soon if that's okay?"

More than okay.

Surely anything that felt this good couldn't be as dangerous as he'd claimed. She reached up and threaded her fingers into his hair and brought his mouth down to hers. His kiss upped the stakes because all of a sudden the zinging deepened at least an inch everywhere beyond the top layer of flesh. And the sensations multiplied a hundredfold.

Samantha hadn't known it was possible to feel too good. Too much sensation. A yearning so powerful that she felt as though she was riding a runaway train. Her ears roared. Her heart pumped.

Oh . . . my . . . God. She could now feel his heart hammering inside her own chest. His sex also inside her. Pure heat boiled through her. Her heat. His heat.

And they burned.

SIX

Ari had made love before, but never had he merged with a lover. His feelings ran the gamut from exciting and exquisite to terrifying. He'd heard of shape-shifters who'd been caught in one shape with their lovers for all time. He couldn't even imagine the horror of failure. To be stuck in the same shape, unable to communicate with each other or the world would be a terrible fate, but even worse, he would have failed to return to help his people with the force field.

A merge followed by a failed separation would be the equivalent of complete paralysis, only with the exasperating awareness of knowing exactly how to extract himself from her without the means to communicate the process. But he'd seen no reason to share the frightening details.

Unfortunately, he had no words to explain the process. It would be like trying to tell someone how to use their eyes to see, or how to use their nose to smell, or their mouth to taste or their skin to touch. Either she would have the sixth sense to extract herself from their shape—or she wouldn't. She had to figure out a lot all by herself.

He had the power to merge them together, but only she could extract them. And while his dream that she could shape-shift was a true dream, sometimes the women couldn't cope with the changes of their bodies or the intimacy of the merge and they panicked—freezing the couple in one shape. And so Ari had proceeded as slowly as possible, letting her become accustomed to the feel of their cells slipping and sliding within each other before he'd deepened the meld.

Holding back had been more difficult than he'd anticipated. Perhaps soul mates came in an irresistible custom package designed to ignite the senses. Samantha's scent certainly drove him wild with distraction. Her sexy soft skin blended perfectly with his. Even her accelerated pulse urged him on. His blood pumped hot through his veins, and yet when he felt her tightening—despite how ready she'd told him she was—he suspected the merging sensation had begun to panic her.

Worried, he reminded himself that he'd had a lifetime to prepare to give up his identity in the merge. Samantha had had only one day to come to grips with the idea of shape-shifting. He had to pull back.

Slow down.

Cool his motor.

But every primal instinct to mate burned through him. Her incredibly silky skin bewitched, compelled, taunted. Her courage drew him as much as her bold sexuality—because she hadn't once asked him to stop.

Gritting his teeth, he pulled out of her. She gasped as if insulted, but he had to allow her time to understand that after she merged she would once again be her complete and independent self.

"What's wrong?" She lazily trailed her hands over his buttocks and the tingling pleased him.

"How do you feel?"

"Uncertain. Impatient. Edgy."

"We don't have to do this all at once."

Her beautiful eyes narrowed. "We began to merge, didn't we?"

"Yes."

"Did I do something wrong?"

"Why would you think that?" he countered, not wanting to point out that she'd tensed up on him. He certainly didn't want to sound as if he were criticizing. He wasn't. Only he wanted her so badly that stopping had left him with a walloping ache in his groin. "We're doing great."

"Then why did you stop?" She sounded confused and needy, but he heard a thread of relief, too.

"We don't need to rush. And there's more pleasure if we don't force—"

"I am a little anxious. But surely that's to be expected?" She looked straight into his eyes, obviously searching for an honest answer.

Never had she seemed as brave as when she faced her own fear with head-on directness. His heart twisted and he gathered her close. "We should let you become accustomed to the merge before we go all the way."

She wriggled against his hardness. "What about you? Don't you need—"

"I need you to feel at ease with me." He tried not to let pure desire color his tone hot red. "I need *you* to want to continue. Any time you want to stop, up until we totally merge, I will break off."

"All right then." She lifted her head to kiss him and he lazily ran the tip of his tongue over her top lip. She opened her mouth, welcoming him and he kissed her long and hard and deep, until her hands clenched his back and urged him to continue to make love once more.

Ari took his time, grateful that he was no longer an impatient lad in his teens. And finally when flesh once more slid into flesh, he felt no tension in her. She seemed as relaxed and ready to go as far as he was, maybe even eager to see what happened next.

And as his hips pumped into her, as he thrust deep within her body, their surface skin again blended until he couldn't tell where his skin ended and hers began. Ari had shape-shifted many times, but he'd never combined his cells with another living being. It was the most erotic and intimate sensation he'd ever encountered.

Samantha's softness seeped into his hardness. Her warmth combined with his and together they stoked an inferno. Bones shifted, slid, melted into one another.

And all the while, the sexual tension inside him grew. He breathed in ragged breaths, reached down to touch her sex to find that he'd become so much a part of her, and she a part of him, that using his hand to arouse wasn't necessary. His flesh had melted into her heat, encasing her sweet spot, tickling, taunting, teasing.

"You feel so good," she murmured. "I want more."

He gave her a little more and watched her eyes dilate in wonder and need.

She hung on tight. "I feel . . . You feel . . . like part . . . of me."

"Soon, we will be one."

She tensed. He stopped moving. His words might have been a mistake but better to back out now than push before she relaxed into him. He'd been so close. Stopping this time . . . hurt. His balls ached. His sex felt uncontrollably hard, stiff and excruciatingly full.

His pent-up needs demanded release. Just a few more seconds, another few inches and they would have been . . . complete. They would have literally been one heart.

Knowing what was at stake—no less than their lives—pulling back still took every ounce of determination he possessed. Damp with perspiration, muscles on edge, his entire body ordered him to finish. Now.

Sheer willpower alone allowed him to rear back and pull out, before he lost himself in her forever. Chest heaving, muscles straining, he forced himself out of her body and away from her touch.

"Oh . . . this is . . . sweet . . . torture." She panted the words in time to the waves lapping the beach as if the sea's rhythm had become her own. She reached out a hand to him. "Come back. Please."

"Give me a moment." His body trembled and he fought for control.

"Can I . . ." She hesitated.

"What?"

"Can I be on top?"

He shook his head. "I have to be in charge of the merge."

"Can't you do that from under me?" she asked. "I'd feel less trapped if I could control the speed of our merge."

Her suggestion rocked him. He'd never thought about it but her request made sense. He could open the door and then let her decide how quickly she wanted to walk through—if he could hold on that long. "We need to crest together to finish the merge. I may not be able to hold on if you are—"

"I trust you." She grinned, rolled over and straddled him. "Ah . . . so . . . much better."

Samantha was accustomed to running a company. And she much preferred to be the one to decide exactly when and how far they would merge. The entire process was so strange. For a moment there she'd felt as if Ari's heart had been beating for her, that his lungs had breathed for her.

The sensation had been nerve-wrenchingly intimate, yet the sensations had left her with a startling euphoria—as if her body had been created to give both of them pleasure she hadn't imagined. Putting the sensations into words was like trying to describe hot and cold. The intensity had overwhelmed her but now that she had a better idea of what to expect, she planned to push through and keep all doubts at bay.

She could merge with Ari. She wanted to merge with him—not to get her off the island—because being with him gave her a sense of rightness, as if fate had brought them together for a good reason. Also the experience of merging, of giving herself to him had changed her deep down in her soul. Samantha had finally recognized that part of what drove her, part of why she worked so hard, was to escape a loneliness that had always been so much a part of her—so much so that she'd thought it normal. And she'd plugged the empty holes in her life with work.

But Ari didn't merely show her that he could fill the barren parts of her soul, he colored them with a spicy palette that lifted her spirit in a way she had yet to acknowledge or comprehend. If she'd been back in New York safely ensconced in her own world, she would still go through with the merge. Because she wanted to see what she could do, because Ari had earned her respect by yielding to her wishes when he could, and because merging wasn't giving up her identity, merging with him was adding another half to her own to make one whole.

Samantha lifted her hips and took Ari's sex inside her. Her mouth found his and she began to move over him. With his hands on her hips, he helped without trying to take over. As her confidence grew, she scraped her nipples over his chest, rubbed her belly against his, ground her pelvis into him.

And this time when her flesh melted, she welcomed the unity. Reveled in uniting their flesh, their blood, their hearts. She took him deeper, and well-being suffused her. Desire erupted and frothed in a raging river, poured into a welcoming sea, where the waters whipped into a frenzied wave that crested higher than she'd ever imagined. And when that crest broke through her, when all of his desires fused with hers, she shattered into a billion fragments, taking him right with her.

The merge was complete.

She could no longer tell what part of her new shape had come from her and what had once been part of him. Where they'd been two separate beings, there was now only one. The joining, total and complete, was done.

But what had they become?

She wanted to speak but she didn't have a mouth or vocal cords. She didn't seem to have hands or feet, either, but instead, thick stubs that thrashed the sand. Her eyes seemed hooded and it was very dark, but then she flexed her neck and . . .

Oh . . . my. She was on her belly. Heavy. Low to the ground. She moved her front flipper-like stubs, very sensitive flippers that felt every grain of sand, and rear legs that shoved her massive body forward in an awkward, yet oddly powerful movement.

She could hear the low vibrations of the lapping waves and concluded she had ears. And while she possessed eyes, she was quite nearsighted and colors were odd, violets and blue green instead of grays and blacks.

Whatever animal Ari had turned them into was massive. And she longed to immerse herself in the sea to feed. Only a small part of her mind remained in the creature. The rest was in the *Inf*, but as Ari had promised, she could tap into her thoughts.

Yet, the creature's body drove her forward toward the sea in search of food with a primitive urge she couldn't deny. Heavy, full of hard cartilage, Samantha pressed to the sea and the promise of filling her belly.

Slowly, she crawled forward, her walk steady and ungainly. When the full moon came out from behind a cloud, she glimpsed her shadow, startled to see that she and Ari had become a giant tortoise.

seven

Samantha didn't know much about sea turtles or marine biology, but the moment she lumbered into the ocean, she felt as though she'd come home. Her nearsighted eyes could see just fine in the clear dark Caribbean Sea, and she suspected her sight was in the ultraviolet range due to the odd green-violet colors. Her sense of smell acute, she inhaled the sweet scent of shrimp through a pulsating movement in her throat. Mouth open slightly, she drew in water through the nose and then immediately emptied it out again through the mouth in a motion as natural as if she'd been breathing in her human form.

Samantha sensed Ari was with her and wished they could communicate. But they wouldn't be able to speak until they returned to human form, shape-shifting back into their bodies. And as much as she wanted to make sure she could once again become herself, the yen to swim, eat and explore the new underwater world of night fish, coral reefs and spectacular sea creatures pulsed stronger than any desire to return to shore.

She had no idea if sea turtles possessed natural enemies. But when she spied a shark hovering over a school of silver-scaled fish, its ominous dark shadow menacing, she shuddered and swam the other way. Her flippers, which had been short, clumsy and inept on land, now powered her swimming with tireless ease.

And when she spied sweet shrimp on the bottom, she feasted hungrily. Belly full, thirst quenched, she circled the magnificent coral reef that formed an atoll around the island. Sea urchins, their black spines like the quills of porcupines, dotted the sand, along with sea crabs and lobster. She noted a huge variety of fish swimming in and out of her submerged airplane and wondered how many years it would take for the metal to become part of the coral reef ecosystem and was pleased to see no fuel spillage.

But most of all, she thought over the puzzle of how to reverse the shape-shifting process. Ari had told her if she didn't panic, she would succeed, but he hadn't given her detailed instructions. And so eventually, as she headed back to the island, she made a nonspecific plan. She would begin by trying to do what he'd done—in reverse.

At least if she didn't succeed right away, they would have the freedom to swim and eat. She was grateful he hadn't turned them into a rock or an ice cube.

However, as much as she'd enjoyed exploring as a turtle, she certainly didn't wish to spend the rest of her life under a giant shell, unable to communicate, and she certainly didn't wish that fate on Ari, either. Making love with him had been awesome and if both of them got stuck in this turtle's body, she'd never be able to repeat the incredible experience.

She suspected it had been difficult for Ari to place his fate in her hands, or flippers. If she failed, he, too, would be caught in turtle form forever. And she really didn't understand the specifics of the shape-shifting. Was all of Ari's mind and will in the *Inf*? She controlled the turtle's body. Her will decided when to feed, when to swim, when to return to the sand beach.

Their organs and blood and cells had combined, but what of his mind? Was he totally locked away in the Inf or was he aware of what their turtle body was doing? Could he see what she was seeing, feel what she was feeling, read her thoughts?

She should have asked more questions and wondered why he hadn't told her more. She lugged her big torso and heavy shell up the beach and settled near the campfire, but not too close. If she managed to change back, she didn't want to risk a limb landing in the embers.

Closing her eyes, she sought to recall the merge. How had Ari altered their cells to slip and slide into one another? She needed to duplicate the process so they could return to human form.

She imagined the cells re-forming into human shapes, but nothing happened. She tried again. Still nothing.

Now what?

Suspecting Ari's mind was in the *Inf*, knowing most of hers was there, she tried thinking at him. Again nothing happened.

Frustrated, tired, she fought off sleep. What was the answer?

Why hadn't he explained better? He'd told her shape-shifting was a sixth sense. Obviously, she could do it. She'd frickin' changed into a sea turtle. According to Ari she had the ability to go back to her human shape.

But how was she supposed to use her new sense?

The part of her mind that remained in the *Inf* was connected to her turtle brain in ways she didn't understand, and the thinking process was a bit different from human form. It was as if her mind was on a hard drive and she had to call up the information onto a screen in her limited turtle brain where she could only process a limited amount of information at a time.

Maybe she needed all of her mind to figure it out. She tried to force her turtle brain into the *Inf*. Nothing.

Damn.

She had to think outside the box. If she couldn't bring her turtle brain into the *Inf*, perhaps she could bring the *Inf* brain cells into the turtle. Samantha's brain cells felt very compressed inside the turtle. And the *Inf* stretched out forever, but she gathered her mind, condensed it, tried to reel it into herself.

Her brain cells budged. Flipped. Rolled over trying to make room for her *Inf* mind.

Only there was no room. And her turtle body began to morph. Yes. Yes. Yes.

She'd created a change—of sorts. Bringing her mind together seemed to be key. And since there wasn't enough room to hold all of her in the turtle, the extra cells forced the turtle to morph.

Pulling, gathering, merging was hard mental work. She concentrated with fierce determination, fueled by her success that she was on the right track.

And as she sucked her brain back, she noted a hitchhiker clinging to her mind and prayed that was Ari. She had no idea if she could bring back both bodies and accidentally leave behind his mind in the *Inf*, but she was not changing him to human and leaving any delicious part of him behind.

So she grabbed the hitchhiker and used the very last of her mental strength to take him with her. Her mind stretched, expanded, popped.

And then everything went black.

"You did it." Ari raised her beautiful head into his lap, smoothed back her hair and watched her eyes flutter open and slowly focus. "You were wonderful."

She blinked sleepily, muttered a few words he couldn't understand and closed her eyes again, succumbing to a deep but natural sleep. Apparently the shape-shifting had exhausted her, depleted her energy reserves.

Ari's teachers had warned exhaustion might happen. Shape shifting took energy, and she would have to build her mental muscles just as a weightlifter had to create physical ones. He'd go slowly, not tax her too much. But the most dangerous part was over.

She'd brought them both back. And he held her in his arms and let her sleep, rocking her gently, very much content with her and the world. As eager as he was to speak, he could wait for morning.

He held her tenderly through the night, watched the sun rise in the eastern sky to create quiet rose streaks with slashes of hot pink. And this time when Samantha opened her eyes and awakened, she was seemingly back to her normal self.

He smiled. "Hi."

"Hi, yourself." She sat up slowly and held up her hands as if counting her fingers.

"You did great. When you headed into the sea, I was certain you'd lost control—"

"You were there?"

"In the *Inf*. I watched you from there. And now that you've learned what to do, we can morph into two animals and it'll be much—"

"Hold up. You're going too fast." She shoved a stray lock of hair behind her ear.

"Sorry." He grinned. He couldn't seem to stop smiling from ear to ear. He handed her a Powerbar and a water bottle. "Have something to eat and you'll feel—"

She frowned. "I'm still stuffed. I ate . . . shrimp." She screwed up her nose. "I ate *raw* shrimp?"

"You'll get used to it."

"Yuck." She spat into the sand as if she could still taste the shrimp. She couldn't, of course, but this part of the shape-shifting could be almost as dangerous as the actual morphing. Some people couldn't accept themselves in the animal state and literally went insane.

Twisting open the water bottle, she took a healthy swig. Then she peered at him, her eyes narrowing. "Why didn't you tell me I had to take the part of my mind in the *Inf* and fuse it with the part in the turtle in order to shift back to normal?"

His eyes widened. "I've never heard shape-shifting described anywhere near like that. We all do it differently, and if I'd told you what works for me, it probably wouldn't have worked for you."

"What do you do?"

"I shrug into myself."

Her eyebrows raised in disbelief. "You shrug?"

"And a friend of mine can only shift as he's falling asleep. I've heard of shape-shifters who require the taste of sour pickles or the smell of raspberries. Or—"

"But there aren't raspberries or pickles here. If I'd needed them, I would have failed."

"Those stimulants are rare. Most of us use our minds."

"And you watched the entire process of me swimming around as a turtle from the *Inf*?"

"Only the tiniest part of my brain remained with you—just enough to observe."

She dug her toes into the sand. "I don't know if I want to shape-shift again."

Uh-oh. He cocked his head to the side, trying to remain patient. "Was there any part you liked?"

"The sex was good." She half smiled and then it faded. "And once I waddled into the water, the swimming underwater was cool. But you know, now that I've done it, I'm not that eager to repeat the experience."

"What if you were a dolphin?"

She shuddered. "Don't they eat live fish?"

Samantha was having a problem with the eating. He picked his words with care in order not to criticize. "When you're in the animal shape, animal feeding habits will be normal. Once you return to human, you may have a little difficulty adjusting to the idea—"

"You think?"

"But animal feeding habits are part of nature. We aren't doing anything wrong."

"Easy for you to say."

"And imagine what it's like to fly like a bird?" She winced and he recalled that birds ate everything from beetles to worms. "You could eat seeds."

"Somehow the prospect of eating seeds can't compare with a filet mignon."

"Yeah, but wait until you fly under the power of your own wings. It's mind-blowing."

"And addictive?"

He shrugged. "What if it is?"

"I'm not sure I want to become addicted."

"Shape-shifting isn't like taking drugs. It can't harm you."

"When I tossed the firewood at you, you elongated your arms to hold the wood. I'd imagine that it wouldn't take long to become accustomed to the luxury of that kind of shifting."

"So?"

"So if I don't stay with you in New Atlantis, I don't want to rely so heavily on my new skills that I'd be uncomfortable staying in human form."

"Once you shape-shift, you're never the same."

"What do you mean?"

"Once your mind accepts what your body can do, it becomes instinctive. Can you tell yourself not to use your eyes? Or your ears?"

"Are you saying I can never go back to staying in human form?"

EIGHT

 "I don't know." Ari spoke with a sincerity that chilled Samantha. "No one in my people's history has ever shape-shifted then refused to do it again."

Samantha suspected his people had a long and interesting take on history. "So you're telling me that every shape-shifter lives on New Atlantis?"

"We all make our homes there, although some of us travel and spend extended periods of time in your world."

"So there's nothing to stop me from shape-shifting into a bird and flying home and resuming my former life?"

"Nothing unless . . ."

"Unless?" she prodded, fascinated by the changing light in his eyes that made reading his emotions difficult.

"Unless you can give up living with your own kind."

"My own kind live in the world."

He had the good sense not to argue that she no longer fit with those who couldn't shape-shift and instead changed the subject. "Wouldn't you like to visit my home and see New Atlantis for yourself before you make such a decision?"

She noted that he didn't say anything at all about their personal relationship. He hadn't tried to convince her to stay with words of love, or even a mention of their lovemaking. He spoke of being with her own kind. Of seeing his home. And yet he'd said they were soul mates, and she'd felt that connection so strongly that surely he'd felt it, too?

"If we go to New Atlantis, I'd be free to leave at any time?"

His tone was gruff, threaded with hurt. "Do you think so little of me that I'd force you to stay where you'd be unhappy?"

"You forced me to come here," she countered. And then he'd made love to her so sweetly that her heart still beat with joy. She so badly wanted to kiss the hurt from his face, but she also owed it to herself to ask lots of questions.

His eyes darkened. "I thought we'd moved past—"

"We have. I have. I just like to understand all my options so I can make the right decision."

"Don't you ever choose with your heart?"

The question ringing in her ears, she stood, brushed the sand from her palms and realized she was nude and hadn't given it a thought. She'd been naked when making love, naked as a turtle and was carrying on a conversation as if she were fully clothed. And it seemed so natural.

She hadn't particularly noticed his nudity either. She'd become accustomed to seeing his bare chest and with his sitting on the beach, she simply hadn't noted he wasn't wearing his boxers. She could blame the oversight on the distraction of shape-shifting—but in truth, if she hadn't been so damn comfortable with him seeing her own skin, she surely would have reached for her shirt sooner.

One whiff and she scrunched up her nose. The shirt smelled. She picked up her clothes and carried them down to the water and

tossed them into the sea. After swirling them around for a few minutes, she wrung them out and carried them back up the beach and
laid them out in the sand to dry.

"Clothes are a problem for shape-shifters," Ari told her with a
smile. "We're forever leaving them behind and arriving naked."

"How do you cope?" she asked, curious about his lifestyle, but
oddly not the least bit uncomfortable walking around naked in
broad daylight. And it was more than that he'd already seen every
inch of her flesh. She simply didn't feel the least bit self-conscious
around him, no doubt due to his attitude. He wasn't indifferent to
her body but she could tell that the way her body parts went together wasn't his primary concern.

"Sometimes we carry clothing in our mouths. Or have someone
tie them to our animal shape. Or we hide them in a place where we
can shape-shift. On New Atlantis shape-shifters contribute more to
the force field than many of our people with other powers. Perhaps
that has gained us a measure of respect. If we're caught nude in public, people don't make a big deal out of it—although nudity isn't our
practice. Many public places keep robes on hand to offer us."

He'd sounded so happy when he spoke of his world. She lifted
her chin and locked gazes with him. "I'd like to visit New Atlantis."

Warm approval shined in his eyes and he gestured across the sea.
"I'll take you there. We can swim there in a day."

She recalled swimming with fondness—except for the shrimp-
eating incident. "How long would it take to fly?"

"A few hours, but mastering the bird form is more difficult."

Soaring through the sky under her own power excited her. She
couldn't imagine the freedom. Heights had never bothered her. And
if she ate, she could eat seeds, although she'd seen none here. But
she also wondered if what he'd told her was true—that if she kept
shape-shifting she'd never again be satisfied to stay in human form.
However, she had to get off this island—so she didn't have much
choice. She'd have to change shape to leave—of course which ani-

mal form she chose was up to her. "I'd like to try, but I'm not sure I'm ready to greet strangers without any clothes."

"Even dry clothing is too heavy to fly with us. But my home is isolated on a beach. There are no neighbors nearby and I have clothing you can borrow." He took her hand. "I understand you have not yet decided whether you want to remain with me, but I'm glad you're considering it."

His words startled her—not because of what he'd said, but because she hadn't previously considered that once she shape-shifted into a bird, she could fly anywhere. She would be free to leave him.

She hadn't even thought about escaping from him—not since they'd made love. What was happening to her? It was one thing to choose to go with him, but it was unlike her not to consider what spending more time would cost her. She could lose the Miami deal. The theater renovation would come to a complete standstill.

And yet, if she didn't spend more time with Ari, if she didn't take this opportunity to visit New Atlantis, she might never have another. If she didn't go with him, she suspected she'd regret it for the rest of her life.

His warmth and sincerity had gotten to her on levels she hadn't suspected. And unlike other men who admired her for her wealth and her business acumen and her looks, Ari looked deeper to her core. And that's what he wanted. Her wealth didn't matter to him, at least not that she could ascertain. Neither did her looks. Sheesh— once she became accustomed to shape-shifting, she could change to any shape she wished.

Ari looked beyond the usual trappings. No man had ever looked so deep into her character and wanted what was pure Samantha. And it scared her because that kind of love was for life. That kind of love could change her entire world, and thinking it could be hers was both exhilarating and terrifying. She didn't know if she wanted to allow Ari to mean that much to her.

But she couldn't shape-shift and fly away either—not before seeing if they were meant to be together as he'd claimed. Soul mates. She'd never expected to meet a man who understood her as well as Ari. He'd seemed to instinctively know what would convince her to consider staying with him—and it wasn't words, but actions.

Knowing he would welcome her embrace, she stepped into his arms. With him, she felt anything less than giving him real truth about her feelings was dishonest. But he already seemed to know and, therefore, she didn't feel kissing him was leading him on or promising anything she couldn't deliver.

His arms closed around her and his mouth angled over hers, taking what she offered. And with the gentle breeze bathing her flesh, the sunlight warming her with a golden glow, she'd never felt so certain of her attractiveness.

She could see he wanted her by the gleam in his eyes, by the fierce beat of his heart and the pulse throbbing in the cords at his neck. Most of all, she was touched by the tender way he held her, even as his mouth took fierce possession.

Warmth and happiness suffused her from the inside out. And when she imagined waking up beside this man for the rest of her life, giving up her life at home didn't seem so much of a hardship.

"When we make love again, I want to do so on New Atlantis." He pulled back, his nostrils flaring with desire, leaving no doubts how much he wanted her. "And if you want to fly there, we have work to do. Are you sure I can't talk you into swimming?"

"An all-day swim or a few hours' flight?" She grinned at him and arched a suggestive eyebrow. "The sooner we arrive, the sooner we can—"

He cleared his throat. "If you're through distracting me, we should begin."

"All right. But I thought if we made love again, it would lead to shape-shifting."

"You must come to New Atlantis on your own. It's one of our laws."

"So what do I do?"

"Close your eyes."

She followed his directions and enjoyed the smooth cadence of his voice. But she also noted the way her toes dug into the sand, the way her breasts lifted with every breath, the way her hair whipped over her face during a gust of wind. "Now what?"

"Think about how you felt when our cells merged."

"When you were making love to me?" She'd never forget the merging of his breath with hers, his heart with hers. The details remained sharp in her mind, especially how he'd taken such care not to frighten her, how he'd taken such care to arouse her.

"Recall the process of sinking into me. But this time you are sinking into a bird."

She opened her eyes. "What kind of bird?"

"Whatever kind you like. Now close your eyes and imagine your cells shrinking, imagine your mind entering the *Inf*."

She shook her head. "Nothing's happening. I think you're going to have to make love to me again."

"Focus."

She sighed. Obviously he was taking this much more seriously than she was. Samantha had been one of those hit-or-miss students. When a subject interested her, she was at the top of her class, but when she was bored, she'd barely passed.

While shape-shifting did interest her, making love with Ari again interested her more. She wanted to do so without the shape-shifting complication. She wanted to find completion in her own body.

"What are you thinking about?" Ari interrupted her musings, a bit of frustration in his tone.

"You. I was thinking about making love in my own body. It would be—"

"Impossible if we don't fly out of here."

At his sharp tone, she opened her eyes again. "What's wrong?"

His gaze stared to the west at darkening skies and dark gray clouds that cast murky shadows across the sea. "A storm's blowing in. We should leave before it arrives. Fighting wind currents takes practice and you have—"

"Fine. I'll concentrate harder." She turned into the wind so her hair blew back from her face. As the wind gusted and brought in cool air and a mist of fine rain, her nipples tightened.

"Push your mind into the *Inf*. Focus on shrinking your body into a bird. A bird with strong wings and feathers to protect you from the rain. A bird that can fly tirelessly for hours, soaring above the sea."

His voice relaxed, almost hypnotizing Samantha but finally she focused. And her cells felt as if she were melting, shrinking. Pressure on pressure, she coaxed her mind into the *Inf*. If Ari hadn't shown her how, she'd have never been able to start the process, but once initiated, her body took over as if it knew exactly what to do.

She shrank. And her excess mass flipped into the *Inf* along with most of her mind. Her toes became webbed. Her bird body grew feathers with no more thought than her human body grew hair.

And her eyesight . . . oh . . . wow. Her eyesight grew keen. Her only regret was that in animal form she could no longer communicate her thoughts to Ari.

But he whooped at her success and then transformed into a bird beside her. Together, they flapped their wings and with almost no effort, she followed him into the air.

She was flying. She was a bird and she was flying. She'd defied physics and the experience was exhilarating. The entire time she'd taken the shape of a turtle, she'd worried whether she could change back. This time she had no worries.

Her heart was as light as her bird-boned body. And flying was magical. Sure, she'd flown in airplanes and helicopters but machines had powered the metal. Flying under her own power was like the difference between navigating the ocean in a submarine or swimming in the sea.

The wind whistled past her ears. Rain began to fall, but her feathers kept her dry and she wasn't the least bit cold. And with her wings outstretched, she was surprised how little energy it took to keep her in the air.

She could have flown for hours, and without any hesitation, she followed Ari and left the island far below. He flew higher, faster, racing away from the storm. And she stayed on his wing, enjoying a freedom she'd never known before.

NINE

The whipping wind told Ari's keen senses that the storm was catching them. He could smell the change in ions, feel the drop in temperature. The air carried the feel of a dangerous electric charge before a major summer thunderstorm.

Normally, he'd have dived into the sea, morphed into a fish and continued the journey, but Samantha wasn't ready to try the complex change from animal to animal. As the winds lashed them, Ari searched for a smooth slip stream of air to fly in. But despite his best efforts, the wind gusts buffeted them.

As New Atlantis's dark green mountains came into view on the horizon, he increased their speed and hoped they'd make landfall before the storm caught up with them. But as thunder roared and the wind whipped the sea below into a frothing cauldron, slashing rain nicked them. The sudden summer storm had turned what should have been an easy flight into a fight to make landfall.

Sensing Samantha's struggles to make headway, he feared she

might panic and fall into the sea, but he hesitated to decrease their altitude. If they flew lower and she panicked or succumbed to exhaustion and morphed back into human shape, the fall might not kill her, but it would be dangerous to fly so close to the ocean where one strong downdraft could fling them into the waves with enough speed to break a bird's neck.

Ari shouldn't have been in such a hurry to bring her to New Atlantis. After the wind had picked up, he should have known better than to have her solo so far in unpredictable weather. He'd been too anxious for her to see his home, too eager to make love to her again on New Atlantis, and his impatience may have placed her life in jeopardy.

He thought about landing on the water and morphing back into human form. Although she was a strong swimmer he knew from his own efforts how tired he was. Staying afloat in those waves would take a superhuman effort.

Ari worried and fretted and blamed himself as Samantha gamely flew toward New Atlantis. When they were only a mile out, he began to believe they would make it to shore.

But fate was against them.

A lightning bolt caught them in its fringe. The near miss stunned him and as he fought to maintain balance, Samantha plunged toward the sea, her wing bent at a peculiar angle, indicating severe damage.

Fear activated his instincts. Ari pulled in his wings, tucked his head and dived after her. Within seconds his streamlined form caught up to her out-of-control plummet. He flew under her, then shape-shifted into a larger bird and extended his wings. Knowing even at this size he hadn't the strength to fly her to safety, he focused on breaking her fall.

He couldn't stop their plunge into the sea, but he could slow their rate of descent. His muscles burned. His lungs worked triple time. And still they fell sickeningly fast and hard, the wind whistling in his ears.

Just before they crashed into the sea, he morphed, wrapped himself around her still body in a cushioning ball. They struck the water hard. If he'd still possessed lungs, he had no doubt the landing would have knocked the air from his chest.

Had he cushioned her enough? As they dropped into the water, he changed shape once more. This time he altered into a giant manta ray. Spreading his pectoral fins, he floated Samantha to the surface and prayed she was still alive, still breathing.

As a manta he couldn't see her on his back, couldn't tell if she moved or lay on his cartilage broken and hurt. The wave action kept washing her back and forth, but he swam her to the deserted sandy shore of his home, morphed back into human shape and used his last energy to gently pull her into his arms.

"Samantha. Samantha."

She didn't move.

"Are you hurt?"

Damn. Damn. Damn. She looked bad. Her eyes were shut. Blood oozed from her beak. Her chest rose and fell, but erratically. If she tried to morph before she could heal, she'd use up the very last of her life forces.

He gathered her gently against his chest, shielding her from the wind and rain with his body, his heart skipping in despair as he noted her broken wing. "I know you can't talk. I know you're in pain but it's important that you listen to me."

One eye fluttered open.

"Don't try to morph. You're too weak." He tried to keep his voice calm but he wanted to rail at fate, which had hurt her and left him sound. He ached to howl into the wind and cry out his pain.

"Just breathe. Relax. Remember when we spoke about self healing. I'll explain the process and you'll fix the damage."

Samantha closed her eyes but at least she didn't appear to be attempting to morph. But he wasn't certain if she remained conscious, either, and his fear escalated.

"Come on, Sam. Stay with me. Fight. I know you're a fighter and we can do this, sweetheart." Ari's every muscle wound tight and he had to force himself to breathe. He took a calming gulp of air, told himself that to talk her through the process he had to stay coherent, positive and upbeat.

Samantha opened her eyes again.

"Good. Now, focus on your damaged cells, but don't morph. The healing process is more delicate. Think of your cells as torn. Heal the tears. Stop the bleeding first. Try to change just one cell until you get the hang of the process. It's not hard. Repairs take less effort and energy than morphing, and once you stop the internal bleeding, the pain will lessen."

He kept talking, repeating his instructions and adding encouragement. When she closed her eyes to rest, he allowed her a few minutes to recover before urging her to continue. And finally, beneath his hands, her heartbeat strengthened, giving him hope.

"You're doing wonderfully well. You're healing yourself. Your pulse is stronger. Keep going. And when you're done, we'll work on the bones."

Ari had no idea how long the process took. But the storm had passed over them and the sun shone brightly on the beach once again before she healed her broken wing. Knowing she didn't have enough energy to morph back to human, he carried her up the beach in his hands.

"You did great. Now sleep, and I'll take us home."

Samantha awakened in a room she'd never seen before. She tested her wing with a small movement and when she remained pain-free, she morphed back to human. Mouth dry, stomach growling with hunger, naked as the night they'd made love, she stretched and worked the kinks from her neck while she glanced at the room.

She must have slept through the night. Morning sunlight lit the room of white stuccoed walls, a white-stained wood floor, elegant gauze curtains that framed open windows. The only color in the room was Ari's bronze flesh resting on a thick white comforter.

Ari had been sleeping beside her but the moment she altered her shape to human, she must have depressed the mattress with her increased weight. He opened his eyes, sat up and handed her a glass of orange juice that he had waiting on a nightstand.

"How are you feeling?" he asked.

Grateful to wet her parched throat, she gulped greedily, surprised to find the juice was cold, as if he'd just taken it from the fridge. After she'd finished the juice, she discovered the glass remained cold. "Does the glass possess its own refrigeration unit?"

"It's nano technology." He fluffed a pillow and pulled her next to him. "I'm so sorry. I should never have brought you here during a storm."

He sounded sad and she didn't understand why he was blaming himself for her injury. He'd saved her life. After the lightning had shocked her, her last thought had been of death as she plunged to the sea. Yet, he'd risked his own life to break her fall, swam her to shore, taught her to heal herself.

Snuggling against his warmth, she tilted up her head to look at him. "You couldn't have predicted that storm. And you saved my life. Thank you."

"Do you hurt anywhere?" he asked, smoothing her hair from her brow.

"I'm fine. In fact, I've never felt better." She marveled at how good she felt, awake, alert and very alive. Surprisingly, she didn't have one sore muscle, not even a twinge of pain.

"When you healed your injuries, you also revitalized your cells. You can always feel as good as you do right now—every day for the rest of your now extended lifetime."

"Wow." For the first time, his earlier words sank in. She would never go back to what she'd been before she'd learned how to morph. Now that she understood how easy it was to coax all her cells into perfect health, she would repeat the process whenever she felt the need. To do anything less would be like putting sugar in her car's gas tank instead of fuel.

Even if she rejected New Atlantis, she could rejuvenate her cells. But did she want to outlive her friends and associates? If she married, she'd outlive her husband and her children—and she didn't want to think about if her children inherited her abilities. The possibilities were mind-boggling.

The longer lifespan and her health would cause any number of problems in the outside world—certainly ones that could be solved with her wealth—but did she want to live the rest of her life hiding her abilities?

Still, the morphing didn't come without risks. She could have died in that lightning storm. Without Ari beside her, she'd be one dead bird right about now.

"You risked your life to save me, didn't you?"

He pulled her onto his chest. "You are my responsibility. It was my fault you were hurt."

"But—"

"But more important, I wouldn't have wanted to live without my soul mate."

"We've only known each other a short time."

"Time has nothing to do with love." He placed her hand on his chest over his heart. "Can you not feel our connection? Surely I can't be the only one who—"

"Ari, I'm not like you. I'm not certain I believe that there's only one perfect love for me."

His eyes darkened. "You wish to search for another mate?"

"I didn't say that." She didn't want to hurt him but she simply couldn't give him more of her thoughts when she hadn't come to terms with her feelings. "I need more time to decide what I'll do with the rest of my life."

"Why do you need more time?"

His question left her flabbergasted. "We . . . you and I . . . I have no idea what you do for a living."

"And that is important to you? Would you reject me if I was a carpenter?"

"Of course not. I'm not that stupid. Do you know how hard it is to find a good carpenter?"

She teased him, and it felt good to be in this peaceful white room with him. She could hear the waves lapping on the beach, catch a view of the mountains behind them and couldn't have imagined a more perfect location for a house.

He laughed at her. "Does what I do for a living matter so much?"

"My point was that I don't know you."

"Afraid I'm after your money?" He eyed her hungrily. "My family is extremely wealthy. I could keep you in the lifestyle to which you're accustomed by simply living off my trust fund but I prefer to dabble."

"Dabble?"

"In nano technology. That glass is one of my inventions." He spoke with pride. And she didn't blame him. His invention would make him even wealthier.

"I'm impressed, but until you just mentioned them, I didn't know you had a family."

"I have parents, grandparents, great-grandparents and great-great-grandparents. My family is huge. The entire population is related if you go back far enough. That's why we need new blood. That's why we need you."

"Your entire family lives on New Atlantis?"

"Most of us. But we all like our privacy so you needn't worry about—"

"A large family sounds wonderful but you keep missing the point. I don't know what you like to do for entertainment"—her stomach growled—"or what you like for breakfast."

He chuckled in delight. "As for breakfast, I believe I'd like to have you."

"I'm serious. I'm starving."

"So am I." He wriggled his brows suggestively.

Samantha decided she could wait to feed her belly. Leaning forward, she kissed Ari with an abandon that surprised her. She'd never been so relaxed with a man and suspected his simple admission of his feelings for her had a lot to do with it. Ari had the courage to say what he felt and go after what he wanted—her—and she admired him for it.

That he'd been willing to risk his life to save her from that horrific fall out of the sky proved he spoke the truth. For the first time in her life, she felt unconditionally loved—and not for her wealth or her looks but for her true self. Ari's love was a truly liberating feeling and it transferred to making love.

Samantha suddenly wanted to try everything she'd ever fantasized about with Ari. She wanted to spend as much time as possible with him today and tomorrow and as long as it took to be sure she'd never have regrets.

His powerful arms closed around her and his clever fingers skimmed up her back, shooting tingles into her core. He surprised her when he broke their kiss and gazed at her with a twinkle in his eyes. "I have a surprise for you."

"I'm not too certain how many more of your surprises my heart can take," she teased.

"I want to show you the force field that protects New Atlantis."

She narrowed her eyes on him. "I thought you were starving for me."

He chuckled. "I am. I can do two things at once."

"I don't understand."

"You will," he promised and went right back to kissing her, leaving her curiosity aroused while he worked on exciting the rest of her.

Between the magic of his lips and hands, it didn't take long for them to come together physically, but in another way that was totally new. Seemingly in no rush, Ari stoked her embers, until fire licked into a blaze of need.

And then as if she'd always lived in isolation, her mental bubble broke. She sensed thousands of people going about their daily lives . . . and gasped. There was warmth, humanity and love keeping up the force field. And she could feel this elemental connection to others of her kind that didn't intrude or overwhelm but shined down on her like the sun, bathing her in a oneness.

And when Ari wrapped his arms around her and held her close, as he moved inside her, building the tension, taking her with him, she'd never felt so close to anyone in her life. There was intimacy of mind and body. There was sharing, caring. And love.

Later, Ari cooked her breakfast. They ate in silence on his back deck that overlooked the sea, sharing waffles and fresh strawberries and sliced pineapples. She contentedly sipped her coffee, listened to the birds caw, the sea lap to and fro over his pink sand beach, but most of all, she enjoyed looking at Ari.

She didn't think she'd ever met a man so sure of himself, who was both simple and complex. Ari had told her that what he did for a living didn't matter, but his nano technology that kept her coffee hot and her juice cold impressed her as much as the house he'd built with his own hands.

She almost hated to break the perfect morning by speaking. "Can we stay here today instead of going into town?"

"We can do whatever you like, but I thought you were eager to see the island to see if you could live here?"

She put down her coffee cup and took his hand. "The rest of the island doesn't matter."

"It doesn't?"

"If there aren't enough shops or restaurants . . . I'll build them."

He grinned. "Building commercial businesses could take quite a bit of time. You'd have to stay here to oversee the construction."

She gazed straight into his eyes. "I want to stay here. With you."

Ari whooped. Scooped her into his arms and twirled her around, his expression happy and loving. "You won't regret your decision. I'll make sure of it."

Deep in her heart she knew she could count on him to keep his promise. When he kissed her with fierce pride, she knew without a doubt that she'd found her home. Her love. Her soul mate.